More Praise for
A BRIDGE OF YEARS
A *Locus* Bestseller

"In [*A Bridge of Years*] there is beauty, and in it there is truth. . . . [Wilson is] a storyteller of astonishing compassion and understanding."
—Orson Scott Card, *The Magazine of Fantasy and Science Fiction*

"A . . . rewarding time-travel fantasy, which compares favorably with such classics as *Bid Time Return* by Richard Matheson and Jack Finney's *Time and Again*."
—*Atlanta Constitution*

Praise for Robert Charles Wilson's Other Novels:

THE DIVIDE
"A literate thriller, a superbly crafted novel of character."
—*New York Times Book Review*

MEMORY WIRE
"Wilson achieves the perfect balance of tension and invention . . . a creative, roller-coaster tale."
—*Booklist*

A HIDDEN PLACE
"A first novel most other writers would die for."
—*Twilight Zone Magazine*

ROBERT CHARLES WILSON

A Bridge
of Years

BANTAM BOOKS

New York   Toronto   London   Sydney   Auckland

A BRIDGE OF YEARS

A Bantam Spectra Book / published in association with Doubleday

PUBLISHING HISTORY
Doubleday edition published September 1991
Bantam edition / October 1992

SPECTRA *and the portrayal of a boxed "s" are trademarks of Bantam Books, a division of Bantam Doubleday Dell Publishing Group, Inc.*

ISBN 0-553-29892-5
Published simultaneously in the United States and Canada

Bantam Books are published by Bantam Books, a division of Bantam Doubleday Dell Publishing Group, Inc. Its trademark, consisting of the words "Bantam Books" and the portrayal of a rooster, is Registered in U.S. Patent and Trademark Office and in other countries. Marca Registrada. Bantam Books, 666 Fifth Avenue, New York, New York 10103.

PRINTED IN THE UNITED STATES OF AMERICA
OPM   0 9 8 7 6 5 4 3 2 1

For Paul . . . for whom the future is more than theoretical

Woe is me, woe is me!
The acorn's not yet fallen from the tree
That's to grow the wood
That's to make the cradle
That's to rock the babe
That's to grow a man
That's to lay me to my rest.

—Anonymous, "The Ghost's Song"

A Bridge of Years

Prologue: April 1979

Soon, the time traveler would face the necessity of his own death.

He had not taken that decision, however, or even begun to contemplate its necessity, on the cool spring morning when Billy Gargullo burst through the kitchen door into the back yard, heavily armed and golden in his armor.

The time traveler—whose name was Ben Collier—had begun the slow, pleasant labor of laying out a garden at the back of the lawn. He had hammered down stakes and marked the borders with binding twine. Next to this patch of grass and weed he had placed a shovel, a rake, and a tilling device called a "garden weasel," which he had found in a Home Hardware store in the Harbor Mall. Ben was looking forward to the adventure of the garden. He had never gardened before. He understood the fundamentals but wasn't certain what might thrive in this sunny, damp patch of soil. Therefore he had purchased a random selection of seeds from the hardware store rotary rack, including corn, radishes, sunflowers, and night-blooming aloe. In his right hand he held a packet of morning glories, reserved for a space by the fence, where they'd have something to climb on.

He had lived alone on this property—two acres of uncultivated woodland and a three-bedroom frame house—for fifteen years now. A tiny chunk of time by any reasonable scale, but substantial when you lived it in sequence. He had arrived at this outpost in August of the year 1964 and since then he had not held a conversation more prolonged than the necessary hellos and thank yous directed at store clerks and delivery people. Occasionally someone would move into the house down the road, would climb the long hill to introduce himself, and the time traveler would be friendly in return . . . but there was something in his manner that discouraged a second visit. He was an ordinary seeming, round-faced, genial young man (not as young as he seemed, of course; quite the contrary) who smiled and wore Levi's and check shirts and short hair and who, on recollection, would remind you of something superficially pleasant but somehow disturbing: a pool of water in a forest clearing, say, where something old and strange might at any moment rise to the surface.

He had lived alone all this time. For Ben, it was not an especial hardship. He had been chosen for his solitary nature and he possessed hidden resources in advance of contemporary technology: slave mnemonics, tactile memory, a population of tiny cybernetics. He wasn't lonely. Nevertheless he was, in a very real sense, alone. He was a careful and dedicated custodian; but the serenity of the house and the property occasionally seduced him into lapses of attention. Sometimes he caught himself daydreaming.

Now, for instance. Peering into this deep tangle of weeds, he imagined a garden. Gardening is a kind of time travel, he thought. One invested labor in the expectation of an altered future. Blank soil yielding flowers. A trick of time and water and nitrogen and human hands. These seeds contained their own blooms.

He looked at the package in his hand. *Heavenly Blue,* it said. The picture was impossibly gaudy, a riot of turquoise and purple Technicolor. As a species, the morning glory had been endangered for years before his birth. He imagined

2

these flowers rising along the old, fragrant cedar planks of the fence (cedar: another casualty). He imagined their blooms in the summer sunlight. He would step out onto the back porch in the last glimmer of a hot, dry day, and there they would be, laced into the wood like bright blue filigree.

In the future.

He was gazing at the package—filled with these thoughts —when the marauder burst through the kitchen door.

He had had some warning, subliminal and brief, enough to start him turning toward the house. He felt it as a disturbance among the cybernetics, and then as their sudden silence.

The marauder was dressed in what Ben recognized as military armor of the late twenty-first century, an armor rooted deep into the body, a prosthetic armor tied into the nervous system. The marauder would be very fast, very deadly.

Ben was not without his own augmentation. As soon as the peripheral image registered, emergency auxiliaries began to operate. He ducked into the meager cover of a lilac bush growing at the edge of the lawn, some few feet from the forest. He had time to wish the lilacs were in bloom.

He had time for a number of thoughts. His reflexes were heightened to the inherent limits of nerve and muscle. His awareness was swift and effortless. Events slowed to a crawl.

He looked at the intruder. What he saw was a blur of golden movement, the momentary shadow of a wrist weapon poised and aimed. Ben couldn't guess what had brought this man here, but his hostility was obvious, the threat unquestionable.

Ben was weaponless. There were weapons hidden in the house, but he would have to pass by the marauder to reach them.

He stood up and dodged left, beginning a zigzag course that would take him to the side of the house and then around

3

to the front, a window or a door there. As he stood, the marauder fired his weapon.

It was a primitive but utterly lethal beam weapon, common for its era. Ben recalled photographs of bodies burned and dismembered beyond recognition, on a battlefield years from here. As he stood, the beam scorched air inches from his head; he imagined he could taste the bright, sour ionization.

Still, the right sort of armor would have protected him. He possessed such an item—in the house.

This was a sustaining thought; but the house was too far, the lawn an unprotected killing ground. He glimpsed the marauder crouching to take aim; he ducked and rolled forward, too late. The beam intersected his left leg and severed it under the knee.

He felt a brief, terrible burst of pain . . . then numbness as the damaged nerves shut themselves down. Crippled, Ben fetched up against a birch stump projecting from the grass. He had been meaning to pull that stump for years now. The severed portion of his leg—now a barely recognizable tube of flayed meat—rolled past him. Absurdly, he wanted to pull it back to himself. But the leg was gone now—past recovery. He would need a new one.

He felt briefly dizzy as opened arteries clamped themselves shut. The gushing of blood from the blackened wound slowed to a trickle.

Clever programs had been written into the free sequences of his DNA. For Ben, this was not a deadly injury. A grave impediment, however, it most certainly was.

He was helpless here. The birch stump was no cover at all and the marauder was primed for another shot. Ben lurched forward, grinding his bloody knee-end into the dirt, hopped two paces and then rolled again in a drunken tumble that might have succeeded if the marauder had been aiming by line of sight; but the weapon was equipped with a target-recognition device and the beam cut twice across Ben's body

4

—first severing his right hand at the wrist and then slicing deep into his abdominal cavity. Blood and flame flowered across his shirt, which he had bought at the Sears in the Harbor Mall.

Now Ben began to consider dying.

Probably it was unavoidable. He understood how profoundly damaged he was. He experienced waves of dizziness as major arteries locked or dilated in a futile attempt to maintain blood pressure. Numbness spread upward from his hip to his collarbone: it was like slipping into a warm bath. He lay on the grass where his momentum had carried him, loosejointed and faint.

He turned his head.

The marauder stood above him.

His armor was quite golden, blinding in the sunlight.

The intruder gazed down at Ben with an expression so absolutely neutral of emotion that it provoked a pulse of surprise. He doesn't much care that he's killed me, Ben thought.

The marauder leveled his wrist weapon one more time, now at Ben's head.

The weapon was unimpressive, built into the curiously insect-jointed machinery of the armor. Ben looked past it. Saw a flicker of a smile.

The marauder fired his weapon.

Most of the time traveler's head vanished in a steam of bone and tissue.

Billy Gargullo regarded the time traveler's body with a new and sudden distaste. Here was not an enemy any longer but something to be disposed of. A messy nuisance.

He took the corpse by its good arm and began to drag it into the wooded land behind the house. This was a long, hot process. The air was cool but the sun bore down mercilessly. Billy followed a narrow path some several yards, unnerved by the lushness of this forest. He stopped where the path

5

curved away to the left. To the right there was a clearing; in the clearing was a slatboard woodshed, ivy-choked and abandoned for years.

He probed the door of the shed. One hinge was missing; the door sagged inward at a cockeyed angle. Sunlight played into the damp interior. There were stacks of mildewed newspapers, a few rusty garden tools, a hovering cloud of gnats.

Billy wrestled the time traveler—the lacerated meat of his body—into the sour, earthy shade of the building. His motion caused a tower of newspapers to tumble over the corpse. The papers thumped wetly down and Billy grimaced at the sudden reek of mold.

He stepped back from the door, satisfied. Possibly the body would be found, but this would deter suspicion at least for a while. He wasn't planning to spend much time here.

He paused with one hand on the sun-hot wall of the shed.

There was a sound behind him, faint but unsettling—a rustle and chatter in the darkness.

Mice, Billy thought.

Rats.

Well, they can have him.

He closed the door.

Billy's first shot had blown the package of morning glory seeds out of the time traveler's hand.

A stray corner of his beam sliced into the package and scattered its contents across the lawn. The charred paper—the words *Heavenly Blue* still brownly legible—drifted to earth not far from the birch stump where the time traveler lost his leg. The seeds were dispersed in a wide curve between the stump and the fence.

Most were eaten by birds and insects. A few, moistened by the next night's rainfall, rooted in the lawn and were choked by crabgrass before the shoots saw light.

Four of them sprouted in the rich soil alongside the cedar fence.

Three survived into the summer. The few blossoms they produced were gaudy by August, but there was no one to see. The grass had grown tall and the house was empty.

It would be empty for a few summers more.

PART ONE

The Door
in the Wall

One

It was a modest three-bedroom frame house with its basement dug a little deeper than was customary in this part of the country, pleasant but overgrown with bush and ivy and miles away from town.

It had been empty for years, the real estate agent said, and the property backed onto a cedar swamp. "Frankly, I don't see a lot of investment potential here."

Tom Winter disagreed.

Maybe it was his mood, but this property appealed at once. Perversely, he liked it for its bad points: its isolation, lost in this rainy pinewood—its blunt undesirability, like the frank ugliness of a bulldog. He wondered whether, if he lived here, he would come to resemble the house, the way pet owners were said to resemble their pets. He would be plain. Isolated. Maybe, a little wild.

Which was not, Tom supposed, how he looked to Doug Archer, the real estate agent. Archer was wearing his blue Bell Realty jacket, but the neat faded Levi's and shaggy haircut betrayed his roots. Local family, working class, maybe some colorful relative still logging out in the bush. Raised to look with suspicion on creased trousers, which Tom happened to be wearing. But appearances were deceptive. Tom paused as they approached the blank pine-slab front door. "Didn't this used to be the Simmons property?"

Archer shook his head. "Close, though. That's a little ways up the hill. Peggy Simmons still lives up there—she's nearly eighty." He raised an eyebrow. "You know Peggy Simmons?"

"I used to deliver groceries up the Post Road. Came by here sometimes. But that was a long while ago."

"No kidding! Didn't you say—"

"I've been in Seattle for most of twelve years."

"Any connection with Tony Winter—up at Arbutus Ford?"

"He's my brother," Tom said.

"Hey! Well, hell! *This* changes things."

In the city, Tom thought, we learn not to smile so generously.

Archer slid the key into the door. "We had a man out here when the property went up for sale. He said it was in fairly nice shape on the inside, but I'd guess, after it's been closed up for so long—well, you might take that with a grain of salt."

Translated from realty-speak, Tom thought, that means it's a hellacious mess.

But the door eased open on hinges that felt freshly oiled, across a swatch of neat beige broadloom.

"I'll be damned," Archer said.

Tom stepped over the threshold. He flicked the wall switch and a ceiling light blinked on, but it wasn't really necessary; a high south-facing window allowed in a good deal of the watery sunshine. The house had been built with the climate in mind: it would not succumb to gloom even in the rain.

On the right, the living room opened into a kitchen. On the left, a hallway connected the bedrooms and the bath.

A stairway led down to the basement.

"I'll be damned," Archer repeated. "Maybe I was wrong about this place."

The room they faced was meticulously clean, the furniture old but spotless. A mechanical mantel clock ticked away (but who had wound it?) under what looked like a Picasso print. Just slightly kitschy, Tom thought, the glass-topped coffee table, the low Danish Modern sofa; very sixties, but immaculately preserved. It might have popped out of a time capsule.

"Well maintained," he said.

"You bet. Considering it wasn't maintained at all, far as I know."

"Who's the owner?"

"The property came up for state auction a long time ago. Holding company in Seattle bought it but never did anything with it. They've been selling off packets of land all through here for the last year or so." He shook his head. "To be honest, the house was entirely derelict. We had a man out to evaluate these properties, shingles and foundation and so on, but he never said—I mean, we assumed, all these old frame houses out here—" He put his hands in his pockets and frowned. "The utilities weren't even switched on till late last week."

How many cold winters, hot summers had this room been closed and locked? Tom paused and slid his finger along a newel post where the stairs ran down into darkness. His finger came away clean. The wood looked oiled. "Phantom maid service?"

Archer didn't laugh. "Jack Shackley's the listed agent on this. Maybe he was in to tidy up. Somebody did a phenomenal job, anyway. The listing is house and contents and it looks like you have some nice pieces here—maybe a little dated. Shall we have a look around?"

"I think we should."

Tom circled twice through the house—once with Archer, once "to get his own impression" while Archer left his business card on the kitchen counter and stepped outside for a smoke. His impression was the same both times. The kitchen cupboards opened frictionlessly to spotless, uniformly vacant interiors. The linen closet was cedar-lined, fragrant and bare. The bedrooms were empty except for the largest, which contained a modest bed, a chest of drawers, and a mirror— dustless. In the basement, high windows peeked out at the rear lawn; these were covered with white roller blinds, which the sun had turned brittle yellow. *(Time passes here after all,* he thought.)

The building was sound, functional, and clean.

The fundamental question was, did it feel like home?

No. At least, not yet.

But that might change.

Did he *want* it to feel like home?

But it was a question he couldn't answer to his own satisfaction. Maybe what he wanted was not so much a house as a cave: a warm, dry place in which to nurse his wounds until they healed—or at least until the pain was bearable.

But the house was genuinely interesting.

He ran his hand idly along a blank basement wall and was startled to feel . . . what?

The hum of machinery, carried up through gypsum board and concrete block—instantly stilled?

Faint tingle of electricity?

Or nothing at all.

"Tight as a drum."

This was Archer, back from his sojourn.

"You may have found a bargain here, Tom. We can go back to my office if you want to talk about an offer."

"Why the hell not," Tom Winter said.

The town of Belltower occupied the inside curve of a pleasant, foggy Pacific bay on the northwestern coast of the United States.

Its primary industries were fishing and logging. A massive pulp mill had been erected south of town during the boom years of the fifties, and on damp days when the wind came blowing up the coast the town was enveloped in the sulfurous, bitter stench of the mill. Today there had been a stiff offshore breeze; the air was clean. Shortly before sunset, when Tom Winter returned to his room at the Seascape Motel, the cloud stack rolled away and the sun picked out highlights on the hills, the town, the curve of the bay.

He bought himself dinner in the High Tide Dining Room and tipped the waitress too much because her smile seemed genuine. He bought a *Newsweek* in the gift shop and headed back to his second-floor room as night fell.

Amazing, he thought, to be back in this town. Leaving here had been, in Tom's mind, an act of demolition. He had ridden the bus north to Seattle pretending that everything behind him had been erased from the map. Strange to find the town still here, stores still open for business, boats still anchored at the marina behind the VFW post.

The only thing that's been demolished is my life.

But that was self-pity, and he scolded himself for it. The quintessential lonely vice. Like masturbation, it was a parody of something best performed in concert with others.

He was aware, too, of a vast store of pain waiting to be acknowledged . . . but not here in this room with the ugly harbor paintings on the wall, the complimentary postcards in the bureau, pale rings on the wood veneer where generations had abandoned their vending-machine Cokes to sweat in the dry heat. Here, it would be too much.

He padded down the carpeted hallway, bought a Coke so he could add his own white ring to the furniture.

The phone was buzzing when he got back. He picked it up and popped the ring-tab on the soft-drink can.

"Tom," his brother said.

"Tony. Hi, Tony."

"You all by yourself?"

"Hell, no," Tom said. "The party's just warming up. Can't you tell?"

"That's very funny. Are you drinking something?"

"Soda pop, Tony."

"Because I don't think you should be sitting there all by yourself. I think that sets a bad pattern. I don't want you getting sauced again."

Sauced, Tom thought, amused. His brother was a wellspring of these antique euphemisms. It was Tony who had once described Brigitte Nielsen as "a red-hot tamale." Barbara had always relished his brother's bon mots. She used to call it her "visiting Tony yoga"—making conversation with one hand ready to spring up and disguise a grin.

"If I get sauced," Tom said, "you'll be the first to know."

"That's exactly what I'm afraid of. I called in a lot of favors to get you this job. Naturally, that leaves my ass somewhat exposed."

"Is that why you phoned?"

A pause, a confession: "No. Loreen suggested—well, we both thought—she's got a chicken ready to come out of the oven and there's more than enough to go around, so if you haven't eaten—"

"I'm sorry. I had a big meal down at the coffee shop. But thank you. And thank Loreen for me."

Tony's relief was exquisitely obvious. "Sure you don't want to drop by?" Brief chatter in the background: "Loreen's done up a blueberry pie."

"Tell Loreen I'm sorely tempted but I want to make it an early night."

"Well, whatever. Anyway, I'll call you next week."

"Good. Great."

"Night, Tom." A pause. Tony added, "And welcome back."

Tom put down the phone and turned to confront his own reflection, gazing dumbly out of the bureau mirror. Here was a haggard man with a receding hairline who looked, at this moment, at least a decade older than his thirty years. He'd put on weight since Barbara left and it was beginning to show —a bulge of belly and a softness around his face. But it was the expression that made the image in the mirror seem so ancient. He had seen it on old men riding buses. A frown that announces surrender, the willing embrace of defeat.

Options for tonight?

He could stare out the window, into his past; or into this mirror, the future.

The two had intersected here. Here at the crossroads. This rainy old town.

He turned to the window.

Welcome back.

Doug Archer called in the morning to announce that Tom's offer on the house—most of his carefully hoarded inheritance, tendered in cash—had been accepted. "Possession is immediate. We can have all the paperwork done by the end of the day. A few signatures and she's all yours."

"Would it be possible to get the key today?"

"I don't see any problem with that."

Tom drove down to the realty office next to the Harbor Mall. Archer escorted him through paperwork at the in-house Notary Public, then took him across the street for lunch. The restaurant was called El Nino—it was new; the location used to be a Kresge's, if Tom recalled correctly. The decor was nautical but not screamingly kitschy.

Tom ordered the salmon salad sandwich. Archer smiled at the waitress. "Just coffee, Nance."

She nodded and smiled back.

"You're not wearing your realty jacket," Tom said.

"Technically, it's my day off. Plus, you're a solid purchase. And what the hell, you're a hometown boy, I don't have to impress anybody here." He settled back in the vinyl booth, lean in his checkerboard shirt, his long hair a little wilder than he had worn it the day before. He thanked the waitress when the coffee arrived. "I looked into the history of the house, by the way. My own curiosity, mainly."

"Something interesting?"

"Sort of interesting, yeah."

"Something you didn't want to tell me until the papers were signed?"

"Nothing that would change your mind, Tom. Just a little bit odd."

"So? It's haunted?"

Archer smiled and leaned over his cup. "Not quite. Though that wouldn't surprise me. The property has a peculiar history. The lot was purchased in 1963 and the house was finished the next year. From 1964 through 1981 it was occupied by a guy named Ben Collier—lived alone, came into town once in a while, no visible means of support but he paid his bills on time. Friendly when you talked to him, but not *real* friendly. Solitary."

"He sold the house?"

"Nope. That's the interesting part. He disappeared around 1980 and the property came up for nonpayment of taxes. Nobody could locate the gentleman. He had no line of credit, no social security number anybody could dig up, no registered birth—his car wasn't even licensed. If he died, he didn't leave a corpse." Archer sipped his coffee. "Real good coffee here, in my opinion. You know they grind the beans in back? Their own blend. Colombian, Costa Rican—"

Tom said, "You're enjoying this story."

"Hell, yes! Aren't you?"

Tom discovered that he was, as a matter of fact. His interest had been piqued. He looked at Archer across the table—frowned and looked more closely. "Oh, shit, I know who you are! You're the kid who used to pitch stones at cars down along the coast highway!"

18

"You were a grade behind me. Tony Winter's little brother."

"You cracked a windshield on a guy's Buick. There were editorials in the paper. Juvenile delinquency on the march."

Archer grinned. "It was an experiment in ballistics."

"Now you sell haunted houses to unsuspecting city slickers."

"I think 'haunted' is kind of melodramatic. But I did hear another odd story about the house. George Bukowski told me this—George is a Highway Patrol cop, owns a double-wide mobile home down by the marina. He said he was up along the Post Road last year, cruising by, when he saw a light in the house—which he knew was unoccupied 'cause he'd been in on the search for Ben Collier. So he stopped for a look. Turned out a couple of teenagers had broken a basement window. They had a storm lantern up in the kitchen and a case of Kokanee and a ghetto blaster—just having a good old party. He took them in and confiscated maybe an eighth-ounce of dope from the oldest boy, Barry Lindell. Sent 'em all home to their parents. Next day George goes back to the house to check out the damage—the kicker is, it turns out there wasn't any damage. It was like they'd never been there. No matches on the floor, no empties, everything spit-polished."

Tom said, "The window where they broke in?"

"It wasn't broken anymore."

"Bullshit," Tom said.

Archer held up his hands. "Sure. But George swears on it. Says the window wasn't even reputtied, he would have recognized that. It wasn't *fixed*—it just *wasn't broken.*"

The waitress delivered the sandwich. Tom picked it up and took a thoughtful bite. "This is an obsessively *tidy* ghost we're talking about."

"The phantom handyman."

"I can't say I'm frightened."

"I don't guess you have any reason to be. Still—"

"I'll keep my eyes open."

"And let me know how it goes," Archer said. "I mean, if that's okay with you." He slid his business card across the table. "My home number's on the back."

"You're that curious?"

Archer checked out the next table to make sure nobody was listening. "I'm that fucking bored."

"Yearning for the old days? A sunny afternoon, a rock in your hand, the smell of a wild convertible?"

Archer grinned. The grin said, Hell, yes, I *am* that kid, and I don't much mind admitting it.

This man enjoys life, Tom thought.

Heartening to believe that was still possible.

Before he drove out to the house Tom stopped at the Harbor Mall to pick up supplies. At the A&P he assembled a week's worth of staples and a selection of what Barbara used to call bachelor food: frozen entrees, potato chips, cans of Coke in plastic saddles. At the Radio Shack he picked up a plug-in phone, and at Sears he paid $300 for a portable color TV.

Thus equipped for elementary survival, he drove to the house up along the Post Road.

The sun was setting when he arrived. Did the house look haunted? No, Tom thought. The house looked *suburban.* Cedar siding a little faded, the boxy structure a little lost in these piney woods, but not dangerous. Haunted, if at all, strictly by Mr. Clean. Or perhaps the Tidy Bowl Man.

The key turned smoothly in the lock.

Stepping over the threshold, he had the brief but disquieting sensation that this was after all somebody else's house . . . that he had arrived, like Officer Bukowski's juvenile delinquents, without credentials. Well, to hell with *that.* He flicked every light switch he could reach until the room was blisteringly bright. He plugged in the refrigerator—it began to hum at once—and dropped the Cokes inside. He plugged in the TV set and tuned the rabbit ears to a Tacoma station, a little fuzzy but watchable. He cranked the volume up.

Noise and light.

He preheated the ancient white enamel stove, watching the elements for a time to make sure everything worked. (Everything did.) The black Bakelite knobs were as slick as ebony; his own fingerprints seemed like an insult to their polished surface. He slipped a TV dinner into the oven and closed the door. Welcome home.

A new life, he thought.

That was why he had come here—or at least that was what he'd told his friends. Looking around this clean, illuminated space, it was possible—almost possible—to believe that.

He took the TV dinner into the living room and poked at the tepid fried chicken with a plastic fork while MacNeil (or Lehrer, he had never quite sorted that out) conducted a round-table discussion of this year's China crisis. When he was finished he tidied away the foil plate into a plastic bag—he wasn't ready to offend the Hygiene Spirit just yet—and pulled the tab on a Coke. He watched two nature documentaries and a feature history of Mormonism. Then, suddenly, it was late, and when he switched off the set he heard the wind turning the branches of the pines; he was reminded how far he had come from town and what a large slice of loneliness he might have bought himself, here.

He turned up the heat. The weather was still cool, summer still a ways off. He stepped outside and watched the silhouettes of the tall pines against the sky. The sky was bright with stars. You have to come a long way out, Tom thought, to see a sky like this.

Inside, he locked the door behind him and slid home the security chain.

The bed in the big bedroom belonged to him now . . .

but he had never slept in it, and he felt the weight of its strangeness. The bed was made in the same Danish Modern style as the rest of the furniture: subdued, almost generic, as if it had been averaged out of a hundred similar designs; not distinctive but solidly made. He tested the mattress; the mattress was firm. The sheets smelled faintly of clean, crisp linen and not at all of dust.

He thought, *I'm an intruder here* . . .

But he frowned at himself for the idea. Surely not an intruder, not after the legal divinations and fiscal blessings of the realty office. He was that most hallowed institution now, a Homeowner. Misgivings, at this stage, were strictly beside the point.

He switched off the bedside lamp and closed his eyes in the foreign darkness.

He heard, or thought he heard, a distant humming . . . barely audible over the whisper of his own breath. The sound of faraway, buried machinery. Night work at a factory underground. Or, more likely, the sound of his imagination. When he tried to focus on it it vanished into the ear's own night noises, tinnitus and the creaking of small bones. Like every house, Tom thought, this one must move and sigh with the pulse of its heat and the tension of its beams.

Surrounded by the dark and the buzzing of his own thoughts, he fell asleep at last.

The dream came to him after midnight but well before dawn —it was three A.M. when he woke and checked his watch.

The dream began conventionally. He was arguing with Barbara, or bearing the brunt of one of her arguments. She had accused him of complicity in some sweeping, global disaster: the warming of the earth, ocean pollution, nuclear war. He protested his innocence (at least, his ignorance); but her small face, snub-nosed, lips grimly compressed, radiated a disbelief so intense that he could smell the rising odor of his own guilt.

But this was only one more variation of what had become the standard Barbara dream. On another night it might have ended there. He would have come awake drenched in the effluvia of his own doubt; would have rinsed his face with cold tap water and staggered back to bed like a battle-fatigued foot soldier slogging to the trenches.

Tonight, instead, the dream dissolved into a new scenario. Suddenly he was alone; he was in a house that was like this house, but bigger, emptier; he was lying on his back in a room with a single high window. There was a diffuse moonlight that illuminated only his bed and left the margins of the room in cavernous darkness.

Hidden in that darkness, things were moving.

He couldn't tell what sort of things they were. Their feet ticked like cat's claws on the hard floor and they seemed to be whispering to one another in a high, buzzing falsetto—a language he had never heard. He imagined elves; he imagined immense, articulate rats.

But the worst thing was their invisibility—compounded by what he recognized suddenly as his own helplessness. He understood that the room had no door; that the window was impossibly high; that his arms and legs were not just stiff but paralyzed.

He strained forward, peering into the darkness . . .

And *they* opened their eyes—all at once.

A hundred eyes all around him.

A hundred disks of pure, pupil-less, bone-white light.

The whispering rose in a metallic, clattering crescendo—

And he awoke.

Woke alone in this smaller, brighter, but still moonlit and unfamiliar room.

Woke with his heart pounding wildly in his chest.

Woke with the sound still ringing in his ears:
The hiss of their voices. The clatter of their nails.

Of course, it was only a dream.

The morning house was clean, hollow, blank, and prosaic. Tom paced from bedroom to kitchen listening to the unfamiliar shush of his feet against the broadloom. He put together breakfast, fried eggs and a bagel, and stacked the dirty dishes in the sink when he was finished. Bachelor housekeeping. Maybe the Genius Loci would clean up.

Yesterday's overcast had spilled away across the mountains. Tom opened the screen door at the back of the kitchen and stepped out into the yard. The lawn had been slashed down to stubble but was starting to grow back, as much weed as grass. No housekeeping elves out here. A stand of tall pine rose up beyond the margin of the yard, enclosing ferns and fallen needles in its darkness. An overgrown trail led away from the corner of the yard and Tom followed it a few paces in, but the trees closed out the sun and the air was suddenly chill. He listened a moment to the drip of water somewhere in this spongy wilderness. Archer had said the forest ran a long way back, that there was a cedar swamp behind the property. (Archer would know, Tom thought. Archer the car-stalker, trailblazer, rock-climber, truant . . . these childhood memories had begun to freshen.) A damp breeze tickled the pale hair on his arms. A hummingbird darted up, regarded him querulously, and darted away.

He turned back to the house.

Tony called after lunch with another dinner invitation, which Tom could not gracefully decline. "Come on over," Tony said. "We'll stoke up the barbecue." It was an order as much as an invitation: tribute to be paid.

Tom left the dirty dishes in the sink. At the door he paused and turned back to the empty house.

"You want to clean up, go ahead."

No answer.

Oh, well.

It was a long drive to Tony's place. Tony and Loreen lived in the Seaview district, a terrace of expensive family homes along the scalloped bay hills south of town. The neighborhood was prestigious but the house Tony lived in wasn't especially flashy—Tony was very Protestant about overt displays of wealth. Tony's house, in fact, was one of the plainer of these homes, a flat white facade which concealed its real, formidable opulence: the immense plate glass windows and the cedar deck overlooking the water. Tom parked in the driveway behind Loreen's Aerostar and was welcomed at the door by the entire family: Tony, five-year-old Barry, Loreen with cranky eight-month Tricia squirming against her shoulder. Tom smiled and stepped into the mingled odors of stain-proofed broadloom, Pine-Sol, Pampers.

He would have liked to sit and talk a while with Loreen. ("Poor Loreen," Barbara used to say. "Playing Tony's idea of a housewife. All diapers and Barbara Cartland novels.") But Tony threw an arm over his shoulder and marched him through the spacious living room to the deck, where his propane barbecue hissed and flamed alarmingly.

"Sit," Tony said, waving a pair of tongs at a deck chair.

Tom sat and watched his brother paint red sauce over steaks. Tony was five years older than Tom, balding but trim, the creases around his eyes defined more by exercise and sunshine than by age. It would be hard, Tom thought, to guess which of us is older.

It was Tony who had come roaring out to Seattle like an angry guardian angel—six months after Barbara moved out; five months after Tom left his job at Aerotech; three months after Tom stopped answering his phone. Tony had cleared the apartment of empty bottles and frozen food wrappers, switched off the TV that had flickered and mumbled for

25

weeks uninterrupted, scolded Tom into showering and shaving—talked him into the move back to Belltower and the job at the car lot.

It was also Tony who had offered, as consolation for the loss of Barbara, the observation "She's a bitch, little brother. They're all bitches. Fuck 'em."

"She's not a bitch," Tom had said.

"They're all bitches."

"Don't call her that," Tom had said, and he remembered Tony's look, the arrogance eroding into uncertainty.

"Well . . . you can't throw your life away for her, anyhow. There are people out there going on with their business —people with cancer, people whose kids were smeared over the highway by semi trucks. If they can deal with it, you can fucking well deal with it."

This was both unanswerable and true. Tom accepted the chastisement and had been clinging to it since. Barbara would not have approved; she disliked the appropriation of public grief for private purposes. Tom was more pragmatic. You do what you have to.

But here he was in Tony's big house beside the bay, and it occurred to him that he was carrying a considerable load of guilt, gratitude, and resentment, mostly directed at his brother.

He made small talk while the steaks charred over the flames. Tony responded with his own chatter. Tony had bought the propane barbecue "practically wholesale" from a guy he knew at a retail hardware outlet. He was considering investing in a couple of rental properties this summer. "You should have talked to me about that house before running off half cocked." And he had his eye on a new sailboat.

This wasn't bragging, Tom understood. Barbara had long ago pointed out Tony's need for physical evidence of his worth, like the validations punched into bus tickets. To his credit, he was at least discreet about it.

26

The problem was that he, Tom, had no such validation of his own; in Tony's eyes, this must render him suspicious. A man without a VCR or a sports car might be capable of anything. This nervousness extended to Tom's job performance, a topic that had not been broached but which hovered over the conversation like a cloud.

Tony's own reliability, of course, was unquestioned. When their parents died Tony had staked his share of the estate on a junior partnership in an auto dealership out on Commercial Road. The investment was more than financial: Tony had put in a lot of time, sweat, and deferred gratification. And the investment had paid off, handsomely enough that Tom sometimes wondered whether his own use of the same inheritance—for his engineering degree, and now the house—was ultimately frivolous. What had it bought him? A divorce and a job as a car salesman.

But he was not even a salesman, really. "For now," Tony said, carrying the steaks in to the dining room table—Topic A surfacing at last—"you are strictly a gofer, a lot boy, a floor whore. You don't write up sales until the manager says you're ready. *Loreen!* We're gettin' hungry here! Where the hell is the salad?"

Loreen emerged dutifully from the kitchen with a cut-glass bowl filled with iceberg and romaine lettuce, sliced tomatoes, mushrooms, a wooden spoon and fork. She set down the bowl and went about tucking Tricia into a high chair while Barry tugged at her dress. Tony sat down and poured himself iced tea from a sweating jug. "The steaks look wonderful," Loreen said.

Tom spent the salad course wondering what a "floor whore" was. Loreen fed Tricia from a jar of strained peas, then excused herself long enough to install the baby in a playpen. Barry didn't want the steak even after she cut it for him; Loreen fixed him a peanut butter sandwich and sent him out into the back yard. When she sat down again her own steak was surely stone cold—Tony had just about finished his.

A floor whore, Tony explained, was a novice salesman, viewed mainly as a nuisance by the older hands at the lot. Tony shook his head. "The thing is," he said, "I'm already getting some flak over this. Bob Walker—the co-owner—was very much opposed to me putting you in this job. He says it's nepotism and he says it frankly sucks. And he has a point, because it creates a problem for the sales manager. He knows you're my brother, so the question becomes, do I handle this guy with kid gloves or do I treat him like any other employee?"

"I don't want any special treatment," Tom said.

"I know! Of course! *You* know that, *I* know that. But I had to go to the manager—Billy Klein, you'll meet him tomorrow—I had to go to him and say, Hey, Billy, just do your job. If this guy fucks up then tell him so. If he doesn't work out, you tell me. This is not a featherbed. I want the maximum from this man."

"Sure enough," Tom said, inspecting the greasy remains of the steak on his plate.

"There are basically two things I want to make clear," Tony said. "One is that if you screw up, I look bad. So as a favor to me, please don't screw up. The second is that Billy has a free hand as far as I'm concerned. You answer to him from now on. I don't do his job and I don't look out for you. And he is not always an easy man to please. Frankly, he wouldn't piss down your throat if your guts were on fire. If it works out, then fine, but if not—*what the hell are you smiling at?*"

" 'Piss down your throat if your guts were on fire'?"

"It's a *colloquialism*. Jesus, Tom, it's not supposed to be funny!"

"Barbara would have loved it."

Barbara would have repeated it for weeks. Once, during a

28

phone call, Tony had described the weather as "cold as the tits on a brass monkey." Barbara laughed so hard she had to pass Tom the receiver. Tom explained patiently that she'd swallowed her gum.

But Tony wasn't amused. He wiped his mouth and slapped the napkin down on the table. "If you want this job you'd better think a little more about your future and a little less about your hippy-dippy ex-wife, all right?"

Tom flushed. "She wasn't—"

"No! Spare me the impassioned defense. She's the one who ran off with her twenty-year-old boyfriend. She doesn't deserve your loyalty and you sure as shit don't owe it to her."

"Tony," Loreen said. Her tone was pleading. *Please, not here.*

Barry, the five-year-old, had wandered in from the back yard; he stood with one peanut butter–encrusted hand on the armoire and gazed at the adults with rapt, solemn interest.

Tom desperately wanted to be able to deliver an answer—something fierce and final—and was shocked to discover he couldn't produce one.

"It's a new world," Tony said. "Get used to it."

"I'll serve the dessert," Loreen said.

After dinner Tony went off to tuck in Barry and read him a story. Tricia was already asleep in her crib, and Tom sat with Loreen in the cooling kitchen. He offered to help with the dishes but his sister-in-law shooed him away: "I'm just rinsing them for later." So he sat at the big butcher-block table and peered through the window toward the dark water of the bay, where pleasure-boat lights bobbed in the swell.

Loreen dried her hands on a dish towel and sat opposite him. "It's not such a bad life," she said.

Tom gave her a long look. It was the kind of bald statement Loreen was prone to, couched in the slow Ohio Valley cadences of her youth. Her life here, she meant; her life with Tony: not so bad.

"I never said it was," Tom told her.

"No. But I can tell. I know what you and Barbara thought of us." She smiled at him. "Don't be embarrassed. I mean, we might as well talk. It's all right to talk."

"You have a good life here."

"Yes. We do. And Tony is a good man."

"I know that, Loreen."

"But we're nothing special. Tony would never admit it, of course. But that's the fact. Down deep, he knows. And maybe it makes him a little mean sometimes. And maybe *I* know it, and I get a little sad—for a little while. But then I get over it."

"You're not ordinary. You're both very lucky."

"Lucky, but ordinary. The thing is, Tom, what's hard is that you and Barbara *were* special. It always tickled me to see you two. Because you were special and you knew it. The way you smiled at each other and the way you talked. The things you talked about. You talked about the world—you know, politics, the environment, whatever—you talked like it mattered. Like it was up to you personally to do something about it. I always felt just a little bigger than life with you two around."

"I appreciate that," Tom said. In fact he was unexpectedly grateful to her for saying it—for recognizing what Barbara had meant to him.

"But that's changed." Loreen was suddenly serious. Her smile faded. "Now Barbara's gone, and I think you have to learn how to be ordinary. And I don't think that's going to be real easy for you. I think it's going to be pretty tough."

Tony didn't apologize, but he came out of Barry's room somewhat abashed and eager to please. He said he'd like to see the new house and Tom seized on the offer as an excuse to leave early. He let Tony follow him down the coast in the electric-blue Aerostar. Moving inland, up the Post Road and away from the traffic, Tony became a glare in Tom's rearview mirror, lost when the car angled around stands of pine. They parked at the house; Tony climbed out of his van and the two of them stood a moment in the starry, frog-creaking night.

"Mistake to buy so far out," Tony said.

"I like the place," Tom offered. "The price was right."

"Bad investment. Even if the market heats up, you're just too damn far from town."

"It's not an investment, Tony. It's my house. It's where I live."

Tony gave him a pitying look.

"Come on in," Tom said.

He showed his brother around. Tony poked into cupboards, dug a fingernail into the window casements, stood up on tiptoe to peer into the fuse box. When they arrived back at the living room Tom poured his brother a Coke. Tony acknowledged with a look that this was good, that there was no liquor handy. "Fairly sound building for its age," he admitted. "Christ knows it's clean."

"Self-cleaning," Tom said.

"What?"

"No—nothing."

"You planning to have us out for dinner one of these days?"

"Soon as I get set up. You and Loreen and the whole tribe."

"Good . . . that's good."

Tony finished his Coke and moved toward the door.

This is as hard for him, Tom recognized, *as it is for me.*

"Well," Tony said. "Good luck, little brother. What can I say?"

"You've said it. Thanks, Tony."

They embraced awkwardly. "I'll look for you at the lot," Tony said, and turned away into the cool night air.

Tom listened to the van as it thrummed and faded down the road.

He went back into the house, alone.

The silence seemed faintly alive.

"Hello, ghosts," Tom said. "Bet you didn't do the dishes after all."

But the thing was, they had.

Two

It wasn't long before a single question came to occupy his mind almost exclusively: What was madness, and how do you know when it happens to you?

The cliché was that the question contained its own answer. If you're sane enough to wonder, you must be all right. Tom had trouble with the logic of this. Surely even the most confirmed psychotic must sometimes gaze into the mirror and wonder whether things hadn't gone just a little bit wrong?

The question wasn't academic. As far as he could figure, there were only two options. Either he had lost his grip on his sanity—and he wasn't willing to admit that yet—or something was going on in this house.

Something scary. Something strange.

He shelved the question for three days and was careful to clean up meticulously: no dirty dishes in the sink, no crumbs on the counter, garbage stowed in the back yard bin. The Tidiness Elves had no scope for their work and Tom was able to pretend that he had actually done the dishes himself the night he went to Tony's: it must have been his memory playing a trick on him.

These were his first days at Arbutus Ford and there was

plenty to occupy his mind. He spent most of his daylight hours studying a training manual or bird-dogging the senior salesmen. He learned how to greet buyers; he learned what an offer sheet looked like; he learned how to "T.O."—how to turn over a buyer to the sales manager, who could eke out a few more dollars on an offer; who would then T.O. the customer to the finance people. ("Which is where the *real* money's made," the sales manager, Billy Klein, cheerfully confided.)

The lot was a new/used operation down along the flat stretch of Commercial Road between Belltower and the suburban malls. Tom sometimes thought of it as a paved farm field where a crop of scrap metal had sprouted but not ripened—everything was still sleek and new. The weather turned hot on Wednesday; the days were long, the customers sparse. Tom drank Cokes from sweating bottles and studied his system manual in the sales lounge. Most of the salesmen took breaks at a bar called Healy's up the road, but they were a fairly hard-drinking crowd and Tom wasn't comfortable with that yet. Lunchtimes, he scuffed across the blistering asphalt to a little steak and burger restaurant called The Paradise. He was conserving his money. He might make a respectable income on commissions in an average month, Klein assured him—assuming he started selling soon. But it was a grindingly slow month. Evenings he drove inland through the dense, ancient pine forest and thought about the mystery of the house. Or tried not to.

Two possibilities, his mind kept whispering.

You're insane.

Or you're not alone here.

Thursday night, he put three greasy china plates on the counter next to the stainless steel sink and went to bed.

In the morning the dishes were precisely where he had left them—as smooth and clean as optical lenses.

• • • •

Friday night, he dirtied and abandoned the same three plates. Then he moved into the living room, tuned in the eleven o'clock news and installed himself on the sofa. He left the lights on in both rooms. If he moved his head a few degrees to the right he had a good view of the kitchen counter. Any motion would register in his peripheral vision.

This was scientific, Tom reassured himself. An experiment.

He was pleased with himself for approaching the problem objectively. In a way, it was almost exciting—staying up late waiting for something impossible to happen. He propped his feet on the coffee table and sprang the tab on a soda can.

Half an hour later he was less enthusiastic. He'd been keeping early hours; it was hard not to nod off during commercial breaks. He dozed a moment, sat upright and shot a glance into the kitchen. Nothing had changed.

(Well, what had he expected? Gnomes in Robin Hood hats humming "Whistle While You Work"? Or maybe—some perverse fraction of his mind insisted—creatures like rats. With clackety claws and saucer eyes.)

The "Tonight" show was less than engaging, but he wasn't stuck with Carson: the local cable company had hooked him up last week. He abused the remote control until it yielded an antique science fiction film: *Them*, featuring James Whitmore and giant ants in the Mojave. In the movies radiation produced big bugs; in the neighborhood of failed fission reactors it mainly caused cancer and leukemia—the difference, Barbara had once observed, between Art and Life. He was nodding off again by the time the ants took refuge in the storm drains of Los Angeles. He stood up, walked to the kitchen— where nothing had changed—and fixed himself a cup of coffee. Now, mysteriously, it *felt* late: no traffic down the Post Road, a full moon hanging over the back yard. He carried his coffee into the living room. It occurred to him that this was a fairly spooky activity he had selected here: making odds on his own sanity, sometime after midnight. He had done things like this—well, things this *reminded* him of—when he was twelve years old, sleeping in the back yard with a flashlight or staying up with the monster flicks all by himself. Except that by now he would have given up and found some reassuring place to spend the night.

Here, there was only the house. Probably safe. Hardly reassuring.

He found an all-night Seattle station showing sitcom reruns. He propped himself up on the sofa, drained the coffee, and hoped the caffeine would help keep him awake. It did, or at least it put him on edge. Edgy, he remembered what he had come to think of as his father's credo: The world is a cold, thoughtless place and it has no special love for human beings. Maybe this was a mistake. Maybe he should go to bed, let the elves wash up, wake up bright and early and put the house back on the market. No law required him to become the Jacques Cousteau of the supernatural. That wasn't what he'd signed up for.

But maybe there was nothing supernatural about it. Something odd but entirely explainable might be at work. Some kind of bacteria. Insects (nonmutated). Anything. If he had to bet, that's where he'd put his money.

It was just that he wanted to know—really *know*.

He stretched out on the sofa. He meant to rest his head against the padded arm. He had no intention of going to sleep.

He closed his eyes and began to dream.

This time, the dream came without preamble.

In the dream he stood up from the sofa, went to the window and raised the sash.

The moon was low, but it cast a clear fluorescence over the back yard. In the dream, it seemed at first as if nothing had changed; there was the starry sky, the deep shadow of the forest, the bleached cedar fence obscure under ivy. Then he saw the grass moving in the wind, a curious sinewy motion—but there *was* no wind; and Tom understood that it wasn't the grass moving, it was something *in* the grass—something like insects, a hundred or more, moving in a snakelike column from the house into the woods. His heart gave a startled jump and he was suddenly afraid, but he couldn't look away or leave the window . . . somehow, that choice had been taken from him. He watched as the line of insect-things slowed to a stop and each one—and there were more of them than he had guessed—turned simultaneously to look at him with tiny saucer-shaped eyes, and they pronounced his name —*Tom Winter*—somehow *inside his head,* a voiceless chorus.

He woke in a drenching sweat.

The TV was showing fuzz. He stood and switched it off. His watch said 3:45.

In the kitchen, the dishes were flawlessly clean.

He slept four more hours in his bedroom with the door closed, and in the morning he showered and phoned Doug Archer—the number on the back of his business card. "You wanted me to get in touch if I noticed anything strange."

"That's right . . . is it getting weird out there?"

"Just a little weird. You could say that."

"Well, you called at the right time. I'm on vacation. The beeper gets switched off at noon. I was planning to drive up into the Cascades, but I can put it off a little while. How about if I drop by after lunch?"

"Good," Tom said, but he was troubled by the note of happy anticipation in Archer's voice.

If you talk about this, he thought, *you're opening one more door that maybe ought to stay closed—taking one step closer to ratifying your own insanity.*

But was silence any better? There were times (last night,

for instance) when he felt himself stewing in the sour juice of his own isolation. No: he needed to talk about this, and he needed to talk about it to somebody who wasn't family— obviously not Tony or Loreen. Archer would do.

Dreams aside, nothing threatening had happened. Some inexpensive dinnerware had been surreptitiously cleaned: not quite *Ghostbusters* material. But it was the dream that stayed in his mind.

He told Archer he'd expect him soon and replaced the phone in its cradle. The silence of the morning house rang out around him. He walked to the kitchen door, opened it and took a tentative step outside.

The air was bracing; the sky was bright.

Tom had brought home a power mower from Sears on Wednesday but he hadn't used it yet; the grass was ankle high. He was briefly afraid to put his foot down off the back step—a vagrant image of metallic insects with brightly focused eyes ran through his mind. (They might be there still. They might *bite*.)

He took a breath and stepped down.

His ankles itched with anticipation . . . but there was nothing sinister among these weeds, only a few ants and aphids.

He walked to the northern quadrant of the yard where the dream-insects had moved between the house and the woods.

He understood that by looking for their trail he was violating the commonsense assumption that dreams are necessarily separate from the daylight world. But he was past fighting the impulse. Yet another prop kicked from under the edifice of his sanity. (Tom had begun to envision his sanity as one of those southern California hillside houses erected on stilts— the ones that wash into the ocean in a heavy rain.) He examined the deep, seeded grass where the insects had seemed to be, but there was nothing unusual among the dewy grass blades and feathered dandelion heads.

He should have been reassured. Instead, he felt oddly disappointed. Disappointed because on some fundamental level he was convinced last night's dream had been no ordinary dream. (No—but he couldn't say exactly how it was different.)

He walked to the verge of the woods. In his dream this was where the broad trail of bright-eyed insects had passed into the moon-shadow of the trees.

The sun, this time of morning, did not much penetrate the deep Pacific Northwest pinewoods. There was a trail leading back through this tangle, but it began at the opposite end of the yard. Here there were only these old trees and this fern-tangle undergrowth, the smell of rotting pine needles and the drip of hoarded rainwater. The barrier between the forest and the sunlit yard could not have been more distinct. He braced his hands on a tree trunk. Leaning forward, he felt the cool, mushroom dampness of the forest on his face.

He turned back to the house.

In his dream, the insects had moved to the forest from the house. Tom paced back to the nearest wall. It was an ordinary frame wall sided with cedar, well preserved—the paint hadn't blistered or peeled—but hardly unusual. This was the wall at the back of the master bedroom, windowless at this corner.

But if his dream had not been a dream, there must be some sort of opening here.

He sat on his haunches and pulled away handfuls of high, seeded grass from the concrete foundation where it rose some few inches above the soil.

He held his breath, gazing at what he found there.

The concrete was riddled with small, precisely round holes. The holes were all alike, all approximately as wide as the ball of his thumb.

His foot slipped in the wet grass and he sat back with a thump on his tailbone.

39

They must be bolt holes, he thought. Something must have been attached here. A deck, maybe.

But the holes in the chalky, water-stained concrete were smooth as glass.

"Be damned," he said.

He plucked a stem of the tall grass and held it to one of the openings.

Like shoving a stick into a hornet's nest, Tom. Real dumb. You don't know what might be in there.

But when he pushed the long grass stem inside there was no resistance . . . no response.

He bent down and peered into the opening. He didn't put his cheek hard up against the concrete foundation, because he couldn't shake the belief that one of those tiny saucer-eyed creatures from his dream might be inside—that it might possess claws, teeth, a poison sac, a hostile intent. But he bent close enough to smell the rooty earth odor rising from the damp lawn . . . close enough to watch a sow bug trundling up the latticework of a thistle. No light radiated from the many holes in the foundation. He thought he felt a breath of air sigh out, oily and faintly metallic.

He stood up and backed off a pace.

What now? Do we call Exterminex? Dynamite the foundation?

Tell Archer?

No, Tom thought. None of the above. Not yet.

He explained everything else—the dishes, the dream—meticulously to Archer, who sat at the kitchen table drinking instant coffee and running his fingernail along the grain of the wood.

The telling of it made Tom feel foolish. Archer was sanity incarnate in his checkerboard cotton shirt and Levi's: rooted to the earth right through the soles of his high-top sneakers. Archer listened patiently, then grinned. "This has to be the most interesting thing to happen around here since Chuck Nixon saw a UFO over the waste treatment plant."

He *would* say that, Tom thought. Archer had been a legend at Sea View Elementary—"a world-class shit disturber," as the gym teacher had declared on one memorable occasion. Maybe that's why I called him, Tom thought: I still think of him as fearless.

"I mean it," Archer said. "You're obviously upset by this. But it's wonderful. I mean, here's this mundane little house in the woods, one more shitty frame house out along the Post Road—pardon me—then suddenly it's *more* than that. You know the quote from Kipling? 'There was a crack in his head and a little bit of the Dark World came through . . .'"

Tom winced. "Thanks a lot." Kipling?

"Don't misunderstand. I would be disappointed," Archer said, "if you were crazy. Craziness is very common. Very—" He struggled for a word. "Very *K-mart*. I'm hoping for something a little classier."

"You're enjoying this too much."

"It's my hobby," Archer said.

Tom blinked. "It's what?"

"Well, it's hard to explain. The supernatural: it's like a hobby with me. I'm a skeptic, you understand. I don't believe in ghosts, I don't believe in UFOs. I'm not that kind of enthusiast. But I've read all the books. Charles Fort, Jacques Vallee. I don't believe in it, but I decided a long time ago that I *wanted* it to be true. I want there to be rains of frogs. I want statues to bleed. I want it because—please don't repeat this—it would be like God saying, 'Fuck Belltower, Washington, here's a miracle.' It would mean the asphalt down by the car lots might break out in crocuses and morning glories and tie up traffic for a week. It would mean we might all wake up one morning and find the pulp mill crumbled into sand. Half the town would be out of work, of course. But we could all live on manna and red wine. And nobody—absolutely nobody —would sell real estate."

Tom said, "When I was twelve years old I used to pray for nuclear war. Not so that millions of people would die. So that I wouldn't have to go to school in the morning."

"Exactly! Everything would be rubble. Life would be transformed."

"Life would be *easier.*"

"More fun! Yes."

"Sure. But would it? I'm thirty years old, Doug. I don't pray for war anymore."

Archer met his gaze. "I'm thirty-two and I still pray for magic."

"Is that what we're talking about here?"

"Something extraordinary, anyhow. Unless you *are* crazy."

"It's a possibility," Tom said. "Crazy people see things sometimes. I had an aunt Emily who used to talk to Jesus. Jesus lived in the attic. Once in a while he'd move over to the bedroom and they'd have a chat while she combed her hair. Everybody in the family thought this was terrifically funny. Then one day Aunt Emily sliced open her wrists in a warm bath. Her landlord found her a week later. She left a note saying Jesus told her to do it."

Archer reflected on this a moment. "You're saying there are serious things at stake."

"Either way, it seems to me. My sanity. Or sanity in general."

"Screw sanity in general."

"My own in particular, then."

"You want me to take this seriously," Archer said. "Okay. Fine. But I don't know you. You're somebody I sold a house to. Somebody who was a year behind me at Sea View Elementary. You seem like a fairly reasonable guy. But let's be clear, Tom. You called me because you want credentials for your sanity. I want more than that."

Tom leaned back in his chair, considering this. Obviously time had not much tamed Douglas Archer. Maybe it was important to remember you could pull a jail sentence and a stiff fine for throwing stones at Buicks, especially if you were old enough to know better. Tom had no love for Belltower, but neither did he especially want to see morning glories tying up traffic down by the car lots (though it would piss Tony off no end).

Still, there was something seductive about Archer's attitude, especially after a night of nervous hysteria. He said, "You know some of the old trails up through here?"

Archer nodded.

"Let's scout the territory behind the house." Tom stood up. "Then we'll talk about what to do."

They followed an old, nearly overgrown foot trail into the dense woods behind the back yard.

Tom had forgotten what it was like to walk through these big Pacific Northwest pinewoods, this density of moss and fern and dripping water. He followed the broad back of Archer's checkerboard shirt along the trail, bending under branches or stepping over small, glossy freshets of rainwater. The sound of cars passing on the Post Road faded as they climbed a gentle slope westward. All this talk of magic—his own and Archer's—seemed much more plausible here.

Archer said, "There were Indians living in through here a hundred years ago. Used to be an old totem pole in among the cedars, but they dragged that off to the town museum."

"Who uses this trail?"

"The Hopfner kids down the road, but they moved away a long time ago. Hikers sometimes. There are trails all the way up from the housing development along Poplar. It's mostly overgrown down by your place—I don't suppose anybody goes through that way these days."

He paused behind Archer where the trail banked away

43

through an open meadow full of thistles and fireweed, past an old tin shack overgrown with ivy: someone's long-abandoned store of firewood, Tom guessed, the structure obscured and sagging moss-thick to the ground. Archer pushed ahead into the deeper forest and Tom followed until the tree shadows closed around him again.

They hiked for more than an hour, uphill through pine forest until they reached a rocky knoll. Archer clambered up the pinnacle, turned back and extended a hand to Tom. "We've come up a good height," he said, and Tom turned back and was surprised by a sweeping view not just to the Post Road but all the way to the coast—the town of Belltower clustered around the bay, the pulp mill lofting a gray plume of smoke.

"This is why people come up here," Archer said. "It's not a well-known trail. If we'd followed the other branch we would have ended up in some serious swamp. Up this way, it gets nice."

"Is there a name for this place?"

"Somebody must call it something. Everything's got a name, I guess."

"You come here a lot?"

"Once in a while. I come for the perspective. From here— on a nice day—everything looks good. The fucking parking lots look good."

"You hate this town," Tom said.

Archer shrugged. "If I hated it, I'd leave. Though from what I've seen I doubt I could find anything significantly better. Hate is a strong word. But I dislike it a whole lot— sometimes." He paused and looked sidelong at Tom, shading his face against the sun. "I do admit to wondering what brought you back here."

"You never asked."

"It's not polite. Specially when someone obviously doesn't

want to talk about it." He turned back to the view. The sunlight was intense. "So are we still being polite?"

"My wife left me," Tom said. "I lost my job. I was drinking for therapy."

Archer scrutinized him more closely now.

Tom said, "You're wondering whether an alcoholic can be trusted when he sees strange things at night. Fair enough. But it's been more than a month since I touched any kind of liquor. As an explanation, a good case of DTs would be almost comforting."

"How long were you drinking?"

"Seriously? Since the job fell through. Maybe three months."

Archer said, "I can think of a couple of tough questions."

"Such as?"

"Lots of people lose their jobs. Lots of people go through divorce. They don't all jump down a bottle."

There were lots of ways to answer that. The most succinct would be, *It's none of your business.* But maybe he had made it Archer's business; he had raised the issue of his own stability. It wasn't a hostile question.

He could say, *I was married for ten years to a bright, thoughtful woman whom I loved intensely, and whose mistrust grew until it was like a knife between us.*

He could explain about Barbara's political activism, her conviction that the world was teetering on the brink of ecological catastrophe. He could explain that his engineering work at Aerotech had divided them, tell Archer that she'd come to see him as a living example of the technological juggernaut: all his schooling and all his ingenuity plugged into a military-industrial machine so hydra-headed in its aspects and so single-minded in its goals that the earth itself was being strip-mined and forested into a global desert.

He could replay, perhaps, one of their arguments. He could reiterate his endless, patient assertion that the engines he designed were fuel-efficient; that his work, while not exactly a pursuit of the ecological Grail, might help clear the air around major cities. Band-Aid thinking, Barbara called this, a piddling solution to an overwhelming problem. A better combustion engine wouldn't restore the rain forests to Brazil or the redwoods to California. To which Tom would reply that it was a damn sight more productive than chaining himself to the gate of a paper mill or sneaking off with some long-haired anarchists to spike trees in the Cascades. At which point— more often in their last year—the conversation would decline into insult. Barbara would begin on his "complacent hick family," particularly Tony; and Tom, if he was drunk or angry enough, would explore the possible reasons for her recent loss of sexual appetite. ("It's not too complicated," she once told him. "Take a look in the mirror sometime.")

But there was no way to explain any of this. No way to explain his nagging suspicion that she was, after all, right; no way to explain the fundamental upwelling of love he still felt, even after their battles, when she was kneeling in the garden or brushing her hair before bed. He loved her with a loyalty that was animal in its mute persistence. He loved her even when he opened his mouth and called her frigid.

He blinked against the fierce blue sky, the curve of the distant bay.

He said, "I loved my wife a lot. I hated it when she left."

"So why'd she leave?" Archer added, "You're allowed to tell me to fuck off at this point."

"It was a political disagreement. I was doing engineering for a little R and D company out of Seattle. Barbara was into the peace movement, among other things. She came home one day and told me the company was about to be handed a big federal grant for weapons research, something connected with SDI. I told her there was no truth to the rumor. The people I worked for were scrupulous, small-scale, community-minded—I *knew* these guys. I checked out the possibility, asked a few questions, came up totally blank. Stood my ground. Really, it was just one more argument. There'd been more than a few. But it turned out this was the last one. She couldn't bear the idea of being married to a war-economy engineer. As far as Barbara was concerned it was dirty money."

"That's what broke you up?"

"That and the fact that she was seeing somebody else."

"Somebody in the movement," Archer guessed. "Somebody who was feeding her a line about government grants."

Tom nodded.

"Pretty fucking raw deal. So you started drinking—that's how you lost your job?"

"I started drinking later. I lost my job because the rumor turned out to be true. The company had been asked to bid on a satellite contract—a little bit of congressional pork for the Pacific Northwest. There was a lot of secrecy, a lot of paranoia about corporate espionage. It was all those questions I asked when I wanted to reassure Barbara. They figured I was a security risk."

Tom stood up and brushed the dirt off his jeans.

"Offhand," Archer said, "I would guess you're as sane as the next guy. A little bit bruised, maybe. Aside from what we've talked about, you hear voices?"

"Nope."

"Are you suicidal?"

"Three A.M. on a bad night—maybe. Otherwise no."

"Well, I'm no shrink. But it sounds like you're a long way from crazy. I think we ought to check out what's been happening in that house you bought."

"Good," Tom said.

He shook hands with Archer and smiled at him, but a new and unwelcome thought had formed at the back of his mind: *If I'm not insane, then maybe I ought to be scared.*

Three

The next morning, Sunday morning, Tom recalled that he hadn't told Archer about the holes in the foundation of the house.

Maybe it was a mistake to withhold this, the only physical evidence that what he'd experienced wasn't an illusion.

But he had held back on purpose, salvaging some fragment of the experience as his own. It was an odd idea: that he should feel possessive about a haunting (or whatever was happening here). But hadn't Archer been possessive, in his own way? All that talk about magic, as if this were his own personal miracle.

But it wasn't Archer who had been called by name in a dream. It wasn't Archer who had stood at the window and watched the shadows of the pines and heard a voice among their sighing voices. *Tom Winter,* the voice had said; and it seemed to him now, after a sounder sleep, that there had been another message, less obvious then but clarified some how by memory:

Help us, the voices had said.

Help us, Tom Winter. Please help us.

Archer arrived that afternoon with a VCR, a Sony video camera, and a tripod packed into the trunk of his car.

Tom helped him unload and erect all this paraphernalia in the living room, where it loomed like a selection of props from a science fiction movie. He said so to Archer, who shrugged. "That's what we're playing at, isn't it?"

"I don't think of this as playing. I *live* here."

"You live here. I'm playing."

"This is not a Huck Finn adventure, Doug. In case you haven't noticed, I'm not enjoying it."

"Something happen during the night, or are you just in a bad mood?"

"No, nothing happened." The question made him uncomfortable. "What's all this for?"

"Surveillance. The unsleeping eye. Take a look."

Tom peered into the eyepiece of the video camera. It was aimed into the kitchen and captured a fairly wide angle of the room, including the stainless steel sink and the tile countertop. A digital clock in the corner of the display read out the date, the hour, the minute, and the second.

Archer said, "The camera's hooked into the VCR and I just set the timer for midnight. At the slowest speed, we've got approximately eight hours of tape. You leave everything alone, you sleep soundly, and in the morning you see what we've got."

Tom shook his head. "They won't stand for this."

Archer regarded him curiously.

Tom pulled back from the eyepiece. "So what do we do in the meantime?"

"I think the logical thing would be to mess up the kitchen."

Archer had brought more than electronics. From the back seat of his car he produced two six-packs of beer, a bag of potato chips and a quart of sour cream and avocado dip his girlfriend had made.

"You eat like an undergraduate," Tom said.

"Is there any other way?" Archer opened the six-pack and

popped the tab on a can. "We can order a pizza for dinner." He handed a can to Tom, then looked suddenly dubious. "Oh, hey, are you AA or anything like that? I don't want to make life difficult."

"I was a hobby drinker," Tom said, "not a professional." But he left the beer alone.

The afternoon droned on. It was a sunny, warm day and Tom opened the front and back doors to let a breeze sweep through the house. The air smelled of hot, tarry pine.

Archer kicked back and put his Reeboks on the kitchen table. "You went to Sea View Elementary. Then the high school over on Jackson, I guess, just like everybody else. Shit-awful schools, both of them," and then they were off on a round of skewed nostalgia—what Barbara had once called "the hideous past, relived at leisure." It turned out that the trouble Archer had gotten into in high school had been more serious and more personal than preadolescent rock throwing. He had waged a war of attrition against his high school principal and his father—two staunch disciplinarians who happened to be poker buddies. Archer had spent plenty of nights listening to them vent their hatred of children over pretzels and a well-shuffled pack of Bicycle playing cards. His father was an appliance repairman who hated kids, Archer explained, out of some fundamental quirk of personality; the principal, Mr. Mayhew, had professional reasons and was deemed to be an expert on the matter. Jackson Archer, belt-whipping his only son, liked to explain that Mr. Mayhew did this for a living and could probably do a better job of it. In fact Mr. Mayhew confined himself to the use of a ruler on the back of the hand, which was painful without incurring the kind of visible injuries that brought mothers howling down to the school—maybe this was what made him an expert. Archer had a theory that they took out their poker losses on him; he learned to avoid whoever had lost money on Sunday night.

"Didn't stop you from getting in trouble," Tom observed.

"Didn't stop me from drinking, smoking, and riding in fast cars. Nope. But I never figured they really *wanted* to stop me. They were having too much fun."

"Does this story have a punch line?"

"When I was sixteen I drove my father's Pontiac into a tree. Totaled it. I wasn't hurt, but I was driving without a license. They sent me to a so-called military school upstate, with the happy consent of the Juvenile Court. What it was, of course, was a concentration camp for adolescent psychotics."

"What did you do *there?*"

Archer ceased smiling. "I ate shit, like every other inmate. These institutions live up to their rep, Tom. They can turn a sullen, rebellious teenager into a sullen, submissive one—like *that.* I ate shit for a couple of semesters and came back when my dad died. My mother said, 'I couldn't leave you in that place.' I thanked her politely, and when she marched me past the casket—in full parade dress, for Christ's sake—I looked down and said, 'Screw you and your poker game and your cardiac arrest too.'"

The silence rang out in the kitchen for a few awkward moments. Tom said, "You never forgave him?"

"He was a lonely, hostile man who never forgave me for being born and complicating his life. Maybe I'll be more generous than that. One of these days." He took a long pull from his beer. "So how about you? Another casualty of childhood?"

"I had a reasonably happy childhood. Nobody sent me to military school, anyway."

"That's not the only way to suffer."

"I can't say I *did* suffer. Not substantially. Dad wouldn't have stood for it."

"Ah—wait a minute. Winter? *Doctor* Winter? Used to have a practice over on Poplar Street?"

"That's us."

"Shit, I knew Doc Winter! I went there with a ruptured appendix when I was ten years old. My father said, 'The kid's complaining about a bellyache.' Of course, I had a raging fever, my abdomen was hard as a rock, I was convulsing from the pain. Your dad took a look at me and phoned the hospital for an ambulance. When he put down the phone he turned to my old man and said, 'You nearly killed your child by waiting this long. If there was a license for fatherhood, I would have yours revoked.' Sick as I was, I remembered that. It felt good. My God, Doc Winter's son! But didn't he—?"

"Both my parents died in a car accident," Tom said. "It was about twelve years ago. A log truck sideswiped them coming around a turn on the coast highway."

"You were how old?"

"Just finishing high school."

"Tough situation," Archer said.

"I lived. The insurance paid for my engineering degree. Much good it's doing me. But, you know, it was kind of ironic. I always figured Dad got into medicine because he believed the world was a bad, dangerous place. He had a real sense of human vulnerability—the basic fragility of a human body. He once told me the human body was a sack of skin containing the vital organs and something even more fragile, which was life."

"Maybe not a good attitude to grow up with," Archer said.

"But he was right. I understood that when the police showed up at the door, the night the truck accordioned his car. There's no forgiveness built into the system. I told Barbara so, dozens of times. She was always marching off to save the whales, save the trees, save some goddamn thing. It was endearing. But in the back of my head I always heard Dad's voice: 'This is only a holding action. Nothing is ever really saved.' Barbara thought the greenhouse effect was like a virus, something you could stop if you came up with the right vaccine. I told her it was a cancer—the cancer of humanity on the vital organs of the earth. You can't stop that by marching."

"Isn't that a little like giving up?"

"I think it's called acceptance."

Archer stood and walked to the door, where his silhouette obscured the motion of the trees.

"Very bleak attitude, Tom."

"Experience bears it out."

Around six, when the sun began to slant through the window over the sink and the kitchen bloomed with summer heat, they moved into the cooler dimness of the living room. Tom phoned Deluxe Pizza in Belltower and was assessed a five dollar delivery charge, " 'Cause we don't ordinarily come out that far." The order arrived an hour later—pepperoni pizza with anchovies, room temperature. After he paid the delivery driver Tom opened the curtains onto a view of the back yard, shadows lengthening among the pines. His appetite had vanished. He ate a little and took his plate to the kitchen. Coming back he negotiated around the video camera looming on its tripod like an alien sentinel. "They won't stand for it," he said again.

Archer looked up from his intense involvement with the pizza. "Yeah, you said that before. Who's *they?*"

"I don't know." Tom shrugged. "But don't you get a sense of it—a sort of intelligence at work?"

"I didn't think we'd admitted that much. Maybe you just have exceptionally tidy roaches."

"I'm beginning to think otherwise."

"For any particular reason?"

The dreams, Tom thought. The dreams, the holes in the foundation of the house . . . and a feeling, an intuition. "No, no particular reason."

"What you've described," Archer said, "sounds less like

intelligence than it does like a machine. The kind of idiot machine that keeps running when the owner's on vacation."

"Its owner being who? The guy who lived here—Ben Collier?"

"Maybe. Unfortunately, it's impossible to find out anything about him. Totally anonymous. Joan Fricker at the grocery store up at the highway must have seen him more than anybody else, and I doubt she could give you a good description. He never participated in public affairs, never held office, never wrote letters to the editor—never said more than hello, as far as anybody can remember. The only person with a special memory of Ben Collier is Jered Smith, who delivered his mail."

"He had memorable mail?"

"According to Jered, Ben Collier subscribed to every magazine published, or it seemed that way. Some not even in English. Every business day Jered delivered five or ten magazines and newspapers to this address. Magazines, he says, are heavy—and he was delivering on foot back then, though the Postal Service gave him a truck last year. That was the first hint that Ben Collier had vanished: Jered complained that there was a stack of magazines deep enough to block the mail slot."

"What kind of magazines?"

"Everything from *Time* to the *Manchester Guardian*. Heavy on current events, but not exclusively."

Tom was bemused. "It's an eccentricity, but—"

"Not just eccentricity. There's some pattern here. It's not a random set—more like a linear equation." Tom raised his eyebrows; Archer added, "Math is my *other* hobby. Math was the only high school class I never cut—you remember Mr. Foster? Tall guy, gray hair? Said I had a talent for it. I'm the guy who always reads the puzzles column in *Scientific American*."

Douglas Archer, JD mathematician. *Don't underestimate this man.* "It's not much to go on."

"It's absolutely nothing. Nothing at all. Just kind of interesting." Archer put his plate aside and stood up. "Well, anyway. Don't touch the equipment—it'll turn itself on. But you might want to play back the tape in the morning."

"Count on it. Can you stay for coffee?"

"I have a date for a late movie. But let me know what shows." His smile was mischievous. "Or what doesn't."

Archer closed the door behind him, and suddenly the house was hollow and empty.

That night, Tom made the disturbing discovery that he was afraid to go to sleep.

He showered and wrapped himself in a bathrobe and tuned in the "Tonight" show. The chatter was tedious, but he left it on for the sound of human voices. That's why we all own these boxes, he thought: because they talk to us when there's no one else home.

But maybe "afraid to sleep" was overstating the case: he wasn't jittery. It was more like a reluctance to close his eyes in the midst of these curious events. He had convinced himself something was happening here, a kind of subterranean industry, maybe something (if Archer's history was accurate) that had been happening for a hundred years or more on this spot. Something insectile, something out of the ground; something that loved holes and hidden places. He was developing a sense of it that was almost frighteningly precise. The eyes that regarded him in his dreams were the eyes—not of *machines,* Archer was wrong; but of something nearly mechanistic in its single-mindedness. A *builder's* eyes. But what exactly were they building?

Not something dangerous. Tom felt this to be true; the insects in his dreams weren't hostile or deadly. But they were fundamentally, utterly strange. It was as if he had reached

55

into a tide pool and touched something that lived there: a variegated, many-limbed polyp so unlike himself that it might have been extraterrestrial.

And of course there was Archer's video machinery, almost as alien, already whirring away. It had recorded no event and probably wouldn't. Or maybe—here was a disturbing thought —he would wake up and find the camera dismantled, its useful parts carried away and its carapace open and gutted on the carpet.

He made himself go to bed before the end credits rolled on the "Tonight" show. He lay in the darkness a long time and imagined he could hear the camera whirring in the next room —but surely that was impossible? It was the whirring, more likely, of his own nerves. His own blood pulsing through his ears. He could not stop turning over these questions in his mind, of *machines* and *intelligence* and what might have been a faint cry for help; but in time his thoughts tumbled away in odd, skewed directions and he was asleep.

For a second night Tom Winter slept dreamlessly. He woke to the noise of the clock radio, a Seattle AM station emitting prophecies about weather and traffic. Sunlight streamed in through the margin of the curtains, but he felt as if he had just gone to bed. Nothing remained of the night in his memory—except, dimly, the echo of a pervasive hum. It was the sound he imagined a buried dynamo might make.

The sound of his thoughts.

Possibly, the sound of *their* thoughts.

But he put that idea away.

The kitchen was clean again.

This trick was familiar enough by now that it had ceased to impress him. It was the small details that fascinated. For instance, every minor dot of organic matter had been cleansed from the cardboard pizza sleeve but the box itself was still open at a random angle on the table. Decisions had been made: this is refuse, this is not. And not simple mechanical decisions. Food in the refrigerator was never disturbed. Unopened packages were off limits. There was a logic in it. Repetitive, maybe, but complex and odd. A maid would have tidied away the empty box. A robot would not. But a robot wouldn't care whether it was caught in the act; a robot wouldn't wait for the small hours of the night.

The video recorder was still running, still minutes away from eight o'clock. Tom bent past the camera lens and switched it off.

He ejected the tape and discovered his hand was trembling. It took him a good fifteen minutes to hook up the VCR to his TV set . . . a minute more to rewind the cassette.

He switched on the monitor and when the screen brightened he punched the Play button of the VCR. An image formed and stabilized—the kitchen, rendered odd and sterile by the static camera angle. The phantom numbers at the top left of the screen ticked off *12:01, 12:02*—he had still been awake then and when he turned up the sound he could hear the Carson show playing in the background. Somewhere behind the picture tube he was watching the "Tonight" show in his bathrobe. A sort of time loop—*but then they'd know all about that.*

This was another phantom thought, unbidden and peculiar. He shook it off.

He punched the Fast Forward key.

A noise bar rolled up the screen; the picture flickered. Minutes rolled by too fast to read. But it was the same messy kitchen he had abandoned last night.

1:00 A.M. blinked past.

2:00.

3:00. Nothing happened. Then—

3:45.

He stabbed the Pause key, too late, and backed up.

3:40:01.

3:39:10.

3:38:27.

At exactly 3:37:16 A.M., the kitchen lights had gone off.

"God*damn!*" Tom said.

The camera was built to function in ordinary house light but not absolute darkness. The screen remained a gray, impenetrable blank. It was so obvious as to be painful. They had fucking *turned the lights out.*

He hit Rewind and watched the sequence in real time. But there was nothing to see: only the static picture . . . and, faintly, the sound of the switch being thrown.

Tock.

Darkness.

And in the background . . . buried in tape hiss, elusive and barely audible . . . something that might have been *their* sound.

A chitinous whisper. The brush of metallic cilia on cold linoleum. The sound of a razor blade stroking a feather.

He didn't even try to call Archer. He was already late; he locked the front door and climbed into his car.

Leaving the house was like shaking off the influence of a long, hypnotic dream. It lingered at the edge of perception and it influenced his decisions. Because he was late he attempted a shortcut through Belltower, only to discover that the through street he remembered (Newcastle down past Brierley) had been widened and diverted to the highway. He hadn't come this way before and the trip was disorienting, a journey through the familiar to the jarringly new. Here was Sea View Elementary on its green hillside, and the high school a quarter mile south, similar buildings of salmon-colored brick so substantial and so immediate in memory that it would not have surprised him to see nine-year-old Doug Archer rush out to launch a fusillade at the car. But the neighborhood newsstand had become a video arcade and the

Woolworth's had evolved into a Cineplex. Once again, the world had changed while his back was turned.

Declined, his father might have said. Like the earth itself, Barbara would have reminded him. Debris clouding the atmosphere and melting the icecaps. Barbara was one of the few individuals Tom had met who both believed in the greenhouse effect and believed it could be stopped: the precarious balance of the activist. Bad thermodynamics, his father would have told her. You can delay a death but not make a man immortal. The same was surely true for a planet: it didn't improve with use. Things decline; the evidence was all around him. The evidence was his life.

Maybe so, Barbara would have said, *but we can go down fighting.* She had believed that half measures were better than none; that even an ineffectual morality was useful in the decade of Reaganomics, the homeless, and the video church. Her voice rang out in his memory.

She was your conscience, Tom thought.

But morality—the morality of weapons research or the morality of selling cars—had a way of twisting out of his grasp. He was twenty minutes late when he arrived at the lot, but there were no buyers waiting and nobody seemed to notice the time; the salesmen were clustered around the Coke machine telling jokes. Tom had clocked in and was standing helplessly on the lot watching cars roar past—thinking about Barbara, thinking about the house—when Billy Klein, the manager, eased up behind him and draped an arm over his shoulder. Klein was wide all over his body, big shouldered and big hipped and broad in the face; his smile radiated predatory vigor and automatic, fake heartiness—an entirely carnivorous smile. Tom turned and took a blast of Tic-Tac–scented breath. "Come with me," Klein said. "I'll show you what selling *really* means."

It was the first time since his interview that he had been allowed into Klein's sanctuary, a glass-walled room that looked into three sales offices where contracts were written up. Tom sat nervously in what Klein called the customer chair, which was cut an inch or two lower than an ordinary office chair; troublesome deals were often T.O.'d to Klein, who felt he benefited from the psychological edge of gazing down from a height. "Strange, but it works. The salespeople call me 'sir' and practically shit themselves bowing out of the room. The customer looks up and he sees me frowning at him—" He frowned. "How do I look?"

Like a constipated pit bull, Tom thought. "Very imposing."

"You bet. And that's the point I want to make. If you're going to work out in sales, Tom, you need an edge. You understand what I'm saying? Any kind of edge. Maybe a different edge with different customers. They come in and they're nervous, or they come in and they're practically swaggering— they're going to make a killer deal and fuck over this salesman —but either way, deep down, some part of them is just a little bit scared. That's where your edge is. You find that part and you work on it. If you can convince them you're their friend, that's one way of doing it, because then they're thinking, Great, I've got a guy on my side in this terrifying place. Or if they're scared of *you,* you work on *that.* You say stuff like 'I don't think we can do business with that offer, we'd be losing money,' and they swallow hard and jack up their bid. Simple! But you need the edge. Otherwise you're leaving money on the table every time. Listen."

Klein punched a button on his desktop intercom. Tinny voices radiated from it. Tom was bemused until he realized they were eavesdropping on the salesroom behind him, where Chuck Alberni was writing up a deal for a middle-aged man and his wife.

The customer was protesting that he hadn't been offered enough on his trade-in, an '87 Colt. Alberni said, "We're being as generous as we can afford to be—I know you appreciate that. We're a little overstocked right now and lot space is at a premium. But let's look at the bright side. You can't beat the options package, and our service contract is practically a model for the industry."

And so on. Focusing the customer's attention on the car he obviously wants, Klein said. "Of course, we'll make money on the financing no matter what happens here. We could practically give him the fucking car. His trade-in is very, very nice. But the point is that you don't leave money on the table."

The customer tendered another offer—"The best we can do right now," he said. "That's pretty much my final bid."

Alberni inspected the figure and said, "I'll tell you what. I'll take this to the sales manager and see what he says. It might take some luck, but I think we're getting close."

Alberni stood up and left the room.

"You see?" Klein said. "He's talking them up, but the impression he gives is that he's doing them a favor. Always look for the edge."

Alberni came into Klein's office and sat down. He gave Tom a long, appraising look. "Toilet training this one?"

"Tom has a lot of potential," Klein said. "I can tell."

"He's the owner's brother. That's a whole lot of potential right there."

"Hey, Chuck," Klein said disapprovingly. But Alberni was very hot in sales right now and he could get away with things like that.

Tom said nothing.

The intercom was still live. In the next room, the customer took the hand of his nervous wife. "If we put off the cedar deck till next year," he said, "maybe we can ante up another thousand."

"Bingo," Alberni said.

"See?" Klein said. "Nothing is left on the table. Absolutely nothing at all."

Tom said, "You eavesdrop on them? When they think they're alone?"

"Sometimes," Klein said, "it's the only way to know."

"Isn't that unethical?"

Alberni laughed out loud. Klein said, *"Unethical?* What the hell? Who are you all of a sudden, Mother Teresa?"

He clocked out at quitting time and took the highway to the Harbor Mall. At the hardware store he picked up a crowbar, a tape measure, a chisel, and a hammer. He paid for them with his credit card and drove the rest of the way home with the tools rattling in his trunk.

The northeastern end of the house, Tom thought. In the basement. *That's where they live.*

He microwaved a frozen dinner and ate it without paying attention: flash-fried chicken, glutinous mashed potatoes, a lump of "dessert."

He rinsed the container and threw it away.

Nothing for them tonight.

He changed into a faded pair of Levi's and a torn cotton shirt and took his new tools into the basement.

He identified a dividing wall that ran across the basement and certified by measuring its distance from the stairs that it was directly beneath a similar wall that divided the living room from the bedroom. Upstairs, he measured the width of the bedroom to its northeastern extremity: fifteen feet, give or take a couple of inches.

In the basement the equivalent measurement was harder to take; he had to kneel behind the dented backplate of the Kenmore washing machine and wedge the tape measure in place with a brick. He took three runs at it and came up with the same answer each time:

The northeastern wall of the basement was set in at least three feet from the foundation.

He pulled away storage boxes and a shelf of laundry soap and bleach, then the two-by-four shelves themselves. When he was finished the laundry room looked like Beirut, but the

62

entire wall was exposed. It appeared to be an ordinary gypsum wall erected against studs, painted flat white. Appearances can be deceptive, Tom thought. But it would be simple enough to find out.

He used the chisel and hammer to peel away a chunk of the wallboard. The wallboard was indeed gypsum; the chalk showered over him as he worked, mingling with his sweat until he was pasty white. Equally unmistakable was the hollow space *behind* the wall, too deep for the overhead light to penetrate. He used the crowbar to lever out larger chunks of wallboard until he was ankle-deep in floury rubble.

He had opened up a hole roughly three feet in diameter and he was about to go hunting for a flashlight for the purpose of peering inside when the telephone buzzed.

He mistook it at first for some angry reaction by the house itself, a cry of outrage at this assault he had committed. His ears were ringing with the effort of his work and it was easy to imagine the air full of insect buzzing, the sound of a violated hive. He shook his head to clear away the thought and jogged upstairs to the phone.

He picked up the receiver and heard Doug Archer's voice. "Tom? I was about to hang up. What's going on?"

"Nothing . . . I was in the shower."

"What about the videotape? I spent the day waiting to hear from you, buddy. What did we get?"

"Nothing," Tom said.

"Nothing? Nada? Zip?"

"Not a thing. Very embarrassing. Look, I'm sorry I got you involved in this. Maybe we ought to just let it ride for a while."

There was a silence. Archer said, "I can't believe I'm hearing this from you."

"I think we've been overreacting, is all."

"Tom, is something wrong up there? Some kind of problem?"

"No problem at all."

"I should at least drop by to pick up the video equipment—"

"Maybe on the weekend," Tom said.

"If that's what you want—"

"That's what I want."

He hung up the phone.

If there's treasure here, he thought, *it's mine.*

He turned back to the basement.

The house hummed and buzzed around him.

Four

Because it was Monday, because she had lost her job at Macy's, because it was a raw and intermittently rainy spring day —and maybe because the stars or Kismet or karma had declared it so—Joyce stopped to say hello to the strange man shivering on a bench in Washington Square Park.

The gray, wet dusk had chased away everybody but the pigeons. Even the nameless bearded octogenarian who had appeared last week selling "poetry" on cardboard box bottoms had moved on, or died, or ascended to heaven. Some other day the square might be thronged with guitar strummers, NYU kids, teenage girls from uptown private schools making (what they imagined was) The Scene; but for now the park belonged to Joyce and to this odd, quiet man who looked at her with startled eyes.

Of course, it was silly and maybe even dangerous to stop and talk. This was New York, after all. Strange men were hardly in short supply; their strangeness was seldom subtle or interesting. But Joyce had good intuition about people. "Sharp-eyed Joyce" Lawrence had called her. "The Florence Nightingale of love." She rejected the implication (though here she was again, perhaps: taking in strays), but accepted the judgment. She knew who to trust.

"You're lost," she said.

He looked up at her and managed a smile. A certain effort there, she thought.

"No," he said. "Not really. I figured it out. New York City. I'm in New York. But the date . . ." He held out his hands in a helpless gesture.

Oh, Joyce thought. But he wasn't an alcoholic. His eyes were bright and clear. He might have been schizophrenic, but his face didn't radiate the pained perplexity Joyce had seen in the faces of the schizophrenics she'd met. (There had been a few, including her uncle Teddy, who was in a "care home" upstate.) Not an alcoholic, not a schizo—maybe he had taken something. There were some odd pills circulating around the Village these days. Dexadril was popular, LSD-25 was easy to come by. An out-of-towner who had picked up something at the Remo: that was possible. But not really a tourist. The man was dressed in jeans and a cotton shirt open at the collar, and he wore the clothes comfortably; they weren't some outfit he had cobbled together for an afternoon of slumming. So perhaps he is One of Us after all, Joyce thought, and this fraternal possibility moved her to sit down next to him. The bench was wet and the rainwater soaked through her skirt; but she was already wet from dashing out of the West Fourth Street station of the IND. Okay to be wet on a cold afternoon at dusk because eventually you'd find a comfortable place to get dry and warm and then it was all worth it. "You look like you could use a cup of coffee."

The man nodded. "Sure could."

"You have money?"

He touched his left hip. Joyce heard the change jingle in his pocket. But his face was suddenly doubtful. "I don't believe I do."

She said cautiously, "How do you feel?"

He looked at her again. Now there was focus in his eyes—he understood the drift of the question.

"I'm sorry," he said. "I know how this must seem. I'm sorry

I can't explain it. Did you ever have an experience you just couldn't take in all at once—something so enormous you just can't comprehend it?"

The LSD, she thought. Down the rabbit hole for sure. A naïf in chemical wonderland. *Be nice,* she instructed herself. "I think coffee would probably help."

He said, "I have money. But I don't think it's legal tender."

"Foreign currency?"

"You could say that."

"You've been traveling?"

"I guess I have." He stood up abruptly. "You don't have to buy me a coffee, but if you want to I'd be grateful."

"My name is Joyce," she said. "Joyce Casella."

"Tom Winter," he said.

Early in the month of May 1962.

She bought coffee at an unfashionable deli where no one would recognize her: not because she was embarrassed but because she didn't want a crowd chasing this man—Tom Winter—away. He was dazed, numbed, and not entirely coherent; but beneath that she was beginning to sense a curious edge, perhaps the legacy of whatever journey had brought him here, or some ordeal, a tempering fire. She talked about her life, the job she'd lost at Macy's book department, her music, relieving him of the need to make conversation and at the same time letting her eyes take him in. Here was a man maybe thirty years old, wearing clothes that were vaguely bohemian but not ragged, a traveler with traveler's eyes, who wasn't skinny but had the gauntness of someone who had ignored meals for too long.

He didn't want to talk about himself or how he'd arrived here. Joyce respected that. She'd met a lot of folks who didn't care to talk about themselves. People with a past they wanted to hide; or people with no past, refugees from the suburbs with grandiose visions of the Village inferred from television and all those self-righteous articles in *Time* and *Life*. Joyce herself had been one of these, an NYU undergraduate in a dirndl skirt, and she respected Tom's silence even though his secrets might be less prosaic than hers.

He did say where he was from: a little coastal town in Washington State called Belltower. She was encouraged by this fracture in his reticence and ventured to ask what he did there.

"Lots of things," he said. "Sold cars."

"It's hard to picture you as a car salesman."

"I guess other people thought so, too. I wasn't very good at it."

"You lost your job?"

"I—well, I don't know. Maybe I still have it. If I go back."

"Long way to go back."

He smiled a little. "Long way to come here."

"So what brought you to the city?"

"A time machine," he said. "Apparently."

He had hitchhiked or ridden boxcars, Joyce guessed, a sort of Woody Guthrie thing; maybe that was what he meant. "Well," she said, "Mr. Car Salesman, are you planning to stay awhile?"

He shook his head no, then seemed to hesitate. "I'm not sure. My travel arrangements are kind of vague."

"You need a place to stay?"

He glanced through the window of the deli (STRICTLY KO-SHER, like the sign in the Peace Eye Bookstore over at 10th and Avenue C). Evening now. Traffic labored through the shiny wet darkness.

"I've got a place," he said, "but I'm not sure I can find the way back."

Joyce suspected he was right. Coming down off some towering LSD kick, he'd probably bounce around Manhattan like the little steel ball in a pachinko machine. Joyce asked herself whether she was convinced of his harmlessness; she decided she was. *Taking in strangers,* she scolded herself—but it was one of those acts Lawrence had called "blinks of connection" in a poem. The grace of an unexpected contact. A kind of touch. "You can sleep on my sofa if you want. It's not much of a sofa."

The offer seemed to provoke fatigue in him. "I would be very happy to sleep on your sofa. I'm sure it's a wonderful sofa."

"Very courtly," she said. "It came from the Salvation Army. It's purple. It's an ugly sofa, Tom."

"Then I'll sleep with my eyes closed," he said.

She lived in a little railroad apartment in the East Village where she had moved from the dorm at NYU. It was two flights up in a tenement building and furnished on no budget at all: the ugly purple sofa, some folding chairs, a Sally Ann standing lamp from the Progressive Era. The bookcases were made of raw pineboard and paving bricks.

Tom stood awhile looking at the books. They were nothing special, her college English texts plus whatever she'd picked up at secondhand stores since then. Some C. Wright Mills, Frantz Fanon's *The Wretched of the Earth,* Aldous Huxley—but he handled them as if they were specimens in a display case.

"Read anything you want," she said.

He shook his head. "I don't think I could concentrate."

Probably not. And he was shivering. She brought him a big bath towel and a cotton shirt Lawrence had left behind. "Dry off and change," she said. "Sleep if you want." She left him stretched out on the sofa and went into the "kitchen"—a corner of the room, really, with a sink and a reconditioned Hotpoint and a cheap partition—and rinsed a few dishes. Her rent was due and the severance check from her department store job would cover it; but that would leave her (she calculated) about seven dollars to live on until she picked up

69

some music work or another job. Neither was impossible, but she would have to find a gig or go hungry. But that was tomorrow's problem—today was today.

She left the kitchen passably clean. By the time she'd finished Tom was asleep on the sofa—stark stone unconscious, snoring a little. She picked up his watch from the wooden crate table where he'd left it, thinking, It must be late.

Then she did a double-take at the face of the watch, which wasn't a watch face at all but a kind of miniature signboard where the time was written in black numerals over a smoke-gray background.

9:35, it said, and then dissolved to *9:36.* The little black colon winked continuously.

Joyce had never seen such a watch and she assumed it must be very expensive—surely not a car salesman's watch. But it wasn't a foreign watch, either. It said "Timex" and "Quartz Lithium" (whatever that was) and "Water Resistant."

Very *very* strange, she thought.

Tom Winter, Man of Mystery.

She left him snoring on the couch and moved into the bedroom. She undressed with the light off and stretched out on the narrow spring-creaking bed, relishing the cold air and the clank of the radiator, the rattle of rainwater on the fire escape. Then she climbed under the scratchy brown blanket and waited for sleep.

Mornings and evenings, she loved this city.

Sometimes she slept five hours or less at a time, so she could have more morning and more night.

Nights, especially when she was out with Lawrence and that crowd, she would simply let herself be swept up in the urgency of their conversation, talking desegregation or the arms race in some guitar cafe; swept up by the music, too, legions of folk singers arrowing in on Bleecker and MacDougal from all over the country these days; in sawdust-floored rooms filled with her poet friends and folk friends and "beat" friends, earnest Trotskyites and junkies and jazz musicians and eighteen-year-old runaways from dingy Midwest Levittowns, all these crosscurrents so fiercely focused that on some nights she believed the pitch-black sky might open in a rapture of the dispossessed and they would all ascend bodily into heaven. Nights like that had been common enough this winter and spring that she was eager for summer, when the pace would double and redouble again. Maybe Lawrence would publish his poetry or she would find an audience for her music. And they would be at the eye, then, of this luminous vortex.

But mornings were good, too. This was a good morning. It was good to wake up and feel the city waking up around her. Since she had lived in New York the rhythm of the city had become a stabilizing pattern. She had learned to distinguish the sound of morning traffic from the sound of afternoon traffic, both distinct from the lonelier siren sound of the traffic late at night. Morning traffic woke her with promises. She did not dislike the city until noon; at noon it was coarse, loud, unruly, plain, and chokingly dull. Lunch hours at Macy's she had written songs about the night and morning city, little spells against the crudity of midday.

Tom was still asleep on the sofa. Joyce was faintly surprised by this. She had imagined him vanished in the morning, like a dream, like smoke. But here he was: substantial in his rumpled clothes. She heard the clank and moan of the bathroom plumbing; he stepped into the kitchen with his face freshly washed and his eyes as wide and dazed as they had been the day before.

"New York," he said. "Nineteen sixty-two."

"Congratulations."

"It's amazing," he said.

"You really *are* from out of town."

"You could say that." His grin was big and a little silly.

"Feeling better this morning?"

"Better. Giddy, in fact."

"Uh-huh. Well, don't get *too* giddy. You probably need breakfast."

"Probably." He added, "I'm still broke."

"Well—I can buy us breakfast. But I have to meet Lawrence at noon. Lawrence might not appreciate knowing you slept here." Tom nodded his acceptance without asking who Lawrence might be—very courteous, Joyce thought.

She locked up and they descended to the street. The sky was bright and the air was almost warm—which was good, because Tom didn't have a coat to throw over his cotton shirt. She started to recommend a thrift shop she knew about —"Once you get some cash." But he shrugged off the problem. "I'll worry about money later."

"That's a good attitude."

"First I have to see about getting home."

"You don't need money for that?"

"Money's not the problem."

"So what *is* the problem?"

"The laws of physics. Mechanical mice." Joyce smiled in spite of herself. He went on, "I can't explain. Maybe I will someday. If I find my way back here."

She met his eyes. "Seriously?"

"Seriously."

She ordered up a coffee-shop breakfast for both of them. Cutting into her budget a little—but what was money for? Tom insisted on buying a newspaper and then he sat marveling at it, turning the pages reverently . . . not reading it so much as *inspecting* it, Joyce thought. Personally, she hadn't picked up a paper since the John Glenn launch in February. She said, "Are you just a car salesman or are you a poet too?"

"I've never been accused of poetry before."

"What you said about mechanical mice. And, hey, this is the Village. Poets are like cockroaches around here."

"My God, it *is*, isn't it? 'The Village.'" He looked up from the paper. "You play music?"

"Sometimes," Joyce allowed.

"I noticed your guitar back at the apartment. Twelve-string Hohner. Not too shabby."

"You play?"

"A little bit. From college. It's been a few years, though."

"We should play sometime. If you come back."

"Guitar players must be as common as poets around here."

"Well, they're like snowflakes. No two the same." She smiled. "Seriously, if you come around this way again . . ."

"Thank you." He looked at his watch and stood up. "You've been awesomely generous."

"De nada. Besides, I like you."

He touched her hand for a moment. The touch was fleeting but warm, and she felt a little internal tingle—mysterious, unexpected.

"I might be back," he said.

"Goodbye, Tom Winter."

He walked into the pale sunlight, wavered a moment in the doorway, then headed unsteadily east.

Find what you're looking for, she thought. A parting wish. Though it didn't seem too likely.

Probably, she thought, *I'll never see him again.*

She sipped her coffee and glanced at the paper, but it was all bad news: two men had been murdered in an alley not a block from her apartment. While she slept, Death had been out walking the streets.

This was a shivery thought and she looked up once more, craned her neck to spot Tom down the street; but he was already gone, lost in the morning traffic and out of reach.

Five

The desk clerk glanced at the ledger as he handed her the key. "Room 312, Mrs. Winter."

Barbara was startled. Had she really signed that name? She took the key and shot a sidelong glance at the page where she had, yes, written *Mrs. Barbara Winter* in neat script.

The motel was a three-story brick bivouac set back from a dismal stretch of highway maybe an hour's drive from Belltower. She had considered driving straight through; but Tony's call had reached her this afternoon at a conference in Victoria, B.C., and it was late now; she was tired; her car was tired, too. So she had stopped at this bleak roadside place at 10:30 P.M. in a light rain and signed her married name to the register.

Room 312 smelled of dry heat and disinfectant. The bed creaked and the window blinds opened on a view of the neon VACANCY sign reflected in the slick wet parking lot. Cars and trucks passed on the highway in clusters of three or four, their tires hissing in the rain.

Maybe it's stupid to see him.

The thought was unavoidable. She'd been having it intermittently since she climbed into the car. It echoed as she shrugged out of her jeans and blouse and stepped into the shower stall, washing away road dirt.

Maybe it *was* stupid to see him; maybe useless, too. Rafe had taken it well, with a minimum of pouting; but Rafe, twenty-three years old, saw the six-year gap between them as a chasm, was threatened by the notion of her lingering affection for Tom. She had obliged him by keeping contacts to a minimum . . . until now.

It was stupid to risk her relationship with Rafe—which was all the relationship she had at the moment, and one she was desperate not to lose. But she remembered what Tony had said on the phone:

I can't do anything for him this time.

The words had gone through her like a shot of cold air.

"Please," she said out loud. "Please, Tom, you dumb bastard, please be okay."

Then she climbed under the cold motel sheets and slept till dawn.

In the morning, she tried the phone. He didn't answer.

She panicked at first. Scolded herself for having spent the night here: it wouldn't have been that much farther to drive. She could have gone on, could have knocked at his door, saved him from—

What?

Well, that was the question, wasn't it? The great unanswered question.

She checked out, stowed her luggage in the trunk of the car, pulled into the sparse dawn traffic droning down the highway.

Since she left Tom she had spoken to his brother Tony exactly twice. On both occasions he had asked for her help with Tom.

The first call had been months ago. Tom had been drinking, the job had fallen through, he owed back rent on his apartment. If Barbara had known she might have tried to help . . . but by the time Tony put in his call the situation was nearly resolved; Tony had arranged for a job in Belltower and Tom had dried out. "I don't think there's anything I could do to help," she'd said.

"You could come back to him," Tony had said. "Much as it pains me to say so. I think that would help."

"Tony, you know I can't do that."

"Why the hell not? For Tom's sake, I mean."

"We broke up for a reason. I have another relationship."

"You're shacked up with some teenage anarchist. I heard about it."

"This isn't helping, Tony."

And Tony responded, "You must be the best cooze in Washington State, Barbara, because I can't figure out why else my brother would be racked up over you," and hung up. Barbara hadn't expected to hear from him after that. Surely only desperation would lead him to call again.

Presumably, desperation had. Tony's second call—yesterday's call—had been routed up to the Conference on Forestry and the Environment in Victoria by one of the board members at World Watch, an advocacy group Barbara worked for. First came a warning call from Rachel, her coworker: "Barb, do you really *know* this guy? He says he's related to your ex. He says, 'I know she works for this pinko organization and I need to talk to her *now*.' Some *family* thing. He said it was urgent so I gave him the hotel number, but I wondered—"

"It's okay," Barbara said. "That's fine, Rachel. You did the right thing."

She waited ten minutes by the phone, standing up Rafe at the Jobs or Oxygen seminar.

Then Tony's call came up from the switchboard.

"It's about Tom," he said.

Barbara felt a sudden weight at the back of her neck: a headache beginning. She said, "Tony . . . didn't we have this conversation once?"

"It's different this time."

"What's changed?"

"Just listen to me, Barbara, will you do that? Save up all the psychological crap until I'm finished?"

Barbara bit her lip but said nothing. Underneath the insult was some urgency: from Tony, a new thing.

"Better," he said. "Thank you. I'm calling about Tom, and the reason I'm calling is that I think he's going off the deep end in a serious way and this time I don't know what to do about it."

Urgency and this confession. Barbara said, "Is he drinking again?"

"That's the weird thing. I don't think he is. He'll disappear for days at a time—but he comes back clean and he's not hung over. He's holed up in this house he bought out on the Post Road. Hardly sees anybody. Reclusive. And it's cutting into his life. He's missed time at the lot and the sales manager is seriously pissed at him. Plus, it's things I don't know how to explain. Did you ever meet somebody who just didn't give a fuck? You could say hello, you could tell them your uncle died, and maybe they say something sympathetic, but you can tell they just don't care?"

"I've met people like that," Barbara said. Like you, you asshole, she thought.

"Tom ever strike you as one of those?"

"No."

"Well, that's what he is now. He has no friends, he has no money, he's on the brink of losing his job—and none of this *matters*. He's out in some other dimension."

Didn't sound like Tom at all. Tom had always been a second-guesser—obsessed with consequences. Because of the way his parents had died, she guessed, or maybe it came from some deeper chamber of his personality, but Tom had always feared and distrusted the future. "It could still be alcohol."

"I'm not stupid," Tony said. "I don't care how subtle he is about it, I know when my brother is juicing. This is something altogether else. Last time I went to the house, you know what happened? He wouldn't let me in. He opened the door, flashed me a big smile and said, 'Go away, Tony.'"

"He's happy, though?"

"Happy isn't the word. *Detached.* You want me to say what I think? I think he might be suicidal."

Barbara swallowed hard. "That's a big leap."

"He's signing off, Barbara. He won't even talk to me, but that's the impression I have. He doesn't care what happens in the world because he already said goodbye to it."

The phone was a dead weight in her hand. "What does Loreen think about this?"

"It was Loreen who convinced me to call you."

Then it *was* serious. Loreen was no genius but she had a feeling for people. Barbara said, "Tony, *why?* What brought this on?"

"Who knows? Maybe Tom could tell you."

"You want me to talk to him?"

"I can't tell anybody what to do anymore. I'm way past that. If you're worried, you know where to find him."

Buzz and hum after Tony hung up.

Her marriage was over. She didn't owe Tom anything. Unfair, to have this dumped in her lap.

She packed her bag and took it to the lobby, found Rafe and explained the situation as kindly as possible. He said he understood. He was probably lying.

Her hand shook when she put the key in the ignition.

She had to pull over a couple of times to check the gas station map of Belltower. By the time she found Tom's house it was almost ten o'clock, Sunday morning. Peaceful out here along the Post Road, clear skies and summer coming on fast. Barbara stepped out of the car and took a deep lungful of cedar-scented air.

The house looked peaceful, too. Very clean, almost pristine. The roof was moss-free and the siding looked practically scrubbed. Tom had let the lawn go a little bit, however.

She put her car keys in her purse. *I didn't think I'd be this nervous.*

But there was no turning away. Up the walk, knock on the door. Primly, *tap-tap-tap.* Then, when no answer came, harder.

The sound echoed and died in the Sunday morning air. No response but the shushing of the trees.

She had bolstered herself for every eventuality but this. *Maybe he went out somewhere.* The garage door was down and locked—no way to tell if his car was inside.

No way to tell if he was still alive. Tony's words came back like a curse: *I think he's suicidal.* Maybe she had come too late. But that thought was gruesome and unwarranted, a product of her own fears; she put it firmly out of mind. Probably he had gone out for a while. She decided to wait in the car.

After half an hour trying to find a comfortable place on the upholstery—and getting a little hungry around the edge of her nerves—she caught a glimpse of motion in the nearest window of the house.

Angry at him for ignoring her knock—but maybe he hadn't heard it—she ran to the window and peered up over the sill.

Into the kitchen. She cupped her hand against the window and saw Tom with his back to her. His shirt was untucked and he was wearing a ragged pair of jeans. He bent down toward something on the floor; she saw it dash away—a cat, perhaps? But that was odd: Tom had never liked pets.

People change, she told herself.

She knocked at the door again, as hard as she could.

Moments later, Tom answered.

His smile faded when he saw her. He said, "My God."

"I've been here a little while," she said. "I knocked—"

"I must have been downstairs. My God. Come in."

She entered the house almost apologetically—cowed by his astonishment. *I should have phoned.* "I didn't mean to surprise you like this, but—"

He waved his hand. "It's all right. I've been out of the house—I don't always pick up the phone."

She allowed this excuse, disturbing as it was. He gestured at the sofa. She sat down.

The room was neutrally furnished, almost impersonal. Barbara recognized a few items from the old Seattle apartment—a rack of jazz LPs, the stereo amplifier Tom had put together during his electronics-hobbyist phase. But the furniture was old-fashioned, styleless, and spotlessly clean; she guessed it came with the house.

"I ought to tell you why I came."

Tom shook his head. "I can guess. Tony called you, right?" She nodded; he said, "I should have expected it. I'm sorry, Barbara. Not sorry to see you again. Sorry you dragged yourself all the way out here for nothing."

"Tony's worried. He has a decent impulse now and then. Loreen's worried, too, he says."

"They shouldn't be."

She didn't want to press the subject. She said, "It's a nice house."

"I guess I ought to show you around."

He showed her the kitchen, the bedroom, the spare room, the bath—all immaculate, old-fashioned, and a little bit sterile. She hovered at the stairs but Tom hung back. "That's just the basement. Nothing of interest."

She sat at the kitchen table while he brewed a pot of coffee. "This doesn't look like bachelor housekeeping."

His smile was secretive. "Guess I've learned a few things since the college dorm."

"Tony said you're working down at his lot."

"Yup."

"How's it going?"

He brought two cups of coffee to the table and passed one to her. "Lousy. Maybe Tony mentioned that, too. I don't have a knack for taking people's money."

"You were always a rotten card player, too. Are you going to quit?"

He said, "I'm thinking of leaving."

This distinction—not "quitting" but "leaving"—struck an odd chord. "So you don't answer the phone, the job's no good . . . Are you moving?"

"I don't have any firm plans."

"You mean you don't want to talk about it."

He shrugged.

She said, "Well, I can't blame Tony and Loreen for worrying. I don't think I've ever seen you like this."

His mood, she meant, but it was the way he looked, too. All his flabbiness had been stripped away. He moved as if he'd tapped some secret well of energy. She considered checking his medicine cabinet for stimulants—but this wasn't a chemical nerviness. Something deeper, she thought: a *purposeful* energy.

"I'm not sick," he said. "And I'm not crazy."

"Can you tell me what's going on?"

He hesitated a long time. Finally he said, "I chose not to talk about this with Tony or Loreen or anyone else. I think I have that right."

"And you don't want to talk about it with me."

A longer pause. He wasn't smiling anymore.

"I waited a long time to see you," he said. "I wanted you to come back. I wanted to see you come through that door. To come and to stay. But that's not why you're here."

"No," she said.

"We don't share secrets anymore. I think that's a fact of life."

"I suppose so. But you understand why I came?"

"Yes."

"You would have done the same—right?"

"Yes. I would."

They sipped coffee in the silence of the kitchen. A breeze lifted the curtains over the sink.

By noon, Barbara understood that, yes, he was preparing to go away for a long time; that he was secretive but probably not suicidal; that she might not see him again.

Adjusting to this last nugget of information was harder than she'd anticipated. She had left him months ago, and the break had been final; she had never made plans to meet him again. The separation had been difficult but not traumatic. But maybe that was because, at the back of her mind, he was still there, as solid and invulnerable as a monument, a part of her life cast in stone.

His bout with alcoholism had disturbed that complacency and now it had been shaken to the roots. This wasn't Tom as she'd left him. This was some new Tom. A wilder Tom, deep in some enterprise he wouldn't explain.

Selfish, of course, to want him never to change. But she was afraid for him, too.

He fixed a little lunch, omelettes, ham and onion—"I don't live entirely on TV dinners." She accepted gratefully but understood that the meal was a gesture; she would have to leave soon.

"Whatever it is you're doing," she said, "I hope it's good for you. I mean that."

He thanked her; then he put down his fork. His face was solemn. "Barbara," he said, "how much do you love the year 1989?"

It was a weird question. "I think it sucks," she said. "Why?"

"It's bad because—well, why?"

"I don't know. Where do you start? It's a bad time for the world because people are starving, because the climate is tough, because we've stripped away the ozone layer—all kinds of reasons. And it's a bad time in America because everybody is very, very nervous and very, very careful. Except the bad guys. Remember Yeats? 'The best lack all conviction, while the worst are full of passionate intensity.' Why do you ask?"

"What if you had a choice?"

"What?"

"I'm serious. What if you could step out of the world? What if you knew a place—not a perfect place, but a place where you could live without some of the uncertainties? A place where you knew for sure there wouldn't be a nuclear exchange in the next thirty years. Where there was disease, but not AIDS. All the human agony—repression, pain, ugliness—but on a slightly less massive scale. And suppose you could predict some of it. Maybe not stop it, but at least stay away from it—floods, plane crashes, terrorist raids. What do you think, Barb, is that a good offer?"

She said, "I don't know. I don't know what you're talking about."

"It's a hypothetical question."

"Even hypothetically, it doesn't make sense."

"But if there *were* such a place. If you *could* go there."

She thought about it. She meant to answer carefully: the question might be hypothetical but it certainly wasn't casual. She read the intensity in Tom's face. "I might be tempted," she said. "Well, hell. I *would* be tempted. Who wouldn't? But in the end—no, I don't think I'd go."

He seemed disappointed. "Why not?"

"Lots of reasons. I have business here."

"Saving the world?"

A small vein of sarcasm. She ignored it. "Maybe doing my share. And there are people—"

"Rafe, for instance?"

"Rafe. Among others, yes. I have a lot to live for, Tom."

"I wasn't talking about dying."

I hope not, she thought.

But then, what?

Had somebody *made* him such an offer?

Too weird, she thought. Absolutely too weird. "I would stay here," she said firmly.

Tom looked at her a long time. She guessed he was weighing the claim, turning it over, judging it. Finally he nodded. "Maybe you would."

"Is that the wrong answer?"

"No . . . not really."

"But it's not *your* answer."

He smiled. "No."

She stood up. "Tell me again. Before I leave. Tell me you're all right."

He walked her to the door. "I'm fine. Just going away for a while."

"You mean that?"

"I mean that."

She inspected his face. He was holding something back; but he meant what he said. Her fear had retreated a little— he wasn't suicidal—but a small nugget of anxiety remained firmly lodged, because *something* had got hold of him, obviously—some strange tide carrying him beyond her reach.

Maybe forever beyond her reach.

He touched her arm, tentatively. She accepted the gesture and they hugged. The hard part was remembering how much she had loved being held by him. How much she missed it.

She said, "Don't forget to feed the cat."

"I don't have a cat."

"Dog, then? When I looked in the window—I thought I saw—"

"You must have been mistaken."

His first real lie, Barbara thought. He'd always been a truly lousy liar.

In the corner of the room his TV set flickered into life—by itself, apparently. She guessed he had a timer on it.

He said, "You'd better go."

"Well, what can I say?"

He held her just a little tighter. "I think all we can say is goodbye."

Six

Tom Winter woke refreshed and ready for the last day he meant to endure in the decade of the 1980s.

It occurred to him that he was checking out only a little ahead of schedule. A few more months, January 1, the ball would drop, the crowds would cheer in the nineties. It was a kind of mass exodus, rats deserting the sinking ship of this decade for the shark-infested waters of the next. He was no different. Only more prudent.

Assuming, of course, the machine bugs would allow him to go.

But he wasn't afraid of the machine bugs anymore.

He showered, dressed, and fixed himself a hearty meal in the kitchen. It was a fine early-summer day. The breeze through the screen door was just cool enough to refresh, the sky blue enough to promise a lazy afternoon. When he switched off the coffee machine he heard a woodpecker tocking on one of the tall trees out back. Sweet smell of pine and cedar and fresh grass. He'd mown the lawn yesterday.

Almost too lovely to leave. Almost.

He wasn't really afraid of the machine bugs anymore, and they weren't afraid of him. Familiarity had set in on both sides. He spotted one now—one of the tiny ones, no bigger than a thumbnail—moving along the crevice where the tile met the wall. He bent down and watched idly as it worked. It looked like a centipede someone had assembled out of agate, emerald, and ruby—a Christmas ornament in miniature. It discovered a fragment of toast, angled toward it, touched it with a threadlike antenna. The crumb vanished. Vaporized or somehow ingested—Tom didn't know which.

Carefully, he picked up the machine bug and cradled it in the palm of his hand.

It ceased all motion at his touch. Inert, it was prickly and warm against his skin. It looked, Tom thought, like a curio from a roadside gem shop somewhere in Arizona—an earring or a cuff link.

He put it back on the kitchen counter. After a moment it righted itself and scuttled away, taking up its task where he'd interrupted it.

A few nights ago the machine bugs had crawled inside his little Sony TV set, modifying and rebuilding it. He moved into the living room and switched the set on now, sipping coffee, but there was only a glimpse of the "Today" show—thirty seconds of news about a near miss over O'Hare International—and then the picture blanked. The screen turned an eerie phosphorescent blue; white letters faded in.

HELP US TOM WINTER, the TV set said.

He switched it off and left the room.

The TV had almost caught Barbara's attention yesterday. And his "cat"—one of the bigger bug machines.

In a way, he was grateful to her for seeing these things. The idea still lingered—and was sometimes overwhelming—that he had stepped across the line into outright lunacy; or at least into a lunacy confined to the property line of this house, a *focal* lunacy. But Barbara had glimpsed these phenomena and he'd been forced to usher her out before she could see more; they were real events, however inexplicable.

Barbara wouldn't have understood. No, that was the wrong word—Tom couldn't say he understood these events, either; enormous mysteries remained. But he accepted them.

His acceptance of the evidently impossible was almost complete. Had been sealed, probably, since the night he broke through the basement wall.

He thought about that night and the days and nights after: bright, lucid memories, polished with use.

□ □

□ □

He pried away big, dusty slabs of gypsum board until the hole was big enough to step through.

The space behind it was dark. He probed with the beam of his flashlight, but the batteries must have been low—he couldn't find a far wall. There didn't seem to be one.

What it looked like . . .

Well, what it looked like was that he had broken into a tunnel approximately as wide as this basement room, running an indefinite distance away under the side yard into the slope of the Post Road hill.

He took another step forward. The walls of the tunnel were a slick, featureless gray; as was the ceiling; as was the floor. It wasn't a clammy subterranean chamber. It was dry, clean, and dustless—except for the mess he'd made with his crowbar.

And, increasingly, it was *light*. The tunnel began to brighten as he stood in it. The light was sourceless, though it seemed to radiate generally from above. Tom glanced down, switched off his flashlight, discovered he was casting a diffuse shadow around his feet.

The light expanded down the corridor, which began at the back of his basement and swept in a gentle leftward curve—paralleling the Post Road for some yards and then veering westward somewhere in the area of the highway, if he was any judge of distance. Maybe a quarter mile away.

Tom stood a long time regarding this vista.

His first reaction was a giddy, nervous elation. By God, he'd been right! There *was* something down here. Something mysterious, strange, large scale, possibly magical. Something he had never read about in a newspaper, never witnessed on TV, never heard about from a friend, never experienced or expected to experience. Something from the deep well of myth, fairy tale, and wild surmise.

Maybe ogres lived here. Maybe angels.

His second reaction, nearly as immediate, was a deep shiver of fear. Whoever had made this place—the machine bugs or whatever force operated them—must be immensely powerful. A powerful force that preferred to remain hidden. A powerful force he might have disturbed with his prybar and his hammer.

He backed out of the corridor through the hole in the basement wall—slowly and silently, though discretion at this stage was fairly ridiculous. If he hadn't alarmed any Mysterious Beings by breaking into their lair with a tire iron, what was the point of holding his breath *now?* But he couldn't fight the instinctive urge to creep quietly away.

He stepped back into the somewhat less mysterious environment of the basement of his house.

The house he owned—but it wasn't his. The lesson? It wasn't his when he bought it; it wasn't his now; and it wouldn't be his when he left.

He wiped his forehead with the sleeve of his shirt. The cloth came away chalky and wet.

I can't sleep here tonight.

But the fear was already beginning to fade. He had slept here lots of nights, knowing something odd was going on, knowing it didn't mean to hurt him. The tunnel and his dreams were part of a single phenomenon, after all. *Help us,* his dreams had pleaded. It wasn't the message of an omnipotent force.

Beyond the hole in the wall, the empty corridor grew dark and still again.

He managed to fall asleep a little after four A.M., woke up an hour before work. His sleep had been dreamless and tense. He changed—he had slept in his clothes—and padded down to the basement.

Where he received a second shock:

The hole in the wall was almost sealed.

A line of tiny insectile machines moved between the rubble on the floor and the wall Tom had torn up last night. They moved around the ragged opening in a slow circle, maybe as many as a hundred of them, somehow *knitting it up*—restoring the wall to its original condition.

They were the insect machines he had seen moving from the foundation to the forest across the moonlit back yard. Tom recognized them and was, strangely, unsurprised by their presence here. Of course they were here. They simply weren't hiding anymore.

The work they were performing on the wall wasn't a patch; it was a full-scale reconstruction, clean and seamless. He understood intuitively that if he scratched away the paint he'd find the original brand names stamped in blue ink on the gypsum panels, the drywall nails restored in every atom to their original place in the two-by-fours, the studs themselves patched where he'd gouged them with the butt of his prybar —wood fiber and knot and dry sap all restored.

He took a step closer. The machine bugs paused. He sensed their attention briefly focused on him.

Silent moving clockwork jewels.

"You were here all along," Tom whispered. "You did the goddamn dishes."

90

Then they resumed their patient work. The hole grew smaller as he watched.

He said—his voice trembling only a little—"I'll open it up again. You know that?"

They ignored him.

But he didn't open it up—not until a week had passed.

He felt poised between two worlds, unsure of himself and unsure of his options. The immensity of what he had discovered was staggering. But it was composed of relatively small, incremental events—the insects cleaning his kitchen, his dreams, the tunnel behind the wall. He tried to imagine scenarios in which he explained all this to the proper authorities —whoever *they* were. (The realty board? The local police? The CIA, NASA, the National Geographic Society?) Fundamentally, none of this was even remotely possible. Stories like his made the back pages of the *Enquirer* at best.

And—perhaps even more fundamentally—he wasn't ready to share these discoveries. They were his; they belonged to him. He didn't have Barbara, he didn't have a meaningful job, he had abandoned even the rough comfort of alcohol. *But he had this secret . . .* this dangerous, compulsive, utterly strange, and sometimes very frightening secret.

This still unfolding, *incomplete* secret.

He stayed out of the basement for a few days and contemplated his next step.

His dream about the machine bugs hadn't been a dream, or not entirely. Breaching the wall, he had stepped inside their magic circle. They stopped hiding from him.

For two nights he watched them with rapt attention. The smallest of them were the most numerous. They moved singly or in pairs, usually along the wallboards, sometimes venturing across the carpet or into the kitchen cabinets, moving in straight lines or elegant, precise curves. They were tiny, colorful, and remorseless in their clean-up duty; they stood absolutely still when he touched them.

Friday night, after he came home from the car lot, he discovered a line of them disappearing into the back panel of his TV set. With his ear next to the screen he could hear them working inside: a faint metallic clatter and hiss.

He left them alone.

Larger and less numerous was a variation Tom thought of as "machine mice." These were rodent sized and roughly rodent shaped: bodies scarab blue and shiny metallic, heads the color of dull ink. They moved with startling speed, though they seemed to lack legs or feet. Tom supposed they hovered an eighth of an inch or so over the floor, but that was only a guess; they scooted away when he tried to touch or hold them. He saw them sometimes herding the smaller variety across the floor; or alone, pursuing duties more mysterious.

Saturday—another moonlit night—he dosed himself with hot black coffee and sat up watching a late movie. He switched off the lights at one A.M. and stepped cautiously into the damp grass of the back yard, with a heavy-duty flashlight in his hand and a pair of wading boots to protect his ankles.

The machine bugs were there in great numbers—as they had been in his not-a-dream—fluorescing in the moonlight, a tide of them flowing from the foundation holes into the deep woods. In pursuit of what?

Tom debated following them, but decided not to: not now. Not in the dark.

They wanted his help. They had asked for it.

Disturbing, that he knew this. It was a form of communication, one he didn't understand or control. HELP US TOM WINTER, they had said, and they were saying it now. But it wasn't a message he heard or interpreted, simply a silent understanding that this was what they wanted. They didn't mean to hurt him. Simply wanted his help. *What* help, *where?* But the only answer was a sort of beckoning, as deeply understood as their other message: FOLLOW US INTO THE WOODS.

He backed away in the darkness, alarmed. He recalled with sudden vividness the experience of reading Christina Rossetti's "The Goblin Market," years ago, in one of his mother's books, a leather-bound volume of Victorian poetry. Reading it and shivering in his summer bedroom, terrified by the spidery silhouette of the arbutus outside his window and by the possibilities of nighttime invitations too eagerly accepted. *No thank you,* he thought, *I believe I'll stay out of the forest for now.*

The machine bugs conveyed no response—except perhaps the dim mental equivalent of a shrug—and carried on their strange commerce between the house and the depths of the woods.

The next morning, when he turned on the TV set, it emitted a crackle of static, flared suddenly brighter, and displayed a message:

HELP US TOM WINTER

Tom had just stepped out of the shower; he was wearing a bathrobe and carrying a cup of coffee. He failed to notice when the coffee splashed over his hand and onto the carpet, though the skin around the web of his thumb was red for the rest of the day.

The letters blinked and steadied.

"Jesus Christ!" he said.

The TV responded,

HELP US

His first instinct was to get the holy hell out of the house and bolt the door behind him. He forced himself to resist it.

He knew the machine bugs had been inside his set; this, he supposed, was why.

He took a large step backward and sat down, not quite voluntarily, on the sofa.

He licked his lips.

He said, "Who are you?"

HELP US faded out. The screen was blank a few seconds; then new letters emerged:

WE ARE ALMOST COMPLETE

Communication, Tom thought. His heart was still battering against his ribs. He remembered a toy he'd once owned—a Magic 8-Ball; you asked it a question and when you turned it over a message appeared in a little window: *yes* or *no* or some cryptic proverb. The letters on his TV screen appeared the same way, welling up from shadowy depths. The memory was peculiar but comforting.

He set aside his coffee cup and thought a moment.

"What do you want from me?"

Pause.

PROTEINS
COMPLEX CARBOHYDRATES

Food, he thought.

"What for?"

TO FINISH BUILDING US

"What do you mean—you're not *finished?*"

TO FINISH US

Apparently, it was the only answer they meant to give. He considered his next question.

"Tell me where you come from."

The pause was longer this time.

"I'm curious. I *want* to know."

Well, maybe not.

He sat back, managed a sip of coffee, and tried to assemble in his mind all the questions that had been vexing him since he moved in.

"What happened to the man who used to live here?"

BROKEN

It was an odd word, Tom thought. "What do you mean, broken?"

NEEDS TO BE REPAIRED

"Is he here? Where is he?"

FOLLOW US

Into the woods, they meant. "No. I don't want to do that yet. Are you—*repairing* him?"

NOT FINISHED

"I found the tunnel behind the wall," Tom said. "Tell me what it is. Tell me where it goes."

The pause now was very long indeed—he began to think they'd given up. Then more letters appeared:

TOM WINTER A MACHINE

"The *tunnel* is a machine? I don't understand."

THE TUNNEL IS A MACHINE

"Where does it go? Does it go anywhere?"

IT GOES WHERE IT IS

"No, I mean—where does it *lead?*"

WHERE IT WAS AIMED

This was wonderfully uninformative. They couldn't hide from him; they wanted his help; but they weren't willing—or weren't able—to answer his most basic questions.

Not a good deal, he thought. No bargain.

He said, "I'll think it over."

HELP US TOM WINTER

Which reminded him. One more question. He said, "When you talked to me before—when we communicated—how did you do that? Before this, I mean."

HELP US faded out and the new message appeared moments later—stark, vivid, matter-of-fact.

WE WERE INSIDE YOU

He sat sharply upright, horrified.

"What do you mean—those little bug machines, like inside the TV? They were inside *me?*"

He pictured them performing secret surgery in the night. Cutting him open—crawling around. *Changing* him.

SMALLER

"There are smaller ones?"

TOO SMALL TO PERCEIVE

Microscopic, Tom interpreted. Still—! "They went *inside me?* Doing what?"

TO TALK

"Inside my head?"

TO COMMUNICATE OUR NEEDS

Pause.

He was cold, sweating—he needed to understand this. *"Are they inside me now?"*

NO

"Am I different? Did they change something?"

NOTHING CHANGED
NOT VERY SUCCESSFUL

Pause.

WE CAN CHANGE YOU IF YOU LIKE
TALK MORE DIRECTLY

"No! Jesus, no thank you!"

Empty screen.

Tom ran his hand over his face. Too much information to absorb, here. He thought about machine bugs small enough to slip into his bloodstream. Machine *germs*. It was a terrifying concept.

He conceived another question . . . then wondered whether it would be wise to ask.

He said, "If you *could* have changed me—changed me so we could talk—why didn't you?"

The TV set hummed faintly.

TOO INTRUSIVE

"What are you saying, that it's *unethical?*"

NEED PERMISSION

"Permission not granted!"

HELP US

Tom stood and approached the television in small, cautious sidesteps. Pushing the power switch, he felt like a man trying to disarm a potent, unfamiliar bomb. His hands were still shaking when the screen faded to black.

He stood staring at it a long, frozen moment; then—an afterthought—he reached down and pulled out the plug.

The invasion of his television set left him shaken and ambivalent. On three different occasions he picked up the phone and began dialing Doug Archer's number. He wanted to talk to someone about this—but "wanted" was too pallid a word. The need he felt was physical, almost violent. But so was its parallel urge: the urge to keep silent. The urge to play these strange cards very close to his chest.

He dialed Archer's number three times, and once he let it ring a couple of times; but he ended up dropping the receiver in its cradle and turning away. His motives were mixed, and he didn't want to examine them too closely, but he reasoned that Archer—desperate for some kind of metaphysical revenge on Belltower, Washington—would intrude on what had been exclusively Tom's magical playground.

He liked Archer. Liked him instinctively. But—and here was a thought he didn't want to consider too closely—maybe that was another reason for not calling him up. He liked Archer, and he sensed that getting him involved in all this wouldn't be doing him a favor. *Help us,* the machine bugs had said. *Broken,* they had said. *Need to be repaired.* The implication? Something was wrong here. Something had gone wrong with some very powerful machinery. Tom couldn't turn away; he'd made his choice. But if he liked Archer—the unwelcome thought persisted—then maybe he ought to keep him well away from this house up along the Post Road.

He went to work during this time—he was even punctual—but his performance suffered; he couldn't deny it, couldn't help it. The act of selling secondhand automobiles to even the most willing customer had begun to seem nonsensical, ludicrous. Tom noticed Klein watching him on the lot, his face screwed up into something like The Frown, but this was another irrelevancy. During the hot afternoons Tom achieved a sort of Zen quiescence, as if he were surveying all this bustle from a hot-air balloon. Abstractly, he understood that he needed this job to eat; but he could coast awhile even if he lost it, and there were other jobs. Above all, there was an impossible tunnel hidden behind the sheetrock in his basement; his home was full of gemlike creatures the size of his thumb; his bloodstream carried benign microscopic robots and his TV had begun to talk to him. In the face of which, it was extremely difficult not to smile cheerfully and suggest some alternative ways of disposing of that troublesome '76 Coronet.

At home, he kept the TV unplugged most of the time. He called it the TV, but he supposed it wasn't that anymore; it was a private phone line for the creatures (or devices) with whom he shared the house. He resolved to use it only when he had a specific question—not that the answers were likely to be helpful.

He plugged it in one evening and asked what was at the *other* end of the tunnel in the basement—what he would find if he went there. DESTRUCTION, the machine replied. The answer was chilling and it prompted Tom to ask, "For me? You mean I would be destroyed?"

THE TERMINAL HAS BEEN DESTROYED
NOT YOU
ALTHOUGH THAT POSSIBILITY EXISTS

The tunnel continued to occupy his thoughts. He guessed it was inevitable that he would reopen that passage, enter it, follow its distant curve. He had been postponing the act, fearing it—but *wanting* it, too, with a ferocity that was sometimes alarming. It had gone past curiosity. Buying this house had been the beginning of a tide of events which wouldn't be complete until he followed the tunnel as far as it would take him.

But that was frightening, and this razor-thin balance of fear and obsession kept him out of the basement—postponing what he couldn't resist.

His dreams had ceased to beg for help . . . but when he came home Friday night and found the clock radio on his bedside table pronouncing the words "Help us, Tom Winter" in the voice of a popular Seattle AM radio announcer, he yanked the appliance's wall cord and went looking for his crowbar. He had waited too long already. It was time to live out this peculiar dream his life had become, to ride it down to its conclusion.

He opened the healed wallboard. A line of machine bugs sat watching him from the lid of the automatic dryer, with wide, blank eyes and no perceptible expression. He supposed he only imagined their patient, grim disapproval of what he was doing.

Events began to happen quickly then.

Within the next week, he made three separate journeys down the tunnel.

The first—that night—was exploratory. His doubts came flooding back when he saw the tunnel again, as its illumination flowed around him. He took a few tentative steps into its luminous white space, then stopped and looked back. Here was the frame wall of his basement standing exposed and absurd, as if it had interrupted this continuous flow of space almost by accident—as incongruous as Dorothy's farmhouse in Munchkinland. (But the tunnel couldn't have been here when the house was erected, could it? The contractors would have had a word or two to say.) The tunnel itself was broadly rectangular; its walls were smooth and warm to the touch; the air felt pleasant and not at all stale. He took a tentative step, then began to walk with more confidence. The floor was faintly elastic and gave back no echo of his footsteps. Every few yards, Tom turned and tried to gauge the distance he had come.

By his own estimate he had traveled several hundred yards —well under the Post Road hill and presumably deep in the earth—when the curve of the tunnel was finally great enough to hide any glimpse of home. As strange as that sight had been, it had also been a comfort. He stood a moment while fresh uncertainties crowded his mind. "Fucking crazy place to be," he said aloud—expecting an echo; but the tunnel absorbed the sound. There was nothing in either direction now but this bland curve of wall.

He walked on. He had no way to measure the angle of the tunnel's ellipse, but the curve was remorseless—he could swear in fact, that he had turned a full 180 degrees. He should have carried a compass . . . but he had a notion that a compass might not work here; that its needle would swing wildly, or perhaps point consistently *forward*. The idea was spooky and he thought again about turning back. He was way out of his depth in this pale, featureless artery. A cold sweat began to bead out on his forehead. He was taking tiny silent cat-steps, straining to hear any sound ahead of him—the fear setting in again, with a strong rider of claustrophobia. The tunnel was a few feet higher than his head with as much as a yard's clearance on each side: not much room to turn around. And nowhere to run, except that long circle back.

But then the curve eased ahead of him and within a couple of minutes he saw what appeared to be the end of the line: a gray obstructing mass rendered obscure by distance. He picked up his pace a little.

The wall, when he reached it, was not a wall but a ruin. It was a tumble of masonry, concrete blocks and dust spilling over the pristine white floor. There seemed to be no way through.

DESTRUCTION, the machine bugs had said.

101

But not, at least, *recent* destruction. This collapse had scattered dust in a broad fan across the tunnel floor—Tom's runners left distinct prints in it—the only prints, he was relieved to note. Nothing had come this way for a long time. Not since the DESTRUCTION.

Experimentally—and still with that prickly sensation of playing at the feet of a sleeping giant—he pulled away a chunk of concrete from the collapse. A haze of dust rose up; new rubble trickled in to fill the vacancy. Some of this was the stuff of which the tunnel itself was made; but some of it appeared to be commonplace concrete block.

And on the other side—what?

Another basement? Somebody *else's* basement? He might be as far away as Wyndham Lane or even the shopping center near the bypass. He checked his watch and thought, *I could have come that far in forty-five minutes.* But he suspected—well, fuck it, he pretty much *knew*—that this tunnel didn't lead to the storeroom under the Safeway. You don't build a tunnel like this unless you have a destination somewhat more exotic than Belltower, Washington.

Gnomeland, maybe. The pits of Moria. Some inner circle of heaven or hell.

Tom pulled away another fragment of brick and listened to the dusty trickle behind it. No way through . . . although he felt, or imagined he felt, a whisper of cooler and wetter air through the tangle of masonry.

Speculation was beside the point: he knew what he had to do.

He had to leave here, to begin with. He was tired, he was thirsty—he hadn't had the foresight to bring so much as a can of Coke. He would have to leave, and sleep; and when he was ready he would have to come back. He would have to bring a picnic lunch, which he would pack in a knapsack along with some tools—his trusty crowbar—and maybe one of those paper masks they sell in paint stores, to keep the dust out of his nose.

Then he would pick and pry at this obstruction until he found out what was behind it—and God help him if it was something bad.

Which was possible, because something bad had definitely happened here: some DESTRUCTION. But the matter had passed beyond curiosity. He had clasped both hands around the tiger's tail and braced himself for the ride.

He came back the next day fully equipped.

Tom decided he must look more than a little strange, hiking down this luminous mineshaft with his prybar and thermos bottle and his sack of ham-and-cheese sandwiches, like one of the dwarfs in Disney's *Snow White*. Of course, there was no one to see him. With the front door locked, the house a mile away, and this end of the tunnel securely barricaded, he was about as alone as it was possible to get. He could take off his clothes and sing an aria from *Fidelio* if the spirit so moved him, and no one would be the wiser.

After three hours of dirty, sweaty work he managed to open a gap between the piled rubble and the abraded ceiling of the tunnel. The space was approximately as large as his fist and when he aimed the flashlight into it the beam disclosed a mass of vacant, cool air. He could see dust motes moving in the light; and farther on he could distinguish what appeared to be a cinderblock wall . . . but he couldn't be certain. He forced himself to stop and sit down with a sandwich and a plastic thermos-top of coffee. The coffee was gritty with dust.

He ticked off the discoveries he had made. One, this tunnel had a destination. Two, that destination had been violently closed. Three, there was nothing on the other side waiting to jump him—nothing obvious, anyhow.

All this would have been much more frightening except for

his conviction that whatever happened here had happened long ago. How many years since the last tenant had vanished from the house on the Post Road? Almost ten—if what Archer had told him was true. A decade. And that felt about right. Ten years of dust on this floor. Ten quiet years.

He balled up his empty lunch bag and plastic wrap and tucked them into his knapsack.

He worked steadily and without much conscious thought for another three hours, by which time there was enough room for him to wedge his body over the pile of rubble.

It was late afternoon back at the house. But the word was meaningless here.

Tom straddled the rubble and probed the inner darkness with his flashlight. In the dim space beyond:

A room. A small, cold, damp, unpleasant stone room with a door at one end.

Ploughing through this barricade had not required much courage. But at the thought of opening that ugly wooden door just beyond it—that, Tom thought, was an altogether different kettle of fish.

The tunnel itself was antiseptic, very Star Wars; this cinderblock room was much more Dungeons and Dragons.

You could pile all these stones back up, Tom told himself. *Pile them up and maybe add a little concrete to buttress everything. Seal the wall at your end. Sell the fucking house.*

Never look back.

But he *would* look back. He'd look back for the rest of his life and wonder about that door. He would look back, he would wonder, and the wonder would be a maddening and unscratchable itch.

Still, he thought, this was serious business. Whatever had destroyed and barricaded this wall could surely destroy him.

THAT POSSIBILITY EXISTS, the TV had said.

Life or death.

But what on God's green earth did he have to live for, at this moment?

Back at the house—back in the real world—he was a lonesome, ordinary man leading a disfigured and purposeless life. He had lived for his work and for Barbara. But his work was finished and Barbara was living in Seattle with an anarchist named Rafe.

If he opened that door and a dragon swallowed him up—well, it would be an *interesting* death.

The world would not much notice, not much mourn.

"What the hell," Tom said, and scrambled forward.

Beyond the door, stone steps led upward.

Tom followed them. His sneakers squealed against damp concrete.

The flashlight revealed a landing barely wide enough to stand on, and a second door.

This door was padlocked—from the other side.

He remembered his crowbar, reached for it, then cursed: he had left it at the excavation.

He climbed down the stairs, through the first door, out across the rubble; he retrieved the iron bar and his knapsack and turned back. By the time he reached the door at the top of the stairs he was winded, his breath gusting out in pale clouds in the cold wet air.

He wasn't frightened now, nor even cautious. He simply wanted this job done. He inserted the crowbar between the door and its stone jamb and leaned on it until he heard the gunshot crack of a broken hasp. The door swung inward—

On one more dark stone room.

"Christ!" Tom exclaimed. Maybe it went on forever, room after ugly little chamber. Maybe he *was* in hell.

But this room wasn't entirely empty. He swept the flashlight before him and spotted two canisters on the floor, next to a flight of wooden stairs leading (again) upward.

Some clue here, he thought.

The canisters were about a hand high; and one of them had a wire handle attached to it at the rim.

He stood above them and shone the flashlight down.

The label on the can on the left said VARSOL.

The label on the can on the right said EVERTINT PAINT. In smaller print, *Eggshell Blue.*

Tom turned and was startled by a string dangling in front of his face. He tugged it, and above his head a naked forty-watt bulb flared on.

Ahead of him—up the stairs—he heard a whisper of traffic and rain.

This was so disorienting—so *disenchanting*—that he stood motionless for a long while in the glare of the overhead light. If anyone had seen him they might have said he was stunned. He looked like a man who had taken a powerful blow to the skull—still standing, but barely.

Let's see, he thought, I headed south from the basement and then circled back, walked half an hour or so . . . maybe as far as the mall or the shops down by the highway. He climbed the stairs expecting nothing, passed another door into a seedy lobby he didn't recognize; then a thought struck him:

It wasn't raining when I left the house.

Well, that was a good long time ago now, wasn't it? Plenty of time for some weather to roll in from the sea.

But he recalled the weekend weather forecast: sunshine all the way to Tuesday.

Wouldn't be the first time they'd made a bad call; coastal weather could be unpredictable.

Still, it was coming down pretty hard out there.

Tom had emerged into what seemed to be the lobby of an apartment building: peeling linoleum, a row of buzzers, an inner and outer door—the outer door cracked in a starry pattern. He fixed the lobby in his mind as a landmark, then stepped outside.

Into the rain.

Into another world.

Tom's first groping thought was that he had walked into a movie set—this was the most coherent explanation his fumbling mind could produce. Professional set dressing: a period piece.

All the cars in the street were antiques, though some appeared virtually new. Must have cost a fortune, he thought dazedly, assembling all this collectible transportation and parking it in a part of town that wasn't familiar *(that isn't Belltower,* one agitated fraction of self insisted), where all the buildings were period buildings and where the people were period *people,* or actors, or extras, dozens of them, scurrying through the rain. And no cameras. And no lights.

He cowered back into the rain shadow of this grubby building.

It was very difficult to think. A part of him was giddy, elated. He had arrived at this unimaginable destination by unimaginable means, he had fucking *done it.* Magic! Elation meanwhile doing battle with its partner, stark animal fear of the unknown. One step in the wrong direction and he would be lost, as lost as it was possible to be. All he really knew was that he had arrived somewhere where the shiniest vehicle on the street was what appeared to be a '61 Buick—or something like it—and all the men braving the rain this cold evening were wearing for Christ's sake *hats,* not rain hats but dress hats—trilbies or fedoras or whatever they were called —the kind of hats you saw in old Cary Grant comedies. Planet of the Hats!

It was very, very strange but also very, very real. A cold wind gusted rain into his face. Real rain. A woman bent under her umbrella shot him a sidelong glance as she passed, and Tom understood that *she* was at home here, *he* was the intruder—a strange, distraught, disheveled man wearing a packsack. He glanced down at himself. His jeans were gray with dust, streaked where the rain had penetrated the dirt. His hands were almost completely black.

The thought persisted: *I'm the stranger here.*

And, on some even deeper level, he knew exactly what this place was. He had traveled a mile or so down a featureless tunnel (MACHINE, the television had called it)—and maybe thirty-odd years into the past.

Not the past of Belltower, Washington. It was a dark night, but he knew at once this was a bigger and busier city than Belltower had ever been. But an American city. The cars were American. The people *looked* American. An American city . . . in or around the year of his birth.

He didn't accept this explanation, not entirely. Logic objected. Sanity was outraged. But logic and sanity had been forced into the back seat quite a while ago, hadn't they? He wouldn't have been too surprised if the tunnel had opened onto the surface of Mars. Was a thirty-year-old rainstorm really such a surprise?

Well, *yes.* It was. A surprise and a shock. But he was beginning to get a handle on it.

He thought, *I can't stay here.* In fact, the feeling was more urgent. *You're a long way from home and it's a long, dark crawl back to the tunnel. What if somebody seals up one of those doors? What if the Machine doesn't work anymore? What if—* and here was a truly chilling thought—*what if it's a one-way Machine?*

Anxiety veered toward panic.

Lots here to figure out, Tom thought, lots of possibilities, lots to absorb, but the *wise* thing would be to turn back and contemplate his options.

Before he did that, however, he took three long steps out into the frigid rain—past a miserable man with umbrella, unlit pipe, dog on a leash—to a newspaper box occupying curb space next to the shiny-wet Buick. He put three dimes into the paper box and pulled out the *New York Times*. Paused to inspect the date.

May 13, 1962.

Raindrops spattered across the front page.

"It's a fucking miracle," he said out loud. "You were right all along, Doug. Miracles up along the Post Road."

He turned and saw the dog-walker regarding him a little suspiciously, a little fearfully, while the dog, a springer spaniel, left its scent on a gray lamp standard. Tom smiled. "Nice weather!"

"For lunatics," the man offered.

Tom retreated past him into the sad lobby of this old building, its smell of mildew and ancient plaster and the unimaginable secret in its foundation. Still *my* secret, he thought. He turned away from the man on the street, away from the rain and the traffic, clutching his souvenir newspaper in one hand, down and away and home; or, if not home, at least *back*.

Back, as they say, to the future.

One more thing caught his attention before he began the long, fatiguing hike back to the basement. As he clambered over the stacked rubble into the tunnel, his flashlight reflected from an object half buried under the masonry and turned up, no doubt, by his movement: a machine bug.

It was inert. He picked it up. The device had lost its shine; it wasn't just dusty, but dull, somehow empty.

Dead, he thought. What it is, is *dead.*

So the machine bugs must have been here, too, in the building behind him, cleaning and maintaining it . . . but something had killed them. At least, something had killed this one. And the wall had never been repaired, unlike the wall in Tom's basement.

He put the broken creature in his pocket—in a strange way, the gesture was respectful—and took a deep breath, bracing himself for the long walk back.

Home, he slept for twelve hours straight. He woke up to a sunny afternoon. He had missed a day at the lot; Klein would be, in Tony's immortal phrase, shitting bricks—but he dismissed the thought as soon as it came to him; he had other things to think about. He fixed himself a huge meal, bacon and fried eggs and buttered toast and a fresh pot of coffee. And sat down at the kitchen table, where the *New York Times* waited for him.

He read it meticulously. He read the headline story: Laos had declared a state of emergency and eighteen hundred marines were en route to Indochina. Troops of the South Vietnamese Seventy-fifth Infantry had ambushed some guerrillas in Kien Phong Province, and President Kennedy had addressed a Democratic Jefferson-Jackson Day dinner in Milwaukee, mainly about the economy. The Mets had won both games of a doubleheader, defeating the Braves at the Polo Grounds. The weather? Cloudy, cool, occasional rain.

He read the fashion ads, the movie ads, the sports pages. Then he folded the paper and set it neatly aside.

He took a pad of paper and a pencil from a kitchen drawer and opened the pad to its first fresh page.

At the top he wrote, *Troubling Questions.* He underlined it twice.

He paused, sipped coffee, then picked up the pencil.

Something is wrong here, he wrote.

Something is wrong or I would never have found the tunnel. The previous owner vanished. The machine bugs talked about "repairing" him/it. The machine bugs are running on autopilot, I think. The lights left on but the premises empty.

Question of rubble at the end of the tunnel. "Destruction." But why, and committed by whom or what?

Well, that was the *real* question, wasn't it?

He wrote, *The tunnel is an artifact. The tunnel is a time machine. It was built by someone. Someone owns it.*

Which would imply someone *from the future,* since they weren't assembling time tunnels down at General Dynamics these days. It was hard to come to grips with that idea, in part because of the echo of too much juvenile fantasy, too many comic books and bad movies. People from the future, very familiar: bald guys in pastel tights.

The trouble was that such thinking was dangerously useless. He would have to think about these numbingly strange events with as much sobriety and clarity as he could muster. The stakes—he remembered DESTRUCTION—might be very high.

Some destructive force caused problems at this end of the tunnel, he wrote, *bad enough that the owners bugged out and left the property running on automatic. The same force, presumably, did an even better job at the Manhattan end.*

But there was so much he still didn't know. Why a tunnel between Belltower and New York City? Were there more tunnels to other places? Did the tunnels always go to the same place? When they functioned normally, what were they for? Who used them?

He wrote these questions down.

Then paused, refilled his coffee cup and sat down again. He reached into his pocket and took out the dead machine bug.

It lay pallid and empty-seeming on the inky front page of the *Times.*

Death by misadventure. Most likely, he thought, it had been murdered.

Ten years have passed, he wrote. *If the passing of time means anything at all, under the circumstances.*

Chewed his pencil.

You could walk away from this.

After all: what was he really doing here? Tempting himself? Daring himself?

This is dangerous, and you could walk away.

It was undeniable.

Maybe the only question is which way to walk.

Because he had a choice now, didn't he? He felt a tingle of excitement, the pleasure of this secret option, this new ace that had been dealt him. He hadn't dared to consider it. He considered it now.

You could leave it all behind.

You could leave the car lot and the divorce and the polite pink slip and the greenhouse effect all behind. The sensation of writing the words made him dizzy. *You could walk out on it. Everybody else on the face of the earth is being dragged into the future an hour at a time but you can walk out. You found the back door.* Forcing some rationality here: *Not the door to paradise. Thirty years ago. They have the Bomb. Think about it. They have industrial pollution. They have racism, ignorance, crime, starvation—*

They have the Bomb, he thought, but maybe the important thing was, *they didn't use it.* He could live three decades, if he wanted to, knowing for a stone fact that the air-raid siren wouldn't go off. He could laugh at the newspapers. If he was diligent, if he did his homework, he'd know the plane he stepped onto wasn't going to fall out of the sky; he'd be out of town when the earthquake hit . . .

And even if someone died, it would be a death already entered into the history books. No graves would be filled that weren't already full. The tragedy of the world would march on, but at least he would have its measure.

He heard an echo of Barbara from that chamber in his head where memories lived and sometimes spoke: *Are you really so frightened of the future?*

After Chernobyl, after Tiananmen Square, after his divorce? In a world where tritium regularly disappeared from scheduled shipments, where the national debt was coming due, where the stock market resembled an Olympic high-dive competition? Scared of the future, here in the world of teen suicide and the cost-effective assault rifle? Scared?—while the Brazilian rain forests clouded the atmosphere with their burning and the skin cancer rate had become an artifact of the evening news? What, *frightened?*

Who, *me?*

I'll go back one more time, he wrote. *At least to look. To be there. At least once.*

Any other questions?

Yes, he thought. Many. But he chose not to write them down.

When Tom glanced up from the paper he saw that several of the larger machine bugs had climbed the table leg and were carrying their dead compatriot away.

Maybe to replace it, Tom thought. Maybe to repair it: they were big on repairing things. Or maybe to *bury* it, to inter it in some metallic grave while they gathered around and sang electromagnetic hymns.

They made a bright, glassy line against the kitchen tiles as they marched away. He didn't interfere.

One more time, he promised himself, at least to see—all decisions postponed until then. He decided he'd provision himself for a weekend trip and in the meantime lead a normal life, as impossible as that sounded.

Astonishingly, the charade was a success. He put in good hours at work. Tony invited him for a family dinner and that worked out well, too, with Tony and Loreen making casual but pointed inquiries about his health and his "attitude," Tom fending them off with carefully fuzzy answers. Time passed easily except at night, when his doubts came sneaking back like guilty prodigals. He installed a hardware store

113

deadbolt on the door leading into the back basement—not that this would stop any serious traffic coming up the tunnel, but it was a useful psychological prop, a sleeping aid, like the small white pills he bought at the Valu-Save Pharmacy. He found some popular histories of the 1960s in the library and invested some study in the first third of that decade, everything up to the Kennedy assassination. It struck him as an oddly quiescent time, large events jostling in the wings but not quite ready to put in an appearance on stage. Call it a nervous appendage of the fifties. He began to recognize names: Gagarin, Khrushchev, John Glenn, Billie Sol Estes—but history paled in the face of this enormity, his secret shortcut through the maze of years and death. The week wheeled on.

He woke up before dawn Saturday morning, marked the space between the wall studs and carved an opening with a keyhole saw—he was getting good at this.

At the opposite end of the tunnel he noted with relief that the rubble had not been disturbed—only his own footprints in the dust—and that the broken lock on the adjoining door had not been replaced.

No one knows yet.

He was safe here still.

He left the tunnel and ventured into the street on a cool and cloudy spring morning. Time passed at the same rate, he noted, here and at home, though the seasons were out of synchronization by a couple of months. He wrote down the street number of the tenement building he emerged from and then the street as he passed the sign at an intersection. Then simply walked. He was a tourist. That was what he'd say if anyone asked. *I'm from out of town.* Basic and quite true.

Of course, he got lost.

He had been to New York on business trips for Aerotech but his grasp of the city's geography was vague at best. He walked across Fourteenth Street to Fifth Avenue with the notion that he might find some familiar landmarks . . . but he didn't want to stray that far from the tunnel.

Not that he would have a hard time finding his way back; the address was there in his pocket. But he couldn't hail a cab and he couldn't even buy a tourist map in a dimestore; his money was useless—or at least ran the risk of being mistaken for counterfeit—unless he put it in a vending machine. He told himself that getting lost wasn't such a bad thing; that he had planned to spend the day wandering—aimlessly or otherwise.

But it was hard to navigate coherently. He walked in a daze, blinded by the miraculous. The most prosaic object—a woman's hat in a milliner's window, a billboard, a chromium hood ornament—would suddenly capture all his attention. They were tokens of the commutation of time, bodies risen from the grave. He could not say which was stranger, his own numbing awareness of the transiency of these things or the nonchalance of the people he passed—people for whom this was merely *the present,* solid as houses.

It made him grin. It made him shiver.

Of the people he passed, many must have died by 1989. *These are the lives of the dead,* Tom thought. *These are their ghost-lives, and I've entered into them.* If they'd known, they might have looked at him twice. He was a cold wind from the land of their children . . . one more cold wind on a cold afternoon.

It *was* afternoon now, and colder than it had been, and the rain started again; a bitter, squalling rain that ran down his collar and seemed to pool, somehow, at the base of his spine. From Fifth Avenue he crossed Washington Square North into the park. He recognized the arch from one of his visits to the city, but that arch had been a canvas for spray-paint graffiti; this arch was visibly marble, if not pristine. He found a bench (the rain had subsided a little) and occupied it while he calculated his route home; then a young woman in harlequin-rimmed glasses and a black sweater stopped and looked at him—really looked—and asked him his name, and wondered whether he had anywhere to go.

Her name was Joyce Casella. She bought him coffee.

She took him home.

He woke once in the night. Waking, he unfolded his memory of the day and examined it—read it like a text, for clues. The mystery was what he ought to do next. He had come a great distance without a compass.

A siren wailed in the outer darkness. He stood up, here in this shabby room in the city of New York in the Year of Our Lord Nineteen Hundred and Sixty-two, stumbled through a dim wash of streetlight to the bathroom and pissed into the rusty porcelain bowl. He was embedded in a miracle, he thought, not just the miracle of 1962 but the miracle of its *dailiness,* of this toothpaste-stained 1962 medicine cabinet, this 1962 bottle of aspirin, this leaky 1962 faucet . . .

He rinsed his face and shook off a little sleep. Three forty-five in the morning, according to the digital watch he'd bought at a Kresge's a quarter century or so in the future. He leaned against the tiled wall and listened to the rain beat against a narrow window. He was full of thoughts he hadn't allowed himself for a long, long time.

How much he missed sharing his home with a woman, for instance.

He liked Joyce and he liked the sensation of being in her apartment, of seeing—for the first time in nearly a year—a bathroom shelf stocked with Midol and a tampon box; seeing her hairbrush, her toothpaste (neatly rolled from the bottom), a Sloan Wilson novel splayed open on the back of the toilet tank. Sharing these small, quotidian intimacies reminded him how thirsty he had been for intimacy in general. This tiny oasis. Such a dry and formidable desert.

"Thank you, Joyce," he said—aloud, but not loud enough that she might hear him in her bedroom. "Shelter from the storm. That's really nice."

Cold rain spattered against the window. The radiator clanked and moaned. Outside, in the dark, the wind was picking up.

In the morning he found his way home.

"I might be back," he told Joyce. It wasn't a promise, but it startled him when he said it. *Would* he be back? This was a miracle; but was it possible to *inhabit* a miracle? Miracles, like Brigadoon, had a way of disappearing.

Later, he would think that perhaps it *had* been a promise, if only to himself . . . that he had known the answer to these questions all along.

☐ ☐

☐ ☐

His last day in Belltower. His last day in the 1980s.

He drove to work prepared to quit, but Klein finessed that by handing him a pink slip. "You're a fuck-up in general," Klein informed him, "but what made up my mind was that deal you wrote on Wednesday."

The Wednesday deal had been a retired County Court judge. The customer might have had an illustrious career on the bench, but he suffered from what Tom had learned to recognize as a common malady: big-purchase panic. The judge regarded the offer form as if it were a writ of execution and offered full sticker price for a car he'd barely looked at. "Let's write up a lower offer," Tom said, "and see what the sales manager has to say."

He told Klein, "We made money on that deal."

"I know the son of a bitch," Klein said. "He comes in every other year. He just toddles in and pays list."

"Nobody pays list."

"If they're giving away money," Klein said, "it's not your job to turn it down. But I don't want to argue with you. I just want you off the lot." He added, "I cleared this with your brother, so don't go running off to him and expect any help. He told me, 'Hey, if Tom fucked up, he's history. That's all there is to it.'"

Tom couldn't help smiling. "I guess that's right," he said. "I guess I'm history."

He phoned Tony and said he was going away for a while. Tony wanted to talk—about the job, about the future. Tom said, "I have to get things sorted out by myself. Thank you for everything, though, Tony. Don't expect to hear from me for a while."

"You're acting crazy," Tony said.

"This is something I have to do."

He packed a change of clothes into his knapsack. Money was a problem, but he was bringing along some items he thought he might be able to pawn: the guitar he'd owned since college (bulky but potentially valuable, a Gibson); a set of silver spoons. By Friday noon he was ready to go.

He hesitated when he noticed the TV had been plugged in again. It seemed to sense his presence; as he watched, it flickered to life.

"You're too late," he said. "I'm leaving."

TOM WINTER, WE DON'T THINK YOU SHOULD GO.

Their punctuation had improved. He considered the statement, considered its source. "You can't stop me," he said. Probably this was true.

IT'S NOT SAFE WHERE YOU'RE GOING.

"It's not safe where I am."

118

YOU WANT IT TOO BADLY. IT ISN'T WHAT YOU THINK.

"You don't know what I want. You don't know what I think."

Of course, maybe they *did*—it was entirely possible. But they didn't contradict him.

YOU CAN HELP US.

"We talked about that."

WE NEED PROTEINS.

"I don't know what you mean by that."

MEAT.

"Meat?" Here was an unforeseen development. "Ordinary meat? Grocery store meat?"

YES, TOM.

"What are you building out in the woods that needs *meat?"*

WE'RE BUILDING US.

He wanted to dismiss the whole disturbing notion; but it occurred to him that he owed these creatures something. It was their territory he was about to trespass through. And more than that: he'd been in their power for a long time. They had implied that they could have changed him; if they'd wanted a slave they could have made him one. They hadn't. He owed them.

Nevertheless—"building us"? And they wanted *meat?*

He said, "I have some steaks in the freezer—"

THAT WOULD BE FINE, TOM.

"Maybe I can leave them on the counter."

THANK YOU.

"How come you can talk so much better now?"

WE'RE ALMOST REPAIRED. THINGS ARE MUCH CLEARER. THE END OF THE WORK IS VERY CLOSE.

Something ominous about that, Tom thought. When the sleeping giant woke, this might not be a safe place to be.

The implication? *Get out now.*

He tried to pull the plug on the TV set but it wouldn't come out of the wall—they must have welded it there. But the screen remained blank. He hurried to the kitchen, left a stack of frozen steaks and ground beef on the countertop—a little queasy at the thought of them wanting it—then gathered up his baggage.

The phone rang once more. He debated letting it ring, then relented and picked up the handset. He expected Tony with some last-minute badgering, but it was Doug Archer's voice he heard.

"I heard you got fired."

"News travels fast," Tom said.

"It's a small town. I've done business with a lot of these people. Yeah, everybody talks."

"Keeping tabs on me?"

"Hell, no. If I had been, I would have noticed you aren't looking for another job. So are you taking a vacation, Tom, or just bugging out?"

"The property's not for sale."

"I'm not calling as your fucking realtor. Are things okay up there?"

"Things are okay."

"You know what I'm talking about."

He sighed. He liked Doug, he didn't want to hurt Doug's feelings—but he didn't want Doug involved, not at this stage. "I'll be out of town for a while."

"Son of a bitch," Archer said. "You *found* something, didn't you? You don't want to talk about it, but you found something."

Or something found me. "You're right . . . I don't want to talk about it."

"How long are you gone for?"

"I honestly don't know."

"The guy who lived there before—you're going where *he* went, right?"

"No, I don't think so."

"When you come back," Archer said, "will you talk to me about this?"

Tom relented a little. "Maybe I will."

"Maybe I should drive by while you're gone—make sure the place is in reasonable shape."

"I don't think that's necessary." A thought occurred. "Doug, promise me you won't try to get in." He lied, "I had the locks changed."

"I promise I won't try to get in if you promise you'll explain this one day."

"Deal," Tom said. "When I get back." *If I get back.*

"I mean to hold you to that," Archer said. There was a pause. He added, "Well, good luck. If you need luck."

"I might need a little," Tom admitted.

He hung up the phone, pulled the shades, turned off the lights, and left the world behind.

PART TWO

Ghosts

PART TWO

Seven

For a long, lost span of years, the time traveler was dead.

Ben Collier's death was not absolute, but it was nothing less than death. The marauder's weapon had opened his skull and scattered much of his brain matter in a bloody rain across the lawn. His heart had given one final, convulsive pump, fibrillated for thirty seconds as wild impulses radiated from his traumatized brainstem, then fallen silent, a lump of static tissue in the cooling cavern of his chest.

Throughout his body emergency repair systems stuttered and shut down. Auxiliary circulatory pumps responded to his failing heart, then failed in turn as blood pressure dropped below maintainable levels. He continued to take huge, ratcheting breaths—like yawns—for nearly a minute. The lungs were the last major system to give up their independent life, and they did so with a final sigh of resignation. By then the body had begun to cool.

Nanomechanisms were trapped in his arteries by clotting blood. Oxygen-starved, they radiated emergency signals and shut themselves off one by one.

Billy Gargullo dragged the body into the woods and left it in an abandoned woodshed under a scatter of mildewed newspaper. Decay organisms—thick in the rainy forest—began to attack the corpse at once.

Billy hurried back to the house. When he arrived here he had disoriented the cybernetics with a pulse of electromagnetic radiation; now he triggered a second burst to keep them out of his way. He paused a moment in the kitchen and consulted his auxiliary memories for a rough estimate of his whereabouts. America, the Pacific Northwest—distinguished by the fiercely dense biomass of the forest, which appalled and frightened him—sometime after 1970: too close to the nightmare he'd left behind. He wanted a more effective buffer, even if it meant greater risk. He moved back to the basement and operated the tunnel's hidden controls the way the dying woman had taught him. Destination was relatively unimportant: he wanted a place to hide. He would run, he would hide, he would never be found and he would never go back.

That was all of his plan. His only plan. The only plan he needed.

Billy's EM pulses interrupted TV and radio reception throughout the town of Belltower and two neighboring counties. Along the Post Road the effect was most violent and startling. Peggy Simmons, the widow who lived a quarter mile from the house Tom Winter would eventually inhabit, was astonished to see her Zenith color television emit a vivid blue spark while the picture tube turned an ominous, fractured gray. Repairs, that summer of 1979, cost her almost three hundred dollars—the set was just out of warranty. She paid the repair bill but reminded the man at Belltower Audio-Video that the Crosley set she'd bought in 1960 lasted her fifteen years with only a tube to replace now and then, and perhaps standards of manufacture had fallen while the price of repairs had zoomed up, which was precisely the sort of thing you'd *expect* to happen, wouldn't you—the world being what it was. The repairman nodded and shrugged. Maybe she was right: he'd been out on a lot of calls just recently.

The rash of electrical failures became a brief sensation in Belltower, reported in the local paper, discussed to no conclusion, and finally forgotten.

Many of the cybernetics died or were rendered hopelessly dysfunctional by the EM burst; but many survived. They were disoriented for days afterward. Severed paths of information needed to be patched and restored; a comprehensible memory of the day's events had to be assembled.

Most damaging was the loss of Ben Collier. For the cybernetics, he had combined the functions of clearinghouse, lawmaker, and God. Without him they were forced to fall back on primitive subroutines. This was unavoidable but limiting. Without Ben, and with their numbers greatly reduced, they possessed only a rudimentary intelligence. They were able to perform routine tasks; all else was groping in the dark.

Many of the nanomechanisms intimately associated with the time traveler's body had been destroyed by the impact of Billy's weapon or the physical shutdown that followed. Some had been scattered to the winds; damaged or swept out of the range of collective mentation, they died. A few—following subroutines of their own—managed an orderly escape; in time, they made their way back to the house. They transferred their significant memory to the larger cybernetics in the manner of bees feeding pollen to the hive. The community of machines, sharing this new wisdom, understood that there were measures to be taken.

Armies of insect-sized cybernetics, following vectors the nanomechanisms described, delved into the forest behind the house. This was risky and had been the subject of debate; territory beyond the perimeter of the house had been forbidden to them—until this emergency. But their first priority (they reasoned) was the restoration of Ben Collier; other issues could be deferred until he was in a position to clarify his wishes.

Restoration was no simple task, however. Cybernetic emissaries found the body in a state of decomposition. Great numbers of microorganisms, mainly bacteria and fungi, had established themselves on the wounds, in the extremities, throughout the body. The putrefaction was extensive and would be impossible to reverse if allowed to continue much longer. Work began at once. Old nanomechanisms were enlisted and new ones created to enter the body as sterilants. The heart was isolated and meticulously restored to a potentially functional state. Open veins and arteries were sealed. Old, infected skin was sloughed off and replaced with extruded synthetics.

What they preserved in this fashion was not the time traveler's body, precisely, but the rough core of it—the skeletal system (minus a leg and most of the skull); crude reductions of the major organs; some sterile meat. An observer walking into the woodshed would have seen what looked like a freshly flayed, naked, and brutally incomplete corpse. It was not in any sense functional.

It never would have been, except that the cybernetics maintained among themselves a blueprint of the time traveler's body and had shared a map of his brain and its contents. This information was shared among them holographically; some detail had been lost in the EM pulse, but it was nothing they couldn't infer from genetic data still preserved in the body. They had salvaged what parts they could and they were ready to begin rebuilding the rest.

The problem was raw material: raw material for the reconstruction and raw material for their own maintenance. Much needed to be done. For now, they simply sterilized the corpse and sealed its perimeters. They maintained a watch over the body of Ben Collier to guarantee the continued viability of his meat; but the main phalanx of the cybernetics retreated to the house to consider their resources and rebuild their material base.

128

Many new nanomechanisms would be needed. These could be assembled—albeit slowly—from material in the house and surrounding soil. The nanomechanisms were intricate but very nearly massless; this was their advantage. With this new army, work could proceed on the restoration of the body . . . a task unfortunately much more massive.

Their sole ally was the body itself. Once primitive cardiovascular function had been restored, the time traveler's own digestive functions could begin to work. In effect, he could be nourished, and the nourishment directed into building and healing. The problem was that he would require a vast amount of protein for maintenance alone.

The cybernetics had established a broad path between the house and the woodshed, and within this space they taught themselves to scavenge food. Much acceptable protein was available in this temperate rain forest. Much that was not acceptable could be rendered so, with modification. They learned how to harvest the forest without denuding it. They took deer fern and horsetail, red huckleberries, bracket fungus from a tall, mossy hemlock. They competed with the frogs and the thrushes for insects. On one occasion they discovered the fresh body of a raccoon. This was a banquet, skinned and liquefied with enzymes. They could have killed a deer and speeded their task immensely; but the cybernetics were deeply inhibited against the taking of vertebrate life. They acquired most of their meat by theft—a mouse or frog stolen from the beak of an owl on moonlit summer nights.

If their numbers had been greater this might have sufficed. Restrained by their material base, they were able to preserve the time traveler but only occasionally to upgrade a major function. In July 1983 he regained an operational kidney. In October 1986 he took his first real breath in seven years.

Consciousness was the last great hurdle—so much brain tissue had been destroyed. The reconstruction was more delicate and required more raw material. Consequently it was slow.

The work was painstaking but the cybernetics were infinitely patient. Nothing intruded on their labor until the arrival of Tom Winter—a complication that was not merely distracting but possibly dangerous. Since they couldn't evict him they attempted to use him to their advantage . . . but there was so much they didn't know, so much wisdom that had been lost, and working with Tom Winter culled away too many of their essential nanomechanisms. For a time, the work was slowed . . . but it hastened once again when Tom Winter donated several packages of proteins from his freezer; hastened again when a cougar killed a deer within range of the woodshed. The cougar was easily frightened away and the deer was a vast, warm repository of useful food.

The work hurried toward completion.

Ben Collier experienced odd moments of wakefulness.

His awareness, at first, was tenuous and small, like the flickering of a candleflame in a vast, dark room.

The first experience strong enough to linger in his memory was of pain—a scalding pain that seemed to radiate inward from all the peripheries of his body. He tried to open his eyes and couldn't. The eyes weren't functional and the lids felt sutured shut. He tried to scream and lacked this function also.

The nanomechanisms inside him sensed his distress and alleviated it at once. They closed his sensorium, blocking nerve signals from his raw and mending skin. They triggered a flood of soothing endorphins. Almost immediately, Ben went back to sleep.

The next time he was allowed to wake, the fundamental mechanisms of self and thought were more nearly healed. He knew who he was and what had happened to him. He was paralyzed and blind; but the nanomechanisms reassured him and monitored his neurochemicals for panic.

Ben was mindful of his custodial duties, doubtless neglected during the period of his death. He had one overriding thought: *Tell me what's happened at the house.*

In time, the nanomechanisms responded. He had made great progress but he wasn't ready to assume his former status. For that, he would need to be entirely healed.

Sleep now, they said. He was grateful, and slept.

The next time he woke he woke instantly, alert and buzzing with concern.

Someone is here, the nanomechanisms told him.

Ben knew where he was. He was in the ancient woodshed in the forest behind the house. The cybernetics had restored his memory, including the memory of his own murder and beyond: really, their memories were his memories. The cybernetics had been designed for Ben as his personal adjuncts —appendages—and he was pleased at how well they had functioned without him. For a moment much briefer than a second he savored the details of his own reconstruction.

Which was miraculous but unfortunately not complete. His mind was almost fully functional, but his body needed work. His skull was still partial, large chunks of it replaced with a gluey, transparent caul; his left leg was a venous flipper; muscle tissue stood exposed over large parts of his body where the skin and decay had been stripped and sterilized.

At least his eyes were functional. He opened them.

He was supine in the rotted mass of newsprint. Sunlight glimmered through gaps in the southern wall of the shed. Everything was green here, the color of moss and lichen. The air was full of dust motes, pollen and spores.

He looked at the door of the shed, a crudely hinged raft of barnboards held together with rusty iron nails.

His ears worked. He was able to hear the rasp of his own

131

breathing . . . the faint scuttle of cybermechanisms in the detritus around him.

The sound of footsteps in the high meadow weeds beyond the door.

Now, the sound of a hand on the primitive latch that held the door closed.

The sound of the latch as it opened.

The door as it squealed inward.

Ben couldn't move. He drew a deep breath into his raw lungs and hoped he would be able at least to speak.

Eight

Greenwich Village, Manhattan, in the gathering heat and tidal migrations of the summer of 1962: by the end of June Tom Winter had learned a few things about his adopted homeland.

He learned some of its history. "The Village," named Sapokanican by the Indians and Greenwich by the British, had been a fashionable section of Manhattan until its prestige migrated north along Broadway at the end of the nineteenth century. Then an immigrant population had moved in, and then radical bohemians drawn by low rents in the years before the First World War. If his time machine had dropped him off in the 1920s he could have walked into Romany Marie's in one of its several incarnations—on Sheridan Square or later on Christopher Street—and found Eugene O'Neill making notes for a play or Edgard Varèse dining on a *ciorba* aromatic with leeks and dill. Or he might have arrived in 1950 and encountered Dylan Thomas drunk in the White Horse or Kerouac at the Remo considering California—these public lives only an eddy of the deeper current, a counterpoint to American life as it was understood in the movies.

Rents had climbed since then; a slow gentrification had been proceeding ever since the subway linked the Village to the rest of the city in the 1930s. Genuinely poor artists were already being shouldered into the Lower East Side. Nevertheless, it was 1962 and the scent of rebellion was strong and poignant.

He learned that he liked it here.

Maybe that was odd. Tom had never considered himself a "bohemian." The word had never meant much to him. He had gone to college in the seventies, smoked marijuana on rare occasions, worn denim and long hair in the last years that was fashionable. None of this had seemed even vaguely rebellious—merely routine. He moved into a white-collar job without anxiety and worried about his income like everybody else. Like everybody else, he ran up his credit debt and had to cut back a little. He was troubled—like everybody else—when the stock market tottered; he and Barbara had never set aside enough for an investment portfolio, but he worried about the economy and what it might mean for their budget. Barbara was deeply committed to ecological activism but she was hardly bohemian about it, despite what Tony thought—her approach, he sometimes thought, was brutal enough to put a hard-nosed corporate lawyer to shame. She told him once that if she had to wear a Perry Ellis skirt to be credible, she'd fucking wear it: it wasn't an issue.

And when the structure of life and job collapsed around him, it didn't occur to Tom that the system had failed; only that he had failed it.

He was surprised and delighted to discover another attitude here, not only in Joyce but generally, in the Village: a consensus that the world outside was a sterile laboratory and that its only interesting products were its failures, its rejects, and its refugees.

He was as poor, certainly, as any refugee. Joyce put him up for a few days when he arrived—until Lawrence objected—and persuaded him not to sell his guitar. She had found a part-time job waitressing and lent him enough cash for a room at the Y. She told her friends he was looking for a day job and one of them—an unpublished novelist named Soderman—told Tom there was a radio and hi-fi shop on Eighth with a Help Wanted sign in the window. The store was called Lindner's Radio Supply, and the owner, Max Lindner, explained that he needed a technician, "somebody to work in the back," and did Tom know anything about electronics? Tom said yeah, he did—he'd done a couple of EE courses in college and he knew his way around a soldering iron. Most of what Max's customers brought in for repair would be vacuum tube merchandise, but Tom didn't anticipate any trouble adapting. "The back" was a room the size of a two-car garage; the walls were lined with tube caddies and testers and there was a well-thumbed RCA manual attached to the workbench on a string. The smell of hot solder flux saturated the air.

"My last guy was a Puerto Rican kid," Max said. "He was only eighteen, but there was nothing he couldn't strip and put back together twice as nice as the day we sold it. You know what they did? They fucking drafted him. Six months from now he'll be building radar stations in Congo Bongo. I did my bit on Guadalcanal and this is how the army repays me." He looked Tom up and down. "You can really do this work?"

"I can really do this work."

"You start tomorrow."

After work, his first priority was a place to live.

Joyce agreed. "You can't stay at the French Embassy. It's not safe."

"The what?"

"The Y, Tom. It's nothing but faggots. Maybe you noticed."

She grinned a little slyly, expecting him to be shocked by this information. He wondered what to say. *My ex-wife was politically correct—we attended all the AIDS fundraisers.* "I think my virtue is intact."

She raised her eyebrows. "Virtue?"

To celebrate his job they had come to Stanley's, a new bar on the Lower East Side. Tom had begun to sort out the geography of the city; he understood that the East Village was even more subterranean than the West, a crosstown bus away from the subways, the Bearded Artist a recent immigrant, which was why Stanley's sometimes offered free beer in an effort to build a clientele. Lawrence's apartment was nearby and Joyce's not too far from it and anyway nothing was happening tonight in the gaudier precincts of Bleecker and MacDougal.

Tom was pleased about the job, a little nervous about the evening.

Joyce offered him a cigarette. He said, "I don't."

"You're very light on vices, Tom." She lit one of her own. The office where he worked at Aerotech had been designated smoke-free; none of Barbara's friends smoked and the salesmen at the car lot had been encouraged not to. He'd forgotten what a fascinating little ritual it could be. Joyce performed it with unconscious grace, waving the match and dropping it in an ashtray. In an hour, when the bar filled up, the air would be blue with smoke. The stern disapproval of C. Everett Koop was a quarter century away.

"At least you drink."

"In moderation." He was nursing a beer. "I used to drink more. Actually, I wasn't a very successful alcoholic. My doctor told me it was too hard for me to drink seriously and too easy to stop. He said I must not have the gene for alcoholism —it just isn't in my DNA."

"Your which?"

"I'm not cut out that way."

"Hopelessly Presbyterian." She drew on the cigarette. "Something's bothering you, yes?"

"I don't want to fend off a lot of questions tonight."

"From me, or—?"

He waved his hand—no, not her.

"Well, people are curious. The thing is, Tom, you're not a *label*. People come here and talk about nonconformity and the Lonely Crowd and all that jazz, but they're wearing labels all the same. You could hang signs on them. Angry young poet. Left-wing folksinger. Ad executive reclaiming his youth. So on. The real, true ciphers are very rare."

He said, "I'm a cipher?"

"Oh, definitely."

"Isn't that a label too?"

She smiled. "But no one likes it. If you don't want to hang around, Tom, you have some options."

"Like?"

"Like, you could go somewhere else. Or you could tell everybody to fuck off. Or *we* could go somewhere else. Now or later."

She sat across the table from him, one hand cocked at an angle and the smoke from her cigarette drifting toward the ceiling. The light was dim but she was beautiful in it. She had tied her long hair back; her eyes were pursed, quizzical, blue under the magnification of her glasses. He could tell she was nervous about making the offer.

Nor was there any mistaking what the offer meant. Tom felt as if the chair had dropped out from under him. Felt weightless.

He said, "What about Lawrence?"

"Lawrence has some problems. Or, I don't know, maybe they're my problems. He says he doesn't want to own me. He doesn't want anybody else to, either. He says he's ambivalent. I'm what he's ambivalent about."

Tom was considering this when the door opened and a crowd rushed in from the hot evening on Avenue B. Her friends. "Joyce!" one of them sang out.

She looked at Tom, shrugged and smiled and mouthed a word: it might have been *"Later."*

Like any immigrant—any refugee—he was adjusting to his new environment. It was impossible to live in a state of perpetual awe. But the knowledge of where he was and how he had come here was seldom far from his mind.

Nineteen sixty-two. The Berlin Wall was less than a year old. John F. Kennedy was in the White House. The Soviets were preparing to send missiles to Cuba, precipitating a crisis which would not, finally, result in nuclear war. In Europe, women were bearing babies deformed by thalidomide. Martin Luther King was leading the civil rights movement; this fall, there would be some trouble down at Oxford, Mississippi. And the Yanks would take the World Series from the Giants.

Privileged information.

He knew all this; but he still felt edged out of the conversation that began to flow around him. For a while they talked about books, about plays. Soderman, the novelist who tipped Tom off to the radio-repair job, had strong opinions about Ionesco. Soderman was a nice guy; he had a young, round chipmunk face with a brush cut on top and a fringe of beard under his chin. Likable—but he might have been speaking Greek. Ionesco was a name Tom had heard but couldn't place, lost in a vague memory of some undergraduate English class. Likewise Beckett, likewise Jean Genet. He smiled enigmatically at what seemed like appropriate moments.

Then Lawrence Millstein performed a verbal editorial on folk music versus jazz and Tom felt a little bit more at home. Millstein was of the old school and outnumbered at this table; he hated the cafe-folk scene and harbored nostalgia for the fierce gods of the tenor sax.

He looked the part. If Tom had been casting a movie version of *On the Road* he might have picked Millstein as an "atmosphere" character. He was tall, dark-haired, lean, and there was something studied about his intensity. Joyce had described him as "a Raskolnikov type—at least, he tries to come on that way."

Millstein performed a twenty-minute monologue on Charlie Parker and the "anguish of the Negro soul." Tom listened with mounting irritation, but kept silent—and drank. He knew the music Lawrence was talking about. Through his breakup with Barbara and after the divorce, he had sometimes felt that Parker—and Thelonious Monk, and Miles Davis of the *Sketches of Spain* era, and Sonny Rollins, and Oliver Nelson—were the only thing holding him together. He had traded in his scoured LPs for the CD versions of some of these records. It was an anomaly, he sometimes thought, these old monophonic recordings deciphered by laser-beam technology. But the music just rolled on out of the speakers. He liked it because it wasn't crying-in-your-beer music. It was never pathetic. It took your hurt, it acknowledged your hurt, but sometimes—on the good nights—it let you soar out somewhere beyond that hurt. Tom had appreciated this strange way the music translated losses into gains and it bothered him to hear Millstein doing a self-righteous tap dance on the subject.

Joyce ventured, "Nobody's putting down Parker. Folk music is doing something else. It's just different. There's no antagonism."

Tom sensed that they had had this argument before and that Millstein had his own reasons for bringing it up. "It's white people's music," Millstein said.

"There's more social commentary in the folk cafes than in the jazz bars," Soderman said.

"But that's the point. Folk music is like a high school essay. All these earnest little sermons. Jazz is the *subject*. It's what the sermon is *about*. The whole Negro experience is wrapped up in it."

"What are you saying?" Tom asked. "White people shouldn't make music?"

Eyes focused on him. Soderman ventured, "The repairman speaks!"

Millstein was full of beery scorn. "What the fuck do you know about the Negro experience?"

"Not a damn thing," Tom said amiably. "Hell, Larry, I'm as white as you are."

Lawrence Millstein opened his mouth, then closed it. A moment of silence . . . then the table erupted in laughter. Millstein managed to say something—it might have been *fuck you*—but it was lost in the roar and Tom was able to ignore him.

Joyce laughed, too, then steered the conversation down a less volatile alleyway: she'd had a letter from somebody named Susan who was doing political organization in rural Georgia. Apparently Susan, a Vassar graduate, had been pretty wild during her Village days. Everybody trotted out Susan stories. Joyce relaxed.

She leaned over and whispered in Tom's ear, "Try not to make him mad!"

He whispered back, "I think it's too late," and ordered another beer.

He had reached that subtle turning point at which he was not quite drunk but definitely a little past sober. He decided these were good people. He liked them. When they left Stanley's, he followed them. Joyce took his hand.

The night air was warm and stagnant. They moved past tenement stoops full of people, bleak streetlights, noise, a barber shop reeking of Barbasol, to an old building and inside and up to a long room cluttered with bookshelves and bad, amateurish paintings. "Lawrence's apartment," Joyce confided. He asked, "Should I be here?" and she said, "It's a party!"

The books were poetry, *Evergreen Review,* contemporary novels. The record collection was large and impressive—there were Bix Beiderbecke 78s in among the LPs—and the hi-fi looked expensive: a Rek-O-Kut turntable, an amplifier bristling with tubes. "Music!" somebody shouted, and Tom stood aside while Millstein eased a John Coltrane record out of its sleeve and placed it on the turntable—the gesture was faintly religious. Suddenly the room was full of wild melody.

Tom watched Soderman pull down the blinds, cutting off a view of the Con Ed stacks on Fourteenth Street, while someone else produced a wooden box containing a quarter ounce of seeded brown marijuana and a package of Zig-Zag rolling papers. Tom was amused by the solemnity of this ritual, including a few doubtful glances in his direction—was this new guy trustworthy? He bustled over and said, "Let me roll it."

Smiles. Joyce asked, "Do you know how?"

He pasted together two papers to make a double-wide. His technique was rusty—it had been a long time—but he produced a creditable joint. Soderman nodded his approval. "Where did you learn that?"

He answered absently, "In college."

"So where'd you go to college?"

"In the agricultural heartland of the Pacific Northwest." He smiled. "A match?"

He meant only to establish his camaraderie, but the dope went instantly to his head. Coltrane's sax, radiating from a single speaker, became a great golden bell-like instrument. He decided he liked Lawrence Millstein for liking this music, then remembered the diatribe in the bar and Joyce's warning —*Don't make him mad*—implying something about his temper and what she might have seen of it. He looked at Joyce where she stood silhouetted in the door to Lawrence's ugly kitchen. He recalled the half promise she had made him and thought about the possibility of holding her in his arms, of taking her to bed. She was very young and not as sophisti-cated as she liked to believe. She deserved better than Law-rence Millstein.

The Coltrane ended. Millstein put on something Tom didn't recognize, fierce bop, an angry music recorded with the microphone too close to the trumpet—it sounded like a piano at war with a giant wasp. The party was getting noisier. Disoriented, he moved to a vacant chair in one corner of the room and let the sound wash over him. There was a knock at the door; the dope was carefully hidden; the door eased open —it was some friend of Soderman's, a woman in a black turtleneck carrying a guitar case. Shouts of welcome. Joyce went to the turntable and lifted the tonearm. Millstein shouted, "Careful with that!" from the opposite end of the room.

Joyce borrowed the guitar, tuned it, and began picking out chords and bass runs. Pretty soon there were five or six peo-ple gathered around her. She was flushed—from the drink-ing or the dope or the attention—and her eyes were a little glassy. But when she sang, she sang wonderfully. She sang traditional folk ballads, "Fannerio," "Lonesome Traveler." When she spoke she was tentative, or shy, or sardonic, but the voice that issued out of her now was utterly different, a voice that made Tom sit up and stare. He had liked her without guessing she had this voice bottled up inside. The look on his face must have been comical; she smiled at him. "Come play!" she said.

He was startled. "Christ, no."

"I heard you diddling that guitar you carried into town. You're not too bad."

Soderman said, "The repairman plays guitar?"

If he'd been a little more sober he would never have ac-cepted. But what the hell—if he was lousy it would only make Joyce look good. Making Joyce look good seemed like a fairly noble ambition.

For years he'd taken his guitar out of its box maybe once a month, so he wouldn't lose what little skill he had. He'd been serious about it in college—serious enough to take lessons with a semialcoholic free-lance teacher named Pegler, who claimed to have led a folk-rock outfit in the Haight in 1965. (Pegler, where are you *now?*) He took the guitar from Joyce and wondered what he could possibly play. "Guantanamera"? Some old Weavers ballad? But he recalled a song he'd taught himself, years ago, from an old Fred Neil album—counted on inspiration and luck to bring back the chord changes.

His singing voice was basically charmless and the dope had roughened it, but he managed the lyrics without groping. He looked up from his fingering halfway through the song and realized Joyce was beaming her approval. Which made him fumble over a chord change. But he picked it up and finished without too much embarrassment. Joyce applauded happily. Soderman said, "Impressive!"

Lawrence Millstein had drifted over from a dark corner of the room. He offered, "Not bad for amateur night."

"Thank you," Tom said warily.

"Sentimental shit, of course."

Joyce was more rankled by the remark than Tom was. "Must be a full moon," she said. "Lawrence is turning into an asshole."

"Reckless," Soderman observed quietly.

Tom sat up.

"No, that's all right," Millstein said. He made an expansive gesture and spilled a little Jack Daniel's from the glass in his hand. "I don't want to interrupt your lovefest."

Tom handed away the guitar. It was dawning on him that he was in the presence of an angry drunk.

Don't make him mad. But Joyce seemed to have forgotten her own advice. "Don't do this," she said. "We don't need this shit."

"*We* don't need it? Who—you and Tom here? Joyce and the repairman?"

Soderman said, "You spilled your drink, Lawrence. Let's get another one. You and me."

Millstein ignored him. He turned to Tom. "You like her? Are you fond of Joyce?"

"Yes, Larry," he said. "I like Joyce a lot."

"Don't you fucking call me Larry!"

Instantly, the party was quiet. Millstein picked up the attention focused on him; he forced a smile. "You know what she is, of course," he went on. "But you *must* know. It's an old story. They come in from Bryn Mawr wearing these ridiculous clothes—ballet flats and toreador pants. They have bohemian inclinations but they all shop at Bonwit Teller. They come here for intellectual inspiration. They'll tell you that. Of course, they really come to get laid. Isn't that right, Joyce? They see themselves in the arms of some nineteen-year-old Negro musician. You can get laid in Westchester just as easily, of course, but not by anyone nearly as *interesting.*" He peered at Tom with a fixed, counterfeit smile. "So just how interesting *are* you?"

"Right now," Tom said, "I guess I'm a little bit more interesting than you are."

Millstein threw down his glass and balled his fists. Joyce said, "Stop him!" Soderman stood up in front of Millstein and put a conciliatory hand on his shoulder. "Hey," he said. "Hey, calm down. It's nothing. Hey, Larry—I mean, *Lawrence*—"

Joyce grabbed Tom's hand and pulled him toward the door.

"The party is fucking over!" Millstein screamed.

They ducked into the hall.

"Come home with me," Joyce said.

Tom said that sounded like a good idea.

· · · ·

She undressed with the unselfconsciousness of a cat.

Pale streetlight came glowing through the dusty window. He was startled by her small breasts and pink, pleasant aureoles; by the neat angle of her pubic hair. She smiled at him in the dark, and he decided he was leading a charmed life.

The touch of her was like a long, deep drink of water. She arched against him as he entered her; he felt rusty springs unwind inside him. She had put her glasses on the orange crate by the bed and her eyes were fiercely wide.

Later, as they were drifting into sleep, she told him he made love like a lonely man.

"Do I?"

"You did tonight. *Are* you lonely?"

"Was lonely."

"Very lonely?"

"Very lonely."

She curved against him, breasts and hips. "I want you to stay here. I want you to move in."

He experienced another moment of pure free-fall. "Is the apartment big enough?"

"The bed is big enough."

He kissed her in the dark. *Charmed life,* he thought.

Nineteen sixty-two, a hot summer night.

It was night all over the continent now, skies clear from the Rockies east to the coast of Maine, stars shining down from the uncrowded sky of a slightly younger universe. The nation slept, and its sleep was troubled—if at all—by faint and distant dreams. A dream of Mississippi. The dream of a war that hadn't quite started, somewhere east of the ocean. The dream of dark empires moving on its borders.

JFK slept. Lee Harvey Oswald slept. Martin Luther King slept.

Tom Winter slept and dreamed of Chernobyl.

• • • •

145

He carried this nugget of discontent from the night into the morning.

I am a cold wind from the land of your children, he had thought. But he looked at Joyce—eating a late breakfast at a cheap restaurant at the end of a dirty, narrow, sunlit street— and didn't want to be that anymore. This was history and history was good because it was immutable; but he worried that he might have brought an infection from the future— not a literal disease but some turbulence in the timestream. Some dark, stalking irregularity that would unravel the fabric of her life. Maybe his certainties were absolutely false. Maybe they would all die in the Soviet attack that followed the missile crisis.

But that was absurd—wasn't it?

"Sometime soon," she said, "you're going to have to tell me who you are and where you came from."

He was startled by the suggestion. He looked at her across the table.

"I will," he said. "Sometime."

"Sometime soon."

"Soon," he said helplessly. Maybe it was a promise. Maybe it was a lie.

Nine

His name was Billy Gargullo, and he was a farmboy.

He had lived in New York City for ten years now, but hot nights like this still reminded him of Ohio.

Hot nights like this, he couldn't sleep. Hot summer nights, he left his tiny apartment and moved like a shadow into the streets. He liked to ride the subway; when the subway was crowded, he liked to walk.

Tonight he rode a little, walked a little.

He had left his shiny golden armor safe at home.

Billy seldom wore the armor, but he often thought about it. The golden armor was at home, in the tenement apartment where he had lived for the last decade. He kept the armor in his closet, behind a false wall, in a box no one else could open.

He wore the golden armor seldom; but the golden armor was a part of him, profoundly his own—and that was troublesome. He had left a great many things behind when he came to New York. Many ugly, many shameful things. But some ugly and shameful things had come with him. The armor itself was not ugly or shameful—in its own way it was beautiful, and when Billy wore it he wore it with pride. But

he had come to suspect that his *need* for it was shameful
. . . that the things he did when he wore it were ugly.

This wasn't entirely Billy's fault, or so he told himself. The
Infantry had performed certain surgeries on him. His need
for the armor was real, physical; he wasn't whole without it.
In a sense, Billy *was* the armor. But the armor wasn't entirely
Billy: the armor had its own motives, and it knew Billy better
than any other creature in the world.

It sang to him sometimes.

Most often, it sang about death.

Billy emerged from the roaring machine caves of the subway
into the night wilderness of Forty-second Street and Broadway. Midnight had come and gone.

Now as ever, he was startled by the wild exuberance of the
twentieth century. All these lights! Colored neon and glaring
filaments, powered, he had learned, by mechanical dams
spanning rivers hundreds of miles away. And most of this—
astonishingly—in the name of *advertising*.

He paced through Times Square, where the lights were so
bright he could hear them sizzle and spit.

Where Billy came from—back on the farm—this frivolous
use of electricity would have been called *promiscuous*. A very
bad word. But the word meant something else here . . . a
dissipation of some other energy entirely.

Words had troubled him from the day he arrived in New
York.

He had arrived in a fury of blood and noise, disgorged into
the sub-basement of an old building through a fracture in the
firmament of time—frightened of what he had seen there;
frightened of what might be waiting for him. He detonated
EM pulses, brought a wall tumbling down, and killed the
man (a time traveler) who tried to stop him.

148

When the dust settled, he crouched in a corner and considered his options.

He thought about the monster he'd encountered in the tunnel.

The monster was called a "time ghost"—Ann Heath had warned him about it before she died.

The fiery apparition had terrified Billy even through the haze of chemical courage pumped into him by his armor. The time ghost was like nothing he had ever seen and Billy sensed—he couldn't say how—that its interest in him was particular, personal. Maybe it knew what he'd done. Maybe it knew he had no place in this maze of time; that he was a deserter, a criminal, a refugee.

The monster had appeared as he reached the end of the tunnel, and Billy felt the heat of it and the subtler weight of its hostility; and he had run from it, a terrified sprint through the terminal doorway to this place, a safe place where the monster couldn't follow—or so Ann Heath had told him.

Nevertheless, Billy was still frightened.

He had a rough idea where he was. Mid–twentieth century. Some urban locus. He had killed the custodian of this place and a few more pulse detonations would sweep it clean of cybernetics. But Billy crouched in the corner of the dimly lit sub-basement—in the stench of fused plaster and cinderblock and a fine gray dust from the damaged tunnel—and understood that his exile was permanent.

He powered down his armor and performed a private inventory.

Things he had run away from:
The Infantry.
The Storm Zone.
Murder.
The woman Ann Heath with a wedge of glass in her skull and a hemotropic tube embedded in her chest.
Things he had left behind:

Ohio.

His father, Nathan.

A town called Oasis.

Miles of kale and green wheat and a sky empty of everything but heat and dust.

Things he couldn't leave behind:

His armor.

And, Billy realized, this place. This building, whatever it was. This tunnel entrance, which he had sealed but which he could not *trust:* because it contained monsters, because it contained the future.

What had seemed at the time like inspiration, this feverish escape into the past, troubled him now. He had tampered with mechanisms he didn't understand, mechanisms more powerful than he could imagine. His encounter with the time ghost had been disturbing enough; who *else* might he have angered? There was so much Billy didn't understand. He believed he was safe here . . . but the belief was tempered with fresh new doubts.

But here you are. That was the plain fact of it. Here he was and here he would stay. At least no Infantry; at least no Storm Zone. A place away from all that. Not Ohio with its deserts and canals and the miracle of the harvest, but at least a safe place.

A city in the middle years of the twentieth century.

That night, his first night in the city of New York, Billy undressed the body of the time traveler and used a fan beam to turn the corpse into a dune of feathery white ash.

The clothes were bloodstained and a poor fit, but they allowed Billy to move without attracting attention. He explored the corridors of the tenement building above the sub-basement chamber which contained the tunnel; he explored the nearby streets of the night city. He deduced from the contents of the dead man's wallet that the time traveler had occupied an "apartment" in this building. Billy located the entrance, one numbered door among many, and fumbled keys into the primitive lock until the door sprang inward.

He slept in the dead man's bed. He appropriated a fresh suit of clothes. He marveled at the dead man's calendar: 1953.

He found cash in the dead man's wallet, more cash in a drawer of his desk. Billy understood cash: it was an archaic form of credit, universal and interchangeable. The denominations were confusing but simple in principle: a ten-dollar bill was "worth" two fives, for instance.

He stayed in the apartment a week. Twice, someone knocked at the door; but Billy was quiet and didn't answer. He watched television at night. He ate regular meals until there was nothing left in the refrigerator. He sat at the window and studied the people passing in the street.

He kept his armor hidden under the bed. As vulnerable as Billy felt without the armor, he would have been grotesquely conspicuous in it. He supposed he could have worn the body pieces under his clothing and looked only a little peculiar, but that wasn't the point; he hadn't come here to wear the armor. He planned not to wear the armor at all . . . at least, only to wear it when he had to, when the peculiar needs of his altered body demanded it. In a month, say. Two months. Six months. Not now.

When there was nothing left to eat Billy gathered up his cash and left the building. He walked three blocks to a "grocery" and found himself in a paradise of fresh fruit and vegetables, more of these things than he had ever seen in one place. Dazzled, he chose three oranges, a head of lettuce, and a bunch of bright yellow speckled bananas. He handed the checkout clerk a flimsy cash certificate and was nonplussed when the man said, "I can't change that! Christ's sake!" Change it to *what?* But Billy rooted in his pocket for a smaller denomination, which proved acceptable, and he understood

151

the problem when the cashier handed him a fresh selection of bills and coins: his "change."

Words, Billy thought. What they spoke here was English, but only just.

He acquired his new life by theft.

The custodian, a time traveler, had owned the block of tenement flats above the sub-basement which concealed the tunnel. The deeds were stored in a filing cabinet in the bedroom. For years the time traveler had operated the building strictly as a formality and most of the apartments were empty. Billy passed himself off as "new management" and accepted the monthly rent checks. The charade was almost ridiculously easy. There was no family to mourn the dead man, no business partners to inquire about his health. By reviewing the documents he learned that the time traveler had registered his business under the name Hourglass Rentals, and Billy was able to discern enough of the local financial customs to manipulate bank deposits and withdrawals and pay the tax bills on time. Hourglass Rentals didn't generate enough revenue to cover its debts, but the amount of money banked in the company name was staggering—enough to keep Billy in food and shelter for the rest of his life. Not only that, but the management of these fiscal arcana had been streamlined for a single individual to operate without help— an hour of paperwork an evening, once Billy mastered the essentials of bookkeeping and learned which lies to tell the IRS, the city, and the utility companies. By the end of 1952, Billy *was* Hourglass Rentals.

It suited him to commandeer the life of a loner. Billy was a loner, too.

He guessed the armor had made him that way. He knew the Infantry surgeons had made him dependent on the armor —that without it he was less than a normal human being. Sexually, Billy was a blank slate. He remembered a time when he had wanted the touch of a woman—back in his brief adolescence, before he was prepped, when the physical need had burned like a flame—but that was long ago. Nothing burned in him now but his need for the armor. Now he saw women all the time: women on television, women on city streets, bank tellers, secretaries, women available for money. Occasionally they looked at him. Their looks seldom lingered. Billy guessed there was something about him they could sense—a blankness, a deferral, an inertia of the soul.

It didn't matter. By the snowy January of 1953 Billy had established a life he was content to lead.

He was far from the Infantry, the Storm Zone, and the prospect of imminent death or court martial. He wasn't hungry and he wasn't in physical danger. When he stopped to think about it, it felt a little bit like paradise.

Was he happy here? Billy couldn't say. Most days passed in blissful oblivion, and he was grateful for that. But there were times when he felt the pangs of a brittle, piercing loneliness. He woke up nights in a city more than a century away from home, and that impossible distance was like a hook in his heart. He thought about his father, Nathan. He tried to remember his mother, who had died when he was little. He thought about his life in exile here, stranded on this island, Manhattan, among people who had been dead a hundred years when he was born. Thought about his life among these ghosts. He thought about time, about clocks: clocks, like words, worked differently here. Billy was accustomed to clocks that numbered time and marked it with cursors, linear slices of a linear phenomenon. Here, clocks were round and symbolic. Time was a territory mapped with circles.

Time and words. Seasons. That January, Billy was caught in a snowstorm that slowed the buses to a crawl. Tired and cold, he decided to check into a hotel rather than walk the distance home. He found an inexpensive boarding hotel and asked the desk clerk for a room with a slut; the clerk showed him a strange smile and said he would have to arrange that himself—he recommended a bar a few blocks away. Billy disguised his confusion and checked in anyway, then realized that in 1953 the word "slut" must have some other meaning —he didn't *need* a heated bed; the entire room, the entire hotel was heated. Probably every room in the *city* was heated, even the vast public spaces of banks and the cavernous lobbies of skyscrapers, all through the bitter winter. He had a hard time grasping this simple fact; when he did, the sheer arrogant monstrosity of it left him dazed and blinking.

Asleep in the snowbound hotel, Billy dreamed of all that heat . . . a hundred summers' worth, bubbling up from this city and a dozen cities like it, hovering for decades in invisible cloudbanks and then descending all at once in a final obliteration of the seasons.

He dreamed about Ohio, about a farm in the desert there.

His need for the armor was quiet at first, a barely discernible tickle of desire, something he could ignore—for a time.

The armor, with its power off and its tensor fields collapsed, lay in the box Billy had found for it like yardcloth from some fairy-tale haberdashery. It looked like spun gold, though of course it wasn't really gold; it was woven of complex polymolecules grown in the big East Coast armaments collectives. Parts of it were electronic and parts of it were vaguely alive.

The Infantry doctors had told Billy he'd die without his armor—that he would go mad without the essential neurochemicals generated in the elytra. Billy was frankly aware that without the armor he was slow, languorous, sleepy, and sexless. But he endured that—in a way, the condition was even sedating. For six months he moved through the city with his eyelids heavy and his mouth turned up in an empty narcotic smile.

Then came the Need.

At first it was only a tingling dissatisfaction, pins and needles in his fingers and toes. Billy ignored it and went about his business.

Then the tingling became an itch, the itch a fiery burning. The skin of his face felt drawn tight, as if it had been clamped and sutured to his hairline. He woke up in the bitter late winter of that year with the disquieting sensation that he could feel the gaps and contours of his own skull under the skin, the grinding of bones and ligaments like dry chalk inside him. He was thirsty all the time, but tap water tasted sour in his mouth and burned his throat when he swallowed. He felt sudden blooms of panic, irrational fears: of heights, open spaces, disease.

He knew what this was all about.

The armor, Billy thought.

The sleek and deadly armor.

He wanted it, or *it* wanted *him* . . . Billy was inclined to the latter belief.

This discomfort, this pain, this vertigo: it was the sound of the armor calling to him from its box under the bed.

Billy resisted it.

He was afraid of what the armor might want.

Well, he *knew* what it wanted. It wanted motion, light, heat. It wanted to be brought alive. It wanted to be the creature that Billy was when he wore it, a powerful nightmare-Billy to be summoned and let loose.

He dreamed he was a dog chasing rabbits through a field of wheat by the bone-white light of a harvest moon. He dreamed of cracking the rabbit's spine with his sharp teeth and of the gush of warm rabbit blood on his muzzle.

He dreamed of the armor. The armor was a presence in all his dreams now, the flash of it like something dazzling at the periphery of his vision. He couldn't bear to look directly at it;

like the sun, it might blind him—but, like the sun, it was always there.

Some nights, sweating and shivering, he dreamed of Ohio.

In the main, Billy's childhood memories were sunny. He had grown up in a farm town called Oasis, one of the soil reclamation collectives that had sprung up along the diversion canals drawing water south from the Great Lakes. Founded in a mood of optimism during the Dry Fifties, operated by a consortium of food distributors out of Detroit, the town had lost some of its civic spirit in the hard decades after. But if you grew up there, you didn't notice. For Billy, it was only a place.

He carried a few vivid memories of that time. He remembered the sky, a hazy blue vastness that had seemed as big as time itself. He remembered the miracle of water, water gushing up from sprinkler heads embedded in the dust-dikes that ran in lazy whorls through the fields—water raining down over a thousand acres of new green leaves. The town grew wheat and cabbage and kale and alfalfa and a patchwork of minor crops. Twice, Billy had been allowed to ride out on the big tending machines; and it made him proud and giddy to sit beside his father in the crow's-nest seat, emperor of all this fragrant green foliage and dusty blue sky. He remembered one scorching summer when a work battalion from AgService came to install what they called "UV screens"—huge banners of some nearly invisible film, tethered on poles and anchored with fat steel cables. For a few days it was cooler in the fields, and the clinic reported exposure trauma down a percentile. But then—pretty much as Billy's father had predicted—a hot wind came blowing from the west and the UV film broke free of its tethers. It balled up and tangled in the crops like so much cellophane discarded by a thoughtless giant. Acres of winter wheat were bent and broken. Nathan, surveying the battered fields, had startled Billy by falling on his knees.

Billy remembered Nathan as a large man—large, bearded, generous, often quiet, and deeply unhappy. His father always followed the news on the big screen in the civic center; and Billy gleaned that it was Nathan who received the *other* news, microwave databursts not sanctioned by the federal information services—news, especially, on the movement of conscription battalions across the Midwest.

Every two or three years the recruiters swept into Oasis. Nathan said they were like the locusts in the Bible, a plague. They would bunk in the labor barracks, stay a few days, maybe leave some of the more impressionable young girls with a new baby inside them; and when they rode away in their huge hovertrucks they would take a few draftees—boys barely old enough to shave, mainly.

Nathan and the town council usually had some warning when the battalions were coming, time enough to tamper with the town's birth records—to delete or alter certain documents. The likeliest young recruits would be hidden away in a supply cellar under the machine shed and the women would sneak them food. The battalions complained about the slim pickings, and sometimes they ran crude tamper-check routines on the civic computers . . . but if you got them drunk enough, Nathan said, they'd leave happy.

But if they came without warning—if they had destroyed the pirate relay towers on their way west—then they took what they wanted.

Billy remembered a summer when the news from the Storm Zone was very bad, tremendous loss of life all through the Caribbean and the occupation forces scattered. That summer, the Infantry came without warning. They arrived in a phalanx of black hovercraft, raising a cloud of dust that must have reddened sunsets all the way to Sandusky. Billy remembered his father's face when he climbed an embankment and saw that gray-black line approaching from the west —dismay as substantial as a weight on his shoulders.

He turned to Billy and said, "Go to the machine shed. Hurry."

It was the first time Billy had been old enough to hide with the other boys. It might have been exciting . . . but this time things were different. This time, he had seen his father's fear.

The cellar was hot and smelled of ancient cottonseed and burlap. He crouched there with a dozen other boys. "I'll come get you," Nathan had said, "when the Infantry are gone," and the words had reassured him a little. But it wasn't Nathan who came.

He never saw Nathan again.

It was a soldier who came.

An Infantryman. Billy woke blinking and bewildered in the clockless depths of cellar night, startled awake by the sound of footsteps. The Infantryman smiled down from the doorway. His name, he said, was Krakow. He was wearing his armor—a command breastplate, radiantly golden. Billy gazed up with no little awe as Krakow touched his chest. "This is my armor," he said. "This is the part of it you can see. Some of it is inside me. My armor knows who I am, and I know my armor. My armor is a machine, and right now it isn't fully powered. But if I switched it on I could kill you all before there was time enough to blink. And I would enjoy it."

Billy didn't doubt the truth of this. Krakow ran his fingers over the mirror-bright surface of the breastplate and Billy wondered exactly *how* you turned the armor on—he hoped Krakow wouldn't do it by mistake.

"My armor is my best friend." Krakow's voice was gentle, confiding. "An Infantryman's armor is always his best friend. Your armor will be your best friend."

Billy knew what that meant. It meant he was leaving home.

Curled in the womb of his apartment, Billy ate canned tuna and watched television and sat up nights shivering, listening

158

to the snow rattle on the window. His temperature crept upward; his joints ached; his body felt as if the skin had been flayed from it. Billy endured this until it was unbearable. He was surprised at how distinct that moment was: the tick of a second hand on the wheel of a clock, a single thought. *No more.*

He took the box from under the bed and opened it.

The golden armor was inside—all the large and small pieces of it.

Billy recalled the catechism of his training.

Sir, this is my armor, sir.

Sir, these are the body pieces, which are called the *elytra*. (Like cloth, quite golden, rigid only when impacted at high velocity. Bulging here and there with instrumentation, power packs, processing units.)

These are the arm pieces, sir, which are called the *halteres*. (Molding to the contour of his skin. They feel warm.)

Sir, these are the leg pieces, which are called the *setae*. (Snug against his thighs.)

Sir, this touchplate controls the *stylet* and the *lancet*, which connect the armor to my body. (To the liver, to the spine, to the lumen of the aorta.)

Hollow micropipettes burrowing in, wet with contact anesthetic.

Motion under his skin.

It felt funny.

Sir, this touchpiece activates the lancet.

Ah.

He moved in the snowbound night streets like a ghost.

He wore loose clothes over his armor, a long gray coat and a broad-brimmed hat to shadow his face.

He moved among the snowy lamp standards and the blinking traffic lights. Past midnight, before dawn, 1953.

159

He was supple and powerful and quite invincible.

He was intoxicated with his own hidden strength and dizzy with the need to kill a human being.

He did not resist the urge but he tantalized himself with it. The streets were empty and the snow came down in dry, icy granules. Wind flapped at the hem of his chalk-gray overcoat and erased his footprints behind him. The few pedestrians he saw were bent against the wind, scurrying like beetles for shelter. He followed one, maintaining a discreet distance, until the man vanished into a tenement building. Billy reached the stoop . . . paused a long moment in the winter darkness . . . then walked on.

He chose another potential victim, a small man spotlit by the beam of an automobile headlight; Billy followed him two blocks east but allowed this one, too, to vanish behind a door.

No hurry. He was warm in his armor. He was content. His heart beat inside him with the happy regularity of a finely tuned machine.

He smiled at a man who stepped out of an all-night delicatessen with a paper bag tucked under his arm. This one? Tall man, sleepless, red-eyed, suspicious, a cheap cloth coat: not a rich man; bulk of arms and chest: maybe a strong man.

"Hell of a night," Billy said.

The man shrugged, smiled vaguely, and turned to face the wind.

Yes, this one, Billy thought.

Billy took him with his wrist beam in an alley half a block away.

The killing took all of twenty seconds, but it was the nearest thing to an orgasm Billy had experienced since he came through the tunnel from the future. A brief and blissful release.

He mutilated the body with a knife, to disguise the cauterization of the wounds; then he took the man's wallet, to make the death seem like a robbery.

He dropped the wallet in a trash bin on Eighth Street. The money—five dollars in ones—he took home and flushed down the toilet.

Soothed and sweetly alive in the dark of his apartment, Billy relaxed his armor and folded it into its box. By dawn, the clouds had rolled away. A winter sun rose over the snow-bound city. Billy showered and raided the refrigerator. He had lost a lot of weight in the last few months, but now his appetite had returned with a vengeance. Now he was very hungry indeed.

He went to bed at noon and woke in the dark. Waking, he discovered something new in himself. He discovered remorse.

He found his thoughts circling back to the man he'd killed. Who had he been? Had he lived alone? Were the police investigating the murder?

Billy had watched police investigations on TV. On TV, the police always found the killer. Billy knew this was a social fiction; in real life the opposite was probably nearer to the truth. Still, fiction or not, the possibility nagged at him.

He developed new phobias. The tunnel in the sub-basement was suddenly on his mind. He had sealed that tunnel at both ends: according to Ann Heath, the dead woman with the wedge of glass in her skull, that act would guarantee his safety. No one would come hunting him from the future; no time ghost would carry him off. The tunnel, after all, was only a machine. A strange and nearly incomprehensible machine, Billy admitted privately, but a *powerless* machine, too —inaccessible.

Nevertheless, it made him nervous.

He patrolled the sub-basement daily. He thought of this as "checking the exits." The city of New York and the meridian of the twentieth century had become in Billy's mind a private place, a welcoming shelter. The natives might be a nuisance, but they weren't gravely dangerous; the real dangers lay elsewhere, beyond the rubble where the tunnel had been. Billy piled the rubble higher and installed a door at the foot of the stairs; on the door he installed an expensive padlock. If—by some magic—the tunnel repaired itself, any intruder would have to disturb these barricades. If Billy found the lock broken or the door splintered it would mean his sanctuary had been invaded . . . it would mean the twentieth century wasn't his own anymore.

The effort reassured him. Still, his *proximity* to the gateway made him nervous. It was hard to sleep some nights with the thought of that temporal fracture buried in the bedrock some few yards under the floor. By the summer of 1953 Billy decided that this building didn't need his nightly presence—that he could move a few streets away without harming anything.

He rented an apartment on the other side of Tompkins Square, three streets uptown. It was not much different from his first apartment. The floor was a crumbling, ancient parquet; Billy covered it with a cheap rug. The windows were concealed by yellow roll blinds and dust. Cockroaches lived in the gaps in the wallboard and they came out at night. And there was a deep closet, where Billy kept his armor in its box.

His life fell into a series of simple routines. Every week, sometimes more often, Billy walked the short distance between the two buildings—or, when he was restless, took a long night walk uptown and back—to collect his rent money and check the exits.

The rent was often late and sometimes his few tenants failed to pay at all. But that didn't matter. What mattered was that the padlock in the basement was never disturbed—a fact more reassuring as the years began to stack up behind him.

Time, Billy often thought, tasting the word in his mind. Time: small circles of days and the great wheel of the seasons. Seasons passed. Engrossed in television news—watching his small Westinghouse TV set the way Nathan had monitored the immensely larger screen in the civic center—he learned a parade of names: Eisenhower, Oppenheimer, Nixon; and places: Suez, Formosa, Little Rock. He numbered the years although the numbers still seemed implausible, one-nine-five-four, one-nine-five-five, one thousand nine hundred and fifty-six years in the wake of a crucifixion which seemed to Billy just as ludicrously unreal as the fall of Rome, the treaty of Ghent, or the Army-McCarthy hearings.

His armor continued to call to him from its hiding place, a small voice which sometimes grew shrill and unbearable. The need seemed to follow the seasons, an irony Billy failed to appreciate: if time was a wheel then in some sense he had been broken on it. Two killings *per annum,* winter and summer, dark nights or moonlit, as irresistible as the tides. And each killing was followed by a grinding remorse, then numbness, then weeks of dull torpor . . . and the Need again.

Nineteen fifty-eight, 'fifty-nine, 'sixty.

Nixon in Moscow, sit-ins in Greensboro, Kennedy in the White House by a fraction of the vote.

Billy grew older. So did the armor—but he tried not to think about that.

Tried not to think about a lot of things, especially tonight, as he was checking the exits: early summer of Anno Domini 1962, a hot night that reminded him of Ohio.

Billy entered the groaning front door of the old building near Tompkins Square where the time traveler had once lived and where nobody lived now except a few aging relics.

He had developed a perverse fondness for these people, human detritus too fragile or tenacious to abandon a building he had allowed to crumble around them. Two of them had been there long before Billy arrived—an arthritic old man named Shank on the fourth floor and a diabetic pensioner on the second. Mrs. Korzybski, the pensioner, sometimes forgot her medication and would stumble out to the street in insulin-shock delirium. This had happened once when he was checking the exits, and Billy had helped the woman inside, using his passkey to open the apartment door she had somehow locked behind her. He didn't like the police or an ambulance coming to the building, so he rummaged in the kitchen drawers among her cat-food cans and cutlery and fading photographs until he found her diabetic kit. He used the syringe to inject a measured dose of insulin solution into the crook of her flabby arm. When she came to, she thanked him. "You're nice," she said. "You're nicer than you look. How come you know how to use that needle?"

"I was in the army," Billy said.

"Korea?"

"That's right. Korea."

He had seen Korea on television.

She said she was glad now that she paid her rent on time, and how come nobody had moved in for such a long while? "Since that Mr. Allen was the manager. It gets kind of lonely these days."

"Nobody wants to rent, I guess."

"That's funny. That's not what I hear. Maybe if you painted?"

"One day," Billy explained solemnly, "all this will be under water."

Nowadays, when he came, he came at night, when Mrs. Korzybski was asleep. Her apartment was dark tonight. All the apartments were dark except for 403: Amos Shank, who lived on his retirement fund from the H. J. Heinz Company in Pittsburgh. Mr. Shank had come to New York to find a publisher for his epic poem *Ulysses at the Elbe*. The publishing industry had disappointed him, but Mr. Shank still liked to talk about the work—three massive volumes of vellum paper bound with rubber bands, still not entirely finished.

Mr. Shank left the light on in case inspiration struck in the depths of the night . . . but Mr. Shank was probably asleep by now too. Everyone in Billy's building was lonely and asleep.

Everyone but Billy.

He whistled a formless tune between his teeth and stepped into the entranceway. The paint on the walls had faded to gray a long time ago. The mirrored wall by the stairs was fogged and chipped and some of the floor tiles had turned up at the corners, like leaves.

Billy went directly to the basement.

The stairway leading down smelled hot and stale. These old wooden steps had grown leathery in the humid air. Silent in the dim light, Billy passed the bizarre and inefficient oil furnace with its many arms, the groaning water heater; through an unmarked access door and deeper, past the storage cellar with its lime-green calcinated walls and its crusted cans of paint, to the door he had sealed with a sturdy Yale padlock. The light was dim—the light here was always dim. Billy took a chrome Zippo lighter out of his hip pocket.

He felt strange down here so close to the tunnel. He had been deeply frightened when he first understood how vast this warren of temporal fractures really was—what it implied and what that might mean to him. He couldn't think about the tunnel without considering the creatures who had made it . . . beings, Billy understood, so nearly omnipotent that they might as well be called gods. And he remembered what he'd seen in this tunnel the day he arrived here, something even stranger than the godlike time travelers, a creature as bright and hot as a living flame.

He flicked the igniter on the Zippo. Time for a new flint, Billy told himself.

He brought the light down closer to the padlock—then drew a sharp breath and stepped back.

Dear God! After all these years—!

The lock had been broken open.

Billy's first thought was of Krakow gazing down at him through another door, the night he was recruited. He had the same feeling now: discovered in hiding.

He was defenseless, weaponless, and the walls were much too close.

He touched his throat, instinctively reaching for the touchplate that would trigger his armor—but the armor was at home.

He backed away from the door.

Someone had been here! Someone had come for him!

He considered going upstairs, dragging Mrs. Korzybski out of her sleep, Amos Shank from his senile slumber, beating them until they told him who had come and who had gone. But they might not know. Probably didn't. Maybe no one had seen.

I need help, Billy told himself. The sense of imminent danger had closed around him like a noose. *(Not alone anymore!)* He pocketed his lighter, climbed the stairs, and left the building.

He stood alone in the sweaty darkness of the street, his eyes patrolling the sawtooth shadows between the tenement stoops.

He hurried away, avoiding streetlights.

The armor, Billy thought. The armor would know what to do.

Ten

Catherine Simmons drove into Belltower after the cremation of her grandmother, Peggy Simmons, who had lived out along the Post Road for many years and who had died a week ago in her sleep.

Summer made Belltower a pretty little town, at least when the wind wasn't blowing from the mill. Catherine knew the town from her many visits; she didn't have any trouble finding the Carstairs Funeral Home on a side street off Brierley, between an antique shop and a marine electronics store. She parked and sat in her Honda a few minutes—she was early for her appointment.

Gram Peggy's fatal stroke had been unexpected and the news of her death still seemed fresh and unreasonable. Of all Catherine's family, Gram Peggy had seemed most like a fixture—the solidest and most fun of the sorry lot. But Gram Peggy was dead and Catherine supposed she would have to adjust to that fact.

She sighed and climbed out of the car. The afternoon was sunny and the air carried a whiff of ocean. Pretty little dumb little smelly little town, Catherine thought.

There was no ceremony planned and no other Simmonses at the funeral home. Catherine's father—Gram Peggy's only son—had died in 1983, of liver cancer, and the rest of the

167

family was hopelessly scattered. Only Catherine had ever come to visit these last several years. Apparently Gram Peggy had appreciated those visits. Her lawyer, Dick Parsons, had phoned to say that the entire estate, including the house, had been left to Catherine: another stunning piece of news, still somewhat indigestible.

The funeral director at Carstairs turned out not to be the unctuous vulture Catherine was expecting; he was a big-shouldered man who looked a little like a football coach. He handed Catherine the bronze urn containing Gram Peggy's ashes in a gesture that was almost apologetic. "This is the way your grandmother wanted it, Miss Simmons. No ceremony, nothing solemn. She arranged all this in advance."

"Gram Peggy was very practical," Catherine said.

"That she was." He managed a sympathetic smile. "Everything's been paid for through her lawyer. I hope we've been of some small help?"

"You did fine," Catherine said. "Thank you."

There was a woman in the lobby as Catherine left, a gray-haired woman roughly Gram Peggy's age; she stepped forward and said, "I'm Nancy Horton—a friend of your grandmother's. I just want to say how sorry I am."

"Thank you," Catherine said. Apparently death involved thanking people a lot.

"I knew Peggy from the shopping trips we took. She still drove, you see. I don't drive if I can help it. She used to drive me down to the mall on the highway, Wednesday mornings usually. We'd talk. Though she was never a big talker. I liked her a lot, though. You must be Catherine."

"Yes."

"Are you going to be staying in the house?"

"Gram's house? For a little while. Maybe for the summer."

"Well, I'm not far away if you need anything." She glanced at the urn in Catherine's hand. "I don't know about cremation. It seems—oh, I'm sorry! I shouldn't be saying this, should I? But it seems like so little to leave behind."

"That's okay," Catherine said. "This isn't Gram Peggy. We talked about that before she died. These are just some ashes."

"Of course," Nancy Horton said. "Will you keep them? Oh, my curiosity! I'm sorry—"

"Gram loved the forest out in back of her property," Catherine said. "She once asked me to scatter her ashes there." She took the urn protectively into the crook of her left arm. "That's what I'll do."

Of course, she couldn't keep the house. It was a big old house up along the Post Road and a long way from anywhere Catherine wanted to live, as much as she sometimes liked Belltower. Once the will was probated, she would probably try to sell the property. She had said as much to Dick Parsons, who had given her the number of the local realty company. One of their agents was supposed to meet her outside the funeral home.

The agent turned out to be the man lounging against a mailbox by the front steps—he straightened up and announced himself as Doug Archer. Catherine smiled and shook his hand. "Everybody's running against type," she said.

"I'm sorry?"

"The funeral director doesn't look like a funeral director. You don't look much like a real estate agent."

"I'll take that as flattery," Archer said.

But it was true, Catherine thought. He was a little too young, a little too careless about his clothes. He wore floppy high-top Reeboks tied too low, and he grinned like an eight-year-old. He said, "Are you still thinking about putting the house on the market?"

"It's a firm decision," Catherine said. "I'm just not sure

about when. I'm thinking of spending the rest of the summer here."

"It may not be a quick sale in any case. The market's a little slow, and those houses out on the Post Road are kind of lonely. But I'm sure we can find a buyer for it."

"I'm in no hurry. Dick Parsons said you'd probably want to look at the house?"

"It'll help when we're thinking about setting a price. If you want to make an appointment? Or I can drive out today—"

"Today is fine. I have to stop by Mr. Parsons' office and pick up the keys, but you can come by later if you like."

"If that's all right." He looked at his watch. "Around three?"

"Sure."

"I'm sorry about your grandmother, Miss Simmons. I handle a lot of those houses up the Post Road, so I had the occasion to meet her once or twice. She was a unique woman."

Catherine smiled. "I don't imagine she had much patience with real estate agents."

"Not too damn much patience at all," Doug Archer said.

Catherine picked up the keys, signed papers, said another round of thanks, then braced herself for the drive to Gram Peggy's house.

The word "holiday," in Catherine's memory, was associated with this road. When she was little they would drive down from Bellingham in her father's station wagon, circle through Belltower to the bottom of the Post Road hill, then up a long corridor of fragrant pines to the door of Gram Peggy's house. Gram Peggy who cooked wonderful meals, who said wonderful and irreverent things, and whose presence imposed a magical truce between Catherine's mother and father. At Gram Peggy's house, nobody was allowed to smoke and nobody was allowed to fight. "Everything else is permitted. But I *will not* have the house stinking of tobacco smoke and I *will not* allow bickering—both of which poison the air. Isn't that right, Catherine?"

The Post Road hadn't changed much. It was still this green, dark, faintly magical corridor—the highway and the malls might have been a thousand miles away. Houses on the Post Road were barely more than outposts in the wilderness, Catherine thought, set in their little plots of landscape, some grand and many humble, but always overshadowed by the lush Douglas firs.

Gram Peggy's house, at the crest of the hill, was the only one of these homes with a view. The house was an old and grandly Victorian wood frame structure, two stories high with a gabled attic above that. Gram Peggy had always been meticulous about having it painted and touched up; otherwise, she said, the weeds would think they had an open invitation. The house had been built by Gram Peggy's father, a piano maker, whom Catherine had never met. The idea of selling the property—of never coming back here—felt like the worst kind of sacrilege. But of course she'd be lost in it herself.

She parked and unlocked the big front door. For now, she left her paints and supplies in the trunk of the Civic. If she stayed for the summer—the idea was steadily more attractive —she could set up a studio in the sunny room facing the woods out back. Or in the guest room, where the bay window allowed glimpses of the distant ocean.

But for now it was still Gram Peggy's house, left untidied at the end of what must have been a tiring day. Crumbs on the kitchen counter, the ficus wilting in a dry pot. Catherine wandered aimlessly through some of these rooms, then dropped into the overstuffed sofa in front of the TV set. Gram Peggy's *TV Guide* was splayed open on the side table —a week out of date.

Of *course* I'll be here all summer, Catherine thought; it

would take that long to sort out Gram Peggy's possessions and arrange to have them sold. None of this had occurred to her. She had assumed, by some wordless logic, that Gram Peggy's things would have vanished like Gram Peggy herself, into the urn now resting by the front door. But maybe this was where the real mourning started: the disposition of these letters, clocks, clothes, dentures—a last, brutal intimacy.

Catherine slipped off her shoes, reclined on the sofa, and napped until Doug Archer knocked at the door.

Before he left, Doug Archer said a strange thing.

His visit went well, otherwise. He was friendly and his interest seemed genuine, more than just businesslike. He asked about her work. Catherine was shy about her painting even though she had begun to earn some money through a couple of small Seattle galleries. She'd taken fine arts courses at college, but the work she produced was mainly intuitive, personal, meticulous. She worked with acrylics and sometimes with montage. Her subjects were usually small—a leaf, a water drop, a ladybug—but her canvases were large, impressionistic, and layered with bright acrylic washes. After her last show a Seattle newspaper critic said she "seemed to coax light out of paint," which had pleased her. But she didn't tell Archer that; only that she painted and that she was thinking of doing some work here during the summer. He said he'd love to see some of her work sometime. Catherine said she was flattered but there was nothing to show right now.

He was thorough about the house. He inspected the basement, the water heater and the furnace, the fuseboard and the window casements. Upstairs, he made a note about the oak floors and moldings. Lastly, he went outside and gazed up at the eaves. Catherine told him Gram Peggy had had the roof inspected every year.

She walked him to his car. "I suppose we'll have to put it

on the market pretty soon. I don't even know what that involves. I guess people come to see it?"

"We don't have to hurry. You must be upset by all this."

"Dazed. I think I'm dazed."

"Take as long as you need. Call me when you're ready to talk about it."

"I appreciate that," Catherine said.

Archer put his hand on the door of the car, then seemed to hesitate. "Do you mind if I ask you something?"

"Shoot."

"Did your grandmother ever talk much about her neighbors?"

"Not that I remember. I did meet Mrs. Horton from around the corner. Apparently they used to drive to the mall together."

"How about the house down the other direction—the man who lived there? She ever mention him? This would have been ten or more years ago."

"I don't remember anything like that. Why?"

"No real reason." Something personal, she guessed. He was obviously embarrassed to have asked. "Will you do me one favor, Catherine? If you notice anything strange happening, will you give me a call? My number's on the card. You can reach me pretty much anytime."

"What do you mean, anything strange?"

"Odd occurrences," Archer said unhappily.

"Like what? Ghosts, flying saucers, that kind of thing? Is there a lot of that around here?" She couldn't help smiling.

"Nothing like that. No, look, forget I asked, okay? It's nothing important. Just kind of a hobby with me."

He thanked her, she thanked him, he drove away. How odd, Catherine thought as his car vanished into the tree shadows along the Post Road. What an unusual man. What a strange thing to ask.

• • • •

173

She didn't think more about it. A bank of clouds moved in and a steady, sullen rain fell without interruption for most of a week. Catherine stayed in the house and began to itemize some of Gram Peggy's possessions, room by room. It was depressing weather and depressing work. She felt lost in this big old house, but the rhythms of it—the ticking of the mantel clock and the morning and evening light through the high dusty windows—were familiar and in their own way reassuring.

Still, she was glad when the sun came out. After a couple of warm days the ground had dried and she was able to move around the big back lawn and some distance down a trail into the woods. She remembered taking some of these walks with Gram Peggy and how intimidating the forest had seemed—still seemed, in fact. There was enough red cedar behind the house to make her feel very small, as if she'd shrunk, Alice-style, to the size of a caterpillar. The trail was narrow, probably a deer trail; the forest was cool and silent.

She took these walks almost every day and before long she began to feel a little braver. She ranged farther than Gram Peggy had ever taken her. Some of this woodland was municipal property, and farther east it had been staked out by the timber interests, but nobody up along the Post Road cared too much about property lines and Catherine was able to wander fairly freely. Most days she hiked south down the slope of the hill, keeping east of the road and the houses.

She bought a guidebook and taught herself to identify some of the wildlife. She had seen a salamander, a thrush, and something she believed was a "pileated woodpecker." There was the tantalizing possibility of encountering a black bear, though that hadn't happened yet. Sometimes she brought her lunch with her; sometimes she carried a sketchbook.

She had already found favorite places in the woods. There was a meadow where she could sit on a fallen log and gaze

174

across a thicket of salal and huckleberry, where the forest sloped away toward Belltower. There was a sandy spot by a creek where she thought she might scatter Gram Peggy's ashes. And another meadow, farther south, riddled with deer trails, where an abandoned woodshed sagged under a growth of moss.

The woodshed fascinated her. There was something inviting about the cockeyed slant of the door. Surely there was nothing inside, Catherine told herself; or only a cord of moldy firewood. But then again there might be an old plough or spinning wheel, something she could clean up and peddle to the antique shops in Belltower. Unless this was somebody's property, in which case she would be stealing. But she could at least *peek.*

She had this thought vaguely in mind Wednesday morning, her second week in Belltower, when she packed a bag lunch and went wandering. It was a warm day and she was sweating by the time she passed the creek. She pressed on south, paused to tie her hair up off her neck, hiked past the huckleberry thicket and on down to the woodshed in its sunny meadow.

She approached the door of the ancient structure, high-stepping through berry-bush runners to avoid a stand of fireweed . . . then she hesitated.

It seemed to her she could hear faint motion inside.

Curiosity killed the cat, Gram Peggy used to say. But she always added the less salutary rider—*Satisfaction brought it back.* Gram Peggy had been a big believer in satisfied curiosity.

So Catherine opened the creaking woodshed door and peered inside, where a stack of newspapers had moldered for decades, and where something hideous moved and spoke in the darkness.

Eleven

How did it feel to begin life over again, thirty years in the past?

Giddy, Tom thought. Strange. Exhilarating.

And—more often now—frightening.

It wasn't clear to him when or why the fear had started. Maybe it had been there all along, a subtler presence than now. Maybe it had started when he moved into the house on the Post Road, a steady counterpoint to all the raucous events since. Maybe he'd been born with it.

But it wasn't fear, exactly; it was a kind of systematic *disquiet* . . . and he felt it most profoundly on a hot Thursday afternoon in July, when he could have sworn, but couldn't prove, that somebody followed him from Lindner's Radio Supply to Larry Millstein's apartment.

The day had gone well. Since he'd taken this job Tom had turned in enough reliable work that Max mainly left him alone. The cavernous back room of Lindner's had begun to feel homey and familiar. Hot days like this, he tipped open the high leaded windows to let the alley breezes through. He was working on a Fisher amplifier a customer had brought in; the output tube had flashed over and one of the power-supply electrolytics was leaking. The capacitors were oil-filled,

176

the kind eliminated under an EPA edict—some years in the future—for their PCB content. The danger, at least at this end of the manufacturing process, was far from mortal. At lunch, Max asked him why he kept the fan so close to his work. "I don't like the smell," Tom said.

Toxins aside, Tom had developed a respect for these old American radios and amplifiers. The up-market models were simple, well built, and substantial—the sheer weight of them was sometimes astonishing. Iron-core transformers, steel chassis, oak cabinets, a pleasure to work with. The job was underpaid and offered absolutely no opportunity for advancement, but for Tom it functioned as therapy: something pleasant to do with his hands and a paycheck at the end of the week.

And still—long since the novelty should have worn off— he would look up from his soldering at the calendar on the wall, where the year 1962 was inscribed over a picture of a chunky woman in a lime-green one-piece bathing suit, and he would feel a dizzy urge to laugh out loud.

What was time, after all, except a lead-footed march from the precincts of youth into the country of the grave? Time was the force that crumbled granite, devoured memory, and seduced infants into senility—as implacable as a hanging judge and as poetic as a tank. And yet, *here he was*—almost thirty years down a road that shouldn't exist; in the past, where nobody can visit.

He was no younger than he had been and he was nothing like immortal. But time had been suborned and that made him happy.

"You're always looking at that calendar," Max said. "I think you're in love with that girl."

"Head over heels," Tom said.

"That's the calendar from Mirvish's. They use the same picture every year. Every summer since 1947, the same girl in the same bathing suit. She's probably an old lady now."

177

"She's a time traveler," Tom said. "She's always young."

"And you're a fruitcake," Max explained. "Please, go back to work."

Certain other implications of this time travel business had not escaped him.

It was 1962 in New York. Therefore it was 1962 all over the country—all over the world, in fact; therefore it was 1962 in Belltower, Washington, and both his parents were alive.

Somewhere in the Great Unwinding—perhaps at step number forty-eight or sixty-three or one hundred twenty-one in the tunnel between the Post Road and Manhattan—a log truck had swerved backward up a mountain road; a bright blue sedan had vaulted an escarpment onto the highway; two bodies had shuddered to life as the dashboard peeled away from the seats and the engine sprang back beneath the hood.

In 1962, in Belltower, a young GP named Winter had recently opened a residential practice serving the middle-class neighborhood north of town. His wife had borne him two sons; the younger, Tommy, had his fourth birthday coming up in November.

They are all living in the big house on Poplar Street, Tom thought, with Daddy's offices downstairs and living quarters up. If I went there, I could see them. Big as life.

He pictured them: his father in a black Sunday suit or medical whites, his mother in a floral print dress, and between them, maybe a yard high in baby Keds, something unimaginable: himself.

One morning when Joyce was off doing restaurant work and he was home feeling a little lonely, he picked up the telephone and dialed the long-distance operator. He said he wanted to place a call to Belltower, Washington, to Dr. Winter's office on Poplar Street. The phone rang three times, a distant buzzing, and a woman answered. *My mother's voice.* It was a paralyzing thought. What could he possibly say?

But it wasn't his mother. It was his father's nurse, Miss Trudy Valasquez, whom he dimly remembered: an immense Hispanic woman with orthopedic shoes and peppermint breath. Dr. Winter was out on call, she said, and who *was* this, anyway?

"It's nothing urgent," Tom said. "I'll try again later."

Much later. Maybe never. There was something perverse about the act. It felt wrong, to disturb that innocent household with even as much as an anonymous call—too tangled and Oedipal, too entirely strange.

Then he thought, *But I have to call them. I have to warn them.*

Warn them not to go traveling up the coast highway on a certain date some fifteen years from now.

Warn them, in order to save their lives. So that Tom could go to med school, as his father had insisted; so that he wouldn't meet Barbara, wouldn't marry her, wouldn't divorce her, wouldn't buy a house up the Post Road, wouldn't travel into the past, wouldn't make a phone call, wouldn't warn them, wouldn't save their lives.

Would, perhaps, loop infinitely between these possibilities, as ghostly as Schroedinger's cat.

This was the past, Tom told himself, and the past *must* be immutable—including the death of his parents. Nothing else made sense. If the past was fluid and could be changed, then it was up to Tom to change it: warn airliners about bombs, waylay Oswald at the Book Depository, clear the airport lobbies before the gunmen arrived . . . an impossible, unbearable burden of moral responsibility.

For the sake of sense and for the sake of sanity, the past must be a static landscape. If he told Pan Am a plane was going to go down, they wouldn't believe him. If he flew to Dallas to warn the President, he'd miss his plane or suffer a heart attack at the luggage carousel. He didn't know what unseen hand would orchestrate these events, only that the alternative was even less plausible. If he tried to change history, he would fail . . . that was all there was to it.

Dangerous even to *experiment*.

But he thought about that call often. Thought about warning them. Thought about saving their lives.

It was hardly urgent. For now and for many years to come they were alive, happy, young, safer than they knew.

But as the date drew closer—if he stayed here, if he lived that long—then, Tom thought, he might *have* to make the call, risk or no risk . . . or know they had died when he could have saved them.

Maybe that was when the fear began.

He slept with these thoughts, woke chastened, and rode the bus to Lindner's. He regarded the girl on the calendar with a new sobriety. Today her expression seemed enigmatic, clouded.

"You're still in love with her," Max observed.

"Look at her face, Max. She knows something."

"She knows you're a lunatic," Max said.

He lost himself in his work. The day's biggest surprise was a call from Larry Millstein: apologies for the incident at the party and would he come over that afternoon? Meet Joyce at the apartment, the three of them could go to dinner, make peace. Tom accepted, then phoned Joyce to make sure she was free. "I already talked to Lawrence," she said. "I think he's reasonably sincere. Plus, you're too popular these days. Avoiding you is beginning to interfere with his social life."

"Should I be nice? Is it worth the trouble?"

"Be nice. He's neurotic and he can be mean sometimes. But if he were a total loss I would never have slept with him in the first place."

"That's reassuring."

"You both like jazz. Talk about music. On second thought, don't."

He left the shop at six. It was a warm afternoon, the buses were crowded; he decided to walk. The weather had been fine for days. The sky was blue, the air was reasonably clean, and he had no reason to feel uneasy.

Nevertheless, the uneasiness began as soon as he stepped out of Lindner's front door and it intensified with every step he took.

At first he dismissed it. He'd been through some novel experiences in the last few months and a little paranoia, at this stage, was perhaps not too surprising. But he couldn't dismiss the uneasiness or the thoughts it provoked, memories he had neglected: of the tunnel, of the machine bugs, of their warning.

He recalled the rubble in the sub-basement of the building near Tompkins Square. Someone had been there before him, someone dangerous. But Tom had passed that way safely, and his anonymity would be guaranteed in a city as vast as New York—wouldn't it?

He told himself so. Nevertheless, as he walked east on Eighth toward Millstein's shabby East Village neighborhood, his vague anxiety resolved into a solid conviction that he was being followed. He paused across the street from Millstein's tenement building and turned back. Puerto Rican women moved between the stoops and storefronts; three children crossed the street at a light. There were two Anglos visible: a large, pale woman steering a baby stroller and a middle-aged man with a brown paper bag tucked under his arm. So who in this tableau was stalking him?

Probably no one. Bad case of coffee nerves, Tom thought. And maybe a little guilt. Guilt about what he'd left behind. Guilt about what he'd found. Guilt about falling in love in this strange place.

He stepped off the curb and into the path of an oncoming cab. The driver leaned into his horn and swerved left, passing him by inches. UNIDENTIFIED MAN KILLED ON CITY STREET—maybe that was history, too.

After some nervous overtures they adjourned to Stanley's, where Millstein drank and relaxed.

They talked about music in spite of Joyce's warning. It turned out Millstein had been an avid jazz fan since he arrived here, "a callow youth from Brooklyn," at the end of the forties. He was an old Village hand; he'd met Kerouac once or twice—an observation which plunged Tom into one more "time travel" epiphany. Giants had walked here, he thought. "Though of course," Millstein added, "that scene is long dead."

Joyce mentioned her friend Susan. Susan had written another letter from the South, where she was getting death threats because of her affiliation with the SNCC. One enterprising recidivist had delivered a neatly wrapped package of horse manure to the door of her motel room.

Millstein shrugged. "Everybody's too political. It's tiresome. I'm tired of protest songs, Joyce."

"And I'm tired of passive pseudo-Zen navel-gazing," Joyce said. "There's a world out there."

"A world run by men in limousines who don't much listen to music. As far as the world is concerned, guitar playing is a minor-league activity."

Joyce inspected the depths of her beer. "Maybe Susan's right, then. I should be doing something more direct."

"Like what? Freedom riding? Picketing? Essentially, you know, it's still guitar playing. It'll be tolerated as long as it serves some purpose among the powerful—federalism, in the present instance. And tidied up when they're done with it."

"That's about the most cynical thing I've heard you say,

182

Lawrence. Which covers some territory. Didn't Gandhi make a remark about 'speaking truth to power'?"

"Power doesn't give a flying fuck, Joyce. That should be obvious."

"So what's the alternative?"

"Il faut cultiver notre jardin. Or write a poem."

"Like Ginsberg? Ferlinghetti? That's pretty political stuff."

"You miss the point. They're saying, here's the ugliness, and here's my revulsion—and here's the mystery buried in it."

"Mystery?"

"Beauty, if you like."

"Making art out of junk," Joyce interpreted.

"You could say that."

"While people starve? While people are beaten?"

"Before *I* starve," Millstein said. "Before *I'm* beaten. Yes, I'll make these beautiful objects."

"And the world is better for it?"

"The world is *more beautiful* for it."

"You sound like the Parks Commission." She turned to Tom. "How about you? Do you believe in poetry or politics?"

"Never gave much thought to either one," Tom said.

"Behold," Lawrence said. "The Noble Savage."

Tom considered the question. "I suppose you do what you have to. But we're all pretty much impotent in the long run. I don't make national policy. At most, I vote. When it's convenient. Henry Kissinger doesn't drop in and say, 'Hey, Tom, what about this China thing?'"

Millstein looked up from his drink. "Who the hell is Henry Kissinger?"

Joyce was a little drunk and very intense, frowning at him across the table. "You're saying we don't make a difference?"

"Maybe some people make a difference. Martin Luther King, maybe. Khrushchev. Kennedy."

"People whose names begin with K," Millstein supplied.

"But not *us*," Joyce insisted. "*We* don't make a difference. Is that what you mean?"

"Christ, Joyce, I don't know what I mean. I'm not a philosopher."

"No. You're not a repairman, either." She shook her head. "I wish I knew what the hell you *were.*"

"There's your mistake," Millstein said. "Dear Joyce. Next time you go to bed with somebody, make sure you're formally introduced."

Millstein drank until he loved the world. This was his plan. He told them so. "It doesn't always work. Well, you know that. But sometimes. Drink until the world is lovable. Good advice." The evening wore on.

They parted around midnight, on the sidewalk, Avenue B. Millstein braced himself against Tom's breastbone. "I'm sorry," he said. "I mean, about before. I was an asshole!"

"It's okay," Tom said.

Millstein looked at Joyce. "You be good to her, Tom."

"I will. Of course I will."

"She doesn't know why we love her and hate her. But it's for the same reason, of course. Because she's this . . . this *pocket of faith.* She believes in virtue! She comes to this city and sings songs about courage. My God! She has the courage of a saint. It's her element. Even her vices are meticulous. She's not merely good in bed, she's *good*—in bed!"

"Shut up," Joyce said. "Lawrence, you shit! Everybody can hear you."

Millstein turned to her and took her face between his hands, drunkenly but gently. "This is not an insult, dear. We love you because you're better than we are. But we're jealous of your goodness and we will scour it out of you if we possibly can."

"Go home, Lawrence."

He wheeled away. "Good night!"

184

"Good night," Tom said. But it didn't feel like such a good night. It was hot. It was dark. He was sweating.

He walked home with Joyce leaning into his shoulder. She was still somewhat drunk; he was somewhat less so. The conversation had made her sad. She paused under a street-light and looked at him mournfully.

She said, "You're not immortal anymore!"

"Sorry to disappoint you."

"No, no! When you came here, Tom, you were immortal. I was sure of it. The way you walked. The way you looked at everything. Like this was all some fine, wonderful place where nothing could hurt you. I thought you *must* be immortal—the only explanation."

He said, "I'm sorry I'm not immortal."

She fumbled her key into the front door of the building.

The apartment was hot. Tom stripped down to his T-shirt and briefs; Joyce ducked out of her shirt. The sight of her in the dim light provoked a flash of pleasure. He had lived in this apartment for more than a month and familiarity only seemed to intensify his feelings about her. When he met her she had been emblematic, Joyce who lived in the Village in 1962; now she was Joyce Casella from Minneapolis whose father owned Casella's Shoe Store, whose mother phoned twice monthly to plead with her to find a husband or at *least* a better job; whose sister had borne two children by a decent practicing Catholic named Tosello. Joyce who was shy about her thick prescription lenses and the birthmark on her right shoulder. Joyce who carried a wonderful singing voice concealed inside her, like a delicate wild bird allowed to fly on rare and special occasions. This ordinary, daily Joyce was superior to the emblematic Joyce and it was this Joyce he had come to love.

But she was ignoring him. She rummaged through a stack

of papers by the bookcase, mainly phone bills; Tom asked her what she was looking for.

"Susan's letter. The one I was telling Lawrence about. She said I could call. 'Call anytime,' she said. She wants me to go down there. There's so much work to do! Jesus, Tom, what time is it? Midnight? Hey, Tom, is it midnight in Georgia?"

He felt a ripple of worry. "What do you mean—you want to call her *tonight?*"

"That's the idea."

"What for?"

"Make arrangements."

"What arrangements?"

She stood up. "What I said wasn't just bullshit. I meant it. What good am I here? I should be down there with Susan doing some real work."

He was astonished. He hadn't anticipated this.

"You're drunk," he said.

"Yeah, I'm a little drunk. I'm not too drunk to think about the future."

Maybe Tom was a little drunk, too. The future! This was both funny and alarming. "You want the future? I can give you the future."

She frowned and set aside the papers. "What?"

"It's dangerous, Joyce. People get killed, for Christ's sake." He thought about the civil rights movement circa 1962. What he recalled was a jumble of headlines filtered through books and TV documentaries. Bombs in churches, mobs attacking buses, Klansmen with riot sticks and sawed-off shotguns. He pictured Joyce in the midst of this. The thought was intolerable. "You *can't.*"

She held out the letter, postmarked Augusta.

"They need me."

"The hell they do. One more earnest white college graduate isn't going to turn the tide, for Christ's sake. They have TV. They have pinheaded southern sheriffs beating women

186

on all three networks. They have friends in the Kennedy administration. After the assassination—" He was drunker than he'd realized. He was giving away secrets. But that didn't matter. "After the assassination they'll have Lyndon Johnson signing civil rights legislation while Vietnam escalates. You want the future? Vietnam, Woodstock, Nixon, Watergate, Jimmy Carter, Ayatollah Khomeini, the whole fucking parade of clichés, with or without the help of Joyce Casella. Please," he said. "Please don't go get killed before we know each other better."

"Sometimes I wonder if I know you at all. What's all this shit about the future?"

"That's where I'm from."

She looked at him fiercely. "Tell me the truth or get out of my apartment."

He described in broad and clumsy outline the train of events that had carried him here.

Joyce listened with focused patience but didn't begin to believe him until he brought out his wallet and unpacked his ID from the card windows—his Washington State driver's license, his Visa card, an expired American Express card, a card to access bank machines; from the billfold, a couple of tens bearing a mint date twenty years in the future.

Joyce examined all these things solemnly. Finally she said, "Your watch."

He hadn't worn it since his first visit; it was in the left-hand pocket of his jeans. She must have seen it. "It's just a cheap digital watch. But you're right. You can't buy those here."

He backed off and let her contemplate these things. He was a little more sober for the telling of it and he wondered whether this had been a terrible mistake. It must be frightening. God knows, it had frightened *him.*

187

But she fingered the cards and the money, then sighed and looked at him fearlessly.

"I'll make coffee," she said. "I guess we don't sleep tonight."

"I guess we don't," Tom said.

She held the cup in both hands as if it were anchoring her to the earth.

"Tell me again," she said. "Tell me how you came here."

He rubbed his eyes. "Again?"

"Again. Slower."

He took a deep breath and began.

By the time he finished it was past two A.M. The street outside was quiet, the light of the room seemed strange and sterile. He was dazed, sleepy, hung over.

Joyce, however, was wide awake.

"It doesn't make sense," she said. "Why a tunnel between here and—what's it called? Bellfountain?"

"Belltower," Tom said. "I don't know. I didn't build it, Joyce. I found it."

"Anybody could have found it?"

"I suppose so."

"And no one else used it?"

"Someone must have. At least once. Used it and, I guess, abandoned it. But I don't know that for a fact."

She shook her head firmly. "I don't believe it."

He felt helpless. He had shown her all the evidence he possessed, explained it as calmly as possible—

"No, I mean—I know it's *true*. The cards, the money, the watch—maybe somebody could fake all that, but I doubt it. It's true, Tom, but I don't *believe* it. You understand what I'm saying? It's hard to look at you and tell myself this is a guy from the year 1989."

"What more can I do?"

"Show me," Joyce said. "Show me the tunnel."

This wasn't the way he had meant it to happen.

He walked with her—it wasn't far—to the building near Tompkins Square.

"This place?" Joyce said. Meaning: a miracle—here? He nodded.

The street was silent and empty. Tom took his watch out of his pocket and checked it: three-fifteen, and he was dizzy with fatigue, already regretting this decision.

Later Tom would decide that the visit to the tunnel marked a dividing line; it was here that events had begun to spiral out of control. Maybe he sensed it already—an echo of his own future leaking through zones of fractured time.

He was reluctant to take her inside, suddenly certain it was a mistake to have brought her here at all. If he hadn't been drunk . . . and then weary beyond resistance . . .

She tugged his hand. "Show me."

And there was no plausible way to turn back. He took one more look at the bulk of the building, all those rooms and corridors he had never explored, a single window illuminated in the darkness.

He led her inside. The lobby was vacant, silent except for the buzzing of a defective fluorescent lamp. He grasped the handle of the door that led to the basement.

It wouldn't turn.

"Trouble?" Joyce inquired.

He nodded, frowning. "It wasn't locked before. I don't think it *had* a lock." He bent over the mechanism. "This looks new."

"Somebody installed a new lock?"

"I think so."

"What does that mean?"

"I don't know. Could mean somebody knows I've been

189

here. Could mean the janitor found some kids in the basement and decided it was time for new hardware."

"Is there a janitor?"

He shrugged.

She said, "But somebody must own the building. It's a matter of record, right? You could look it up at City Hall."

"I suppose so." It hadn't occurred to him. "Might be dangerous. This isn't a Nancy Drew mystery. I don't think we should draw attention to ourselves."

"If we don't open that door," Joyce pointed out, "you can never go home again."

"If we *do* open it, maybe they'll put in a better lock next time. Or post a guard." This was a chilling thought and he couldn't help looking past her, through the cracked glass of the outer door. But the street was empty.

"Maybe we can open it without being too obvious," Joyce said.

"We shouldn't even try. We should get the fuck out of here."

"Hey, no! I'm not backing out now." Her grip on his hand tightened. "If this is true . . . I want to *see.*"

Tom looked at the lock more closely. Cheap lock. He took out his Visa card and slipped it between the door and the jamb. This worked on television but apparently not in real life; the card bumped into the bolt but failed to move it. "Give me your keys," he said.

Joyce handed him her key ring.

He tried several of the keys until he found one that slid into the lock. By twisting it until it caught some of the tumblers he was able to edge the bolt fractionally inward; then he forced the card up until the door sprang open an inch.

A gust of cool, dank air spilled through the opening.

· · · ·

190

He felt the change in Joyce as they descended. She had been cocky and reckless, daring him on; now she was silent, both hands clamped on his arm.

In the first sub-basement he tugged the cord attached to the naked forty-watt bulb overhead—it cast a cheerless pale circle across the floor. "We should have brought a flashlight."

"We probably should have brought an elephant gun. It's scary down here." She frowned at him. "This is real, isn't it?"

"As real as it gets."

The second lock, on the wooden door in the lowest sub-basement, had also been replaced. Joyce lit a series of matches while Tom examined the mechanism. Whoever had installed the lock had been in a hurry; the padlock was new and sturdy but the hasp was not. It was attached with three wood screws to the framing of the door; Tom levered the screws out with the edge of a dime and put them in his pocket.

Down into darkness.

They climbed over rubble. Joyce continued striking matches until Tom told her to stop; the light was too feeble to be useful and he was worried about the flammable debris underfoot. She let the last match flicker out but flinched when the darkness closed over them. She said, "Are you sure—?"

But then they were in the tunnel itself. A sourceless light illuminated the slow, precise curve of the walls ahead.

Joyce took a few steps forward. Tom hung back.

"It's really all true," she said. "My God, Tom! We could walk into the future, couldn't we? Just stroll a few decades down the road." She faced him. "Will you take me some-time?" Her cheeks were flushed. She looked fragile and fever-ish against these blunt white walls.

"I don't know if I can promise that. We're playing with something dangerous and we don't know how it works. I can't guarantee we're safe even just standing here. Maybe we're exposed to radiation. Maybe the air is toxic."

"None of that stopped you from coming here."

But that was before, Tom thought. When I had nothing to lose.

She touched the walls—smooth, slightly resilient, utterly seamless. "I wonder who built it? Haven't you thought about it?"

"Often," he said. "It must have been here at least ten years. Maybe longer." Maybe since the Indians occupied Manhattan. Maybe since Wouter van Twiller operated the Bossen Bouwerie in this district. Maybe Wouter had had a tunnel under his cowshed hereabouts. Maybe he knew it and maybe he didn't.

"People from the future," Joyce said. "Or Martians or something like that. It's like a 'Twilight Zone' episode, isn't it?" She drew a line in the dust with the point of her shoe. "How come it's broken at this end?"

"I don't know."

She said, "Maybe it was hijacked."

He blinked at the idea. Joyce went on, "The people who are supposed to use it aren't here. So somebody used it who *wasn't* supposed to . . . maybe fixed it so nobody could find him."

Tom considered it. "I suppose that's possible."

"There must be other tunnels. Otherwise it doesn't make sense. So maybe this one used to be connected somewhere— a junction. But somebody hijacked it, somebody sealed it off."

This was plausible; he couldn't formulate a better explanation. "But we don't really know."

"Hey," she said. "Nancy Drew is on the case."

Maybe, Tom thought, this would turn out all right. He had convinced her to turn around and go back—but then the strange thing happened.

Joyce saw it first.

"Look," she said. "Tom? What *is* that?"

He turned where she was pointing, already afraid.

What he saw was only a vague blur of luminescence against the uniform brightness of the tunnel, far away. He thought at first it might be some malfunction of the lights. Then Joyce squeezed his hand. "It's moving," she said.

Slowly but perceptibly, it was. It was moving toward them.

He guessed it might be a hundred yards away—maybe more.

He turned back to the rubble at the near end of the tunnel. They had wandered maybe thirty feet from it. Sprinting distance, Tom thought.

Joyce repeated, "What *is* that?" There was only a tremor of uncertainty in her voice—she wasn't frightened yet.

"I've never seen anything like it," Tom said. "Maybe we should get out while we can."

What he felt was not quite awe, not yet fear. The luminescence was bright and had taken on the suggestion of a shape. Tom hustled Joyce toward the exit, aware that he was in the presence of something he didn't understand, something akin to the tunnel itself: strange, powerful, beyond his comprehension.

This was the tunnel under the world, where demons and angels lived.

He paused at the place where the broken brick and old lathing and plaster had collapsed, because it was impossible to resist the urge to turn and look.

Joyce did the same.

But the phenomenon had moved much faster than he'd guessed.

It was almost on top of them.

He drew a breath, stepped back instinctively—and caught his heel on a brick, and fell.

Joyce said, "Tom!" and tried to drag him up.

The creature hovered over them both.

Tom couldn't find a word for the thing suspended in the air above him, almost close enough now to touch. Briefly, his fear was crowded out by a kind of abject wonder.

The shape of the apparition was indistinct—blurred at the edges—but approximately human.

Later, Tom reviewed his memory of the event and tried to reconstruct the creature in his mind. If you took a map of the human nervous system, he thought, modeled it in blue neon and surrounded it with a halo of opalescent light—that might come close.

It was translucent but not ghostly. There was no mistaking its physical presence. He felt the heat of it on his face.

Joyce crouched beside him.

The creature had stopped moving. It was watching them, he thought—perhaps with the two opaque spots which occupied the position of eyes; perhaps in some other fashion.

This was terrifying—bearable only because the creature was utterly motionless.

Tom counted silently to ten, then backed up the piled rubble an inch or so.

The creature's *attention* followed him. But only that.

Joyce looked at him. He could tell by the grip of her hand that she was deeply frightened but still in control. He whispered, "Back up slowly. If it moves, stand still."

He didn't doubt the creature's immense power; he felt it all around him, felt it in the radiant heat on his exposed skin.

Joyce nodded tightly and they began to inch up the rubble and out of the tunnel. It occurred to Tom that this was the instinctive response to a dangerous large animal, no doubt wildly inappropriate here. He stared into the creature's eyespots and knew—absolutely wordlessly—that its interest in them was intense but momentary; that it could kill them if it wished; that it hadn't decided yet. This wasn't the random indecision of an animal but something much more focused, more intimate. A judgment.

Gazing into that pale blankness, he felt naked and small.

They had almost reached the welcome darkness of the basement when the creature vanished.

Later, he argued with Joyce about the way it had disappeared. Tom maintained that it simply blinked out of existence; Joyce said it had *turned sideways* in some way she couldn't describe—"Turned some corner we couldn't see."

They agreed that its absence was as sudden, absolute, and soundless as its appearance.

Joyce scrambled through the dark basement, pulling Tom up the stairs. He felt her trembling. This is my fault, he thought.

He made her wait while he put the hasp of the lock back on the wooden door. He fumbled in his pocket for the three screws and the dime to drive them with, sank the first two home and then dropped the last. Joyce said, "Christ, Tom!" —but held a match in one unsteady hand while he groped on his knees. The screw had rolled under the edge of the door and for one sinking moment he thought he'd have to pry off the hasp a second time to get the last screw back, which would be next to impossible in this dark bad-smelling basement full of who-knows-what-kind-of-impossible-monsters—but then he caught the head of the screw with his fingernail and managed to retrieve it.

He was as meticulous as his shaking hands would allow. He didn't want anyone to know he'd been here—though maybe that was impossible. But the idea of one more barrier between himself and the tunnel, no matter how flimsy, was reassuring.

195

He tightened the last screw and pocketed the dime. They climbed the stairs toward the lobby, Joyce leading now.

He pictured the top door, the one he'd opened with a credit card and Joyce's key. A terrifying thought: what if it had slipped shut? What if the bolt had slammed home and he couldn't open it again?

Then he saw the crack of light from the lobby, saw Joyce groping for the door, saw it open; and they tumbled out together, unsteady in the light, holding each other.

Twelve

Billy's nerves were steadier by the time he got home, and for two days after that he resisted his urgent need for the armor.

He told himself he needed time to think; that there was nothing to be gained by acting impulsively.

The truth was, he feared the armor almost as much as he feared the violation of the tunnel.

Feared it as much as he wanted it.

The days grew long, hot, sullen-bright and empty. His apartment was sparsely furnished; he owned a sofa, a brass bed, a Westinghouse TV set and an alarm clock. He left the windows open and a warm breeze lifted the skirts of the white lace curtains. Through the endless afternoon Billy listened to the ticking of the clock and the sound of traffic on the street below.

Listened to the hollow keening of his own unbearable hunger.

He was afraid of his armor because he needed it.

He would never *stop* needing it . . . but here was a fact Billy didn't like to think about: the armor was getting old.

Billy did all the maintenance he could. He kept the armor clean and dry; he ran all the built-in diagnostics. But there was no way to repair any serious damage in this extravagant but technically primitive era. Already some of the more com-

197

plex subroutines had begun to function sporadically or not at all. Eventually the armor's main functions would begin to falter, despite their multiple redundancies—and Billy would be left with his fierce hunger, his terrible need, and no way to satisfy or end it.

To postpone that apocalypse Billy had taught himself to hoard the armor, to use it sparingly and only as often as his body demanded.

He resisted the urge, now, because he wanted to think. It occurred to him that there were lots of ways to handle this crisis. The obvious fact was that another time traveler had entered the city. But the time traveler might be anyone or anything; might have an interest in Billy or might not. Maybe no one really cared about him. Maybe this intruder would leave him alone.

The other (and, Billy thought, more likely) possibility was that the time traveler knew all about Billy and the secrets he had prised from the woman with the wedge of glass in her head—that the time traveler wanted to punish or kill him. He had no evidence of this and some to the contrary; the intruder hadn't tried to conceal his presence, and a good hunter would, wouldn't he? Unless the hunter was so omnipotent he didn't *need* to.

The idea frightened him.

Billy thought, *I have two options.*

Run or fight.

Running was problematic. Oh, he could get on a plane to Los Angeles or Miami or London; he knew how to do that. He could make a life for himself in some other place . . . at least as long as the armor continued to function.

But he couldn't live with the knowledge that *they* might still find him—the time travelers, the tunnel builders, unknown others. Billy didn't relish living the rest of his years as prey. That was why he had stayed in New York in the first place: to mind the tunnel, check the exits.

Therefore, he could fight.

True, he didn't know who or what the intruder might be. But maybe that was only a temporary difficulty. Much of his armor's forensics were still working; Billy guessed he could learn a great deal if he examined the tunnel for clues.

It all depended on the armor, didn't it?

His lifeline. His life.

At last, he took it out of its hiding place.

He had traded its cardboard box for a wooden chest of approximately two cubic feet in volume—he'd found it in a Salvation Army thrift shop. The chest was closed with a pad-lock. Billy placed great faith in padlocks; they seemed so much more substantial than the electronic locks of his own era. He wore the key attached to a belt-loop of his pants. Billy lifted the chest from the back of his closet and used the key to open it.

The holes where the lancet and the stylet entered his body had almost healed—but it only hurt for a minute.

He wore loose, layered clothing over the armor to conceal it.

Billy knew how this made him look. He looked like an alcoholic, a bum. Seeing him, people would turn their faces away. But that wasn't a bad thing.

Underneath, the armor regulated his skin temperature, kept him cool, kept him alert.

The armor was "turned off"—well below full combat ca-pability. But its regulatory functions were automatic. The ar-mor sampled his blood, his nervous impulses. A gland in one of the elytra synthesized new hormones and drip-released them into his body. He was alert, happy, confident.

He was awake.

Life is sleeping, Billy thought. The armor is waking up. Funny how he always forgot this in the long gray passages of his life; how he remembered it when he put the armor on. It was like coming out of a trance.

All his doubts dissolved. He felt the way he imagined a wolf must feel: fiercely focused and dizzy with the pleasure of the hunt.

He went to the building where his pensioners lived, at the junction of time and time.

He installed two new locks he'd bought at a hardware store yesterday: a new knob set for the door in the lobby and a new padlock for the door farther down. If one of the tenants happened to see him while he was working Billy was prepared to offer an excuse for the way he was dressed—but no one came by except a delivery boy with a box of groceries for Amos Shank, up the stairs and out again without speaking.

Then Billy was in the basement, where no one ever went.

He installed the new padlock and hooked the key to the loop on his belt. Now Billy jingled when he walked.

Then he followed the stone stairs down to the lowest level of the building, the sub-sub-basement where the tunnel began, where one of his concussion grenades had taken out a wall and sealed the empty space behind it—where the rubble had been cleared away again to make a passage.

He didn't like coming down here. Armor or not, he didn't like the tunnel. The tunnel made him think of the time ghost he had encountered in it, a mystery even Ann Heath had not been able to explain, a fiery monstrosity with a queasily organic internal structure pulsing under the bright membrane of its skin. Ten years ago now: but the memory was still painfully fresh. The creature had come close enough to singe the hair from the right side of his head. He had smelled the stink of his own burning for days afterward.

Was it a time ghost that had come after him now?

Billy didn't think so. Ann Heath had said they never appeared outside the tunnels; the tunnels were their habitat; they lived in these temporal fractures the way certain bacteria lived in the scalding heat of volcanic springs. Whatever had come through the door, Billy thought, it must be at least approximately human.

He clambered over the scattered rubble into the mouth of the tunnel. He looked apprehensively into the blank, white distance; but there was no time ghost, not now, and he guessed there probably wouldn't be; Ann Heath had said they were dangerous but seldom seen. Nevertheless, Billy stayed close to the entranceway. How strange to have made this transition so easily. Billy had damaged the tunnel so that it had a single destination, a house in the Pacific Northwest some thirty years in the future, and he had sealed *that* entranceway and killed *that* time traveler and therefore no one should have come through . . . but there were footprints in the dust.

Sneaker-prints.

There was a great confusion of these prints and Billy wondered—nervous in the brisk, pale light of the tunnel—whether the intruder might have come from the other direction: discovered the tunnel in Manhattan and followed it into the future.

But no—the lock on the door had been broken from the *inside*.

Someone who had stumbled onto the tunnel at its other terminus, somewhere near the end of the century?

That was possible—even encouraging. Billy had assumed that gateway was all but unusable; still, after a decade, he supposed someone might have opened it somehow. This new possibility made him more optimistic. He would have to hunt the intruder down and kill him, of course; he needed to be the tunnel's only proprietor. It was a secret too important to share. But an unsuspecting civilian from the near future would be easy prey.

Still, he shouldn't count on that. Prepare for hard battle, hope for a vulnerable target.

He cast a final glance down the empty tunnel, then switched on his forensic programs.

He was able to learn a great deal.

His armor detected and memorized fingerprints from the cellar walls, skin samples where the intruder had cut himself on a shard of glass projecting from the rubble. The intruder was quite human, a male, type O+ blood. Back home, a competent laboratory might have been able to put together a portrait of the man from a simple genome projection, assuming the samples were more or less intact. But Billy didn't have that capacity; he needed another means of tracking his prey.

The enormity of the task was daunting. It might be impossible—a civilian joyriding from the future might be anywhere. Might have jumped a plane to some familiar place. Invested money in the stock market and set off on a tour of his own recent history.

But the man had arrived here less than a month ago and Billy guessed he would need more time than that to adjust. After all: his money was no good, his knowledge was valuable but difficult to cash in on. He might still be close by.

But how to identify him?

Billy ran a finger through the dust on the floor. Dust from his concussion grenade, dust from the foundation of the building. He opened a pouch in one of the elytra of his armor and withdrew the armor's headset, a leathery black mask that covered his face entirely. He clipped an optical cable between the headset and the armor's processors while his forensics sampled the dust and announced its constituents to Billy in a flickering eyepiece readout: limestone, sand, bedrock . . . and microscopic fragments *of the tunnel itself:* strange long-chain molecules that fluoresced in dim light, absorbing background radiation and leaking photons.

Billy narrowed the bandwidth of his eyepiece to the frequency of strongest emission, then clambered back into the dark chamber of the basement.

With his opticals adjusted, the dust was plainly luminescent.

He stood in a starry blue limbo, very strange. The tip of his forefinger radiated light like a small constellation.

How much of this dust had the intruder carried out of the building? How much would cling to him? To his shoes? To his clothes? For how long?

Interesting questions.

He stood in the tunnel a moment before he left.

He took a step forward, his heart pounding. This was not a place, he reminded himself. It was a time machine. Each step carried him a measured distance forward: a week? a month? And what am I doing out there? Take a step: February? March? Is it snowing? Am I out in the snow? Am I hunting? Is the armor alive? Am I?

Suppose he ran a hundred yards forward. 1963? 1964? Had the elytra failed? The gland dried up? *Have I convulsed and died somewhere?* Suppose he went even farther. Suppose he stood in some sheltered part of this tunnel where 1970 raged overhead, 1975, 1980: was Billy in his coffin in some potter's field, buried a century before his own birth?

He felt a sudden weightlessness, a kind of vertigo.

It was better not to think about these things.

Home, he showered away all the dust still clinging to him; then he washed and shined the armor. He disliked taking the armor off. He hadn't powered up entirely and the physical need was still urgent and unsatisfied. The lancet had left a painful sore on the right side of his abdomen; without the hormone drip he felt small, vulnerable, and nervous. But he needed to sleep. And it would be wasteful to sleep in his armor.

Tomorrow, he promised himself. In the night.

He dreamed of the Storm Zone, of armored combat, in the future, where he had once lived; and then of Ohio, the fierce summers and cold, snowless winters there. He dreamed of the bed he had slept in as a child, with a heater he was allowed to switch on in January and February; of bitter nights walking from the common store to the housing plex, frost on the ground and a horned moon overhead.

He dreamed these things with a clarity so absolute and a sadness so piercing they could be sustained only in a dream. And then, finally, he dreamed the face of Nathan, his father.

He woke wanting the armor.

Even in New York City—even in 1962, in a city that was the axis around which much of the world revolved—the night was quieter than the day.

Billy chose the stillest hours of the night, between three A.M. and dawn, to begin his search.

He wore the armor snug to his body. He pulled on loose, filthy pants over the leggings. Over the elytra and the halteres he wore a torn athletic sweatshirt marked *NYU,* which he had found in a bin at a secondhand shop. He pulled up the hood to help disguise the headset; the headset was conspicuous but he needed its eyepiece. Over the sweatshirt Billy wore a slate-gray, threadbare coat that reached to his knees, the high collar turned up at his throat.

Before he left the apartment he looked at himself in the chipped bathroom mirror.

The black headset with its calibrated goggles projected from the hood of his sweatshirt like the muzzle of an animal.

A rat, Billy thought. He looked like some kind of leathery, robotic sewer rat attempting to pass for human.

I look like someone's nightmare.

The thought was disquieting. It troubled him until he activated the armor's lancet; then everything was simple, everything was clear.

He kept to the shadows.

He tuned his eyepiece to the radiant frequency of the tunnel dust. He was able to follow his own footprints—a faintly blue, faintly luminous path—back to the building near Tompkins Square.

The lobby of the building was alive, starry with ghostlight.

But the intruder had come through here long ago and there was no clear trail to follow. Well, Billy had expected that. There had been rain since then; there had been wind, air pollution, foot traffic, a thousand scatterings and adulterations.

He stood in the street outside the building. Faint blue light glimmered here and there. A brush of it adhered to a lamppost. A scatter of it stood like snow crystals along the filthy curb.

No trail, only clues: dim, ambiguous.

He looked up at the building, dark except for Mr. Shank's apartment. Amos Shank chose that moment to pull back his blinds—awake in some delirium of creativity—and Billy gazed up calmly at him. Mr. Shank returned his look for one long breathless moment . . . then pulled away from the window; and the blinds slashed down again.

Billy smiled.

What did you see, Mr. Shank? What do you think I am, out here in the lonely dark?

Billy imagined himself old and senile in 1962, lost in a dream of antiquity and Napoleonic Europe, peering from his slum apartment into a nighttime world inhabited by monstrosities.

Why, Billy thought, I must look like Death.

Good guess, Mr. Shank.

Billy laughed quietly and turned away.

He moved in a crude spiral away from the tunnel, avoiding Fifth Avenue and the late-night crowds in the Village, hoping for some substantial clue, an arrow of blue light, that would lead him to the intruder.

He found none. He found traces of the dust here and there almost at random—a big deposit clinging to an oil slick at Ninth and University Place, a smaller one smudged into the yellow grass at the foot of a bench in Washington Square Park. Billy lingered at the bench a moment, but there was nothing coherent, only a suggestion that his prey had passed this way. He frowned and decided to move south, avoiding the west side of the park where a few hustlers and homosexuals still lingered in the darkness. That part of the park was a familiar hunting ground when his armor needed a killing—like Times Square and Union Square at night, places where disposable nonpersons gathered. Billy's armor wanted a killing *now;* but there wasn't time and he suppressed the urge.

He paused a moment, adjusted his opticals and gazed up at the sky.

Ordinarily the city sky was featureless, but Billy's opticals showed him too many stars to count. It was like an Ohio sky, Billy thought.

He felt a sudden pang of longing, so intense it worried him. The armor was pumping out complex neurochemicals to make him alert, to help him hunt—to keep him alive. There shouldn't have been room for nostalgia. Unless the elytra or the lancet or the strange, false gland in the armor had begun to fail.

But they hadn't, really; or if they had, the effect was purely transient. Billy sat on a park bench until the pang of home-sickness faded. Then the sky was only the sky, clean and blank of meaning. He retuned his opticals and crossed the empty space of Washington Square South at Sullivan, hunting.

And came up empty. And sweated through another day.

In the early evening he went out without his armor to wander the busy streets of the Village. He sat for a time on the terrace at the Cafe Figaro, mistaken by its regulars for one more middle-aged tourist, wondering whether the intruder had strolled past him in the crowd or might even be sitting at the next table, smug with thirty years' worth of cheap prescience. Or might after all have left the city: that was still a real possibility. In which case Billy's prey would be hopelessly beyond reach, no trace of him but a residue of fading phosphorescence.

But Billy hadn't given up yet.

He went home, donned the armor, wandered toward midtown in a ragged pattern for three hours without result.

He finished the night without killing anything—a profound disappointment.

And dreamed of blue light.

Three nights later, ranging west along Eighth Street, he discovered a smoky luminescence around the doorway and interior of a tiny retail shop called Lindner's Radio Supply.

Billy smiled to himself, and went home, and slept.

He woke in the heat of the afternoon.

He put on his golden armor, activated the lancet, and dressed to conceal himself. He didn't wear the headset; today he didn't need it.

He felt a little strange, going outside in daylight.

He walked to Lindner's in his overcoat, attracting a few stares but nothing more. He paused on the sidewalk in front of the store and pressed his face against the window.

It wasn't a big store, but business seemed reasonably good. There was a hi-fi set in the window bristling with vacuum tubes, a hand-lettered card announcing the word STEREO-PHONIC! Beyond that, in the dimness, an old man stood patiently behind a wooden counter. Billy felt a tinge of disappointment: was this feeble thing his prey?

Maybe. Maybe not. It was too soon to say.

He crossed the street to a delicatessen, ordered a ham sandwich and coffee, and occupied a table by the window.

Lindner's was moderately busy. People came, people went. Any of them might be the intruder. But Billy guessed from the smoky nimbus of the glow last night that the man had come here often. The dust—by this time a few motes still clinging to his shoes or cuffs—could only have been deposited by repeated traffic. Probably he's an employee, Billy thought. A deliveryman, say, or a sales assistant.

The sandwich was very good. He hadn't eaten much for days. He bought a second one, a second coffee. He ate slowly and watched the traffic in and out of Lindner's.

He counted fifteen individuals in and fifteen individuals out, all of them customers, Billy guessed. Then a truck pulled up to the curb and a sweating man in a blue shirt unloaded three cardboard boxes on a dolly. Billy watched with heightened interest: here was a possibility. There was no way to follow the truck, but he made a note of the license number and the name of the distribution company.

And continued to watch.

A little after four o'clock the counterman at the deli approached his table. "You can't just sit here. This is for paying customers."

The place was nearly empty. Billy slid a ten-dollar bill across the table and said, "I'd like another coffee. Keep the change." Thinking, *If I wanted to kill you I could do it right now.*

The counterman looked at the money, looked at Billy.

He frowned and came back with the coffee. Cold coffee in a greasy cup.

"Thank you," Billy said.

"You're welcome. I think."

The last customer left Lindner's at five-fifteen; the store was scheduled to close at six. Billy divided his attention between the storefront and the clock on the deli wall. By six, his focus was intense and feverish.

He watched as the old man—the proprietor, Billy guessed —ambled to the door with a key ring in his hand and turned the sign around to show the word CLOSED.

Billy left his table at the deli and moved into the street.

Warm, sunny afternoon. He shielded his eyes.

At Lindner's, the proprietor—gray-haired, balding, fat— stepped through the door and pawed at his keys. Then paused, turned back, pronounced some word into the shadow of the store, closed the door, and walked off.

Billy's interest was immediate: the old man had *left someone inside.*

It was hardly likely the fat proprietor was his target, in any case. He looked too much at home here: too bored, too mindlessly familiar. Bide your time, Billy thought. Wait, watch.

He stood at a newsstand and pretended to examine a copy of *Life.*

The second man stepped through the door a moment later and locked it with his own key.

This man, Billy thought. His heart speeded up in his chest.

Billy followed at a discreet distance.

He was working on intuition, but he didn't really doubt this was his prey. Here was a reasonably young man in pale blue jeans, cotton shirt, a pair of sneakers that looked suspiciously anachronistic. Dust in the tread of those shoes, Billy thought. Some dust, maybe, still trapped in the weave of his pants. In the dark, this man would light up like a neon tube. Billy was sure of it.

He lagged back a block or two, following.

The man sensed Billy's presence. Sometimes this happened with prey. Sometimes it didn't; there were people who simply didn't pick up the clues. You could sit next to them on the subway, follow them up an escalator, read over their shoulders; they didn't notice. More often, a victim would feel some warning instinct; he would walk a little faster, cast a nervous glance over his shoulder. In the end, of course, it didn't matter; prey was prey. But Billy wanted to be careful now. He couldn't use the armor too conspicuously and he didn't want to lose this trail.

He crossed the street, came parallel with his prey, then ducked into a liquor store and paid for a bottle—a squat fifth of whiskey, but any bottle would have done; it was only a prop. He put the paper bag under his arm and hurried out. He spotted his target a block away, heading into a seedy neighborhood on the border of the warehouse district.

The target paused once, turned, and gazed back at Billy.

And what do *you* see, Billy wondered. Not what Mr. Shank had seen, certainly. Not naked death, not on a sunny afternoon. Billy crossed at the corner and examined his own reflection in a window. Here was a gray-haired man in a dirty gray overcoat carrying a bottle in a brown paper bag. Ugly but hardly conspicuous. He smiled a little.

The prey—the time traveler—nearly walked into the path of a taxi (Billy contemplated this possibility with a mixture of regret and relief); stepped back at the last minute (Billy felt a different mixture of relief, regret); then hurried into the lobby of a tenement building.

Billy noted the address.

210

Follow him, was Billy's next thought. *Follow him into whatever shabby little room he occupies. Kill him there. Finish with this.* His armor wanted a killing.

Then Billy hesitated—

And the world *dimmed.*

Dimming was how he thought of it later. It *felt like* a dimming —literally, as if someone had switched off a lightbulb in his head.

He was suddenly Billy Gargullo, farmboy, standing on a dirty street on the Lower East Side in the antiquated past, the words *kill him* still echoing in his head like the chorus of an obscene song. He thought of the man he had followed and felt a hot rush of guilt.

Suddenly Billy wasn't a killer. He wasn't a hunter; his senses weren't keen. He felt opaque, thick, frightened, leaden-footed. His clothes were too heavy; he started to sweat.

His armor had malfunctioned.

Billy fled.

It wasn't a problem he could run away from. But running was his first instinct. He ran until he was breathless, bent double and gasping for air, then walked in a cold daze until the streetlights blinked on.

He sought shelter in a movie theater on Forty-second Street, where lonely men masturbated in the balconies or gratified each other in the toilet stalls. Other nights, he had come here looking for victims. But that irony was lost on him now. Billy huddled into a torn seat, terrified in the flickering movie light.

His life might be over.

Maybe it had been a bad bargain all along. Billy had seized the opportunity when it was offered: leap back into the fabulous past, out of the Storm Zone, battle zone, Infantry, mortal fear; seal the exits and check them; live a modest, concealed life with his armor a private and occasional indulgence.

Oh, but Billy (some fraction of himself had objected even then), *the armor won't last forever, there are no replacements where you're going, no parts no labor no repair.* He envisioned a searing, unquenchable, and ultimately deadly Need.

But that might not come (Billy had told himself). Who could tell how long the golden armor might last? Out of combat, preserved, groomed, polished, maintained, diagnosed, coddled—maybe it would last forever. Or as long as Billy lived. The power packs were good for that.

So he told himself.

It hadn't seemed like a fairy tale, then.

It was a calculated risk. Maybe this optimism was a flaw in his mental equipment; maybe some slip of the scalpel at the military hospital had left him too independent of mind or too vulnerable to imagination. Billy had huddled against the noise and fury of the combat zone and told himself, *You don't have to stay here*—and that meant a great deal, with the wind outside, the constant lightning, furtive combat in ruined buildings, in this nightmare wasteland a thousand miles from Ohio.

He remembered that time without wanting to.

Three of them had discovered the time traveler.

Billy killed the two infantrymen while they slept. Then he killed the time traveler herself, the so-called custodian, whose name was Ann Heath.

And journeyed back. And sealed his exits. And checked them.

Exhausted and afraid, Billy fell asleep in the movie theater.

The film—an "art film," mainly of people fucking—droned on around him.

In his dream he unreeled private movies.

• • • •

Billy didn't know much history.

After his conscription, in the tedious hours at training camp, he sometimes picked up the popular novels his buddies read—illustrated historicals about the wild days of the twentieth century. Billy enjoyed these books. There was always a pointed moral about the sins of gluttony or pride; but Billy could tell the writers took as much prurient pleasure in their stories as he did. Some of these books had been banned in California for their frank depiction of tree-burning forest barons, of greedy politicians zooming around the world in gasoline-powered aircraft. As a conscript Billy relished the promiscuity of his ancestors. They had danced on their cliff-edge, he thought, with great style.

These were his first coherent thoughts about the past.

The rest of Billy's knowledge was commonplace. The climate had begun to change long before he was born. In school they'd made him sing pious songs about it. *Sun and water, wind and tree, what have these to do with me? Sun and water, tree and wind, against these, Father, I have sinned.* But climate was Billy's destiny. Long before his birth, a fierce curl of tropical air had formed and stabilized over the waters of the Caribbean and the Gulf of Mexico. The Storm Zone ebbed and strengthened; some years it was hardly more than a knot in the jetstream, some years it generated hurricane after hurricane, battering coastlines already devastated by the rising of the world's oceans and the melting of the poles. And every decade—as the atmosphere warmed another degree or two—the trend was unmistakable: the Storm Zone had become a stable new climatic feature.

By the time Billy was five anyone who could afford to had migrated out of the southeastern coastal states. But the poor stayed behind, joined by refugees from the Caribbean and Central America seeking the relative safety of these ruined

213

American cities. There were food riots, secession riots. Washington dispatched troops.

By the time he was conscripted the war had been going on for nearly a decade. It had turned into one of those festering conflicts all but ignored by the prestigious European news cartels. A senseless effort, some said, to preserve as American territory a swath of land rapidly growing uninhabitable. But the war went on. Billy didn't much care about it, not at first. Recruited at the age of twelve, he was shipped around to various training and indoctrination bases, mainly out west. He spent a couple of years guarding the transcontinental railway tracks where they passed through insurgent territory in Nevada, where water-poor locals had tried to dynamite the trains a couple of times. Billy didn't see any action, but he loved to watch the trains go by. Big silver bullets shimmering in the sun haze, loaded with grain, ingots, armaments, liquid hydrogen. The trains levitated soundlessly from horizon to horizon and left dust-devils dancing in their wake. Billy imagined himself riding one of those trains to Ohio. But it was impossible. He'd be AWOL; there were travel restrictions. He'd be shot. But it was a lovely thing to think about.

He was lonely in Nevada. He lived in a stone barracks with three other recruits and an aging, armored CO named Skolnik. Billy wondered whether he would ever see a woman, hold a woman, marry a woman, have children with a woman. Billy was technically assigned to an armored division of the 17th Infantry, but he hadn't been issued his armor yet; privately, he hoped he never would. Some recruits did a term of menial labor and were released back into their communities. Maybe that would happen to him. Billy was careful to do everything he was asked to do—but slowly, ploddingly. It was a form of silent rebellion.

It didn't work. On his seventeenth birthday, Billy was shipped east for treatment.

They gave him his armor and they posted him to the Zone.

214

• • • •

He woke in the movie theater on Forty-second Street and shuffled outside into a miserably humid night.

Walking home, he felt a surge of energy, like needlepricks on his skin—a trickle from the gland in his elytra, Billy presumed. That was a good sign and it made him optimistic. Maybe the malfunction was temporary.

His thoughts were more coherent, at least.

Home, he attached the headgear to his armor and prayed the diagnostics were still working.

His eyepiece bled graphs and numbers into his field of vision. A complete diagnostic sequence took more than an hour, but Billy knew what all the numbers ought to be. He ran down his electrical systems, then started on the biologicals. Everything came up normal or near normal except for two items: a local blood pressure and the temps on a tiny circulatory pump. Billy finished the general diagnostic, then called back those numbers for a closer look. He asked the armor for a complete sequence on the abdominals and waited nervously for the results.

More numbers appeared, chiefly pressure readings. But Billy understood what these misplaced decimal points implied: a blood clot had lodged in the reedlike lancet.

Billy climbed out of his armor.

He hadn't powered all the way up, though he had worn the armor a great deal in the last week, and maybe that was good—a full power-up would have placed greater demands on the gland in the elytra, perhaps thrown the clot into an artery. He might have died.

But the Need was still very great.

The armor was limp in his hand. He turned the flexible elytra inside out and deployed the lancet—a long, narrow microtube still wet with blood.

Here was where the clot had lodged.

Billy went to the kitchen and put a pot of water on the

215

stove. As it boiled, he shook in a handful of Morton salt to approximate the salinity of human blood. This was "emergency field service," a technique he had never tried, though he remembered it from training.

When the water was cool enough to touch, Billy dipped the lancet in.

Micropumps responded to the heat. Threads of dark blood oozed into the pot.

He couldn't tell whether the clot had dissolved.

He cleaned the lancet and retracted it. Then he wrapped the elytra around his body, sealed them, and ran the diagnostics again.

The numbers looked better. Not perfect—but of course it was hard to tell until he plugged the lancet into his body and allowed his own blood to course through it.

Billy activated that system.

He felt the lancet slide under his skin. It stung a little—perhaps some salt still clinging to the microtube in spite of its own sterilants and anesthetics. But at least—

Ah.

—it seemed to be working.

Billy experienced a dizzy sense of triumph. He set out from the apartment at once.

He had lost a lot of time. It was late now. A street-cleaning truck had passed this way and Billy caught the reflection of a fingernail moon in the empty, wet asphalt.

Only an interruption, he told himself. How childish to have been so frightened of a minor malfunction. But understandable: all his courage came from the armor.

He thought about the secret gland hidden in the folds of the elytra.

It was dormant when the armor was folded away, tissues bathed in life-suspending chemicals. But the gland was a living thing—grown, he supposed, in a factory somewhere, a

216

critically altered mutation of a thalamus or thyroid. When it lived, it lived on Billy's blood—pumped in from an artery through the stylet, processed and pumped back through the lancet. The gland secreted the chemicals that made Billy the fine hunter he was tonight.

But because the gland was alive it might age, might be susceptible to disease, tumors, toxins—Billy simply didn't know. For all the armor's inbuilt diagnostics, such problems were necessarily the business of the infantry doctors.

No infantry doctors here.

He wondered whether his gland had been damaged by the blood clot. Whether it would clot again. Maybe it would . . . maybe this last episode had been a token of his own mortality.

But no, Billy thought, that's wrong. I *am* Death. That's what I am tonight. And Death can't die.

He laughed out loud, an overflow of joy. It felt good to be hunting again.

He went to the place his prey had gone, where the hunt had been interrupted. He adjusted the bandwidth on his eyepiece and saw a dust of blue light in the doorway, very faint. And up the stairs.

Tonight, Billy thought, it would all come together.

Tonight, at last, he would kill someone.

Thirteen

Catherine backed out of the woodshed, turned and ran, stumbling over the berry-bush runners and scratching herself on the thorns. She didn't feel any of this. She was too frightened.

The thing in the shed was—

Was unnameable.

Was not human.

Was a pulsating travesty of a human being.

She ran until she was breathless, then braced herself against a tree trunk, gasping and coughing. Her lungs ached and her unprotected arms were bloody from the nettles. The forest around her was silent, large, and absurdly sunny. Treetops moved in the breeze.

She sat down among the pine needles, hugging herself.

Be sensible, Catherine thought. *Whatever it is, it can't hurt you. It can't move.*

It had been bloody and helpless. Maybe not a monster, she thought; maybe a human being in some terrible kind of distress, skinned, mutilated . . .

But a mutilated human being would not have said "Help me" in that calm and earnest voice.

It was hurt. Well, *of course* it was hurt—it should have been dead! She had been able to see through its skin, into its

218

insides; through its skull into its brains. What could have done that to a human being, and what human being could have survived?

Go home, Catherine instructed herself. Back to Gram Peggy's house. Whatever she did—call the police, call an ambulance—she could do from there.

At home, she could think.

At home, she could lock the doors.

She locked the doors and scoured the kitchen shelves for something calming. What she turned up was a cut-glass decanter of peach brandy, two thirds full—"for sleepless nights," Gram Peggy used to say. Catherine swallowed an ounce or so straight out of the bottle. She felt the liquid inside her like a small furnace, fiery and warming.

In the downstairs bathroom she sponged the blood off her arms and sprayed the lacework cuts with Bactine. Her shirt was torn; she changed it. She washed her face and hands.

Then she wandered through the downstairs checking the doors again, stopped when she passed the telephone. Probably she ought to call someone, Catherine thought.

911?

The Belltower Police Department?

But what could she say?

She thought about it a few minutes, paralyzed with indecision, until a new idea occurred to her. An impulse, but sensible. She retrieved Doug Archer's business card from a bureau drawer and dialed the number written there.

His answering service said he'd call back in about an hour. Catherine was disconcerted by this unexpected delay. She sat at the kitchen table with the peach brandy in front of her, trying to make sense of her experience in the woodshed.

Maybe she'd misinterpreted something. That was possible, wasn't it? People see odd things, especially in a crisis. Maybe somebody had been badly hurt. Maybe she shouldn't have run away.

But Catherine had an artist's eye and she recalled the scene as clearly as if she had sketched it on canvas: dark blur of mold on ancient newsprint, bars of sunlight through green mossy walls, and the centerpiece, all pinks and blues and strange crimsons and yellows, a half-made thing, which pronounced the words *Help me* while its larynx bobbed in its glassy throat.

Sweet Jesus in a sidecar, Catherine thought. *Oh, this is way out of bounds. This is crazy.*

She'd finished half the contents of the brandy decanter by the time Doug Archer knocked. Catherine opened the door for him, a little light-headed but still deeply frightened. He said, "I was out in this neighborhood so I thought I'd just drop by instead of calling . . . Hey, are you all right?"

Then, without meaning to, she was leaning against him. He steadied her and guided her to the couch.

"I found something," she managed. "Something terrible. Something strange."

"Found something," Archer repeated.

"In the woods—downhill south of here."

"Tell me about it," Archer said.

Catherine stammered out the story, suddenly embarrassed by what seemed like her own hysteria. How could he possibly understand? Archer sat attentively in Gram Peggy's easy chair, but he was fundamentally a stranger. Maybe it had been dumb to call him. When he asked her to get in touch if she noticed anything strange, was *this* what he meant? Maybe it was a conspiracy. Belltower, Washington, occupied by hostile aliens. Maybe, under his neat Levi's and blue Belltower Realty jacket, Archer was as transparent and strange as the thing in the woodshed.

220

But when she finished the story she found herself soothed by the telling of it.

Archer said he believed her, but maybe that was politeness. He said, "I want you to take me there."

The idea revived her fear. "Now?"

"Soon. Today. And before dark." He hesitated. "You might be mistaken about what you saw. Maybe somebody really does need help."

"I thought about that. Maybe somebody does. But I know what I saw, Mr. Archer."

"Doug," he said absently. "I still think we have to go back. If there's even a chance somebody's hurt out there. I don't think we have any choice."

Catherine thought about it. "No," she said unhappily. "I don't guess we do."

But it was late afternoon now and the forest was, if anything, spookier. Fortified by the brandy and a great deal of soothing talk, Catherine led Archer downhill past the creek, past the blackberry thickets and the tall Douglas firs, to the edge of the meadow where the woodshed stood.

The woodshed hadn't changed, except in her imagination. It was mossy, ancient, small and unexceptional. She looked at it and envisioned monsters.

They stood a moment in brittle silence.

"When we met," Catherine said, "you asked me to watch out for anything strange." She looked at him. "Did you expect this? Do you have any idea what's going on here?"

"I didn't expect anything like this, no."

He told her a story about a house he'd sold to a man named Tom Winter, its strange history, its perpetual tidiness,

She said, "Is that near here?"

"A few hundred yards toward the road."

"Is there some connection?"

Archer shrugged. "It's getting late, Catherine. We'd better do this while we can."

They approached the crude door of the woodshed.

Archer reached for the latch handle, but Catherine turned him away. "No. Let me." *You found him,* Gram Peggy would have said. *He's your obligation, Catherine.*

Already the thing inside was "he," not "it." She had shut out the image and concentrated on the voice.

Help me.

Catherine took a deep breath and opened the door.

The sun had edged down toward the treetops; the woodshed was darker than it had been this morning. A green, buzzing, loamy darkness. Catherine wrinkled her nose and waited for her eyesight to adjust. Doug Archer hovered at her shoulder; his presence was at least a little bit reassuring.

For a time she couldn't hear anything but the quick beat of her heart; couldn't see anything but dimness and clutter.

Then Archer forced the door to the extremity of its hinges and a new beam of light slanted in.

The monster lay on the pressed-dirt floor, precisely where she had left it this morning.

Catherine blinked. The monster blinked. Behind her, she heard Archer draw a sudden, shocked breath. "Holy Mother of God," he said.

The monster turned its pale, moist eyes on Archer a moment. Then it looked at Catherine again.

"You came back," it said. *(He* said.)

This was the terrible part, she thought dizzily, the truly unendurable, this voice from that throat. He sounded like someone you might meet at a bus stop. He sounded like a friendly grocer.

She forced her eyes to focus somewhere above him, on the pile of moldy newspapers. "You said you needed help."

"Yes."

"I brought help."

It was all she could think of to say.

Archer pushed past her and knelt over the man—if it *was* a man. *Be careful!* she thought.

Catherine heard the tremor in his voice: "What happened to you?"

Now Catherine's gaze drifted back to the man's head, the caul of translucent tissue where the skull should have been, and the brain beneath it—she presumed this whitish, vague mass must be his brain. The creature spoke. "It would take too long to explain."

Archer said, "What do you want us to do?"

"If you can, I want you to take me back to the house."

Archer was silent a moment. Catherine noticed he didn't say *What house?* The Tom Winter house, she thought. These things were connected after all. Mysterious events and living dead men.

She felt like Alice, hopelessly lost down some unpleasant rabbit hole.

But it was at least a thing to do, carrying this monster back to the Tom Winter house, and deciding how to do it brought her back to the level of the prosaic. There was an old camp cot Gram Peggy had kept in the cellar; she hurried and fetched it back with Doug Archer beside her, neither of them talking much. They wanted to be finished before nightfall: already the shadows were long and threatening.

We'll have to touch that thing, Catherine thought. *We'll have to lift it up onto this old cot.* She imagined the injured thing would feel cool and wet to the touch, like the jellyfish lumps that washed up on the beach along Puget Sound. She shuddered, thinking about it.

Archer propped open the door of the shed and did most of the lifting. He supported the thing (the man) with his hands under its arms and brought it out into the fading daylight,

223

where it looked even more horrific. Some of its skin was dark and scabbed over; some was merely flesh colored. But whole chunks of it were translucent or pale, fishy gray. It blinked gray eyelids against the light. It looked like something that had been underwater a long time. One leg was missing. The stump ended in a pink, porous mass of tissue.

At least there was no blood.

Catherine took a deep breath and did what she could to help, lifting the leg end onto the army cot. Here was more pale skin and a fine webbing of blood vessels underneath, like an illustration from an anatomy textbook. But the flesh wasn't cool or slimy. It was warm and felt like normal skin.

Archer took the head end of the army cot and Catherine lifted the back. The injured man was heavy, as heavy as a normal man. His strangeness had not made him light. This was good, too. A creature with this much weight, she reasoned, could not be ghostly.

It was hard to hold the pipe legs of the army cot without spilling the man off, and she was sweating and her hands were cramped and sore by the time they passed out of the deep forest, down a trail nearly overgrown with moss and horsetail fern, into the back yard of what must be the house Archer had described. It was a very ordinary-looking house.

They put the army cot down on the overgrown lawn for a minute. Archer wiped his face with a handkerchief; Catherine kneaded her aching palms. She avoided his look. We don't want to acknowledge what we're doing, she thought; we want to pretend this is a regular kind of job.

The thing on the cot said, "You should be prepared for what's inside."

Archer looked down sharply. "What *is* inside?"

"Machines. A lot of very small machines. They won't hurt you."

"Oh," Archer said. He looked at the house again. "Machines." He frowned. "I don't have a key."

"You don't need one," the monster said.

The door opened at a touch.

They carried the army cot inside, through an ordinary kitchen, into the big living room, which was not ordinary because the walls were covered with the machines the monster had warned them about.

The machines—*there must be thousands of them,* Catherine thought—were like tiny jewels, brightly colored, segmented, insectile, eyes and attention all aimed at the man on the cot. They were motionless; but she imagined them, for some reason, quivering with excitement.

It's like a homecoming, Catherine thought dazedly. That's what it's like.

None of this was possible.

She understood that she had reached an unexpected turning point in her life. She felt the way people must feel in a plane crash, or when their house goes up in flames. Now everything was different; nothing would be the same ever again. In the wake of these events, it wasn't possible to construct an ordinary idea of the world and how it worked. There was no way to make any of this fit.

But she was calm. Outside the context of the decaying woodshed—outside of the woods—even the monster had ceased to be frightening. He wasn't a monster after all; only a strange kind of man who had had some strange kind of accident. Maybe a curse had been placed on him.

They carried him into the bedroom, where there were more of the machine insects. She helped Archer lift him onto the bed. Archer asked in a small voice what else the man needed. The man said, "Time. Please don't tell anyone else about this."

"All right," Archer said. And Catherine nodded.

"And food," the man said. "Anything rich in protein. Meat would be good."

"I'll bring something," Catherine volunteered, surprising herself. "Would tomorrow be all right?"

"That would be fine."

And Archer added, "Who are you?"

The man smiled, but only a little. He must know how he looks, Catherine thought. When your lips are nearly transparent, you shouldn't smile too much. It creates a different effect. "My name is Ben Collier," he said.

"Ben," Archer repeated. "Ben, I would like to know what kind of thing you are exactly."

"I'm a time traveler," Ben said.

They left Ben Collier the time traveler alone with his machine bugs. On the way out of the house Catherine saw Archer pick up two items from the kitchen table: a blue spiral-bound notebook and a copy of the *New York Times*.

Back at Gram Peggy's house, Archer pored over the two documents. Catherine felt mysteriously vacant, lost: what was next? There was no etiquette for this situation. She said to Archer, "Shall I make us some dinner?" He looked up briefly, nodded.

It had never occurred to her that people who had shared experiences like this—people who were kidnapped by flying saucers or visited by ghosts—would have to deal with anything as prosaic as dinner. An encounter with the numinous, followed by, say, linguine. It was impossible. (That word again.)

Step by step, she thought. One thing at a time. She heated the frying pan, located a chicken breast she'd been thawing since morning, took a second one from the freezer and quick-defrosted it in the microwave—she would eat this one herself; Catherine didn't believe in nuked food, especially for guests. She didn't much believe in pan-fried chicken, either, but it was quick and available.

She set two places at the dinner table. The dining room was large and Victorian, Gram Peggy's cuckoo clock presiding over a cabinet stocked with blue Wedgwood. Catherine started coffee perking and served dinner on the Petalware she'd picked up at a thrift shop in Belltower—because it seemed somehow wrong or impertinent to be eating from Gram Peggy's china when Gram Peggy wasn't home. Archer carried his two souvenirs, the notebook and the *New York Times,* to the table with him. But he set them aside and complimented her on the food.

Catherine picked at her chicken. It tasted irrelevant.

She said, "Well, what have we got ourselves into?"

Archer managed a smile. "Something absolutely unexpected. Something we don't understand."

"You sound pleased about that."

"Do I? I guess I am, in a way. It kind of confirms this suspicion I've had."

"Suspicion?"

"That the world is stranger than it looks."

Catherine considered this. "I think I know what you mean. When I was eighteen, I took up jogging. I used to go out after dark, winter nights. I liked all the yellow lighted-up windows of the houses. It felt funny being the only person out on the street, just, you know, running and breathing steam. I used to get an idea that anything could happen, that I'd turn a corner and I'd be in Oz and nobody would be the wiser—none of those people sleepwalking behind those yellow windows would have the slightest idea. I knew what kind of world it was. They didn't."

"Exactly," Archer said.

"But there was never Oz. Only one more dark street."

"Until now."

227

"Is this Oz?"

"It might as well be."

She supposed that was true. "I guess we can't tell anyone."

"I don't think we should, no."

"And we have to go back in the morning."

"Yes."

"We can't forget about it and we can't walk away. He needs our help."

"I think so."

"But what *is* he?"

"Well, I think maybe he told us the truth, Catherine. I think he's a time traveler."

"Is that possible?"

"I don't know. Maybe. I'm past making odds on what's possible and what isn't."

She gestured at the notebook, the newspaper. "So what did you find?"

"They belonged to Tom Winter, I believe. Look."

She pushed aside her chicken and examined the paper. Sunday, May 13, 1962. The Late City Edition.

U.S SHIPS AND 1,800 MARINES ON WAY TO INDOCHINA AREA; LAOS DECREES EMERGENCY . . . DOCTORS TRANSPLANT HUMAN HEART VALVE . . . CHURCH IN SPAIN BACKS WORKERS ON STRIKE RIGHTS

The front page had yellowed—but only a little.

"Check out the notebook," Archer prompted.

She leafed through it. The entries were brief scrawls and occupied the first three pages; the rest of the book was blank.

Troubling Questions, it said at the top.

You could walk away from this, it said.

This is dangerous, and you could walk away.

Everybody else on the face of the earth is being dragged into the future an hour at a time, but you can walk out. You found the back door.

228

Thirty years ago, she read. *They have the Bomb. Think about it. They have industrial pollution. They have racism, ignorance, crime, starvation—*

Are you really so frightened of the future?

I'll go back one more time. At least to look. To really be there. At least once.

She looked up at Doug Archer. "It's a sort of diary."

"A short one."

"Tom Winter's?"

"I'd bet on it."

"What did he do?"

"Walked into a shitload of trouble, it looks like. But that remains to be seen."

Only later did the obvious next thought occur to Catherine: Maybe *we* walked into a shitload of trouble, too.

Archer slept on the sofa. In the morning he phoned the Belltower Realty office and told them he was sick—"Death's door," he said into the phone. "That's right. Yup. I know. I know. Yeah, I hope so too. Thanks."

Catherine said, "Won't you get into trouble?"

"Lose some commissions, for sure."

"Is that all right?"

"It's all right with me. I have other business." He grinned —a little wildly, in Catherine's opinion. "Hey, there are miracles happening. Aren't you a little bit excited by that?"

She allowed a guilty smile. "I guess I am."

Then they drove down to the Safeway and bought five frozen T-bone steaks for Ben, the time traveler.

□ □

□ □

Archer visited the house every day for a week, sometimes with Catherine and sometimes without her. He brought food, which the time traveler never ate in his presence—maybe the machine bugs absorbed it and fed it to him in some more direct fashion; he didn't care to know the details.

Every day, he exchanged some words with Ben.

It was getting easier to think of him as "Ben," as something human rather than monstrous. The bedclothes disguised most of his deformities; and the white, sebaceous caul where his skull should have been had acquired enough pigmentation, by the third day, to pass for human skin. Archer had been scared at first by the machine bugs all over the house, but they never approached him and never presented any kind of threat. So Archer began to ask questions.

Simple ones at first: "How long were you in the shed?"

"Ten years, more or less."

"You were injured all that time?"

"I was dead most of that time."

"Clinically dead?"

Ben smiled. "At least."

"What happened to you?"

"I was murdered."

"What saved you?"

"They did." The machine bugs.

Or he asked about Tom Winter: "What happened to him?"

"He went somewhere he shouldn't have gone."

This was ominous. "He traveled in time?"

"Yes."

"Is he still alive?"

"I don't know."

Brief questions, brief answers. Archer let it rest at that. He was trying to get a sense of who this person really was—how dangerous, how trustworthy. And he sensed Ben making similar judgments about him, perhaps in some more subtle or certain way.

Catherine didn't seem surprised by this. She let Archer sleep in her living room some nights; they ate dinner and breakfast together, talked about these strange events sometimes and sometimes not. Like Archer, she stopped by the Winter house every day or so. "We're like church deacons," Archer said. "Visiting the sick." And she answered, "That's what it feels like, doesn't it? How strange."

It was that, Archer thought. Very strange indeed. And the strangeness of it bolstered his courage. He remembered telling Tom Winter about this, his conviction that one day the clouds would open and rain frogs and marigolds over Belltower. (Or something like that.) And now, in a small way, that had happened, and it was a secret he shared only with Catherine Simmons and perhaps Tom Winter, wherever Tom had gone: absolute proof that the ordinary world wasn't ordinary at all . . . that Belltower itself was a kind of mass hallucination, a reassuring stage set erected over a wild, mutable landscape.

"But dangerous, too," Catherine objected when he told her this. "We don't really know. Something terrible happened to Ben. He was almost killed."

"Probably dangerous," Archer admitted. "You can get out of this if you want. Sell the house, move on back to Seattle. Most likely, you'll be perfectly safe."

She shook her head with a firmness he found charming. "I can't do that, Doug. It feels like a kind of contract. He asked me for help. Maybe I could have walked away then. But I didn't. I came back. It's like saying, Okay, I'll help."

"You *did* help."

"But not just carrying him back to the house. That's not all the help he needs. Don't you feel that?"

"Yes," Archer admitted. "I do feel that."

He let her fix him a meal of crab legs and salad. Archer hated crab legs—his mother used to buy cheap crab and lobster from a fishing boat down by the VFW outpost—but he smiled at the effort she made. He said, "You should let me cook for you sometime."

231

She nodded. "That would be nice. This is kind of weird, you know. We hardly know each other, but we're nursemaiding this—person out of a time machine."

"We know each other all right," Archer said. "It doesn't take that long. I'm a semi-fucked-up real estate agent living in this little town he kind of loves and kind of hates. You're a semisuccessful painter from Seattle who misses her grandmother because she never had much of a family. Neither of us knows what to do next and we're both lonelier than we want to admit. Does that about sum it up?"

"Not a bad call." She smiled a little forlornly and uncorked a bottle of wine.

The night after that she went to bed with him.

The bed was a creaky, pillared antique in what Catherine called the guest room, off the main hall upstairs. The sheets were old, thin, delicate, cool; the mattress rose around them like an ocean swell.

Catherine was shy and attentive. Archer was touched by her eagerness to please and did his best to return the favor. Archer had never much believed in one-night stands; great sex, like great anything, required a little learning. But Catherine was easy to know and they came together with what seemed like an old familiarity. It was, in any case, Archer thought, a hell of an introduction.

Now Catherine drifted to sleep beside him while Archer lay awake listening to the silence. It was quiet up here along the Post Road. Twice, he heard a car pass by outside—one of the locals, home late; or a tourist looking for the highway.

There were big questions that still needed answering, he thought. Archer thought about the word "time" and how strange and lonely it made him feel. When he was little his family used to drive down to his uncle's ranch outside Santa Fe in New Mexico, dirt roads and the Sangre de Cristo Mountains in the distance, scrub pines and sage brush and

232

ancient pueblos. The word "time" made him feel the way those desert roads used to make him feel: lost in something too big to comprehend. Time travel, Archer thought, must be like driving those roads. Strange rock formations and dust devils, and an empty blank horizon everywhere you look.

When he woke, Catherine was dressing herself self-consciously by the bed. He turned away politely while she pulled on her panties. Archer sometimes wondered whether there was something wrong with him, the doubtful way women always looked at him in the morning. But then he stood up and hugged her and he felt her relax in his arms. They were still friends after all.

But something was different today and it was not just that they had gone to bed last night. Something in this project was less miraculous now, more serious. They knew it without talking about it.

After breakfast they hiked down to the Winter house to visit Ben Collier.

The steaks from the Safeway had been doing him good. Ben was sitting up in bed this morning, the blankets pooled around his waist. He looked as cheerful as a Buddha, Archer thought. But it was obvious from the lie of the bedclothes that his leg was still missing.

Archer believed the stump was a little longer, though. It occurred to him that he *expected* the time traveler to grow a new leg—which apparently he was doing.

"Morning," Archer said. Catherine stood beside him, nodding, still a little frightened.

Ben turned his head. "Good morning. Thank you for coming by."

Archer began to deliver the speech he'd been rehearsing: "We really have to talk. Neither of us minds coming down here. But, Ben, it's confusing. Until we know what's really going on—"

233

Ben accepted this immediately and waved his hand: no need to continue. "I understand," he said. "I'll answer all your questions. And then—if you don't mind—I'll ask you one."

Archer said that sounded fair. Catherine brought in two chairs from the kitchen, on the assumption this might take a while.

☐ ☐

☐ ☐

"Who are you really," Archer asked, "and what are you doing here?"

Ben Collier wondered how to respond to this.

Confiding in these people was a radical step . . . but not entirely unprecedented, and unavoidable under the circumstances. He was prepared to trust them. The judgment was only partially intuitive; he had watched them through his own eyes and through the more discerning eyes of his cybernetics. They showed no sign of lying or attempting to manipulate him. Archer, in particular, seemed eager to help. They had weathered what must have been a frightening experience, and Ben credited that to their favor.

But they would need courage, too. And that quality was harder to judge.

He meant to answer their questions as honestly and thoroughly as he could. He owed them this, no matter what happened next. Catherine could have made things infinitely more difficult when she discovered him in the shed—if she had called the police, for instance. Instead, his recovery had been hastened by a significant margin. It would have been pointless and unkind to lie about himself.

He was born (he explained) in the year 2157, in a small town not far from the present-day site of Boulder, Colorado. He had lived there most of his professional life, doing research for a historical foundation.

All this begged the definition of "small town," of "professional life," and of "historical foundation" as these things would be understood by Archer and Catherine—but they were close enough to the truth.

Catherine said, "That's how you became a time traveler?"

He shook his head. "I was recruited. Catherine, if you visited the twenty-second century you would find a lot of marvelous things—but time travel is not among them. Any reputable physicist of my own era would have rejected the idea out of hand. Not the idea that time is essentially mutable and perhaps nonlinear, but the idea that it could be traversed by human beings. The water in the ocean is like the water in a swimming pool, but you can't swim across it. I was recruited by individuals from my own future, who were recruited by others from *their* future—and so on."

"Like stepping stones," Archer supplied.

"Essentially."

"But recruited for what?"

"Primarily, as a caretaker. To live in this house. To maintain it and protect it."

"Why?" Catherine asked, but he imagined she had already surmised the answer.

"Because this house is a sort of time machine."

"So you're not a real time traveler," Archer said. "I mean, you come from the future . . . but you're only a kind of employee."

"I suppose that's a good enough description."

"The machine in this building isn't working the way it's supposed to—am I right?"

He nodded.

"But if it was, and you were the custodian, who would come through here? Who are the *real* time travelers?"

This was a more serious question, more difficult to answer. "Most of the time, Doug, no one would come through. It's not a busy place. Mainly, I collect contemporary documents —books, newspapers, magazines—and pass them on."

"To whom?" Catherine asked.

"People from a time very distant from my own. They look human, but they aren't entirely. They created the tunnels— the time machines."

He wondered how much sense they would make of this. 'The *real* time travelers,' Archer had said: as good a description as any. Ben always trembled a little on the occasions when he was required to interact with these beings. They were kindly and only somewhat aloof; but one remained conscious of the evolutionary gulf. "Please understand, much of this is as far beyond my comprehension as it may be beyond yours. All I really know are legends, passed down by people like myself—other custodians, other caretakers. Legends of the future, you might say."

"Tell us some," Archer said.

What this concerns (Ben explained) is life on earth.

Look at it in the context of geologic time.

In the primeval solar system the earth is fused into coherent shape by the collisions of orbiting planetesimals. It has a molten core, a skin of cooler rock. It exudes gases and liquids —carbon dioxide, water. In time, it develops an atmosphere and oceans.

Over the course of millions of years, life of a sort arises as vermiform crystalline structures in the porous rock of hot mineral-dense undersea vents. In time, these crystalline structures adapt to a cooler environment by incorporating proteins into themselves—so successfully that the crystalline skeleton is discarded and purely proteinoid life comes to dominate the primitive biosphere. RNA and DNA are adopted as a genetic memory and evolution begins in earnest.

236

An almost infinite diversity of structures compete against the environment. There will never again be such complexity of life on earth—the rest of evolution is a narrowing, a winnowing out.

The climate changes. Prokaryotic cells poison the atmosphere with oxygen. Continents ride tectonic plates across the magma. Life flows and ebbs in the long intervals between cometary impacts.

Mankind arises. It turns out that mankind, like the grasses, like the flowering plants, is one of those species capable of transforming the planet itself. It alters the climatic balance and might well have drowned in its own waste products, except for an extraordinary new ability to modify itself and to create new forms of life. These are parallel and complementary technologies. Mankind, dying, learns to make machines in its own image. It learns to change itself in fundamental ways. The two capabilities combine to generate a new form of life, self-reproducing but only marginally biological. It can be called human because there is humanity in its lineage; it's the legitimate heir of mankind. But it's as different from mankind as crystalline life from the rocks it was born in, or protein life from the rocky structures that preceded it. These new creatures are almost infinitely adaptable; some of them live in the ocean, some of them live in outer space. In their diaspora they occupy most of the planets of the solar system. They are very successful. They begin to comprehend, and eventually manipulate, some fundamental constants of the physical universe. They visit the stars. They discover hidden structures in the fabric of duration and distance.

Ben paused, a little breathless. How long since these mysteries had been explained to him? Years, he thought—no matter how you measure it. "Catherine," he said, "would you open the window? There's a nice breeze outside." A little dazedly, she rolled back the blinds and lifted the window. "Thank you," Ben said. "Very pleasant."

Archer was frowning. "These 'new creatures,' these are the folks who travel in time?"

"Who built the machine that operates in this house, yes. You have to understand what time travel means, in this case. They discovered what might be called crevices in the structure of space and time—fractures, if you like, with a shape and duration outside the definable bounds of this universe but intersecting it at certain points. A 'time machine' is a sort of artificial tunnel following the contour of these crevices. In the local environment of the earth, a time machine can only take you certain places, at certain times. There are nodes of intersection. This house—an area surrounding it for some hundreds of yards—is one of those nodes."

Archer said, "Why here?"

"It's a meaningless question. The nodes are natural features, like mountains. There are nodes that intersect the crust of the earth under the ocean, nodes that might open in thin air."

"How many places like this are there, then?"

Ben shrugged. "I was never told. They tend to cluster, both in space and in time. The twentieth century is fairly rich in them. Not all of them are in use, of course. And remember: they have duration as well as location. A node might be accessible for twenty years, fifty years, a hundred years, and then vanish."

Catherine had been sitting in patient concentration. She said, "Let me understand this. People a long way in the future open a pathway to these nodes, yes?"

Ben nodded.

"But why? What do they use them for?"

"They use them judiciously for the purpose of historical reclamation. This century—and the next, and my own—are

238

the birthing time of their species. For them, it's the obscure and distant past."

"They're archeologists," Catherine interpreted.

"Archeologists and historians. Observers. They're careful not to intervene. The project has a duration for them, also. Time passes analogously at both ends of the link. They're conducting a two-hundred-year-long project to restore their knowledge of these critical centuries. When they're finished, they mean to dismantle the tunnels. They're nervous about the mathematics of paradox—it's a problem they don't want to deal with."

Catherine said, "Paradox?"

Archer said, "A time paradox. Like if you murder your own grandfather before you're born, do you still exist?"

She regarded him with some astonishment. "How do you know that?"

"I used to read a lot of science fiction."

Ben said, "I'm told there are tentative models. The problem isn't as overwhelming as it seems. But no one is anxious to put it to the test."

Archer said, "Even the presence of somebody from the future might have an effect. Even if they just crush a plant or step on a bug—"

Ben smiled. "The phenomenon isn't unique to time travel. In meteorology it's called 'sensitive dependence on original conditions.' The atmosphere is chaotic; a small event in one place might generate a large effect in another. Wave your hand in China and a storm might brew up in the Atlantic. Similarly, crush an aphid in 1880 and you might alter the presidential election of 1996. The analogy is good, Doug, but the connection isn't precisely causal. There are stable features in the atmosphere that tend to recur, no matter what—"

"Attractors," Archer supplied.

Ben was pleased. "You keep up with contemporary math?"

Archer grinned. "I try."

"I've been told there are similar structures in historical time—they tend to persist. But yes, the possibility for change exists. It's an observer phenomenon. The rule is that the present is always the present. The past is always fixed and immutable, the future is always indeterminate—no matter *where* you stand."

"From here," Archer said, "the year 1988 is unchangeable—"

"Because it's the past."

"But if I traveled three years back—"

"It would be the future, therefore unpredictable."

"But there's your paradox already," Archer said. "It doesn't make sense."

Ben nodded. He had struggled with this idea himself . . . then submitted to it, a Zen paradox which happened to be true and therefore inarguable. "It's the way time works," he said. "If it doesn't make sense, it's because you haven't made sense of it."

"You said there was a math for this?"

"So I'm told."

"You don't know it?"

"It's not twenty-second-century math. It's several millennia beyond that. I doubt you or I could contain it without a certain amount of neural augmentation."

Catherine said, "This is awfully abstract."

Archer nodded and seemed to struggle a moment with his thoughts.

Ben looked out the window. There was something wonderfully calming about all these Douglas firs. The sound they made when the wind moved through them.

Archer cleared his throat. "There's another obvious question."

The painful question. "You want to know what went wrong."

240

Archer nodded.

Ben sighed and took a breath. He didn't relish these memories.

He had reconstructed this from his own experience, from the fragmentary memories of the cybernetics, from the evidence of the tunnel itself.

There was a house like this house, he told Archer and Catherine, a temporal depot, in the latter half of the twenty-first century, in Florida—in those days a landscape of fierce tropical storms and civil war.

The custodian of that house was a woman named Ann Heath.

(Ann, he thought, I'm sorry this had to happen. You were kind when you recruited me and I never had a chance to repay that kindness. Time may be traversed but never mastered: the unexpected happens and in the long run we are all mortal.)

The Florida house had been scheduled for shutdown. Its environment was growing too unpredictable. But something unexpected happened prior to that closing. As nearly as Ben could deduce from the available clues, the house had been invaded by forces of the American government.

The house had possessed some defenses and so did Ann Heath, but perhaps these had been partially dismantled prior to shutdown; in any case, the soldiers of the grim last decades of that century were formidable indeed, with weapons and armor rooted deep into their bodies and nervous systems.

One of these men must have occupied the house, overpowered Ann, and forced her to reveal some of the secrets of the tunnel. The man had used this information to escape into the past.

(*She must be dead,* Ben thought. *They must have killed her.*)

The marauder had invaded Ben's domain without warning, disabled the cybernetics with an electromagnetic pulse, de-

241

stroyed much of Ben's body, and dumped his corpse in the woodshed. The attack had been quick and successful.

Then the marauder had opened a tunnel some thirty years long, to a nodal point in New York City, where he had committed the same sort of attack but more thoroughly; another custodian and all his cybernetics were irretrievably destroyed.

Finally—as a last, shrewd defense—the marauder had disabled the tunnel's controls so that the connection between Belltower and Manhattan was permanently open.

Catherine said, "Permanently open? Why is that such a great idea?"

Ben was lost a moment in temporal heuristics, then hit on a simple analogy: "Imagine the nodal points as terminals in a telephone network. Simultaneous connections are impossible. I can call a great number of destinations from one phone— but only one at a time. As long as the connection with Manhattan is open, no other connection can be made."

"The phone is off the hook," Catherine said, "at both ends."

"Exactly. He's sealed himself off. And us along with him."

"But a phone," Catherine said, "if it doesn't work, you can always go knock on the door. Somebody from another terminal somewhere else could have shown up and helped. Better yet, they could warn you. Leave a message in 1962: *In seventeen years, watch out for a bad guy.*"

Oh dear, Ben thought. "I don't want to get too deeply into fractal logistics, but it doesn't work like that. Look at it from the perspective of the deep future. Our time travelers own a single doorway; its duration governs duration in all the tunnels. From their point of view, Belltower 1979 and Manhattan 1952 disappeared simultaneously. Since that disappearance, approximately ten years have elapsed—here, and in the New York terminus, and in the future. And there are no overlapping destinations. The portal in this house was created in 1964, twenty-five years ago, when its valency point with Manhattan was the year 1937 . . . Are you following any of this?"

Catherine looked dazed. Archer said, "I think so . . . but you could still leave a message, seems to me. A warning of some kind."

"Conceivably. But the time travelers wouldn't, and the custodians have sworn not to. It would create a direct causal loop, possibly shutting down both terminals permanently."

" 'Possibly'?"

"No one really knows," Ben said. "The math is disturbing. No one wants to find out."

Archer shrugged: he didn't understand this, Ben interpreted, but he would take it on faith. "That's why nobody came to help. That's why the house was empty."

"Yes."

"But *you* survived."

"The cybernetics rebuilt me. It was a long process." He gestured at the stump of his leg under the blanket. "Not quite finished."

Catherine said, "You were out there for *ten years?*"

"I wasn't suffering, Catherine. I woke out of a long sleep, the day you opened the door."

"Then how do you know all this?"

This was easier to demonstrate than explain. He made a silent request and one of the cybernetics climbed the bedsheets and sat a moment in the palm of his hand—a glittering, many-legged jewel.

"My memory," he said.

"Oh," Catherine said. "I see."

□ □

□ □

This was an awful lot to accept all at once, Archer thought. Time as a fragmented structure, like sandstone, riddled with

243

crevices and caverns; twenty-first-century marauders; insect memories . . .

But Ben made it plausible. Plausible not because of his exoticisms—his strange injuries or his tiny robots—but because of his manner. Archer had no trouble at all believing this guy as a twenty-second-century academic recruited into an odd and secret business. Ben was calm, intelligent, and inspired trust. This could, of course, be a clever disguise. Maybe he was a Martian fifth columnist out to sabotage the planet—given recent events, it wouldn't be too surprising. But Archer's instinct was to trust the man.

Questions remained, however.

"Couple of things," Archer said. "If your marauder did such a thorough job at the Manhattan end, why did he screw up here?"

"He must have believed I was dead beyond reclamation. Probably he thought all the cybernetics were dead, too."

"Why not come back and check on that?"

"I don't know," Ben said. "But he may have been afraid of the tunnel."

"Why would he be?"

For the first time, Ben hesitated. "There are other . . . *presences* there," he said.

Archer wasn't sure he liked the sound of this. Presences? "I thought you said nobody could get through."

The time traveler paused, as if trying to assemble an answer.

"Time is a vastness," he said finally. "We tend to underestimate it. Think about the people who opened these tunnels—millennia in the future. That's an almost inconceivable landscape of time. But history didn't begin with them and it certainly didn't end with them. The fact is, when they created these passages they found them already inhabited."

"Inhabited by what?"

"Apparitions. Creatures who appear without warning, vanish without any apparent destination. Creatures not altogether material in constitution."

"From an even farther future," Archer said. "Is that what you mean?"

"Presumably. But no one really knows."

"Are they human? In any sense at all?"

"Doug, I don't know. I've heard speculation. They might be our ultimate heirs. Or something unrelated to us. They might exist—somehow; I find it difficult to imagine—outside our customary time and space. They seem to appear capriciously, but they may have some purpose, though no one knows what it is. Maybe they're the world's last anthropologists—collecting human history in some unimaginable sense. Or controlling it. Creating it." He shrugged. "Ultimately, they're indecipherable."

"The marauder might have seen one of these?"

"It's possible. They appear from time to time, without warning."

"Would that frighten him?"

"It might have. They're impressive creatures. And not always benign."

"Come again?"

"They almost always ignore people. But occasionally they'll take one."

Archer blinked. *"Take* one?"

"Abduct one? Eat one? The process is mysterious but quite complete. No body is left behind. In any case, it's very rare. I've seen these creatures and I've never felt threatened by them. But the marauder may have been told about this, maybe even witnessed it—I don't know. I'm only guessing."

Archer said, "This is very bizarre, Ben."

"Yes," Ben said. "I think so too."

Archer tried to collect his thoughts. "The last question—"

"Is about Tom."

Archer nodded.

"He discovered the tunnel," Ben said. "He used it. He should have known better."

"Is he still alive?"

"I don't know."

"One of these ghost things might have eaten him?"

Ben frowned. "I want to emphasize how unlikely that is. 'Ghost' is a good analogy. We call them that: time ghosts. They're seldom seen, even more seldom dangerous. No, the more present danger is from the marauder."

"Tom could be dead," Archer interpreted.

"He might be."

"Or in danger?"

"Very likely."

"And he doesn't know that—doesn't know anything about it."

"No," Ben said, "he doesn't."

□ □

□ □

This talk worried Catherine deeply.

She had accepted Ben Collier as a visitor from the future; as an explanation it worked as well as any other. But the future was supposed to be a sensible place—a *simplified* place, decorated in tasteful white; she had seen this on television. But the future Ben had described was vast, confusing, endless in its hierarchies of mutation. Nothing was certain and nothing lasted forever. It was scary, the idea of this chasm of impermanence yawning in front of her.

She was worried about Doug Archer, too.

He had crawled into her bed last night with the bashful eagerness of a puppy dog. Catherine accepted this as a gesture of friendship but worried about the consequences. She had not slept with very many men because she tended to care too much about them. She lacked the aptitude for casual sex. This was no doubt an advantage in the age of AIDS, but too often it forced her to choose between frustration and a commitment she didn't want or need. For instance, Archer: who was this man, really?

She stole a glance at him as he sat beside her, Levi's and messy hair and a strange little grin on his face, listening to Ben, the porcelain-white one-legged time traveler: Douglas Archer, somehow loving all this. Loving the *weirdness* of it.

She wanted to warn him. She wanted to say, *Listen to all these frightening words.* A renegade soldier from the twenty-first century, a tunnel populated with time ghosts who sometimes "take" people, a man named Tom Winter lost in the past . . .

But Doug was sitting here like a kid listening to some Rudyard Kipling story.

She looked at Ben Collier—at this man who had been dead for ten years and endured it with the equanimity of a CEO late for a meeting of his finance committee—and frowned.

He wants something from us, Catherine thought.

He won't demand anything. (She understood this.) He won't threaten us. He won't beg. He'll let us say no. He'll let us walk away. He'll thank us for all we've done, and he'll really mean it.

But Doug won't say no. Doug won't walk away.

She knew him that well, at least. Cared that much about him.

Doug was saying, "Maybe we should break for lunch." He looked at Ben speculatively. "How about you? We could fix up some of those steaks. Unless you prefer to eat 'em raw?"

"Thank you," Ben said, "but I don't take food in the customary fashion." He indicated his throat, his chest. "Still undergoing repairs."

"The steaks aren't for you?"

"Oh, they're for me. And thank you. But the cybernetics have to digest them first."

"Ick," Catherine said.

"I'm sorry if this is disturbing."

It was, but she shrugged. "They fed my aunt Lacey through a tube for two years before she died. This isn't any worse, I guess. But I'm sorry for you."

"Strictly temporary. And I'm not in any pain. You two have lunch if you like. I'm quite happy here."

"Okay," Catherine said. Meekly: "But I have a couple of questions of my own."

"Surely," Ben said.

"You told us you were a sort of custodian. A caretaker. You said you were 'recruited.' But I don't know what that means. Somebody knocked at your door and asked you to join up?"

"I was a professional historian, Catherine. A good one. I was approached by another caretaker, from my own near future, also a historian. Think of us as a guild. We recruit our own."

"That puts a lot of power in your hands." *Custodian* was a modest word, Catherine thought; maybe too modest.

"It has to be that way," Ben said. "The tunnel-builders are journeying into their own distant past. Their records of this time are sketchy; that's why they're here. The custodians act as their buffer in a sometimes hostile environment. We provide them with contemporary documents and we help to integrate them into contemporary culture on the rare occasions when they choose to make a physical visit. Could you, for instance, walk into a Cro-Magnon encampment and expect to pass for one of the tribe?"

"I see. You agreed to this?"

"When it was explained to me."

"Just like that?"

"Not without some soul-searching."

"But you must have had a life of your own. It must have meant giving something up."

"Not as much as you might think. I was old, Catherine. An old man. And longevity is something of an art in my time; I was more than a century old. And failing. And quite alone."

He said this with a wistfulness that made Catherine believe him. "They made you young again?"

"Passably young," Ben said. "Young enough to begin another life when I leave here."

"Are you allowed to do that?"

"I'm an employee, not a slave."

"So what you want," Catherine surmised, "is to fix up all this damage. Make the tunnel work again. And eventually go home."

"Yes."

"Is that possible? *Can* you fix it?"

"The cybernetics are repairing as much of the physical damage as they can. Then we can close the connection to Manhattan, isolate it until it can be repaired as well. But that will take some time. Weeks, at least."

"And until then," Catherine interpreted, "the problem is Tom Winter."

"He may be perfectly safe. He may not. The cybernetics tried to warn him, but they were working across a tremendous information barrier—I'm afraid they weren't very specific. He may have alerted the marauder, which puts us at risk; or he may do so if he hasn't yet."

Catherine bit her lip. Here was the crux of it. "You want us to bring him back."

Ben looked very solemn. "That may not be possible at this stage. The cybernetics can help, and they might provide some defense against the marauder, but the danger is obvious. I won't ask you to go—either of you."

You don't have to ask, Catherine thought sadly. She looked at Doug Archer and knew.

249

Archer grinned.

"Tom is a likable sonofabitch," he said. "I expect I can drag his ass back here."

Doug went to the kitchen, leaving Catherine alone with Ben.

She hesitated in the doorway, unnerved by Ben's expressionless patience. Finally she said, "Is this necessary? If you don't get Tom Winter back . . . would the world end?" She added, "Doug is risking his life, I think."

"I'll do everything I can to minimize the risk. Some risk remains. The world won't end if Tom Winter stays in Manhattan . . . but there might be other consequences I can't calculate." He paused. "Catherine, Doug knows the doorway is open. Do you think he'd stay away from it if I told him to?"

"No . . . I don't suppose he would." Catherine resented this but understood that it was true. "This way, at least he's serving a purpose. Is that it?"

"This way," Ben said, "he'll come back."

Fourteen

Tom slept for three hours and woke with Joyce beside him, already feeling as if he'd lost her.

He phoned Max to say he wouldn't be in. "Maybe I can come in Saturday to make up for it."

"Are you sick," Max inquired, "or are you jerking me around?"

"It's important, Max."

"At least you're not lying to me. *Very* important?"

"Very important."

"I hope so. This is bothersome."

"I'm sorry, Max."

"Take care of your trouble soon, please. You do nice work. I don't want to break in a new person."

The trouble wasn't Joyce. The trouble was in the space between them: that fragile connection, possibly broken.

She was asleep in bed, stretched out on her side with one hand cupping the pillow. The cotton sheet was tangled between her legs. Her glasses were on the orange crate next to the bed; she looked naked without them, defenseless, too young. Tom watched from the doorway, sipping coffee, until she uttered a small, unhappy moan and rolled over.

He couldn't begin to imagine what all this might mean to

her. First the interesting news item that the man she'd been living with was a visitor from the future . . . followed by an encounter with something strange and monstrous in a tunnel under the earth. These were experiences nobody was supposed to have. Maybe she would hate him for it. Maybe she ought to.

He was turning over these thoughts when she staggered out of the bedroom and pulled up a chair at the three-legged kitchen table. Tom filled her coffee cup and was relieved that the look she gave was nothing like hateful. She yawned and tucked her hair away from her shoulders. He said, "Are you hungry?" and she shook her head: "Oh, God. Food? Please, no."

Nothing hateful in the way she looked at him, Tom thought, but something new and disquieting: a bruised, wounded awe.

She sipped her coffee. She said she had a gig tonight at a coffeehouse called Mario's, "but I don't know if I can face it."

"Hell of a night," Tom observed.

She frowned into her cup. "It was all real, wasn't it? I keep thinking it was some kind of dream or hallucination. But it wasn't. We could go back to that place and it would still be there."

Tom said, "It would be. We shouldn't."

She said, "We have to talk."

He said, "I know."

They went out for breakfast in the late-morning sunlight and the hot July smell of road tar and sizzling concrete.

The city had changed, too, Tom thought, since last night.

It was a city lost in a well of time, magical and strange beyond knowing, subterranean, more legend than reality. He had come here from a world of disappointment and miscalculation; in its place he had discovered a pocket universe of optimists and cynical romantics—people like Joyce, like

252

Soderman, like Larry Millstein. They said they hated the world they lived in, but Tom knew better. They loved it with their outrage and their poetry. They loved it with the conviction of their own newness. They believed in a future they couldn't define, only sense—used words like "justice" and "beauty," words that betrayed their own fundamental optimism. They believed without shame in the possibility of love and in the power of truth. Even Lawrence Millstein believed in these things: Tom had found a carbon copy of one of his poems, abandoned by Joyce in a kitchen drawer; the word "tomorrow" had been printed with fierce pressure—*"Tomorrow like a father loves his weary children and gathers them up"* —and yes, Tom thought, you're one of them, Larry, brooding and bad tempered but singing the same song. And of all these people Joyce was the purest incarnation, her eyes focused plainly on the wickedness of the world but seeing beyond it into some kind of salvation, undiscovered, a submerged millennium rising like a sea creature into the light.

All in this hot, dirty, often dangerous and completely miraculous city, in this nautilus shell of lost events.

But I've changed that, Tom thought.

I've poisoned it.

He had poisoned the city with dailiness, poisoned it with boredom. The conclusion was inescapable: if he stayed here this would become merely the place where he lived, the morning paper and the evening news not miraculous but predictable, as ordinary as the moving of his bowels. His only consolation would be a panoramic, private window on the future, thirty years wide. And Joyce.

Consolation enough, Tom thought . . . unless he'd poisoned her, too.

He tried to remember what he'd said last night, a drunken recital of some basic history. Too much, maybe. He understood now what he should have understood then: that he wasn't giving her the future, he was stealing it. Stealing the wine of her optimism and leaving in its place the sour vinegar of his own disenchantment.

He ordered breakfast at a little egg and hamburger restaurant where the waitress, a tiny black woman named Mirabelle, knew their names. "You look tired," Mirabelle said. "Both of you."

"Coffee," Tom said. "And a couple of those Danishes."

"You don't need Danishes. You need something to build you up. You need aigs."

"Bring me an egg," Joyce said, "and I'll vomit."

"Just Danishes, then?"

"That'll be fine," Tom said. "Thank you."

Joyce said, "I want to be alone a little bit today."

"I can understand that."

"You're considerate," Joyce said. "You're a very considerate man, Tom. Is that a common thing where you come from?"

"Probably not common enough."

"Half the men around here are doing a Dylan Thomas thing—very horny and very drunk. They recite the most awful poetry, then get insulted if you don't go all weak-kneed and peel off your clothes."

"The other half?"

"Are lovable but queer. You're a nice change."

"Thank you."

"Something's bothering me, though."

"That's not surprising."

"Tom, I know why you lied to me. That part is understandable. And it wasn't even really lying—you just kept a few things to yourself. Because you didn't know whether I would understand. Well, that's fair."

He said, "Now you're being considerate."

"No, it's true. But what I don't understand is why you're here. I mean, if I found a hole in the ground with the year 1932 at the other end I would definitely check it out . . . but why would I want to *live* there? To catch a bunch of

254

Myrna Loy movies, chat with F. Scott Fitzgerald? Maybe get a real close look at Herbert Hoover? I mean, it would be absolutely fascinating, I'll grant you that. But I have a life." She shook her head. "I think it would be different if the tunnel ran the other way. I might be really tempted to jump a few decades down the road. But to take a giant step backward—that doesn't make a whole lot of sense."

She lit a cigarette. Tom watched the smoke swirl up past her eyes. She had asked an important question; she waited for his answer.

He was suddenly, desperately afraid that he might not have one—that there was nothing he could say to justify himself.

He said, "But if you *didn't* have a life . . . if you had a lousy, fucked-up life . . ."

"So is that how it was?"

"Yes, Joyce, that's pretty much how it was."

"Nineteen sixty-two as an alternative to suicide? That's a weird idea, Tom."

"It's a weird universe. The defense rests."

Mirabelle arrived with Danishes and coffee. Joyce pushed hers aside as if they were an irrelevancy or a distraction. She said, "Okay, but let me tell you what worries me."

Tom nodded.

"Back in Minneapolis I went out with a guy named Ray. Ray used to talk about World War Two all the time. We'd go to the movies and then sit at some cheap restaurant while he told me about Guadalcanal or the Battle of Midway. I mean *everything*, every detail—I can tell you more about Midway than you want to know. So after a while this began to seem kind of strange. One day I asked him how old he was when they dropped the bomb on Hiroshima. Ray says, 'I was twelve —almost thirteen.' I asked him how he came to know all this stuff about the war and he told me he got it from books and magazine articles. He was never in the army; he was four-F because of his allergies. But that was okay, he said, because there was nothing happening nowadays, nothing like the *real* war, not even Korea had been like that. He told me how great it must have been, guys risking their lives for a cause they really cared about. I asked him what he would have done if he'd had to invade Italy. He gave me a big smile and said, 'Shit, Joyce, I'd kill all the Nazis and make love to all the women.'"

She exhaled a long wisp of smoke. "My uncle was in Italy. He never talked about it. Whenever I asked him about the war, he got this really unpleasant expression. He'd stare at you until you shut up. So I knew this was basically bullshit. It kind of made me mad. If Ray wanted to live out some heroic existence, why not just do it? It wasn't even what you could honestly call nostalgia. He wanted some magic transformation, he wanted to live in a world where everything was bigger than life. I said, 'Why don't you *go* to Italy? I admit there's not a war on. But you could live on the beach, get drunk with the fishermen, fall in love with some little peasant girl.' He said, 'It's not the same. People aren't the same anymore.'"

Tom said, "Is this a true story?"

"Mostly true."

"The moral?"

"I thought about Ray last night. I thought, What if *he* found a tunnel? What if it led back to 1940?"

"He'd go to war," Tom said. "It wouldn't be what he expected, and he'd be scared and unhappy."

"Maybe. But maybe he'd love it. And I think that would be a lot more frightening, don't you? He'd be walking around with a permanent hard-on, because this was *history,* and he knew how it went. He'd be screwing those Italian girls, but it would be macabre, terrible—because in his own mind he'd be screwing *history.* He'd be fucking ghosts. I find that a little terrifying."

Tom discovered his mouth was dry. "You think that's what I'm doing?"

Joyce lowered her eyes. "I have to admit the possibility has crossed my mind."

He said he'd meet her after her gig at Mario's.

Alone, Tom felt the city around him like a headache. He could go to Lindner's—but he doubted he could focus his eyes on a radio chassis without passing out. Instead he rode a bus uptown and wandered for a time among the crowds on Fifth Avenue. On a perverse whim he followed a mob of tourists to the 102nd-floor observatory of the Empire State Building, where he stood in a daze of sleep-deprivation trying to name the landmarks he recognized—the Chrysler Building, Welfare Island—and placing a few that didn't yet exist, the World Trade Center still only a landfill site in the Hudson River. The building where he stood was thirty years old, approximately half as old as it would be in 1989 and that much closer to its art deco glory, a finer gloss on its Belgian marbles and limestone facades. The tourists were middle-aged or young couples with children, men in brown suits with crisp white shirts open at the collar, snapping photos with Kodak Brownies and dispensing dimes to their kids, who clustered around the ungainly pay-binoculars pretending to strafe lower Manhattan. These people spared an occasional glance for Tom, the unshaven man in a loose sweatshirt and denims: a beatnik, perhaps, or some other specimen of New York exotica. Tom looked at the city through wire-webbed windows.

The city was gray, smoky, vast, old, strange. The city was thirty years too young. The city was a fossil in amber, resurrected, mysterious life breathed into its pavements and awnings and Oldsmobiles. It was a city of ghosts.

Ghosts like Joyce.

He shaded his eyes against the fierce afternoon sun. Some-

257

where in this grid of stone and black shadow, he had fallen in love. This was certain knowledge and it took some of the sting from what Joyce had said. He wasn't fucking ghosts. But he might have fallen in love with one.

And maybe that was a mistake; maybe he'd be better off fucking ghosts. He tried to recall why he had come here and what he had expected. A playground: maybe she was right about that. The sixties—that fabled decade—had ended when he was eleven years old. He'd grown up believing he'd missed something important, although he was never sure what—it depended on who you talked to. A wonderful or terrible time. When the Vietnam War was fought in, or against. When drugs were good, or weren't. When sex was never lethal. A decade when "youth" was important; by the time of Tom's adolescence the word had lost some of its glamour.

Maybe he had expected all these wonders assembled together, served with a side of invulnerability and private wisdom. A vast phantom drama in which he was both audience and actor.

But Joyce had made that impossible.

He had come here wanting love—some salvaging grace—but love was impossible in the playground. Love was a different landscape. Love implied loss and time and vulnerability. Love made all the props and stage sets too real: real war, real death, real hopes invested in real lost causes.

Because he loved her he had begun to see the world the way she did: not the gaudy Kodachrome of an old postcard but solid, substantial, freighted with other meanings.

He raised his eyes to the horizon, where the hot city haze had begun to lift into a comfortless blue sky.

He bought dinner at a cafeteria and showed up at Mario's, a basement cafe under a bookstore, before Joyce was due on stage. The "stage," a platform of two-by-fours covered with

258

plywood panels, contained a cane-backed chair and a PA microphone on a rust-flecked chromium stand—not strictly necessary, given the size of the venue. Tom chose a table by the door.

Joyce emerged from the shadows with her twelve-string Hohner and a nervous smile. Out of some tic of vanity she had chosen to leave her glasses offstage, and Tom was mildly jealous: the only other time he saw her without her glasses was when they were in bed together. Without them, under the stage lights, her face was plain, oval, a little owl-eyed. She blinked at her audience and pulled the microphone closer to the chair.

She began without much confidence, letting the guitar carry her—more certain of her fingers than of her voice. Tom sat among the quieting crowd while she ran a few arpeggios and chord changes, pausing once to tune a string. He closed his eyes and appreciated the rich body of the Hohner.

"This is an old song," she said.

She sang "Fannerio," and Tom felt the piercing dissonance of time and time: here was this long-haired woman in a Village cafe playing folk ballads, an image he associated with faded Technicolor movies, record jackets abandoned at garage sales, moldering back issues of *Life*. It was a cliché and it was painfully naive. It was quaint.

But this was Joyce, and she loved these words and these tunes.

She sang "The Bells of Rhymney" and "Lonesome Traveler" and "Nine Hundred Miles." Her voice was direct, focused, and sometimes inconsolably sad.

Maybe Larry was right, Tom thought. We love them for their goodness, and then we scour it out of them.

What had he given her, after all?

A future she didn't want. A night of stark terror in a hole under Manhattan. A burden of unanswerable questions.

He had come into her life like a shadow, the Spirit of

Christmas Yet to Come, with his bony finger pointed at a grave.

He wanted her optimism and her intensity and her fierce caring, because he didn't have any of his own . . . because he had mislaid those things in his own inaccessible past.

She sang "Maid of Constant Sorrow" under a blue spot, alone on the tiny stage.

Tom thought about Barbara.

The applause was generous, a hat was passed, she waved and stepped back into the shadows. Tom circled around behind the stage, where she was latching the Hohner into its shell. Her face was somber.

She looked up. "The manager says Lawrence called."

"Called here?"

"Said he'd been trying to get hold of us all day. He wants us to go over to his apartment and it's supposed to be urgent."

What could be urgent? "Maybe he's drunk."

"Maybe. But it's not like him to phone here. I think we should go."

They walked from the cafe, Joyce hurrying ahead, obviously concerned. Tom was more puzzled than worried, but he let her set the pace.

They didn't waste any time. They arrived too late, anyhow.

There was a crowd in the stairwell, a siren in the distance —and blood, blood in the hallway and blood spilling from the door of Millstein's apartment, an astonishing amount of blood. Tom tried to hold Joyce back but she broke away from him, calling out Lawrence's name in a voice that was already mournful.

Fifteen

Armored, alert, and fully powered, Billy identified the scatter of blue luminescence on the apartment door and adjusted his eyepiece to wideband operation. His heart was beating inside him like a glorious machine and his thoughts were subtle and swift.

The corridor was empty. The keen apparatus of Billy's senses catalogued the smell of cabbage, roach powder, mildewed linoleum; the dim floral pattern of the wallpaper; the delicate tread and pressure of his feet along the floor.

He burned open the lock with a finger laser and moved through the doorway with a speed that caused the hinges to emit a squeal, as of surprise.

He closed the door behind him.

The apartment was long and rectangular, with a door open into what appeared to be the kitchen and another door, closed, on what was probably a bedroom. A window at the far end of the rectangle showed the night silhouette of the Fourteenth Street Con Edison stacks through a burlap curtain tied back to a nail. The wall on the left was lined with bookshelves.

The room was empty.

Billy stood for a silent moment, listening.

This room and the kitchen were empty . . . but he heard a faint scuffle from the bedroom.

He smiled and moved through that door as efficiently as he had moved through the first.

This room was smaller and even shabbier. The walls were dirty white and bare except for a crudely framed magazine print of an abstract painting. The bed was a mattress on the floor. There was a man in the bed.

Billy ceased smiling, because this wasn't the man he had followed from Lindner's.

This was some other man. This was a tall, pigeon-chested, naked man snatching a cotton sheet over himself and squinting at Billy in the darkness with gap-jawed astonishment.

The man on the mattress said, "Who the fuck are you?"

"Get up," Billy said.

The man didn't get up.

He doesn't know what I am, Billy realized. *He thinks I'm an old man in a pair of goggles. It's dark; he can't see very well. Maybe he thinks I'm a thief.*

Billy corrected this impression by burning a hole in the mattress beside the naked man's outstretched left arm. The hole was wide and deep. It stank of charred kapok and cotton and the waxy smoke of the wood floor underneath. The hole was black and began immediately to burn at the edges; the naked man yelped and smothered the flames with his blanket. Then he looked up at Billy, and Billy was pleased to recognize the fear in his eyes. This was the kind of fear that would make him abject, malleable; not yet a panicked fear that would make him unpredictable.

"Stand up," Billy repeated.

Standing, the man was tall but too thin. Billy disliked his fringe of beard, the bump of his ribs, the visible flare of his hip bones. His penis and shriveled scrotum dangled pathetically between his legs.

Billy imagined burning away that sack of flesh, altering this

262

man in something like the way the Infantry doctors had altered Billy himself . . . but that wasn't good strategy.

Billy said, "Where's the man who lives here?"

The naked man swallowed twice and said, "I'm the man who lives here."

Billy walked to the wall and switched on the light. The light was a sixty-watt bulb hanging on a knotted cord, smoke from the charred mattress swimming around it. Billy's eyepiece adapted at once to this new light, damping its amplification. The naked man blinked and squinted.

He stared at Billy. "My God," he said finally. "What *are* you?"

Billy knew the question was involuntary and didn't require an answer. He said, "Tell me your name."

"Lawrence Millstein," the naked man said.

"Do you work at a shop called Lindner's Radio Supply?"

"No."

This was true. Billy heard its trueness in the quaver of the man's voice; in the overtones of his terror.

"Do you live here alone?"

"Yes."

This was true, also.

"A man came here from Lindner's," Billy said. "Do you know a man who works at Lindner's?"

"No," Lawrence Millstein said.

But this was a lie, and Billy responded to it instantly: he narrowed the beam of his wrist weapon and used it to slice off the tip of Lawrence Millstein's left-hand index finger at the top knuckle. Millstein stood a moment in dumb incomprehension until the pain and the stink of his own charred flesh registered in his brain. He looked down at his wounded hand.

His knees folded and he sank back to the ruined mattress.

Billy said reproachfully, "You know the man I mean."

"Yes," Millstein gasped.

"Tell me about him," Billy said.

All this reminded Billy of that time long ago, in the future, in Florida, and of the woman who had died there.

Those memories welled up in him while he extracted Lawrence Millstein's confession.

Billy remembered the shard of glass and the woman's name, Ann Heath, and the way she had repeated it to herself, *Ann Heath Ann Heath,* with the blood on her face and throat and soaking the front of her shirt like a bright red bib.

He had come northwest from the ruins of Miami with his comrades Hallowell and Piper, a fierce storm on their heels. Cut out of their platoon in an ambush, they had retreated in the face of superior fire through a maze of suburban plexes and windowless pillbox dwellings whipped by a torrent of wild ocean air, the barometer low and falling. The night was illuminated by arcs of lightning along the eastern horizon, where a wall of cloud rotated around the fierce vacuum of its core. They ran and didn't much speak. They had given up hope of finding friendly territory—they wanted only some space between themselves and the insurgency before they were driven to shelter.

Billy had grown used to the wind like a fist at his back by the time they saw the house.

It was a house much like all the other houses on this littered empty street, a low bunker of the type advertised as "weatherproof" after the first disasters in the Zone. Of course, it wasn't. But its roof was intact and the walls seemed secure and defensible and it must have survived a great many storms relatively intact. It was whole; that was what drew Billy's attention.

Most of these buildings were empty, but there was always the possibility of squatters; so Brother Hallowell, a tall man and thick-chested under his armor, vaulted a chain fence and circled to the back while Billy and Brother Piper launched a concussion weapon through the narrow watch slot next to the door. Billy grinned as the door whooshed open and white smoke billowed out into the rain. He stepped inside and felt his eyepiece adjust to the darkness; he pulled a pocket extinguisher from his belt and doused the burning carpet. Brother Piper said, "I'll do the back door for Brother Hallowell," and started for the rear of the house while Billy sealed the front against the gusting rain, thinking how good it would be to be dry for a night . . . but then things turned strange very quickly. Brother Piper began shouting something incomprehensible, Brother Hallowell thumped at the rear door, while machine bugs came pouring out of the walls, out of hiding places in the plasterboard, from crates and boxes Billy had mistaken for squatters' refuse—thousands of glistening jewel-like creatures Billy could only dimly identify as mechanical. Brother Piper screamed as they swarmed up his legs. Billy had heard of Brazilian weapons imported by the insurgents, tiny poisonous robots the size of centipedes, and he reached by instinct for the machine-killer on his belt: a pulse bomb the size of a walnut, which he triggered and tossed against the far wall; it exploded without much concussion but with a burst of electromagnetic radiation strong enough to overload anything close. Even Billy's armor, which was hardened against such pulses, seemed to hesitate and grow heavy; his eyepiece dimmed and read him nonsense numbers for a long second. When his vision cleared the machine bugs were silent and motionless. Brother Piper was shaking them off his leg in a wild dance. Then Brother Hallowell, who was their CO, came through a doorway from the back and said, "What the fuck? I had to dump two pulses just to get in here and I put a third downstairs—this place has a big cellar. Brother Billy, do you know what these little bugs are?"

Billy was the youngest but he read a lot; Piper and Hallowell always asked him questions like that. This time he was stumped. "Sir, I don't," Billy said.

Brother Hallowell shrugged and said, "Well, we walked into something peculiar for sure. You know there's a lady in the next room?"

Billy was reluctant to take a step forward; he didn't relish the sound of the machine bugs crunching under his feet. "A lady?"

"That's right," Brother Hallowell said, "but your concussion grenade just about took her out, Brother Billy. She has a wedge of plate glass in her head. She's not dead, and her eyes are open, but—well, come look."

Billy was dazed but his armor kept him functioning. Even Brother Piper was beginning to calm down. The elytra came back up to full function and Billy felt as if his blood had cooled by two or three degrees. Maybe this place was a weapons dump; maybe they'd get a commendation for discovering it. This was a pleasant idea but Billy disbelieved it even as he thought it—the machine bugs were too strange a product even for the Brazilian ordinance makers.

He followed Brother Hallowell to the next room, where the woman lay slumped in a corner between two boxes. The concussion grenade had slivered a glass dividing wall and driven one long green-tinted wedge into the woman's head between her right ear and her right eye. There was blood, but not as much as Billy had expected. The sight of this young woman with the shank of plate glass projecting from her cranium like a ghastly party hat took Billy strangely; he reached down to touch the glass—a gesture of awe—and as he touched it the woman blinked and gasped . . . not in pain, Billy thought, but as if the tremor of his touch had ignited some pleasant memory, long forgotten. She looked up at Billy with one eye, the left. The right eye, bloodshot, gazed indifferently at some vision not physically present.

"What's your name?" Billy asked.

"Ann Heath," the woman said plainly.

"Back off now." Billy stepped away as Brother Hallowell took a medical package out of his pack and selected a cardiovascular unit. He tore away the woman's shirt, then clamped the wound unit between her breasts. When he switched it on Billy heard the hemotropic tubes crunch into Ann Heath's body, a terrible sound. "Oh," she said calmly, as the wound unit began to regulate her breathing. Now she wouldn't die even if her heart and lungs gave out, though she still might become comatose. Billy understood the purpose of this maneuver: to keep her interrogatable for a little while longer.

Brother Hallowell gave the machine a moment to stabilize, then bent down over Ann Heath. "Ma'am," he said, "can you tell me exactly what this place is?"

Ann Heath responded obediently, as if the shard of glass had severed the part of her brain governing caution and left only obedience:

"A time machine," she said.

Brother Hallowell looked almost comically perplexed. "A *what?*"

"A time machine," Ann Heath said. The cardiovascular machine put a tremor in her voice, as if she had a bad case of the hiccups.

Brother Hallowell sighed. "She's scrambled," he said. "She's brain dead." He straightened and flexed his back. "Brother Billy, will you interrogate the prisoner? See if you can get anything coherent out of her. Meanwhile Brother Piper and I will reconnoiter and try to get some power going."

Wind rocked the building. Billy sat down next to the injured woman and pretended not to see the wedge of green glass in her head. He waited until Brother Hallowell and Brother Piper had left the room.

Ann Heath didn't look like a liar to him. In her condition, Billy thought, it might not be possible to tell a lie.

He said, "Is this building really a time machine?"

"There's a tunnel in the basement," Ann Heath said, tonelessly, except for the hiccupping.

"Where does it go?" Billy asked.

"The future," she said. "Or the past."

"Tell me about it," Billy said.

The storm penned them in the house for two days. Ann Heath grew steadily less intelligible; but in that time, while Brother Hallowell and Brother Piper were cleaning their armor, or heating rations over the building's thermopump, or playing card games, Billy did as he was told: he interrogated the prisoner. He explained to Piper and Hallowell that she was incoherent but he hoped she might still say something useful. Piper and Hallowell didn't really care what she said. They had swept aside the dead machine bugs and seemed to have written them off as some Storm Zone aberration, something the research corps might be interested in—later. Neither Piper nor Hallowell enjoyed mysteries. Nor did Billy; but Billy believed what Ann Heath told him.

What Ann Heath told him was a catalogue of miracles. She told it without passion and with great clarity, as if a door had come unlocked in her head, the answers to Billy's questions spilling out like hoarded treasure.

Late on the third night of their occupation, while the storm plucked at the edges of the house and Brother Hallowell and Brother Piper dozed in the placid heat of their armor, Billy took Ann Heath down to the basement. Ann Heath couldn't walk by herself, the left side of her body curling out from under her as if the joints wouldn't lock, so Billy put an arm around her and half carried her, getting his hands all bloody on the mess of her shirt. He was disappointed by the basement, because it was as plain a cell as the upstairs rooms —no miracles here that he could see. Billy had retained the edge of his skepticism throughout this interrogation and the

268

basement seemed to confirm all his doubts. But then she showed him the control panel set into the blank wall, invisible until she spoke a word in a language Billy didn't recognize; then he held his own hand against the panel while she spoke more words until the panel knew Billy's touch. She taught him which words to say to operate the machine, and Billy and his armor memorized the peculiar sounds. Then her head dropped and she started to drool and Billy put a pillow of wadded rags behind her so she could sleep—if this was sleeping—while the cardiovascular unit bumped steadily against her breastbone. Billy opened the tunnel—it appeared at once, white and miraculous, his final assurance that these miracles were genuine—then he closed it again. Ann Heath had told him how she was getting ready to close this tunnel forever, and Billy wondered what it would have been like if he and Brother Piper and Brother Hallowell had passed by this place and found some other shelter: he would never have guessed, never imagined, lived out his life never knowing about tunnels between time and time. He thought about this and about Ohio and about the Infantry and how much he hated it. He thought about his armor; then he powered his armor up and moved upstairs to the place where Brother Piper and Brother Hallowell were sleeping, and he put his gloved hand down close to Brother Piper's exposed head and beamed a smoky corridor through Brother Piper's skull, then turned and did the same to Brother Hallowell before he was altogether awake; then he ran back downstairs, hurrying because he was afraid this peculiar, mutinous courage might evaporate and leave him weeping.

He paused to bend over Ann Heath. Ann Heath was awake again and followed him with her one bright eye. Billy said, "Are you suffering?" and she answered in her toneless, bleak voice, "Yes." Billy said, "Would you rather be alive or dead?" And when she answered, "Dead," he did her the way he'd done Piper and Hallowell, but looking away, so he wouldn't see the wedge of bloody glass fused into the new wound he'd made.

The cardiovascular machine faltered as her blood volume dropped. Billy turned off the machine before he left.

He remembered that bleak room, sitting in this one with Lawrence Millstein.

Billy had remembered a lot recently. Sometimes the memories came flooding out of him, a river mysterious in its source. Maybe he was getting old. Maybe some flaw in the armor (or in himself) allowed these freshets of remembrance. He had never been a particularly good soldier; he was what the infantry doctors had called an "anomalous subject," prone to unpredictable chemistries and odd neural interactions. Most soldiers loved their armor, and so did Billy, but he loved it the way an addict loves his addiction: profoundly, bitterly.

He extracted from Lawrence Millstein the address of the apartment where his prey—Tom Winter—lived.

He considered going there directly, but the sun had come up now and the morning streets were fiercely bright. He looked through Lawrence Millstein's back window over a landscape of iron fire escapes, across the enclosed courtyard where a gutted TV set glittered like a bottle washed up from the sea. Billy was fully armored now and it would be hard to move in daylight without drawing attention.

But he was comfortable here . . . at least for a while.

Lawrence Millstein had wrapped a wad of toilet paper around the stump of his finger. He sat in a chair staring at Billy. He had not stopped staring at Billy since the moment Billy switched on the bedroom light. "It's going to be a hot day," Billy said, watching Millstein flinch at the sound of his voice. "A scorcher."

Millstein didn't venture a response.

"It gets hot where I come from," Billy said. "We had sum-

270

mers that made this look like Christmas. Not so humid, though."

In a voice that sounded uncomfortably like Ann Heath's voice, Lawrence Millstein said, "Where do you come from?"

"Ohio," Billy said.

"There's nothing like you in Ohio," Millstein said.

"You're right." Billy smiled. "I live in the wind. I'm not even born yet."

Lawrence Millstein, who was a poet, seemed to accept this.

An hour passed while Billy contemplated his options. Finally he said, "Do you know his number?"

Millstein was weary and not paying attention. "What?"

"His telephone number. Tom Winter."

Millstein hesitated.

"Don't lie to me again," Billy cautioned.

"Yes. I can call him."

"Then do that," Billy said.

Millstein repeated, "What?"

"Call him. Tell him to come over. He's been here before. Tell him you need to talk to him."

"Why?"

"So I can kill him," Billy said irritably.

"You evil son of a bitch," Millstein said. "I can't invite him to his death."

"Consider the alternative," Billy suggested.

Millstein did so, and seemed to wither before Billy's eyes. He cradled his wounded hand against his chest and rocked back and forth, back and forth.

"Pick up the phone," Billy said.

Millstein picked up the receiver and braced it against his shoulder while he dialed the number. Billy calculated the number and memorized it, listening to the clatter of the dial each time it spun home. He was a little surprised Millstein was actually doing this; he'd guessed the odds were fifty-fifty that Millstein would refuse and Billy would have to kill him. Millstein held the receiver to his ear, breathing in little sobs, eyes half shut, then hung up the phone with a triumphant slam. "Nobody's home!"

"That's all right," Billy said. "We'll try again later."

Billy's prediction was correct: the day was long and hot.

He opened the tiny window but the trickle of air it admitted was syrupy and stank of gasoline. Billy's armor kept him cool, but Lawrence Millstein turned pale and began to sweat. The sweat ran down his face in glossy rivulets and Billy told him to drink some water before he fainted.

Sunset came late and Billy began to grow impatient. He felt the pressure of the armor; if he didn't take some action soon he would have to power down. When he was up too long he grew edgy, nervous, a little unstable. He looked at Lawrence Millstein and frowned.

Millstein hadn't moved from his chair all day. He sat upright by the phone, and every time he called Tom Winter's apartment Billy pictured Millstein as Ann Heath, the wedge of glass driven in a little deeper with every number he dialed. Millstein was pretty much a wreck.

Billy thought about this.

He said, "Does Tom Winter live alone?"

Millstein regarded him with a dread so familiar it had become tiresome.

"No," Millstein said faintly.

"Lives with a woman?"

"Yes."

"Do you know where *she* might be?"

The silence now was protracted.

"You could call her and just leave a message," Billy suggested. "It wouldn't be hard."

"She might come here with him," Millstein said, and Billy

recognized this as a prelude to capitulation. Not that there was any question of it, really.

"I don't care about her," Billy said.

Millstein trembled as he picked up the phone.

It should have gone easily after that and Billy wasn't sure why it didn't: some flicker of his attention, maybe, or of the armor's.

He waited with Lawrence Millstein through the long evening after sunset, while the air through the window turned cooler and the apartment filled with shadows. He listened to the sound of voices from the courtyard. Not far away, a man was shouting in Spanish. A baby was crying. A phonograph played *La Traviata*.

Billy was distracted a moment by the lonesome sound of the music and by the stirring of the burlap curtains in the breeze. This was a kind of paradise, he thought, this old building where people lived without fighting over rice and corn, where nobody came and took children away and put them in golden armor. He wondered if Lawrence Millstein knew about living in paradise.

Then there was a knock at the door.

Billy turned, but Lawrence Millstein was already standing up, shouting.

He shouted, *"No! Oh, fuck, Joyce, go away!"*

Then Billy killed him. The door opened and a woman stood outlined in the light from the hallway, a huge brown-complexioned woman in a flower-print dress; she peered into the dark apartment through thick lenses. "Lawrence?" she said. "It's Nettie—from next door!"

Billy killed Nettie with his wrist beam, but his hand shook and the beam cut not neatly but like a ragged knife, so that the blood went everywhere, and Nettie made a noise that

273

sounded like "Woof!" and fell back against the faded wall-paper.

Then the hallway was full of voices and distress and although Billy had soothed his armor with these killings he knew his real business would have to wait.

Sixteen

A woman in the crowd tugged Joyce away from the doorway, away from the bodies. Tom understood by the look on her face that Lawrence was inside and that Lawrence was dead.

His first impulse was to comfort her. But the crush of tenants held him back, and the sirens were closer now . . . He edged down the stairwell and out to the sidewalk. He couldn't allow himself to be questioned even casually, with a wallet full of ID from the future and no one to vouch for him but Joyce.

A crowd formed around him as the police cruisers pulled up. Tom stood discreetly back among them. He watched the cops erect a barricade; he watched two medics hustle from an ambulance into the building, then stroll out moments later to stand under a streetlight, smoking and laughing. The red rotary lights on the police cars made the street ominous and bleak. Tom stood a long time even after the crowd began to thin, waiting.

There was a hush when the bodies came out: two amorphous shapes under blankets.

Joyce emerged a little after that, a fat man in a brown suit escorting her toward an unmarked car. The fat man, Tom guessed, was a police detective. He must have asked her whether she knew either of the victims; *yes,* she would have said, *that one* . . . She would cooperate because she'd want to help find the killer.

But Tom knew by the way she looked at him, and then away, that she was confused about his role in all this.

A confusion he shared. Not that he might have committed the crime but that Millstein's death might be connected somehow with his time-traveling. Too many possibilities, Tom thought. A world that contained doorways between decades might contain almost anything else . . . Any kind of evil monster might have tracked him to Millstein's apartment.

The police cruisers began to pull away from the curb; the crowd dispersed. A raft of cloud had moved across the sky from the northwest and the night was suddenly cooler. A wind whipped around the corner from Avenue B.

Rain before morning, Tom thought.

He thought about the walk back to the apartment, dangerous in these night streets.

He felt a hand on his shoulder . . . and spun around, startled, expecting a cop or something worse, and was shocked again:

"Hey, Tom," Doug Archer said. "We have to get out of here."

Tom took a step back and drew a deep breath. Yes, anything was possible. Yes, this was Doug Archer, from Belltower in the state of Washington at the end of the 1980s, as incongruous in this dirty street as a Greek amphora or an Egyptian urn.

Doug Archer, who seemed to have some idea what was going on. Now *there's* a neat trick, Tom thought.

He managed, "How did you find me?"

"Long story." Archer tilted his head as if he were listening to something. "Tom, we have to leave *now*. We can talk in the car. Please?"

276

Tom took a last look at the building where Lawrence Millstein had died. An ambulance pulled away from the curb, headed uptown. Joyce was gone.

He nodded.

Archer drew an oversize Avis keytag out of his pocket.

Tom felt but didn't understand the urgency as Archer hustled him into a boxy rental Ford and pulled away from the curb. The heat had broken and the rain came down in a sudden, gusty wash. Dawn was still hours away.

They drove to an all-night deli in the Village and ducked inside.

"A man was killed," Tom said. He was still trying to grasp the fact of Millstein's death. "Somebody I knew. Somebody I got drunk with."

"Could have been you," Archer said. "You're lucky it wasn't." He added, "That's why we have to go home."

Tom shook his head. He felt too weary to frame a reasonable response. He looked at Archer across the table: Doug Archer in a crewcut and a starched shirt and black leather shoes, his sneakers presumably abandoned in 1989. "How do you know all this?" Millstein dead and Doug Archer in the street outside: not a coincidence. "I mean, what are you *doing* here?"

"I owe you an explanation," Archer said. "I sure as hell hope we have time for it."

An hour ticked by on the wall clock while Archer told him about Ben Collier, the time-traveling custodian.

Much of what Archer told him was barely plausible. Tom believed it, however. He had been numbed to the miraculous a long time ago.

At the end of it he cradled his head on his hands and struggled to put this information into some kind of order. "You came here to take me back?"

"I can't 'take' you anywhere. But yeah, I think it would be the wise thing to do."

"Because of this so-called marauder."

"He knows about you and he obviously means to kill you."

It was a hypothetical threat; Tom was impatient. "The tunnel was intact when I moved into the house on the Post Road. He could have walked in and killed me in my sleep, if he exists . . . if he's still alive. I was in danger then, I'm in danger now—what's the difference? As long as he can't find me—"

"But he *can* find you! Jesus, Tom, he very nearly *did* find you—*tonight.*"

"You think he's the one who killed Lawrence?" Tom was dazed enough to be startled by the idea.

"It would be fucking near suicidal," Archer said, "to doubt it."

"It's a supposition—"

"It's a fact, Tom. He was *there*. He was close by when I found you. Another five minutes, ten minutes, the street empties out, you turn down some alley, he would have had a clean shot at you."

"You can't know that."

"Well, but, that's the thing. I can."

Tom looked blank, felt apprehensive.

"Simple," Archer said. "This guy took out three temporal depots, each one stocked with machine bugs eager to defend it. He killed the cybernetics with an EM pulse weapon. His armor was hardened against the pulse and the machine bugs weren't. Hardly any cybernetics survived—unless they were also protected by his armor."

"How could that be?"

"They were in the air he was breathing. Little bitty ones the size of a virus—you know about those?"

278

"I know about those," Tom allowed. "But if they're inside him, how come they can't stop him?"

"They're like drones without a hive. They're lost and they don't have instructions. But they send out a little narrow-bandwidth data squirt, a sort of homing signal. I can pick up on that."

"You can?"

Archer turned to display a plug in one ear, something like a miniaturized hearing aid. "Ben had his cybernetics whip this up for me. I can tell when he's inside a radius of eight, nine hundred yards . . . reception permitting. You too, by the way."

"They're inside *me?*"

"Completely benign. Don't get your shorts in a knot, Tom. Maybe they saved your life. I drove around Manhattan for three days, Battery Park to Washington Heights, on the off chance I'd come within range." He cocked his head. "You sound kind of like a telephone. A dial tone. The marauder sounds more like a dentist's drill."

"You're telling me he was there at Larry Millstein's apartment building."

"That's why I was in such an all-fired hurry to leave."

"He must have known I was coming."

"I suppose so. But—"

"No," Tom said. "Let me think about this."

It was hard to think at all. If Archer was correct, he had been standing a few yards away from a man who wanted to murder him. Who had murdered Millstein. And if the marauder had been waiting for him, had known he was coming, then Millstein must have cooperated with the marauder.

They had hurried to the apartment because Millstein phoned Joyce at Mario's.

The marauder knew about Mario's. The marauder knew about Tom. Maybe the marauder knew his address. Certainly the marauder knew about Joyce.

Who had left with a cop. Who might be headed home by now. Where the marauder might be waiting.

Tom spilled his coffee, standing up.

Archer tried to soothe him. "What they'll likely do is question her as long as she's willing to sit still. She's probably giving a statement to some sleepy cop as we speak. Safe and sound."

Tom hoped so. But how long would she be willing to answer questions?

She might have a few questions of her own.

He couldn't erase his memory of the hallway outside Lawrence Millstein's door. All that blood.

"Drive me home," he told Archer. "We'll meet her there."

Archer raised his eyebrows at the word "home" but fumbled in his pocket for the keys.

They drove into the narrow streets of the Lower East Side. The city looked abandoned, Tom thought, pavements and storefronts glazed with rain and steam rising out of the sewers. "Here," he said, and Archer pulled up at the curb outside the building.

The rain was loud on the roof of this old car.

Tom reached for the door handle; Archer put a hand on his wrist.

Tom said, "Is he near here?"

"I don't think so. But he could be around a corner, half a block away. Listen, what if she's not home?"

"Then we wait for her."

"How long?"

Tom shrugged.

"And if she *is* here?"

"We take her with us."

"What—back to Belltower?"

"She'll be safe there . . . safer, anyhow."

"Tom, I don't know if that's a real good idea."

He opened the door. "I don't have a better one."

• • • •

He rang the buzzer.

Nobody answered. Then he climbed the stairs—these old, dirty boards complaining under his feet. It must be four A.M., Tom calculated. The light from the incandescent bulb over the landing was stale and fierce.

He opened the door and knew at once the apartment was empty.

He switched on the lights. Joyce wasn't home and he guessed—prayed—she hadn't been. Nothing had been disturbed since this morning. Two coffee cups stood on the kitchen table, brown puddles inside. He walked into the bedroom. The bed was unmade. The rain beat against the window, a lonesome sound.

Yesterday's paper lay open on the arm of the sofa, and Tom regarded it with a stab of longing: if he could step back even a day he could turn this around, keep Joyce safe, maybe even keep Lawrence Millstein alive—he would have a handle on what was happening.

But the thought was ludicrous. Hadn't he proved that already? My God, here he was armed with nearly thirty years of foresight and he couldn't even help *himself*. It had all been a dream. A dream about something called "the past," a fiction; it didn't exist. Nothing was predictable, nothing played the same way twice, every certainty dissolved at the touch.

History was a place where dramas were played out on a ghost stage, the way Joyce's old boyfriend had imagined D-day. But that's not true, Tom thought. This was history: an address, a locality, a place where people lived. History was this room. Not emblematic, merely specific; merely this vacant space, which he had come to love.

He thought about Barbara, who had never much cared about the past but had longed for the future . . . the uncreated future in which there were no certainties, only possibilities.

Everywhere the same, Tom thought. 1962 or 1862 or 2062. Every acre of the world littered with bones and hope.

He was indescribably tired.

He stepped into the hallway and sealed the apartment, which had contained a fair portion of his happiness, but which was empty now. He would be better off waiting with Doug in the car.

He was leaving the building when a taxi pulled up at the curb.

He watched Joyce pay the driver and step out into the rain.

Her clothes were instantly wet and her hair matted against her forehead. Her eyes were obscure behind rain-fogged lenses.

It was raining when they met, Tom recalled, a couple of months ago in the park. She had looked different then. Less tired. Less frightened.

She regarded him warily, then crossed the pavement.

He touched her wet shoulders.

She hesitated, then came into his arms.

"He was dead, Tom," she said. "He was just lying there dead."

"I know."

"Oh, God. I need to sleep. I need to sleep a long, long time."

She moved toward the lobby; he restrained her with his hands. "Joyce, you can't. It's not safe in there."

She pulled away. He felt a sudden tension in her body, as if she were bracing herself for some new horror. "What are you talking about?"

"The thing—the man who killed Lawrence—I believe he meant to kill me. He must know about this place by now."

"I don't *understand* this." She balled her fists. "What are you saying, that you know who killed Lawrence?"

"Joyce, it's too much to explain."

282

"He wasn't stabbed, Tom. He wasn't shot. He was burned open. It's indescribable. There was a big hole burned into him. Do you know about that?"

"We can talk when we've found a safe place."

"There's no end to this, is there? Oh, shit, Tom. I've seen *way* too much ugliness tonight. Don't tell me this shit. You don't have to go inside if you don't want to. But I need to sleep."

"Listen, listen to me. If you spend the night in that apartment you could come out like Lawrence. I don't want it to be that way but that's the way it is."

She looked at him fiercely . . . then her anger seemed to subside, swallowed up in an immense exhaustion. She might have been crying. Tom couldn't tell, with the rain and all.

She said, "I thought I loved you! I don't even know what you *are!*"

"Let me take you somewhere."

"What do you mean, somewhere?"

"A long way from here. I've got a car waiting and I've got a friend inside. Please, Joyce."

Archer put his head out the window of the Ford, shouting against the hiss of the rain—the words were unintelligible—then ducked back inside and revved the engine.

Tom felt his heart bump in his chest. He pulled Joyce toward the car.

She resisted and would have turned back, but a smoking gash opened in the concrete stoop a few inches from her hand. Tom looked at the blackened stone for a few dumb seconds before its significance registered. Some kind of weapon had done this: some kind of *ray gun.* This was ludicrous but quite terrifying. Archer leaned over the seat and jacked open the rear door of the car; Tom pushed Joyce toward it. She didn't push back this time but was too shocked to coordinate her legs. She tumbled inside with Tom behind her, a motion that seemed endless, and the rain came down on the metal roof with a sound like gunfire.

Archer lunged his rental Ford into the street before Tom could close the door. He committed a 180-degree turn that left V-shaped skids on the wet asphalt, tires shrieking.

As the car rotated Tom caught a glimpse of the man who had tried to kill him.

If "man" was the word.

Not human, Tom thought.

Or, if human, then buried under some apparatus, a snout-like headpiece, an old cloth coat humped across his back, oily in the rain and the glare of a streetlight.

His eyes were aimed at Tom through the rear window of the car. Nothing showed of his face except a wide, giddy smile . . . gone a moment later as Archer fishtailed the Ford around a corner.

They abandoned the car on a desolate street near Tompkins Square.

The sky seemed faintly brighter. The rain had slackened a little but the gutters were running and dark water dripped from the torn awning over the lobby of the tenement building which contained the tunnel.

Tom touched his shoulder, where a ferocious pain had just begun: a reflection or glancing shot from the marauder's weapon had blistered a wide patch of skin there.

The three of them stood a moment in the empty lobby.

Tom said, "The last time we came this way there was something in the tunnel—"

"A time ghost," Archer said. "They're not real dangerous. So I'm told."

Tom doubted this but let it pass. "Doug, what if he comes after us? There's nothing stopping him, is there?" He kept an arm around Joyce, who was dazed and passive against his shoulder.

"He might," Archer admitted. "But we know what to expect now. He can't take us by surprise. The house is a fortress; be prepared—you might not recognize it."

"This isn't over," Tom interpreted.

"No," Archer said. "It isn't over."

"Then we ought to hurry."

Tom led the way into the basement, over the heaped rubble and down an empty space into the future.

Seventeen

He slept for twelve hours in a bed he had never really thought of as his own and woke to find a strange woman gazing down at him.

At least, Tom thought, an *unfamiliar* woman—he had grown a little stingy with the word "strange."

She occupied a chair next to the bed, a paperback Silhouette romance in her hands; she put the book splayed open on the knee of her jeans. "You're awake," she said.

Barely. "Do I know you?"

"No—not yet. I'm your neighbor. Catherine Simmons. I live in the big house up by the highway."

He collected his thoughts. "Mrs. Simmons, the elderly woman—you're what, her granddaughter?"

"Right! You knew Gram Peggy?"

"Waved to her once or twice. Delivered her paper when I was twelve years old."

"She died in June . . . I came down to take care of business."

"Oh. I'm sorry."

He took a longer look around the room. Same room, same house, not much changed, at least this corner of it. He didn't remember arriving here. The shoulder wound had gone from painful to incapacitating and he had crossed the last fifty yards of the tunnel with his eyes squeezed shut and Doug Archer propping him up.

The shoulder felt better now . . . He didn't check for blisters but the pain was gone.

He focused his attention on Catherine Simmons. "I guess this isn't the business you meant to take care of."

"Doug and I sort of stumbled into it."

"I guess we all did." He sat up. "Is Joyce around?"

"I think she's watching TV. But you'll need to talk to Ben, I think."

He supposed he would. "The TV's working?"

"Oh, Ben was very apologetic about that. He says the cybernetics managed to scare you without warning you off. They were dealing with a situation way outside their expertise; they went about it all wrong. He made them fix the TV for you."

"That's very thoughtful of Ben."

"You'll like him. He's a nice guy." She hesitated. "You slept a long time . . . Are you sure you're all right?"

"My shoulder—but that's better now."

"You don't seem too pleased to be back."

"Friend of mine died," Tom said.

Catherine Simmons nodded. "I know how that is. Gram Peggy was pretty important in my life. It leaves a vacuum, doesn't it? Let me know if there's something I can do."

"You can bring me my clothes," Tom said.

He reminded himself that he had climbed back out of the well of time and that this was the summer of 1989—the last hot summer of a hot decade, hovering on the brink of a future he couldn't predict.

The house was a fortress, Archer had told him, and some of that showed in the living room: the furniture had been pushed back against the walls and the walls themselves were

287

covered with a mass of gemlike machine bugs. It looked like a suburban outpost of Aladdin's Cave.

Tom followed Catherine to the kitchen, where the machine bugs—a smaller mass of them—were dismantling the stove.

A man, evidently human, sat at the kitchen table. He stood up clumsily when Tom entered the room.

"This is Ben," Catherine said.

Ben the time traveler. Ben who had risen, like Lazarus, from the grave. Ben the custodian of this malfunctioning hole in the world.

He stood with one hand propped against a cane. His left leg was truncated, the denim tied shut between his knee and the place where his ankle should have been. He was pale and his hair was a faint, fine stubble over his scalp.

He offered his hand. Tom shook it.

"You're the time traveler," he said.

Ben Collier smiled. "Let's sit down, shall we? This leg is still awkward. Tom, would you like a beer? There's one in the refrigerator."

Tom wasn't thirsty. "You lived here ten years ago."

"That's right. Doug must have explained all that?"

"You were hurt and you were in that shed out in the woods. I think I owe you an apology. If I hadn't gone haring off down the tunnel—"

"Nothing you've done or haven't done is anybody's fault. If everything had been working correctly the house would never have been for sale. You walked into a major debacle; you didn't create it."

"Doug said you were—he used the word 'dead.' Buried out there for some years."

"Doug is more or less correct."

"It's hard to accept that."

"Is it? You seem to be doing all right."

"Well . . . I've swallowed a fair number of miracles since May; I suppose one more won't choke me."

He gave Ben a closer look. A ray of sunlight from the big back window had fallen across the time traveler and for a moment Tom imagined he saw the outline of the skull under the skin. An optical illusion. He hoped. "Maybe I'll have that beer after all. You want one?"

"No, thank you," Ben said.

Tom took a beer from the refrigerator and twisted off the cap. Welcome to the future: throw away that clumsy old bottle opener.

A stove grill clanked against the floor behind him and a brigade of machine bugs began hauling it toward the basement stairs.

Life, Tom thought, is *very* strange.

"They're using the metal," Ben explained. "Making more of themselves. It's hard on the appliances, but we're in fairly desperate straits at the moment."

"They can do that? Duplicate themselves?"

"With enough raw material, certainly."

"They're from the future," Tom said.

"Somewhat in advance of my own time, as a matter of fact. I found them a little repellent when I was introduced to the concept. But they're extremely useful and they're easy to conceal."

"They can repair the tunnel?"

"They're doing precisely that—among many other things."

"But you said we were in 'dire straits.' So nothing is repaired yet and this so-called marauder—"

"Might choose to follow you here. That's what we're on guard against, yes."

"But he hasn't tried it yet. Maybe he won't."

"Maybe. I hope not. We do have to take precautions."

Tom nodded; this was sensible. "How well protected are we?"

Ben seemed to ponder the question. "There's no doubt we can stop him. What troubles me is that it might take too long."

"I don't understand."

"From what I can reconstruct, the man is an armored conscript soldier, a renegade from the territorial wars at the end of the next century. In a sense, he isn't really our enemy—the enemy is his armor."

"I saw him in New York," Tom said. "He didn't look especially well armored."

"It's a kind of cybernetic armor, Tom. Thin, flexible, very sophisticated, very effective. It protects him from most conventional weapons and interacts with his body to improve his reflexes and focus his aggression. When he's wearing the armor, killing is an almost sexual imperative. He wants it and he can't help wanting it."

"Ugly."

"Much worse than ugly. But in a way, his strength is his weakness. Without the armor he's more or less helpless; he might not even be inclined to do us harm. The fact that he took advantage of the tunnel to flee the war suggests his loyalty isn't as automatic as his surgeons might have liked. If we can attack the armor we can neutralize the threat."

"Good," Tom said. He pulled at the beer. "Can we?"

"Yes, we can, in a couple of ways. Primarily, we've been building specialized cybernetics—tiny ones, the size of a virus. They can infiltrate his bloodstream and attack the armor . . . dismantle and disconnect it from the inside."

"Why didn't they do that in the first place?"

"These aren't the units he was exposed to. They've been built expressly for the purpose. He had the advantage of surprise; he doesn't have that anymore."

"So if he shows up here," Tom interpreted, "if he breathes the air—"

"The devices go to work instantly. But he won't simply fall

over and die. He'll be functional, or partly functional, for some time."

"How much time?"

"Unfortunately, it's impossible to calculate. Ten minutes? Half an hour? Long enough to do a great deal of damage."

Tom thought about it. "So we should leave the machine bugs and clear out of here. If he shows up, they can deal with him."

"Tom, you're welcome to do so if you like. I can't; I have an obligation to protect the premises and direct the repair work. Also, we have weapons that might slow down the marauder while the cybernetics work on him. It's important to keep him confined to the property. The machines inside him aren't entirely autonomous. They need direction from outside, and if he moves beyond a certain radius they'll lose the ability to communicate, might not be able to finish disarming him. He could cause a great deal of havoc if he wandered down to the highway."

No doubt that was true. "Doug and Catherine—"

"Have volunteered to help. They're armed and they know what to do if an alarm sounds."

He asked the central question: "What about Joyce?"

"Joyce is making a difficult adjustment. She's endured a great deal. But she volunteered her help as soon as she understood the situation."

"Might as well make it unanimous," Tom said.

He found Joyce in the back yard, in a lawn chair, reading the Seattle paper in the shade of the tall pines.

It was a cool day for August; there was a nice breeze bearing in from the west. The air carried the smell of pine sap, of the distant ocean, a faint and bitter echo of the pulp mill. Tom stood a moment, savoring all this, not wanting to disturb her.

He wondered what the headlines were. This wasn't precisely the present, not exactly the future; he had come here by a twisted path, a road too complex to make linear sense. Maybe some new country had been invaded, some new oil tanker breached.

She looked up from the editorial page and saw him watching her. He came the rest of the way across the lawn.

She was an anachronism in her harlequin glasses and straight hair, beautiful in the shade of these tall trees.

Before he could frame a sentence she said, "I'm sorry about the way I behaved. I was tired and I was sick about Lawrence and I didn't know how you were involved. Ben explained all that. And thank you for bringing me here."

"Not as far out of danger as I thought it would be."

"Far enough. I'm not worried. How's your shoulder?"

"Pretty much okay. Enjoying the news?"

"Convincing myself it's real. I watched a little TV, too. That satellite news station, what's it called? CNN." She folded the paper and stood up. "Tom, can we walk somewhere? The woods are pretty—Doug said there were trails."

"Is it a good idea to leave the house?"

"Ben said it would be all right."

"I know a place," Tom said.

He took her up the path Doug Archer had shown him some months ago, past the overgrown woodshed—its door standing open and a cloud of gnats hanging inside—up this hillside to the open, rocky space where the land sloped away to the sea.

The sea drew a line of horizon out beyond Belltower and the plume of the mill. In the stillness of the afternoon Tom heard the chatter of starlings as they wheeled overhead, the rattle of a truck out on the highway.

Joyce sat hugging her knees on a promontory of rock. "It's pretty up here."

He nodded. "Long way from the news." Long way from

1962. Long way from New York City. "How does the future strike you?"

The question wasn't as casual as it sounded. She answered slowly, thoughtfully. "Not as gee-whiz as I expected. Uglier than I thought it would be. Poorer. Meaner. More short-sighted, more selfish, more desperate."

Tom nodded.

She frowned into the sunlight. "More *the same* than I thought it would be."

"That's about it," Tom said.

"But not as bad as it looks."

"No?"

She shook her head vigorously. "I talked to Ben about this. Things are changing. He says there's amazing things happening in Europe. The next couple of decades are going to be fairly wild."

Tom doubted it. He had watched Tiananmen Square on television that spring. Big tanks. Fragile people.

"Everything is changing," Joyce insisted. "Politics, the environment—the weather. He says we happen to be living on the only continent where complacency is still possible, and only for a while longer. That's our misfortune."

"I suppose it is. What did he tell you, that the future is some kind of paradise?"

"No, no. The problems are huge, scary." She looked up, brushed her hair out of her eyes. "The man who killed Lawrence, he's the future too. All the horrible things. Conscription and famine and stupid little wars."

"That's what we have to look forward to?"

"Maybe. Not necessarily. Ben comes from a time that looks back on all that as a kind of insanity. But the point is, Tom, it's the future—it hasn't happened yet and maybe it doesn't have to, at least not that way."

"Not logical, Joyce. The marauder came from somewhere. We can't wish him out of existence."

"He's a fact," Joyce conceded. "But Ben says anyone who travels into the past risks losing the place he left. Ben himself. If things happen differently he might be orphaned—might go home and find out it's not there anymore, at least not the way he remembers it. It's not *likely,* but it's *possible.*"

"So the future is unknowable."

"I think the future is something like a big building in the fog—you know it's there, and you can grope your way toward it, but you can't be sure about it until it's close enough to touch."

"Leaves us kind of in the dark," Tom observed.

"The place you stand is always the present and that's all you ever really have—I don't think that's a bad thing. Ben says the only way you can own the past is by respecting it—by not turning it into something quaint or laughable or pastel or bittersweet. It's a real place where real people live. And the future is real because we're building it out of real hours and real days."

No world out of the world, Tom thought.

No Eden, no Utopia, only what you can touch and the touching of it.

He took her hand. She gazed across the pine tops and the distant town site toward the sea. "I can't stay here," she said. "I have to go back."

"I don't know if I can go with you."

"I don't know if I want you to."

She stood up and was beautiful, Tom thought, with the afternoon sun on her hair.

"Hey," she said. "Don't look at me like that. It's just me. Just some fucked-up chick from Minneapolis. Nothing special."

He shook his head, was mute.

"I was a ghost for you," she said. "Ghost of some idea about what life used to be like or could be like or what you wanted from it. But I'm not that. But that's okay. Maybe you were a ghost too. Ghost of whatever I thought I'd find in the city. Somebody mysterious, wise, a little wild. Well, the circumstances are very strange. But here we are, Joyce and Tom, a couple of pretty ordinary people."

"Not all that damn ordinary."

"We hardly know each other."

"Could change that."

"I don't know," Joyce said. "I'm not so sure."

These last few hours—before the marauder attacked, or the time machine was repaired, whichever apocalypse happened first—were a kind of Indian summer.

Archer drove to the Burger King out along the highway and brought home dinner. They ate on the back lawn in the long sunlight; the alarms would sound, Ben said, if anything happened inside.

Ben, who didn't eat prepared food, was an avuncular presence at the edge of the feast, periodically hobbling over to the redwood fence where he had marked a long rectangular patch with string. It was too late in the year to start a garden, he said, but this was where one ought to be. Tom wondered, but didn't ask, whether he planned to start one in the coming year or expected someone else to.

After dark, Archer took Tom down into the basement—what remained of the basement. The false wall in front of the tunnel had been removed entirely, and so had one of the foundation walls—revealing a layer of what must be machinery, pale white and blue crystals swarming with cybernetics. This was the functional heart of the time terminal and the machine insects, he assumed, were repairing it. Periodically, bright sparks erupted from the work.

"We're running a race," Archer said. "The longer that sonofabitch in Manhattan sits on his hands, the closer we come to shutting him out entirely."

"How long until all this is finished?"

"Soon, Ben says. Maybe by this time tomorrow. Here—" He opened a drawer under the workbench: Tom's wood-working bench, the one he'd moved from Seattle. "Ben said you should have one of these."

Archer handed him a ray gun.

No doubt about it, Tom thought, this was a ray gun. It weighed about a pound. It was made of red and black poly-styrene plastic and the words SPACE SOLDIER were stenciled on the side.

He looked at the gun, looked at Archer.

"We had to make 'em out of something," Archer said. "I picked up a bunch of these at the K-mart at Pinetree Mall. The machine bugs worked them over."

The trigger was made of what looked like stainless steel, and the business end featured a glassy protrusion too finely machined to match the rest of the toy. "You're telling me this is functional?"

"It projects a focused pulse that might or might not slow down the gentleman's armor a little bit. Use it but don't de-pend on it. We all have one."

"Jesus Christ, Doug. SPACE SOLDIER?"

Archer grinned. "Looks kind of cool, don't you think?"

Back upstairs, the sun was setting over the ocean and Cath-erine had turned on the living room lights.

Tom helped Archer collect the dinner plates from the back yard. The sky was a deep evening blue; the stars and the crickets had come out.

Archer hesitated a moment in the cooling air.

"Everything's going to be different when this is over," he said. "Suddenly we're out of the picture. Bystanders. But we did something rare, didn't we, Tom? Took a long stroll into

296

the past. Imagine that. I stood on those streets, nineteen sixty-two, Jesus, I was a toddler down at Pine Balm Pre-School! Hey, Tom, you know what we did? We walked straight up to Father Time and we kicked that miserly SOB right in the family jewels."

Tom opened the screen door and stepped back into the warmth of the kitchen. "Let's hope he doesn't return the favor."

Archer and Catherine shared a mattress in the spare bedroom. Ben spent the night in the basement—slept there, if he slept at all.

Joyce had spent two nights on the living room sofa. She came into Tom's bed tonight with what he took to be a mixture of gratitude and doubt.

When he rolled to face her she didn't turn away.

It was a warm night in the summer of 1989, skies clear over most of the continent, oceans calm, the world on some brink, Tom thought, not yet explicit, a trembling of possibilities both dire and bright. Her skin was soft under his touch and she took his kiss with an eagerness that might have been greeting or farewell.

Midnight passed in the darkness, an hour and another.

They were asleep when the alarms went off.

Eighteen

Amos Shank, eighty-one years old, who had come from Pittsburgh to publish his poetry and who had lived for fifteen years amid the stained plaster and peeling wallpaper of this shabby apartment, rose from his bed in the deep of the night, still wrapped in dreams of Zeus and Napoleon, for the purpose of relieving his bladder.

He walked to the bathroom, past his desk, past reams of bond paper, sharpened pencils, leatherbound books, in the stark light of two sixty-watt floor lamps which he kept perpetually lit. The rattle of water in the porcelain bowl sounded hollow and sinister: the clarion call of mortality. Sighing, Amos hitched up his boxer shorts and headed back to his bed, which folded out of the sofa, convolution of night inside day. He paused at the window.

Once he had seen Death in the street outside. A sudden dread possessed him that if he looked he would see that apparition again. He had, in fact, kept vigil for several consecutive nights—ruining his sleep to no good effect. He was torn between temptations: oblivion, vision.

He slatted the blinds open and peered into the street.

Empty street.

Amos Shank pulled his desk chair to the window and nestled his bony rear end into it.

The older he got the more his bones seemed to protrude from his body. Everything uncomfortable. Nowhere to rest. He whistled out a long breath of midnight air and put his head on the windowsill, pillowed on his hands.

Without meaning to, he slept again . . .

And woke, aching and stiff. He moaned and peered into the street where—perhaps—the sound of footsteps had roused him: because here *he* was again, Death.

No mistaking him.

Amos felt his heart speed up.

Death walked down the empty sidewalk in a dirty gray overcoat; paused and smiled up at Amos.

Smiled through his leathery snout and the hood of his shirt.

Then Death did a remarkable thing: he began to undress.

He shrugged off the overcoat and dropped it in the gutter like a shed skin. Pulled the NYU sweatshirt over his head and threw it away. Stepped out of the pants.

Death was quite golden underneath.

Death shone very brightly under the streetlights.

"I know you!" Amos Shank said. He was only dimly aware that he had said it aloud. *"I know you—!"*

He had seen the picture. Which old book?

Wars of Antiquity. The Court of the Sun King. Campaigns of Napoleon. Some ancient soldier in bright armor and cheap lithography.

"Agamemnon," Amos Shank breathed.

Agamemnon, Death, the soldier, masked and armored, entered the building, still smiling.

Ashamed, Amos Shank double-checked the lock on the door, extinguished the lights for the first time in a month, and hid under the blankets of his bed.

Nineteen

Billy entered the tunnel with his armor fully powered and most of his fears behind him.

He had lived too long with fear. He'd been running from things he couldn't escape. This visitation from the future was punishment, Billy thought, for a life lived in exile.

After he killed Lawrence Millstein, after a failed attempt on his legitimate prey, Billy had retired for two days to his apartment; had powered down, hidden his armor, retreated to the shadows. Two days had been enough. He didn't feel safe. There was no security anymore, no anonymity . . . and the Need was deep and intense.

So he took the armor out of its box and wore it with all its armaments and accessories here, to the source of his trouble, this unpatrolled border with the future.

Where his prey had retreated—he knew that by the tangle of footprints amid the rubble.

Here we begin some reckoning, Billy thought. The beginning or the end of something.

He stepped through fallen masonry into the bright and sourceless light of the time machine.

Fear had kept him out of this tunnel for years: fear of what he'd seen here.

The memory was vivid of that apparition, huge and luminous. It had moved slowly but Billy felt its capacity for speed; had seemed immaterial but Billy felt its power. He had escaped it by a hairbreadth and was left with the impression that it had *allowed* him to escape; that he had been evaluated and passed over by something as potent and irresistible as time itself.

Now—under the bravado of his armor, the courage pumped out by the artificial gland in the elytra—that fear remained fresh and intact.

Billy pressed on regardless. The corridor was empty. Here in the depth of it, both exits out of sight, he felt suspended in a pure geometry, a curvature without meaningful dimension.

Beyond these walls, Billy thought, years were tumbling like leaves in a windstorm. Age devoured youth, spines curved, eyes dimmed, coffins leapt into the earth. Wars flashed past, as brief and violent as thunderstorms. Here, Billy was sheltered from all that.

Wasn't that all he had ever really wanted?

Shelter. A way home.

But these were vagrant, treasonous thoughts. Billy suppressed them and hurried ahead.

The cybernetics had entered the tunnel as a fine dust of polymers and metal and long, fragile molecules. They began to infiltrate Billy almost at once.

Billy was unaware of it. Billy simply breathed. The nanomechanisms, small as viruses, were absorbed into his bloodstream through the moist fabric of his lungs. As their numbers increased to critical levels, they commenced their work.

To the cybernetics Billy was a vast and intricate territory, a continent. They were isolated at first, a few pioneers colonizing this perilous hinterland along rivers of blood. They read the chemical language of Billy's hormones and responded with faint chemical messages of their own. They crossed the difficult barrier between blood and brain. They clustered, increasingly numerous, at the interface of flesh and armor.

Billy inhaled a thousand machines with every breath.

The exit loomed ahead of him now, an open doorway into the year 1989.

Billy hurried toward it. He had already begun to sense that something was wrong.

Twenty

Tom was out of bed as soon as the alarm registered. Joyce reached the door ahead of him.

The machine bugs had assembled these alarms from a trio of hardware-store smoke detectors. The noise was shrill, penetrating. Tom and Joyce had slept in their clothes in anticipation of this; but the actual event, like a fire or an air raid, seemed unanticipated and utterly unreal. Tom stopped to fumble for his watch, working to recall what Ben had told him: *If the alarm sounds, take your weapon and go to the perimeter of the property,* but mainly he followed Joyce, who was waving impatiently from the door.

They hurried through the dark of the living room, through the kitchen and out into a blaze of light: fifteen sodium-vapor security lights installed in the back yard, also courtesy of Home Hardware.

Beyond the lights, in the high brush and damp ferns at the verge of the forest, he crouched with Joyce—and Doug and Catherine, who had beaten them out of the house.

The alarms ceased abruptly. Cricket calls revived in the dark of the woods. Tom felt the racing of his own pulse.

The house was starkly bright among pine silhouettes and a scatter of stars. A night breeze moved in the treetops. Tom

303

flexed his toes among the loamy, damp pine needles: his feet were bare.

He looked around. "Where's Ben?"

"Inside," Archer said. "Listen, we should spread out a little bit . . . cover more territory."

Archer playing space soldier. But it wasn't a game. "This is it, isn't it?"

Archer flashed him a nervous grin. "The main event."

Tom turned to the house in time to see the windows explode.

Glass showered over the lawn, a glittering arc in the glare of the lights.

He took a step back into the shelter of the woods. He felt Joyce do the same.

But there was no real retreating.

Here was the axis of events, the absolute present, Tom thought, and nothing to do but embrace it.

Twenty-one

Ben stood calmly in the concussion of the grenade. It was an EM pulse grenade, less useful to the marauder than it had been; the cybernetics were hardened against it. The blast traveled up the stairway from the basement and exploded the windows behind him. Ben felt the concussion as a rush of warm air and a pressure in his ears. He stood with his back to the door, braced on his one good leg, watching the stairs.

He didn't doubt that the marauder could kill him. The marauder had killed him once and was quite capable of doing so again—perhaps irreparably. But he wasn't afraid of death. He had experienced, at least, its peripheries: a cold place, lonesome, deep, but not especially frightening. He was afraid of leaving his life behind . . . but even that fear was less profound than he'd expected.

He'd left behind a great many things already. He had left his life in the future. He had buried the woman he had lived with for thirty years, long before he dreamed the existence of fractal, knitted time. He wasn't a stranger to loss or abandonment.

He had been recruited at the end of a life he'd come to terms with: maybe that was a requirement. The time travelers had seemed to know that about him. Ben recalled their cool, unwavering eyes. They appeared in human form as a

305

courtesy to their custodians; but Ben had sensed the strangeness under the disguise. Our descendants, he had thought, yes, our *children,* in a very real sense . . . but removed from us across such an inconceivable ocean of years.

He listened for the sound of footsteps up the stairs. He hoped Catherine Simmons and the others had deployed outside the house . . . fervently hoped they wouldn't be needed. He had volunteered to defend this outpost; they had not, except informally and in a condition of awe.

But the nanomechanisms were already doing their work, deep in the body of the marauder: Ben felt them doing it.

Felt them as the marauder came up the carpeted stairs. Ben watched him come. The marauder moved slowly. His eyepiece tracked Ben with oiled precision.

He was an amazing sight. Ben had studied the civil wars of the twenty-first century, had seen this man before, knew what to expect; he was impressed in spite of all that. The hybridization of man and mechanism was mankind's future, but here was a sterile mutation: a mutual parasitism imposed from without. The armor was not an enhancement but a cruel prosthetic. Infantry doctors had rendered this man incapable of unassisted pleasure, made his daily life a gray counterfeit, linked every appetite to combat.

The marauder, not tall but quite golden, came to the top of the stairs with small swift movements. Then he did a remarkable thing:

He stumbled.

Dropped to one knee, looked up.

Ben felt the nanomechanisms laboring inside this man. Vital connections severed, relays heating, redundancies overwhelmed . . . "Tell me your name," Ben said gently.

"Billy Gargullo," the marauder said, and fired a beam weapon from his wrist.

But the marauder was slow and Ben, augmented, anticipated the move and ducked away.

306

He fired his own weapon. The focused pulse, invisible, seemed to pull Billy Gargullo forward and down; his armor clenched around him like a fist. He toppled, convulsed once . . . then used his momentum as the armor relaxed to swing his arm forward.

This was a gesture Ben had *not* anticipated. He dodged the beam weapon but not quickly enough; it cut a charred canyon across his abdomen.

Ben dropped and rolled to extinguish his burning clothing, then discovered he couldn't sit up. He had been cut nearly in half.

Precious moments ticked away. Ben felt his awareness ebb. A wave of cybernetics poured out from the walls, covered the wound, sealed it; severed arteries closed from within. For a brief and unsustainable moment his blood pressure rose to something like normal; his vision cleared.

Ben pushed himself up on his elbows and fumbled for his weapon.

He found it, raised it . . .

But Billy had left the room.

Twenty-two

By the time he reached the foot of the basement stairs Billy assumed he was dying.

He knew his armor was crumbling away, somehow, inside him. His eyepiece displayed bright red numerals and emergency diagnostics. He felt cut loose from himself, afloat, hovering over his own body like a bird.

This was very sudden, very strange, unmistakably hostile. He didn't let it slow him down.

He came up the stairs still operational but awash in strange emotions: vivid lightnings of panic; blue threads of guilt. Billy was coherent enough to understand that he'd walked into a trap; that his prey, the time traveler, someone, had interfered with his armor. There was a perpetual high-pitched keening in his ears and the diagnostics in his eyepiece read him a catalogue of major and minor malfunctions. So far, the gland in the elytra was still pumping—though fitfully—and his weapons were functional. But he was vulnerable and he was slow and before long he might be altogether helpless.

None of this affected Billy's resolve. Sensing his panic, Billy's armor flushed potent new molecules into his blood. The killing urge, which had seemed so powerful in the past, blossomed into something new and even more intense: an agony of necessity.

308

At the top of the stairs he faced a man he had killed once before, a time traveler. Billy didn't question this resurrection, merely resolved to kill the man again, to kill him as often as necessary. Some momentary fluctuation caused him to topple forward; he fell, looked up, and the time traveler asked him his name. Billy answered without thinking, startled by the sound of his own voice.

Then he raised his wrist weapon. But the chaos inside him had made him slow and the time traveler was able to aim and fire his own weapon, a beam device that seemed to lock Billy's armor into a momentary rictus, so that Billy toppled forward in a parody of movement, like a statue tumbling off a pedestal.

He didn't waste time regretting his vulnerability; only waited for it to pass. As soon as his arm was mobile he brought it up and forward with all the precision his failing neural augmentation was able to calculate and burned open the time traveler's belly.

The result was impressive. The walls seemed to crumble. Machine bugs rivered across the carpet. A stab of primitive revulsion made Billy leap to his feet and back away. He detonated another pulse grenade—his last—and it slowed the bugs but didn't stop them.

Detonated aboveground, the pulse did have a profound effect on the local electrical grid. The houselights flickered and dimmed, brightened and flickered again. Down the length of the Post Road, three different families would wake to find their television sets fused and useless. In a dozen homes in the east end of Belltower groggy individuals stumbled out of bed to pick up ringing telephones, nothing on the other end but an ominous basso hum.

The cybernetics churned around the body of the fallen time traveler—healing him or devouring him. Billy didn't know which, didn't care.

Dying, Billy hurried for the door.

Twenty-three

Tom had circled to the front of the house when the last intact window—north wall, master bedroom—was blown out by a second concussion.

The floodlights dimmed, brightened, dimmed again. So did the streetlights down along the Post Road.

He cut through the front yard and across the open width of the road to the gully on the far side. Ben was supposed to be covering the front door of the house; but it had occurred to Tom that Ben was not an impenetrable barrier and that the front door was handy to the basement stairs. He left Doug out back with Joyce and Catherine and prayed the three of them would be safe there.

The shock of being roused out of a deep sleep had nearly worn off. He was as awake now as he had ever been, clear-headed and frightened and acutely aware of his own peculiar position: barefoot and carrying a SPACE SOLDIER ray gun from K-mart, modified. Every window in his house had been blown out and he was tempted to reconsider the logic of this adventure. What kept him moving was Joyce—her vulnerability overriding his own—and the single glimpse he had caught of the marauder in an empty street in Manhattan. Those eyes had contained too many deaths, including Lawrence Millstein's. Eyes not vengeful or even passionate, Tom thought; the look had been passive, the distracted stare of a bus passenger on a long ride through familiar territory. Tom had not especially liked Lawrence Millstein, but it hurt to think that Millstein's last sight had been that leathery muzzle, those thousand-mile eyes.

He's already dying, Tom thought. Dying or being dismantled from inside. All we have to do is slow him down.

He was thinking this when the front door opened, spilling light down the gravel driveway and across the road.

Tom ducked into the roadside ditch opposite his front yard.

For the space of three breaths he pressed his face into the wet grass and dewy spiderwebs, no thought possible beyond the panicky need *not to be seen,* to make himself small among the Queen Anne's lace and goldenrod, small in the starlight, let this apparition pass him by.

Then he took a fourth and deeper breath and raised his head.

The marauder walked out of the house with the queasy deliberation of a drunk. One step, two step, three step. Then he tottered and fell.

Tom rose into a crouch with the zap gun ready. The marauder was obviously disabled but probably still dangerous. But Ben: where was Ben? A thread of blue smoke rose from the open doorway past the moth-cluttered light . . . Something bad had happened in there.

He chose a Douglas fir growing in the wild lot south of his property as good cover and began a spring back across the Post Road, still crouched, a posture he'd seen on TV: supposed to make him a smaller target though that didn't seem likely under the circumstances. He had just cleared the gravel margin of the road and felt blacktop under the soles of his feet when the marauder began to move and Tom did a stupid thing in response: turned to watch. He didn't stop running but he slowed down. Couldn't help it. This was some kind of

311

spectacle, this golden man lifting himself to one knee, like a Byzantine icon come creaking to life, like some upscale version of the Tin Man in *The Wizard of Oz,* now standing up, bent back straightening, head swiveling in sudden oiled motion. Tom didn't begin to feel appropriately terrified until those eyes lit on him.

Even in the starlight, the dim glow of a streetlight down the Post Road, dear God, he thought, those eyes! Maybe not even the eyes, Tom thought, just some reflection or refraction in the goggles, the *illusion* of eyes, but he felt pinned by them, trapped here on the tarmac.

The marauder raised his hand, a casual gesture.

Tom remembered his own weapon. He raised it, felt himself raising it, and it was like hoisting an anchor from the bottom of the sea, cranking it up through the weight of the water link by agonizing link. Why was everything so *slow?* He realized he'd never fired this device, not even once, as an experiment; that he had thumbed back the little switch marked Safety without being absolutely sure it was part of the weapon and not part of the toy. There were questions he had neglected to ask: questions about range, for instance; was the weapon effective from this distance?

But there was only time to commit an approximation of aim and pull the trigger. Showdown on the Post Road. Some part of him insisted that the whole thing was too ludicrous to take seriously. Only dreams were conducted like this.

He was hit before he could finish. His shot went wide.

The marauder's shot had gone a little wide, too, a stitch of flame from Tom's hip to his armpit and across the biceps of his left arm. There was no impact, only a sudden numbness and the alarming realization that his clothes were on fire. He fell down without meaning to. Rolled like a dog in the dirt at the verge of the Post Road until the flames were extinguished, though this provoked the first stab of a deep, paralyzing pain.

What kind of burns? First degree? Third degree? He looked down at himself. Under the ashen shirt was a peninsula of charred and blackened skin. He closed his eyes and decided he wouldn't look at the wound again because the sight of that blistered flesh was too scary, not useful.

He felt a little drunk now, a little dizzy.

He hauled himself up with his good arm and looked for the marauder. The marauder had fallen down, too. Tom's shot had missed but the encounter had slowed him. That's why I'm here, Tom recalled. Slow him down so the machine bugs can work inside him. Maybe he was already dead.

It was a faint hope, extinguished at once.

The marauder stood up.

There was some kind of heroism in the act, Tom thought. It was a faltering, tormented motion that reeked of malfunction, of stripped gears, overheated engines, buckled metal. The marauder stood up and moved his head as if the goggles had clouded, a querulous and birdlike gesture. Then he stripped off the headpiece and looked at Tom.

Tom couldn't discern much of his features in the dim light, but it seemed to him this was even worse than the mask had been, the revelation of a human face underneath. With what expression on it? Something like despair, Tom thought. He felt a dizzy urge to call time-out. I'm hurt. You're hurt. Let's quit.

But the marauder took aim, a little raggedly, with his deadly right hand.

Oh shit, Tom thought. What happened to my *gun?*

He'd left it in the road.

Inadequate lump of polystyrene and impossibility. It hadn't done him much good anyhow. It was yards away. The yards might have been miles.

The marauder aimed but held his fire, advancing from Tom's gravel driveway in a crippled but steady lope. If I

313

move, Tom thought, he'll kill me. If I go for the gun or roll into the gully, he'll kill me. And if I stay here—he'll kill me.

He had pretty much decided to go for the gun anyhow, count on surprise and the work of the cybernetics to give him a chance against that deadly right hand—when the miraculous event occurred.

The miracle was heralded by a light.

The light made strange, wide shadows on the pines and the shadows swayed like something huge and alive. Then he heard the sound of the engine, the sound of a car coming down the Post Road from the highway, high beams probing the slow curve south of the Simmons house.

The car was traveling fast.

Tom turned toward it as the marauder did. The lights were blinding. Tom took the opportunity to pitch himself left, into the ditch at the side of the road. He put his head up and saw the marauder dodge toward him as the car seemed at first to veer away . . . Then tires squealed against blacktop, the car swerved again, and the marauder was fixed in the glare of its lights like a fragment of a dream, motionless until the impact lifted him like a strange, broken bird into the air.

☐ ☐
☐ ☐

Ordinarily Billy's armor would have protected him from the impact—at least in part. Maybe it *had* protected him: the collision hadn't killed him. Not quite.

But he was broken. Broken inside. Armor broken, body broken.

Blood oozed out of his armor at the broken joints. The gland in the elytra had been crushed, the last of its stimulants dissolved. Billy was only Billy.

Nevertheless, he stood up.

Felt the shifting of ribs inside his chest.

He turned to the house. He ignored Tom Winter, ignored the pinwheel rotation of the night sky, attempted to ignore his pain. He could not fathom a destination but the tunnel, which he had confused with escape or going home.

He hurried through the open door of the house, this bar of light. This door which contained a door which was a door in time which was all he had ever wanted, an unwinding of his life, a way home. He imagined it as a road, pictured it in his mind with sudden clarity. A dusty road winding into dry, distant mountains under a clean blue sky.

Sanctuary. A door into the unmaking of himself.

Billy peeled off the battered fragments of his armor and entered the house.

□ □
□ □

Past reason, past calculation, Tom picked up his weapon and followed the marauder into the house.

Forced to justify the action, he might have said it was still possible for the marauder to escape, follow the tunnel back to Manhattan, heal himself and repair his armor. The idea that the events he had just endured might not be an ending was too painful to consider. So he rose and followed the marauder into the house under the blinding weight of his own burned flesh. Doug Archer and Joyce and Catherine came around the corner as he was at the door, called out to him to stop, but he barely registered their voices. They didn't understand. They'd missed the main event.

The house was full of a gray, cloying smoke but the cybernetics had extinguished all the fires. Ben Collier lay bloody and prostrate at the top of the stairs. Tom registered this fact but set it aside, something to be dealt with later.

He felt giddy going down the stairs. He was in pain, but

315

the pain was distant from him; he worried about shock. Probably he was in shock. Whatever that meant or might later mean. It didn't matter now. He made himself walk.

He found the marauder some yards into the tunnel.

The marauder had collapsed—probably for the last time, Tom thought—against the blank white wall. He was armorless, weaponless, naked, hurt. Tom felt his fingers open, heard the rattle of his own weapon as it fell to the floor. The marauder didn't look.

Tom reached out a hand to support himself but the wall was too smooth; he lost his balance and sat down hard.

Two of us here on the floor, Tom thought.

He was at the brink of unconsciousness. The pain was very bad. He spared another glance at his ruined left side. His light-headedness lent him some objectivity. *Singed meat,* he thought. He had never thought of himself as "meat" before. *Barbecued ribs.* It made him want to laugh, but he was afraid of the sound his laughter might make in this empty tunnel.

This transit in time. Not a tunnel under the earth; something stranger. Strange place to be lying with what might be a mortal wound, next to the man who had wounded him.

He saw the marauder move. Dismayed, Tom raised his head. But the marauder was not hostile, only frightened, trying to back his broken body away from this:

This sudden apparition.

This halo of light in the shape of a human being.

It came toward the marauder at a terrible speed.

Time ghost, Tom thought, too sleepy to be terrified. Doug had called it that. Ghost of what? Of something native to this fracture in the world. Of a kind of humanity uprooted from duration.

Something too big to be contained by his idea of it. He felt its largeness as it hovered a few feet away. It was large in some dimension he couldn't perceive; it was many where it seemed to be singular.

316

He felt the heat of it wash over his face.

He felt it *consider* him . . . and pass him by.

He saw it hover over the marauder, saw it contain that frightened man in a veil of its own intolerable light.

And then it disappeared, and the marauder was gone with it.

Tom heard voices calling his name, Joyce's voice among them. He turned with a feverish gratitude toward the sound, would have stood up but for the darkness that took him away.

PART THREE

Time

Twenty-four

When he woke there was nothing left of his wound but pink, new skin and an occasional phantom pain. The cybernetics had healed him, Ben explained. He'd been asleep for three and a half weeks.

The house had been healed, too. No trace remained of the smoke and fire damage. The windows had been replaced and reputtied. The house was immaculate—spotless.

The way I found it, Tom thought. New and old. A half step out of time.

"There's someone you need to meet," Ben said.

She was waiting for him in the kitchen.

Dazed with his recovery and events that seemed too recent, he didn't recognize her at first; felt only this powerful sense of familiarity, a sort of déjà vu. Then he said, "You were in the car . . . driving the car that hit him." He remembered this face framed in those lights.

She nodded. "That's right."

She was gray-haired, fiftyish, a little wide at the hips. She was dressed in jeans and a blue cotton blouse and thick corrective lenses that made her eyes seem big.

He looked again, and the world seemed to slip sideways. "Oh my god," he said. "Joyce."

Her smile was large and genuine. "We do meet under the most peculiar circumstances."

He spent a few days at the house undergoing what Doug called "emotional decompression," but he couldn't stay. In effect, the building had been repossessed. The time terminus was repaired; Tom didn't have a place here anymore.

He was homeless but not poor. A sum equivalent to the purchase price of the house had appeared in a Bank of America account in his name. Tom asked Ben how this happy event had occurred—not certain he wanted to know—and Ben said, "Oh, money isn't hard to create. The right electronics and the right algorithms can work wonders. It can be done by telephone, amazingly enough."

"Like computer hacking," Tom said.

"More sophisticated. But yes."

"Isn't that unethical?"

"Do you own this house? Did you really take possession of the chattel goods to which you're entitled under the contract? If not, would it be fair to leave you penniless?"

"You can't just invent money. It has to come from somewhere."

Ben gave him a pitying look.

The tunnel was repaired and the time travelers came through it from their unimaginable future: Tom was allowed a glimpse of them. He stood at the foot of the basement stairs as they emerged from the tunnel, a man and a woman, or apparently so—Ben said they changed themselves to seem more human than they really were. Their eyes, Tom thought, were very striking. Gray eyes, frankly curious. They looked at him a long time. Looked at him, Tom supposed, the way he might look at a living specimen of *Australopithecus*—with the peculiar affection we feel for our dim-witted ancestors.

Then they turned to Ben and spoke too softly for Tom to understand; he took this as his cue to leave.

Archer and Catherine made room for him in the Simmons house at the top of the hill. The bed was comfortable but he planned to leave; he felt too much like an intruder here. They made allowances for his disorientation, tiptoed around his isolation. It wasn't a role he wanted to play.

The Simmons house was for sale, in any case. Archer had left his job with Belltower Realty but refused to employ another agent; the property was "for sale by owner." "It's full of important memories," Catherine said, "but without Gram Peggy this place would be a mausoleum. Better to let it go." She gave him a curious half-sad little smile. "I guess we all came out of this with new ideas about past and future. What we can cling to and what we can't."

Archer said they were moving up to Seattle, where Catherine had a market for her painting. He could find some kind of work there—maybe even audit some college courses. Tom said, "Leaving Belltower after all these years?"

"Cutting that knot, yeah. It's easier now."

"It rained morning glories," Tom said.

"All up and down the Post Road. Morning glories a foot deep."

"Nobody knows it but us."

"Nope. But we know it."

August had ended. It was September now, still hot, but a little bit of winter in the air, colder these nights.

He took his car out of the garage and drove it down to Brack's Auto Body for a tune-up. The mechanic changed the oil, cleaned the plugs, adjusted the choke, charged too much. He ran Tom's Visa card through the slider and said, "Planning a trip?"

Tom nodded.

"Where you headed?"

"Don't know. Maybe back east. Thought I'd just drive."

"No shit?"

"No shit."

"That's wild," the mechanic said. "Hey, freedom, right?"

"Freedom. Right."

He made a couple of phone calls from the booth outside.

He called Tony. It was Saturday; Tony was home and the TV was playing in the background. He heard Tricia crying, Loreen soothing her.

"I was passing through town," Tom said. "Thought I'd call."

"Holy shit," Tony said. "I thought you were dead, I really did. Are you all right? What do you mean, passing through town?"

"I can't stay, Tony. You were right about the house. Not a good investment."

"Passing through on the way to where?"

He repeated what he'd told the mechanic: someplace east.

"This is extremely adolescent behavior. Immature, Tom. This is life, not 'Route 66.'"

"I'll keep that in mind. Listen, is Loreen around?"

"You want to talk to her?" He seemed surprised.

"Just to say hi."

"Well. Take care of yourself, anyhow. Stay in touch this time. If you need anything, if you need money—"

"Thanks, Tony. I appreciate that."

Muffled silence, then Loreen got on the line. "Just checking in on my way through town," Tom said. "Wanted to thank you folks."

They chatted a while. Barry had been down with chicken pox, home from school for two weeks. Tricia was cutting a tooth. Tom said he'd been traveling and that he'd be traveling awhile longer.

"You sound different," Loreen said.

"Do I?"

"You do. I don't know how to describe it. Like you're making peace with something." He couldn't formulate an answer. She added, "It's been a long time since that accident. Since your mama and daddy died. Life goes on, Tom. Days and years. But I guess you know that."

A last call, long distance to Seattle; he charged it to his credit card. A male voice answered. Tom said, "Is Barbara there?"

"Just a second." Clatter and mumble. Then her voice.

She said she was glad to hear from him. She'd been worried. It was a relief to know he was all right. He thanked her for coming to see him back in the spring. It was good that she cared.

"I don't think a person stops caring. We didn't work too well together but we weren't the Borgias, either."

"It was good when it was good," Tom said.

"Yes."

"You're still hooked up with Rafe?"

"We're working things out. I think it's solid, yeah."

"There were times I wanted you back so bad I tried to pretend you didn't exist. Can you understand that?"

"Perfectly," she said.

"But those were real years."

"Yes."

"Good and bad."

"Yes."

"Thank you for those years," he said.

She said, "You're going away again?"

"I'm not sure where. I'll call."

"Please do that," she said.

He drove out of town along the coast highway until he came to the narrow switchback where his parents had died.

He turned off the road at a scenic overlook some yards up

325

the highway, stepped out of his car and sat awhile at the stone barricade where the hillside sloped away into scrub pine and down to the ocean. He had passed this place a dozen times since the accident but had never stopped, never allowed himself to contemplate the event. The knock on the door, the inconceivable announcement of their death—he had considered and reconsidered those things, but never this place. The mythology but never the fact. He reminded himself that the tumbling of their vehicle down this embankment had happened on a rainy day, that the car had crushed itself against the rocks, the ambulance had arrived and departed, the wreckage had been lifted by crane and towed away, night fell, the clouds parted, stars wheeled overhead, the sun rose. Two people died; but their dying was an event among all the other events of their lives, no more or less significant than marriage, childbirth, ambition, disappointment, love. Maybe Loreen was right. Time to take this bone of bereavement and inter it with all the other bones. Not bury it but put it in its place, in the vault of time, the irretrievable past, where memory lived.

He climbed into the car and drove back toward Belltower.

To the hollow central mystery of his life now: Joyce.

He found her on the Post Road, hiking to the little grocery up by the highway.

He stopped the car and opened the passenger door for her. She climbed inside.

By Tom's calculation she had turned fifty in February of this year. She'd gained some weight, gained some lines, gained some gray. She wore a pair of faded jeans a little too tight around her thighs; a plain yellow sweatshirt; sneakers for the long hike up the road. The marks of time, Tom thought. Her voice was throaty and pitched lower than he remembered it; maybe time or maybe some hard living had done that. Her eyes suggested the latter.

She looked at him cautiously. "I wasn't sure you'd be back."

"Neither was I."

"Still planning on leaving town?"

He nodded.

"I was hoping we could talk."

"We can talk," Tom said.

"You haven't been around much. Well, hell. It must be a shock, seeing me like this."

It was true, but it sounded terrible. He told her she looked fine. She said, "I look my age, for better or worse. Tom, I lived those twenty-seven years. I know what to expect when I look in the mirror. You woke up expecting something else."

"You left," he said. "Left before I had a chance to say goodbye."

"I left as soon as I knew you'd be all right. You want to know how it went?" She settled into the upholstery and stared into the blue September sky. "I left because I didn't trust the connection between us. I left because I didn't want to be a freak of nature, here—or make you into one, there. I left because I was scared and I wanted to go home.

"I left because Ben told me the tunnel would be fixed and the choice I made would have to be the final choice. So— back to Manhattan, back to 1962. You always think you can start again, but it turns out you can't. Lawrence was dead. That changed things. And I'd been *here*, I'd had a look at the future. Even just a tiny look, it leaves you different. For instance, you remember Jerry Soderman? Wrote books nobody would publish? He did okay as a trade editor, actually got into print in the seventies—literary novels hardly anybody read, but he was real proud of them. Couple of months after I got back, Jerry tells me he's gay, he might as well be frank about it. Fine, but the only thought I had was, Hey, Jerry, come 1976 or so you better be careful what you do. I actually phoned him around then, hadn't talked to him for years. I said, Jerry, there's a disease going around, here's how to protect yourself. He said no there's not and how would *you* know? Anyhow . . . Jerry died a couple of years back."

"I'm sorry," Tom said.

"It's not your fault, not his fault, not my fault. The point is, I couldn't leave behind what happened with you and me and this place. I tried! I really did. I tried all the good ways of forgetting. And I lived a life. I was married for five years. Nice guy, bad marriage. I did some professional backup vocals, but that was a bad time . . . I drank for a while, which kind of screwed up my voice. And, you know, I marched for civil rights and I marched against the war and I marched for clean air. When things leveled out I took a secretarial job at a law firm downtown. Nine to five, steady paycheck, annual vacation, and I'd be there today if I hadn't quit and bought a ticket west. It's amazing: for the longest time I promised myself I wouldn't do it. What was done here was finished. I'd left; I'd made my decision. But I remembered the date on the newspaper I read in your back yard. Every August, I marked the anniversary, if you can call it that. Then, for the last couple of years, I started watching calendars the way you might watch a clock. Watching that date crawl closer. On New Year's Eve last winter I sat home by myself, one lonely lady approaching the half-century mark. I broke open a bottle of champagne and at midnight I said fuck it, I'm going.

"Bought plane tickets six months in advance. Gave notice. I don't know what I hoped or expected to find, but I wanted it real bad. Well, the flight was delayed. I missed a connection at O'Hare and had to wait overnight in the airport. When I got to Seattle it was already morning; the newspaper, the one I remembered, was sitting in the boxes staring at me. I rented a car and drove too fast down the coast. Blew out a tire and took a long time changing it. Then I got to Belltower and couldn't find the house. Couldn't remember the name of the road. I guess I thought there'd be signs posted: 'THIS WAY TO

THE TIME MACHINE.' I asked at a couple of gas stations, looked at a map until I thought my eyes would pop out of my head. Finally I stopped at a little all-night restaurant for coffee and when the waitress came I asked her if she knew anybody named Tom Winter or Cathy Simmons and she said no but there was a Peggy Simmons out along the Post Road and didn't she have a granddaughter named Cathy? I gave her a twenty and came roaring out here. Caught the bad guy in my headlights and I couldn't help myself, Tom: after all those years he still looked like death. I remembered Lawrence lying in a cheap coffin in some funeral parlor in Brooklyn, where his parents lived, and it still hurt, all these years later. So I turned the wheel. I was crying when I hit him."

"Saved my life," Tom said.

"Saved your life and drove on down the road and checked into a hotel room and sat on the bed shaking until noon the next day. By which time my younger self had gone home."

"Then you came back," Tom said.

"Scared hell out of Doug and Cathy. Ben didn't seem too surprised, though."

"You still wanted something."

"I don't know what I wanted. I think I wanted to look at you. Just look. Does that make any sense? For most of thirty years I'd been thinking about you. What we were. What we might have been. Whether I should love you or hate you for all this."

He heard the weariness in her voice. "Any conclusions?"

"No conclusions. Just memory in the flesh. I'm sorry if I freaked you out."

"I'm the one who should apologize."

He pulled into the lot in back of the grocery store and parked where a patch of sun came shining through a stand of tall pines. Tom decided this woman was Joyce, unmistakably

Joyce despite all the changes; that he had walked into one more miracle, as pitiless and strange as the others.

She squinted at him through a bar of sunlight, smiling. "Catherine said there's a sale on seed packets here. It's too late for a garden, obviously, but the seeds stay good if you keep them in a refrigerator."

"Seeds for Ben to plant? He talked about a garden."

"For me to plant. I might be staying here. Ben offered me a job." She paused. *"His* job."

Tom turned off the engine, looked at her blankly. "I don't get it."

"He's going home. I think he deserves it, don't you? He offered me as a replacement. His employers agreed."

He considered it a moment. "You want this?"

"I think I do. Ben says it's lonely work. Maybe I need some lonely work for a while."

"How long a while?"

"Eight years. Then the terminal's closed for good. There won't be anything in the basement but Gyproc walls. Weird thought, isn't it?"

Eight years, Tom thought. 1997. Just shy of the millennium.

"I can do eight years," she said. "I can hack that."

"What then? They pension you off?"

"They rebuild me. They make me young." She shook her head: "No, not young. That's the wrong word. They make my body young. But I'll be nearly sixty, no matter what I look like. That might be hard to deal with. My theory is that it shouldn't matter. On the inside you're not old or young, you're just *yourself,* right? I won't be a callow youth but I won't be something monstrous, either. At least that's what I believe."

She had been Joyce, would be Joyce, was Joyce now. "I don't think you have anything to worry about."

"It's funny," she said. "We were together for what—ten

weeks, eleven weeks? It's funny how a couple of months can put such a spin on a whole life. Now I'm old, you're young. In a few years it'll be the other way around."

He took her hand. He pictured himself coming back here in seven years' time, knocking on the door, Joyce answering—

She put a finger on his lips. "Don't talk about it. Live your life. See what happens."

So he helped her with the shopping and he drove her home.

During the ride she asked Tom what he meant to do now and he told her more or less what he'd told Tony and Barbara: head east, live on the house money for a while, sort himself out.

He added, "I keep thinking about what Barbara's doing. I can't see myself carrying a picket sign around some toxic waste dump. But maybe I should, I don't know. I think about what Ben said, that the future is always unpredictable. Maybe we don't have to end up with the kind of world that created, you know, *him*—"

"Billy," Joyce said. "Ben said his name was Billy."

"Maybe we can uncreate Billy." Tom pulled into the gravel driveway of this plain house, ugly but well maintained, this lonely house up along the Post Road. "But that's a paradox, isn't it? If Billy doesn't exist, where did he come from?"

"Wherever ghosts come from," Joyce said.

"Hard to believe a ghost could be that dangerous."

"Ghosts are always dangerous. You should have figured that out."

She touched his cheek with her hand, then opened the door and stepped outside. Tom made himself smile. He wanted her to remember him smiling.

Driving east, he discovered a package of seeds in the passenger seat where it must have fallen from her shopping: morning glories, Heavenly Blue.

Epilogue

Billy remembered a sense of upward motion, of expansion, as if he were being drawn into a vacuum. The motion surrounded him, became a place, incomprehensibly large, a blue vastness like the sky. And then it *was* the sky.

A blue sky generous over a dry landscape, powder-white hills in the far distance and in the foreground a farm. Water arced up from a thousand sprinkler-heads, made rainbows over miles of kale and new green wheat and luxurious arbors of grapes.

Ohio!

Billy was astonished.

He stood on a dusty road in civilian clothes. His body wasn't broken. No more pain, no more fear.

A road in Ohio inside a monster inside a tunnel inside time.

He couldn't make sense of this hierarchy of impossibilities. He had been carried here by wish or accident, perhaps by some being altogether timeless, human or not human or human in one of its aspects or all humanity collated together at the end of duration—he didn't know; it didn't matter. He wondered what he would do without his armor, but the thought was less terrifying than it should have been. Maybe he didn't need the armor. He reached under his rough-woven cotton shirt and touched the place where the lancet had entered his skin; but the hole was seamlessly healed.

Billy walked toward the farm until the common buildings loomed ahead of him and he distinguished two figures at the main gate. Now he hurried forward, recognizing the bearded man: Nathan, his father; and the woman beside him was Maria, his mother, who had died of cancer a month after Billy was born; he recognized her from her photographs.

He stood before Nathan, who was as tall as Billy remembered him. Billy said, "What is this place?" And Nathan answered, "This is where we begin again." Then he opened his arms and Billy ran forward.

Nathan and Maria took him home. Their touch pulled memory out of him like a throbbing tooth until there was only the fact of the sky, the water, the heat.

"Saw an Infantry patrol this morning," Nathan remarked, "but it passed well to the south."

"That's good," Billy's mother said.

Billy took her hand and tugged her toward home.

"I'm tired," he said. The sun was hot and made him tired and he felt like he'd walked a very long way.

Here is an excerpt from

THE HARVEST

by Robert Charles Wilson

Coming in December 1992
in Bantam Spectra hardcover and trade
paperback

"Wilson is a fine storyteller . . . the best example I've seen of a writer who is using the techniques and tropes of science fiction to produce significant literary accomplishments."—Orson Scott Card in *The Magazine of Fantasy and Science Fiction*

And once again, critically acclaimed author Robert Charles Wilson does just that. In THE HARVEST, he confronts an issue that defines us as human beings. Throughout history, humanity has struggled to outwit death. Now, the mysterious Travellers have arrived with the answer: Immortality. All across the Earth, humanity is asked, *Do you want to live forever?*

Matt was a doctor because he had been seduced by the idea of healing.

A dozen TV series and a handful of movies had convinced him that the heart of the practice of medicine was the act of healing. He managed to carry this fragile idea through med school, but it didn't survive internship. His internship drove home the fact that a doctor's purpose is bound up with death—its postponement, at best; its amelioration, often; its inevitability, always. Death was the grey eminence behind the caduceus. Healing was why people paid their doctors. Death was why they were afraid of them.

Contrary to myth, the med degree conferred no emotional invulnerability. Even doctors feared death; even successful doctors. Feared it and avoided it. Sometimes neurotically. During his residency, Matt had worked with an oncologist who hated his patients. He was a good doctor, unflaggingly professional, but in a lounge or a cafeteria or a bar—among colleagues—he would explain at length what weaklings people were. "They *invite* their tumors. They're lazy or fat or they smoke, or they inebriate themselves with alcohol or lie in the sun with their skin exposed. Then they bring their abused bodies to me. Cure this, please, doctor. Sickening."

"Maybe they're just unlucky," Matt had ventured. "Some of them, at least."

"The more time you spend on my floor, Dr. Wheeler, the less inclined you will be to believe that."

Maybe so, Matt thought. The contempt was not reasonable, but it served a purpose. It kept death at arm's length. Open the door to sympathy—even a crack—and grief might crowd in behind it.

It was not an attitude Matt could adopt, however, which helped steer him into family practice. His daily work was leavened with mumps, measles, minor wounds stitched, infections knocked out with antibiotics. Healing, in other words. Small benevolent acts. He was a bit player in the minor dramas of ordinary lives, a good guy, not a death angel presiding at the gateway to oblivion.

Seldom, at least.

But Cindy Rhee was dying and there was nothing he could do about it.

He had told the Rhees he would stop in to see their daughter Friday morning.

David Rhee was a forklift driver at the mill south of town. His parents were Korean immigrants living in Portland; David had married a pretty Buchanan girl named Ellen Drew and twelve years ago Ellen had borne him a daughter, Cindy.

Cindy was a delicate, thin child with just a

touch of her father's complexion. Her eyes were large, mysterious, brown. She was suffering from a neuroblastoma, a cancer of the nervous system.

She fell down walking to school one autumn morning. She stood up, brushed the leaf debris off her jacket, carried on. Next week, she fell again. And the week after. Then twice in a week. Twice in a day. Finally her mother brought her in to see Matt.

He found gross anomalies in her reflexes and a pronounced papilledema. He told Mrs. Rhee he couldn't make a diagnosis and referred Cindy to a neurologist at the hospital, but his suspicions were grave. A benign and operable tumor of the brain might be the girl's best hope. There were other possibilities, even less pleasant.

He attended her while she was admitted for tests. Cindy was immensely patient in the face of the unavoidable indignities, almost supernaturally so. It occurred to Matt to wonder where such people came from: the obviously good and decent souls who endure hardship without complaint and cause duty-hardened nurses to weep for them in the hallways.

He was with the Rhees when the neurologist explained that their daughter was suffering from a neuroblastoma. David and Ellen Rhee listened with ferocious concentration as the specialist described the hardships and benefits, the pluses and minuses, of chemotherapy. David spoke first: "But will it *cure* her?"

"It might prolong her life. It might send the tumor into remission. We don't use the word 'cure.'

We would have to keep a close watch on her even in the best case."

David Rhee nodded, a gesture not of acquiescence but of broken-hearted acknowledgement. His daughter might not get well. His daughter might die.

I could have been a plumber, Matt thought, an electrician, an accountant, anything, dear God, not to be in this room at this moment. He couldn't meet Ellen's eyes when she left with her husband. He was afraid she would see his craven helplessness.

Cindy responded to the chemotherapy. She lost some hair but recovered her sense of balance; she went home from the hospital skinny but optimistic.

She was back six months later. Her tumor, inoperable to begin with, had disseminated. Her speech was slurred and her eyesight had begun to tunnel. Matt canvassed the hospital's specialists: surely *some* kind of operation. . . . But the malignancy had colonized her brain too deeply; the x-rays were eloquent, merciless. Surgery, if anyone had been mad enough to attempt it, would have left her speechless, sightless, possibly soulless.

Now she was home to die. The Rhees understood this. In a way, the prognosis was kind; she was functional enough to leave the hospital and with any luck she wouldn't end up DNR in some pitiless white room. Now Cindy was blind and could form only the most rudimentary words, but Ellen Rhee continued to care for her daughter with a relentless heroism that Matt found humbling.

He had promised he would stop by this morning, but he didn't relish the task. It was hard not to care about Cindy Rhee, hard not to hate the disease that was torturing her to death. There was a state of mind Matt called "being the doctor machine," in which he kept his emotions filed for later reference . . . but that was a difficult balancing act at the best of times, and this morning he was feverish and disoriented. He popped a decongestant and drove to the Rhees' house in a grim mood.

There was the question, too, of what Jim Bix had told him. He carried it like a stone, a weight he could not dislodge nor easily bear. Jim was sincere, but he might still be mistaken. Or crazy. Or maybe this really was the beginning of the end . . . in which case, as indecent as the thought sounded, maybe Cindy Rhee was the lucky one.

He parked in the driveway at the Rhees' modest two-bedroom house. Ellen Rhee opened the door for him. She wore a yellow housedress with her hair tied away from her neck. The air in the living room smelled of Pine-Sol; an old upright vacuum cleaner stood sentinel on the carpet. It was Matt's experience that in the homes of the dying housework is performed religiously or not at all. Ellen Rhee had taken to frantic cleaning. In the last few months he had seldom seen her without her apron on.

But she was smiling. That was odd, Matt thought. And the radio was playing. Some AM station. Cheerful pop music.

"Come in, Matt," Ellen said.

He stepped inside. The house was not as dim as

he remembered it; she had opened all the blinds and pulled back all the drapes. A summer-morning breeze swept the odor of antiseptic past him, and a more delicate waft of roses from the backyard garden.

"I'm sorry," she said. "The house is kind of chaotic. I'm in the middle of cleaning up. I guess I forgot you were coming."

She sniffed and dabbed her nose with a Kleenex. The Taiwan Flu, Matt thought. Wasn't that what the papers were calling it?

He said, "I can come back another time—"

"No. Please. Come in." Her smile had not faded.

The clinical word for this kind of behavior was "denial." But maybe it was simply her way of coping. Carry on, smile and welcome the guest. A new wrinkle in the etiology of Ellen Rhee's grief. But it seemed to Matt she *looked* different. Less burdened. Was that possible?

"Is David home?"

"Early shift at the mill. Would you like a coffee?"

"No, thank you, Ellen." He looked toward Cindy's bedroom. "How is she today?"

"Better," Ellen Rhee said. Matt's surprise must have been too obvious. "No, really! She's feeling much better. You can ask her yourself."

It was a macabre joke. "Ellen—"

Her smile softened. She touched his arm. "Go see her, Matt. Go ahead."

Cindy was sitting up in bed, a small miracle in itself. Matt's first astonished thought was: she *did* look better. She was still brutally thin—the delicate bone-and-parchment emaciation of the terminal cancer patient. But her eyes were wide and appeared lucid. The last time he stopped by, she hadn't seemed to recognize him.

Matt parked his medical bag on the bedside table and told her hello. He made it a point to talk to her, though the neurologist had assured him she couldn't understand. She might still take some solace from the tone of his voice. "I came by to see how you're doing today."

Cindy blinked. "Thank you, Dr. Wheeler," she said. "I'm doing fine."

"You look like you've seen a ghost," Ellen said when he emerged from the girl's bedroom. "Come on. Sit down."

He sat at the kitchen table and allowed Ellen to pour him a glass of 7-Up.

"She really is better," Ellen said. "I told you so."

Matt struggled to form his thoughts.

"She spoke," he said. "She was lucid. She understood what I said to her. She's weak and a little feverish, but I believe she may even have gained some weight." He looked at Ellen. "None of that should be possible."

"It's a miracle," Ellen said firmly. "At least that's what I believe." She laughed. "I'm a little feverish myself."

"Ellen, listen. I'm pleased about this. I couldn't be happier. But I don't understand it."

And truly, he did not. Yes, there was such a thing as a remission. He had once seen a lung tumor remit in a way that could be called "miraculous." But Cindy was a vastly different case. Brain tissue had been destroyed. Even if the tumors had somehow vanished, *she should not have been able to speak.* That part of her brain was simply missing. Even without the tumors, she would have been in the position of someone who had suffered a severe stroke. Some recovery of faculties might be possible; certainly not a complete cure . . . certainly not what he had witnessed in the bedroom.

He did not say any of this to Ellen. Instead, he offered: "I want to be sure. I want the hospital to look at her."

Ellen frowned for the first time this morning. "Maybe when she's stronger, Matt. I don't know, though. I hate to put her through all that again."

"I don't want us to have false hopes."

"You think she might get worse?" Ellen shook her head. "She won't. I can't tell you how I know that. But I do. The sickness is gone, Dr. Wheeler."

He couldn't bring himself to argue. "I hope you're right. Cindy said something similar."

"Did she?"

The girl had spoken with deliberation, as if the framing of the words still required enormous effort, but succinctly and clearly.

"Poor Dr. Wheeler," this emaciated child had said to him. "We're putting you out of business."

That night he climbed into bed beside Annie.

It had been a while since they'd slept together, and now he wondered why. He'd missed this, the presence of her, her warmth and what he thought of as her "Annie-ness." She was a small woman, all her vivid energies and enigmatic silences packaged tightly together. She rolled on her side but snuggled closer; he curled himself around her.

The first time Annie came home with him Matt had been guilt-ridden—this had still been very much Celeste's house and Annie an intruder in it, an insult, he worried, to her memory. And he had wondered how Rachel might take it. A rivalry between Annie and his daughter was a complication he had dreaded.

But Rachel had taken to Annie at once, accepted her presence without question. "Because she mourned," Annie suggested later. "She mourned for her mother and I think in some ways she's still mourning, but she isn't hiding it from herself. She's letting go of it. She knows it's all right for me to be here because Celeste isn't coming back."

Matt winced.

Annie said, "But you, Matt, you don't like letting go. You're a collector. You hoard things. Your childhood. This town. Your idealism. Your marriage. You can't bear the idea of giving any of it up."

This was both true and maddening. "I gave Celeste up," he said. "I didn't have a choice."

"It's not that simple. There's a certain way you *shouldn't* let her go—she's a part of you, after all. And there's the giving up you couldn't help, which is her dying. And there's the space in between. Not a very big space right now. But that's the space where I fit in."

Matt wondered, holding Annie close to him, what had provoked this old memory.

You're a collector. You don't like letting go.

He guessed it was true.

Clinging to Annie now. Clinging to Rachel.

Clinging to Jim and Lillian and the practice of medicine and the town of Buchanan.

Everything's changing, Lillian had said.

But it was too much to let go of.

A cool finger of air touched the skin of his shoulder, and Matt pulled up the bedsheet and closed his eyes in the summer dark; and then, like Annie, like Rachel, like Jim and Lillian and everyone else in Buchanan and in the sleeping world, he began to dream.

*　　*　　*

A wave of sleep crossed the globe like the shadow of the sun, a line of dreaming that lagged only a few hours behind the border of the night.

It was a sleep more complete than the planet had known since the human species migrated out of Africa. Sleep tracked across North America from the tip of Labrador westward, and it possessed almost everyone equally: possessed the shift workers, the insomniacs, the wealthy and the homeless; possessed the alcoholic and the amphetamine addict alike.

It possessed farmers, fishermen, the inmates of penitentiaries and penitentiary guards. It possessed methedrine-saturated truckers spinning Waylon Jennings tapes in the cabs of 18-wheelers, who pulled into the breakdown lanes of empty highways and slept in their rigs; possessed airline pilots, who landed 747s on the tarmac of sleeping airports under the direction of air-traffic controllers who methodically emptied the sky, and then slept.

There were isolated, and temporary, exceptions. Medical emergencies were rare, but telephone lines were maintained by a few dazed workers (who slept later); ambulances evacuated injuries to hospitals, where a few residents, functional but dazed beyond wondering at the events that had overtaken them, staunched the few wounds of a few sleeping patients . . . whose injuries, in any case, seemed to heal without much intervention. Fire crews remained functionally alert, though curiously sedated. No one slept until they had attended—without much conscious thought—to the obvious dangers: cigarettes were extinguished, ovens switched off, fireplaces damped. The fires that did break out were accidents of nature, not humanity. In Chicago, a welfare mother named Aggie Langois woke from a powerful and incomplete dream—which was not a dream—to find flames licking out of a 1925-vintage wall socket and kindling the paper curtains of her two-room apartment. She took her sleeping baby and her wakeful but calm three-year-old and hurried them downstairs, two flights to the sidewalk . . . and was surprised to find the other occupants of the building calmly filing out behind her. The crack dealer from 3-A was carrying the legless old man from 4-B; and Aggie's personal nemesis, the neighbor girl who was a cocktail waitress and who liked to party after hours when the children were trying to sleep, had brought out a score of blankets and handed three of them to Aggie without comment.

Someone had paused long enough to dial 911. The fire engines arrived, not just promptly, but in eerie silence; the crew hooked up their hoses with an easy, economical motion. It was as if only a part of them was awake: the fraction necessary to do this job and do it efficiently. A man from the building next door—a stranger—offered Aggie a sofa to sleep on and a bedroll for her babies. Aggie accepted. "It's an unusual night," the man said, and Aggie nodded, mute with wonder. Before an hour had passed the fire was extinguished and the occupants of the building had been dispersed to new locations, all in a strange and dignified silence. Safe and with her children safe beside her, Aggie began once more to dream.

Apart from the telephone exchanges, local communications dwindled and international networks began to fail. Within hours, the Earth had dimmed appreciably in the radio and microwave frequencies. Night overtook the western cities of Lima, Los Angeles and Anchorage, and began to darken the ocean, while Israelis watched their CNN satellite feed shutting down due to "unexpected staff shortages" according to one weary Atlanta announcer; and then there was only a static logo, then only static—as overseas subscribers blinked at the horizon and guessed something was wrong, something must be seriously wrong, and it was odd how *calm* they felt, and later sleepy.

Some resisted longer than others. By some quirk of will or constitution, a few individuals were able to shake off their sedation, or at least postpone it a few moments, a few hours.

A sales rep for the Benevolent Shoe Company of Abbotsford, Michigan, driving a rental Chrysler northbound on 87 from the Denver airport, ponuered the miracle that had overtaken him in the darkness. He was due to check in at a Marriot in Fort Collins and face a convention of western footware retailers, beginning with a Reception Buffet at seven, for Christ's sake, in the morning. The miracle was that some kind of formless disaster had spared him the necessity of scrambled eggs and bacon with a bunch of sleepy entrepreneurs wearing HELLO MY NAME IS stickers.

The miracle had seemed to commence sometime after sunset, when his flight landed at Stapleton. The airport was nearly empty despite the fact that its gates were crowded with motionless aircraft. At least half the passengers on his flight stayed aboard, curled up in their seats . . . flying on to some other destination, he supposed, but it struck him as peculiar nonetheless. The terminal itself was cavernous and weirdly silent; his luggage was a long time arriving and the woman at the Hertz booth was so spaced out he had trouble holding her attention long enough to arrange a rental. Driving north, he was startled by the emptiness of the highway . . . cars pulling over into the emergency lane until he was the last mobile vehicle on the road, humming along like a sleepy wraith, listening to a Eurythmics tune that seemed to rattle in his head like a loose pea. Then the Denver oldies station abruptly signed off, and when he tried to find something else there was only one other signal, a country-and-western station, which promptly faded. Not normal, he admitted to himself. No, more than that. This was *way past* not normal, and it should have been scarier than it was. He pulled into the emergency lane, like everybody else, and climbed out of the car. Then he climbed up *on top* of the car and sat on the roof with his heels kicking at the passenger door, because—well, why not? Because he understood, in a feverish flash, that the world was ending. Ending in some strange and unanticipated and curiously sedate fashion, but ending, and he was alive at the end of it, sitting on top of this dung-colored Chrysler in a cheap suit and hearing for the first time the quiet of an abandoned night, a night without human noises. His own scuffles on the car top seemed achingly loud, and the wind made a hushed sound coming over farmland through the grain, and the smell of growing things mixed with the hot-engine smell of his car and his own rank sweat, and a dog barked somewhere, and the stars were bright as sparks overhead . . . and it was all a single phenomenon, *the quiet*, he named it, and it was awesome, frightening. He thought of his wife, of his seven-year-old son. He knew—another sourceless "knowing"—that whatever this was, it had overtaken them, too. Which made it a little easier to cooperate with the inevitable. He felt suddenly light-headed, too much alone on this immense table of sleeping farmland, so he climbed down and scurried back inside the womb of the car, where the silence was even louder, and curled up on the upholstery and obeyed a sudden and belated urge to sleep.

Among many other things, he dreamed that a mountain had begun to grow from the prairie not far from his car—a mountain as big as any mountain on the earth, and as perfectly round as a pearl.

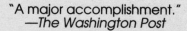